For M and L

DAUGHTERS
of
SHADOW
&
BLOOD

—⚬⚬⚬—

Book III: Elizabeth

J. Matthew Saunders

Saint George's Press

It will have blood; they say, blood will have blood:
Stones have been known to move and trees to speak;
Augurs and understood relations have
By magot-pies and choughs and rooks brought forth
The secret'st man of blood. What is the night?
                              —*William Shakespeare,*
                                 Macbeth, *Act III, scene iv*

DAUGHTERS
of
SHADOW
&
BLOOD

—⫘—

Book III: Elizabeth

PROLOGUE

Târgoviște, Romania
29 December 1989

NO ONE FLEES *TO* DRACULA'S Castle. Not without a very good reason.

When the Romanian people finally rose up against Nicolae Ceaușescu and drove him from Bucharest, the Communist dictator and his wife headed for Târgoviște in a helicopter. When the military forced the helicopter to land, the Ceaușescus commandeered not one but two different vehicles trying to get to the old castle that was once the stronghold of Vlad the Impaler.

Something was there. Maybe something they believed could keep them in power.

But they were gone now, executed after a hasty show trial, one held in the castle.

Why were they so desperate to get here?

Gabriel Popescu planned to find out.

Clouds obscured the night sky, but still the pale light of the full moon filtered through, casting shadows across the stone ruins as Gabriel made his way silently across what once had been a courtyard. Ahead the Chindia Tower loomed, built by Vlad himself. Gabriel covered his mouth with his gloved hand to keep his breath from coming out in white clouds.

Some would consider it ill advised to visit the place at night. Even if one didn't believe in vampires, which Gabriel didn't, most believed the place was best avoided after sunset. Horrible things had happened there and had left a taint in the air. Most people could sense it, even if they didn't have a name for it. Even though Gabriel didn't feel anything unnatural, the stories made him wary.

In his line of work it was good to be wary.

He probed the base of the tower first, trudging around the outside, looking for loose mortar or any obviously newer stones. He didn't really expect such a search to bear fruit. After all, Ceaușescu was wily. He had held onto power for over forty years and had the resources of an entire nation at his disposal. He would not be so careless, but at the same time Gabriel would never forgive himself for missing something obvious.

After circling the tower and finding nothing, he came to a small wooden door. The lock took him only a few seconds to pick. On the other side, a circular set of stairs led upward into the darkness. Gabriel climbed, sweeping his pen light in front of him. About a third of the way up, he found an irregular stone in the wall, but a brief examination proved it to be nothing special. He was about to proceed when he saw a shadow move out of the corner of his eye. Ahead of him a window broke the monotony of the curved stone wall. Charcoal grey clouds moved against the inky sky. Just a cloud drifting in front of the moon, or so he reasoned. He shook his head and continued up.

Running his hands over the stones he had to wonder. Of any place, the tower made the most sense. It would be like Ceaușescu to place something of importance in Dracula's stronghold. Gabriel had spent the last several days speculating, running through the possibilities. Gold was his best guess. If so, he'd have to return another night to retrieve it. Currency was another conjecture, though he doubted Romanian leus would be worth the effort. Better to be Russian rubles or German marks. State secrets offered another possibility. Intelligence the Russians or the Americans might pay for. Imminently more dangerous, but enough to allow him to buy a Greek Island and retire from the burglary business for good.

He had almost reached the top when the shadows moved again in his peripheral vision. He told himself it was merely another trick of the light. No one else was there besides him. Still he continued a little more cautiously. When he came to the end of the stairs, he pushed open the heavy door that led to the roof. The wind bit into him as he emerged. The clouds rushed across the sky. Around him the entire valley spread out.

Gabriel had another view in mind, though.

He scanned the floor for almost an hour until he discovered what he was looking for. One of the stones in the floor appeared worn, as if it had been there for five hundred years—a clever bit of camouflage—but the filtered moonlight revealed the obvious difference. The composition was not the same. The color of the tiny shimmering crystals in the rock was just slightly off. Gabriel smiled. It was nice to know he wasn't out of practice.

He knelt over the stone and ran his fingers around the edges. There didn't appear to be any gaps in the mortar, but looks could be deceiving. He probed the stones around the rock, seeking some hidden mechanism, until he felt one small stone give. He pushed down, and then a hand clamped over his mouth.

ONE

—m—

Sarajevo, Bosnia and Herzegovina
2 December 1999

ADAM DIDN'T LOOK UP WHEN the door opened, or when the cup of coffee appeared on his desk in one of the few places not covered by papers and books. He muttered a thank-you as he reached for the cup, only to have it jerked away. He looked up to find Clara glaring at him.

"What?" he asked.

"Do you even know what time it is?"

Adam glanced out the window of the study into the darkness. "Nighttime."

Clara rolled her eyes. "It's four o'clock in the morning. When was the last time you slept?"

"Not sure. What are you doing up?"

"I couldn't sleep," she replied.

"So, neither can I."

"Really?" She crossed her arms. "In forty-eight hours?"

Adam surveyed the pile of papers on the desk. "I'm almost there."

Clara reached over and shut the book in his hand. "You've said that for over a month. Now you need to get to sleep." She wrinkled her nose. "Right after you take a shower."

Adam smirked. "You're not my mother."

She sighed. "Come on Adam. You've been killing yourself trying to find Dracula's medallion." She picked up a piece of paper with Adam's handwriting, a grid of letters. "What's this?"

"It's a table for a Vigenère cipher."

"You think there's some sort of code in these books?"

Several months earlier, Adam had received a worn copy of *Dracula* from his deceased friend Mihai Iliescu. The book was the first in a string of clues that led him on a scavenger hunt across the Balkans—a scavenger hunt with a high body count. Adam collected several books Mihai had left for him, in addition to confronting Yasamin, one of the women Bram Stoker immortalized as a Bride of Dracula.

"A code makes sense," he replied. "There are random letters and words circled in all the books, including *The Giaour*, the one everyone said was the key, but the problem is that we don't know what exactly the key is."

The Giaour, an epic poem by Lord Byron and one of the first vampire stories in the West, was the last book Mihai wanted Adam to find, but it had been misplaced, and acquiring it meant working with another of Dracula's Brides, the beguiling Elena. That encounter nearly cost Adam his life as well.

"Chances are you're not going to figure it out in the next hour," Clara said. "It can wait until you get some sleep."

"Have you heard from Arkady?" Adam asked.

Clara shook her head. "Not yet, but he said he'd be out-of-pocket for a few days. He'll send word soon I'm sure. Inspector Gavrilović did stop by earlier."

"What did he say?"

"He said you need to go to bed."

Adam sighed and stood up. "Fine. You're probably right. A few more hours won't make a difference at this point."

He trudged out of the room, with Clara close behind. "Thank you," he said.

She cocked her head to the side. "For what?"

"For looking out for me."

The corners of her mouth turned up in a weak smile. "It's what I do, it seems."

Adam shut the door to his room and collapsed onto the bed, realizing only then how tired he was. Clara was right, of course. He had been pushing himself hard, maybe too hard, and he needed a break to get his thinking back on track.

He smiled wistfully as he gazed up at the ceiling. She had ended their relationship, and she'd had good reasons for doing so, but if it weren't for Clara, he'd likely be dead. She came to find him when no one else would, and she stayed even after learning why he had left his entire life in the States behind. He closed his eyes and drifted off to sleep thinking, as always, of what might have been.

WHEN ADAM OPENED HIS EYES again, the sunlight punched through the gaps in his curtains. He pushed himself up and staggered to the bathroom, dutifully following Clara's orders to take a shower and wondering why he didn't hear anyone else in the house.

Usually in the morning the housekeeper came, a dour woman named Greta. The only joy she ever seemed to take was in making as much noise as possible, banging pots in the kitchen and moving furniture emphatically, just to wake him up. Even after Adam stepped out of the shower, there was only silence in the townhouse.

"Clara," Adam called as he came down the stairs. "Clara, are you there?"

Silence still.

When Adam reached the bottom of the stairs, he knew something was wrong. All of the clean, white furniture he had come to accept as part of the Russian government's string of safe houses was overturned, and something even more chilling greeted Adam—smeared in red on the wall, a dragon curved in a circle, with its tail wrapped around its neck, the symbol of the Order of the Dragon, the symbol that gave Dracula his name.

Then he spotted an arm protruding from underneath an overturned chair, and his heart leaped into his throat. He ran over and pulled the chair off to find Greta. Something had ripped her throat out. Something with big teeth. Adam covered his mouth and nose to keep from retching. A piece of paper was stuffed in her hand. Two words written in an exquisitely detailed hand seared into his mind.

Work faster.

TWO

Near Cluj, Romania
2 December 1999

CLARA OPENED HER EYES TO find herself in a room Dracula would have been proud of. She lay in a giant four-poster bed covered in satin and silk and velvet. The room was long, with tall windows on one side. Opposite was a fireplace, framed in stone, in front of it two overstuffed chairs. There was also a bookshelf and writing desk in the room. Deep reds and dark woods dominated.

Clara threw back the covers and stepped across the wood floor to one of the windows. She looked out over a narrow snow-covered lawn, and beyond it a forest of bare trees. She had seen the same scene in any of a thousand paintings of the Eastern European landscape.

Her mind ran over the events that had brought her there. She made Adam go to bed and get some rest. Sleep had been her intention as well when she heard a noise downstairs in the townhouse. She thought Arkady might have returned, or perhaps Greta had chosen to come in early. When she went downstairs, though she didn't see anything. She was about to return to her room when she heard the noise again. This time it was distinct—a knock at the door. She knew better than to answer. A sense of dread crept over her as the knocking continued. She backed away. Her hand went to the crucifix around her neck, the one Arkady had given her.

The knocking continued as shadows moved in front of the windows. Clara was about to call for Adam when a gloved hand closed over her mouth, and a harsh voice whispered in her ear, "You should have been paying attention to the other door."

After that she didn't remember anything until she had awoken in the room. She tested all the windows. The sashes were nailed shut, and in any event, she was on an upper floor, too high to drop to the ground below.

Behind her the room's only door opened. She turned to find a man standing in the doorway. He was dressed more for the nineteenth century than the twentieth, in a black waistcoat with a red cravat. A streak of white ran through his black hair, from the tip of his widow's peak to behind his left ear. He moved like a wolf prowling, and Clara caught herself watching his muscles tensing and flexing underneath his clothes.

He gave a slight bow "Welcome, Dr. MacIntosh. I trust the accommodations are to your liking?"

Clara couldn't place his accent. She knew only it wasn't Eastern European. "Where am I? Who are you?"

"We're in the middle of a forest," the man answered with a lopsided smile, "in a manor house that dates back to the eighteenth century, once owned by Hungarian nobles."

"That's ... that's not what I meant," she stammered, "and you didn't answer my second question."

He grinned again, baring his teeth. "Not now. All you need to know is that I'm your host." He glanced at the table next to the bed. "I'll see you're brought something to eat. Please, try to enjoy your stay. You may as well. You'll probably be here for a while."

He left her, locking the door behind him.

THE SUN HAD JUST SET when the door opened again. Clara sat in the bed with the blankets pulled around her. With the loss of the light, the temperature in the room plummeted. An older man entered and set a tray of food on the table next to the bed. Then he began to stack wood in the fireplace. He barely looked at her.

While the man set about preparing a fire, she forced herself to ignore the rich aroma wafting from the food despite her protesting stomach.

"Excuse me," she said. "What's your name? What is this place?"

The man didn't answer. Clara tried again in German. Still she received no response. When the man left a fire roared in the fireplace, and the room gradually warmed. She turned her attention to the tray of food to discover some sort of meaty red stew and a hunk of crusty bread. Clara almost gagged on the first spoonful at the amount of paprika, but she forced herself to eat, and the second spoonful she found more tolerable. About halfway through she began to enjoy the stew.

After she finished eating, Clara walked to the window again. Outside the crescent moon hung low in the sky, just above the trees, and the stars shone brightly. Frost spiderwebbed its way across the glass. Shadowy figures moved among the naked trees in the woods.

When she turned around, the man in the black waist-coat sat in one of the chairs next to the fireplace.

"Please, have a seat," he said, motioning to the other chair.

"I don't think I want to do that." She did want to, though.

He was dressed much as before, except the cravat was gone, and the collar of his shirt was open. Her eyes traced the line of his collarbone to his broad chest. The light from the fire never quite reached his face. The shadows flickered and darted around him.

"Please," he repeated. "We have much to discuss."

"Like what?"

He stood and walked towards her, his predator's gait even more pronounced. "Really, now, you needn't fear me. If we took some time to get to know one another, I'm sure you'd find we share quite a few of the same goals."

He stood over her looking down, his face just inches from her. He smelled like cinnamon and sage, and even though something in the back of her head told her it ought not be, she could feel the heat coming off his body. She tried to back away, but there was nowhere to go. "I'm not going to hurt you. I want you to trust me."

"That's a little hard to do when I'm being held prisoner."

He reached out and took her hand in his. "Only out of necessity. Maybe, soon we can alter that arrangement."

Clara shivered as a wave of electricity passed through her body. Her heart fluttered, and her cheeks grew hot. "What do you mean? Where are Adam and Arkady? Did you do something to them?"

"I assure you they are alive and healthy, but you needn't worry about them. They may have other worries at the moment." He gave her hand a gentle squeeze. "You could come to like it here."

Her gaze shifted to the moonlit scene outside. "I doubt that."

With his other hand he caressed her cheek. "Perhaps I'm rushing things. I should give you some time. I know you don't understand everything now, but you will soon."

And with that he backed out of the room and closed the door, leaving her alone again. Only she didn't feel like she was alone.

Clara climbed back into the bed and pulled the covers over her head. As she drifted off to sleep, a wolf howled, and when she dreamt, she dreamt she was someone else, somewhere else, in a time long past. Wolves howled there, too, and shadows moved in the darkness more dangerous than the wolves by far.

THREE

Near Berlin, Germany
6 June 1878

THE BUMP IN THE ROAD jolted Elizabeth awake. The slow rocking of the carriage and the rhythm of the horses' hooves had lulled her to sleep. She looked out the window and immediately knew something was wrong. Even the light of the full moon wasn't enough to penetrate the murky woods crowding the road on either side. Friedrich, the driver, had said they would make Berlin by sundown.

She leaned out as far as she dared and called to him. "Friedrich, where are we?"

He didn't answer.

"Friedrich, is something wrong? Shouldn't we be in Berlin by now?"

Again no answer.

Elizabeth tried one last time. "Friedrich, are we lost?"

At that moment, she caught a glimpse of something in the woods out of the corner of her eye, something that worried her more than Friedrich's failure to answer. A few seconds later, it appeared again, a shadow, darker than the darkness itself, keeping pace with the carriage. It was following them, and it wasn't the only one. All around her, yips and hoots pierced the night, and then a full-throated howl. The horses whinnied. The carriage lurched. Friedrich struggled to keep it under control.

The wolf howled again, joined by others this time. The carriage pitched to one side and then the other as the horses panicked. Friedrich fought as hard as he could to keep them from bolting, but ultimately lost. The carriage careened to the left and crashed onto its side.

Elizabeth lay there momentarily, listening to the horses' hooves as they galloped away. Something warm and wet ran down her cheek. She winced when she reached up to touch it.

Elizabeth twisted herself around until she could stand. With some effort, she managed to push open the door on the side of the carriage facing up, and with even more effort, more than Elizabeth thought she was capable of, she lifted herself out of the overturned vehicle.

The horses were gone, and there was no sign of Friedrich. Elizabeth gingerly placed a foot on the carriage's running board in order to climb down, but the barks and the yips returned. All around her in the woods, pairs of yellow eyes glowed. Emerging from the dimly lit tree line, a dozen smoke-grey wolves surrounded the ruined carriage. Teeth bared and growling, they inched toward her, making the circle smaller and smaller.

The largest lunged at her, catching the hem of her dress in its teeth. It tried to pull her off the carriage, but her dress tore, and the animal fell back. Elizabeth fell, too, and almost met her end at the jaws of another wolf taking the opportunity to spring at her. Sooner or later, one of them would succeed in pulling her down.

A gunshot shattered the night. The wolves broke rank, turning their attention from her. A moment later, another gunshot sent the pack scattering back into the woods. Elizabeth looked in the direction of the shots to see three men on coal-black horses emerge from the darkness. Gypsies.

The one in front barked something in a language she didn't understand, and the three of them stopped. The leader dismounted and walked toward her. His piercing green eyes and long nose gave his face a hawk-like appearance, even over an ample brown mustache. At the base of the carriage, he made a dramatic bow and offered his hand to her. Elizabeth slipped her hand in his, and he helped her down off the carriage.

"Are you all right, my lady?" he asked in strangely accented German.

"Yes," Elizabeth replied in her own tentative German. "Thank you for scaring off the wolves."

The man smiled. "I simply could not let you be devoured. It would have been ungentlemanly." His smile melted away, replaced by a look of concern. He reached up to touch her cheek. "My lady, we must get you some help. You have been hurt."

"It's just a scratch," Elizabeth said.

The man shook his head. "No, our camp is not far from here. I insist that you come with us. We'll have someone look at it there."

He helped her onto the back of his horse. They followed the road for a while, then without warning turned off into the undergrowth. The Gypsy's companions did the same. Startled, Elizabeth clutched the man's midsection.

She could feel his compact and powerful muscles as he guided the horse over a trail she never would have seen on her own. They wound their way deeper into the woods, into a world completely foreign to Elizabeth. The moon shown down in patches through the trees, spotlighting odd vignettes—a half-fallen tree with its branches turned to grow upward toward the sky, a thicket of shrubs with bright red berries, a massive oak tree with branches so heavy, they almost touched the ground. Unfamiliar sounds filled the air around her, too—not the night noises of the city, but crickets, owls, and bats.

The nearly invisible trail reminded Elizabeth of the stories her father used to tell her about fairy roads in England that appeared and disappeared without warning. If a hapless traveler took one of them, he would find himself in a different realm entirely, where the fairies ruled and where our world's rules of logic held no sway. Only a very few ever came back from that world.

Soon, an orange glow emerged from the darkness ahead. They came upon a clearing where the Gypsies had set up camp. The man dismounted and helped Elizabeth off the horse. He walked over to a group of women and spoke to them in the same language he had used with the men earlier.

A few minutes later, he returned and spoke to her in his accented German, "Magda will show you where you can sleep tonight. Tomorrow, we will take you into the city."

"Thank you," Elizabeth said again.

He took her hand and kissed it. "I would not be a man if I did not give aid to a beautiful woman in distress."

As he turned to walk away she called after him. "Wait. I have to know your name. Please."

"Alexej," he replied before disappearing among the others in the camp.

A plump older woman led her to a small tent with blankets and pillows, and almost immediately, someone thrust a cup of some hot liquid into her hands. It smelled like cloves and honey. Elizabeth sipped while the Gypsy woman carefully dabbed the blood from her cheek with a cloth soaked in warm water. She stayed up listening to the Gypsy music as they played their instruments and sang in their peculiar language. She drifted to sleep with the music's rhythms running through her head.

"Lady James."

Elizabeth woke with a start. She looked up to see Friedrich's concerned face from where she still lay in the overturned carriage. The sky overhead was several shades lighter than she remembered.

"Lady James," Friedrich repeated. "Don't worry. Help has arrived."

FOUR

—⁂—

Sarajevo, Bosnia and Herzegovina
2 December 1999

A DAM PACED THE STUDY OF the safe house like a caged tiger. Arkady Danilovich Markov, special agent for the Russian Orthodox Church, sat in one of the chairs, staring sullenly out the window. Inspector Nikola Gavrilović of the Sarajevo Police sat in the other chair, his fingertips pressed together.

"I'm beginning to share Clara's opinion of your 'safe' houses," Adam snapped at the Russian.

"So am I, for what it's worth," Arkady replied.

"How exactly does something like this happen?" Adam asked. "It was almost dawn. And this place, it has a threshold. A vampire shouldn't have been able to cross."

"Humans can, though. If a vampire had helpers like Stjepan did ..." Inspector Gavrilović offered.

Stjepan, going by the name of Dragomir, was the three-hundred-year-old vampire leader of the Chetniks, a Serbian ultranationalist organization that had been after

Dracula's medallion. To complicate matters, he was also Elena's former lover. *Yasamin. Elena.* A hard lump formed in the pit of Adam's stomach. In *Dracula*, there were three brides.

"Also remember, a strong enough vampire can tolerate sunlight for a short amount of time," Inspector Gavrilović continued, "especially at sunrise, when the light is not too strong. That's one thing Bram Stoker got right."

"In any event," Arkady added, "Greta's wounds could also have been made by something other than a vampire."

Adam shook his head. "We didn't find any blood."

Arkady shrugged. "She could have been killed somewhere else and brought here."

Adam narrowed his eyes. "So what are you saying? You don't think there are any vampires involved in this? Need I remind you what is pained on the wall downstairs?"

Arkady sighed. "What I'm saying is that we don't know. Jumping to conclusions could get us killed. Or Clara."

"So what do you suggest we do?"

"Inspector Gavrilović and I will work our contacts for now, and you should do what the note said, work faster."

"That's it? Clara is in danger. She could be anywhere now." Adam plumbed the depths of his rage. "You could at least act like you care."

Arkady shot up from the chair, his face suddenly red, his teeth clenched. "Do not ever question me again about that." His face fell, and he sat back down. "I care. I'm just responsible for keeping you from doing something stupid."

Adam grabbed his coat and headed for the door.

"What are you doing?" Arkady asked.

"Something stupid," Adam replied. "I'm going for a walk. I need some air."

"You really shouldn't," the inspector said, "until we

know what we're facing—"

Adam jabbed a finger in the inspector's direction. "Don't you start, too. I'll be back before dark, and then I'll 'work faster.'"

He slammed the door behind him a little harder than he intended. Outside the air was crisp, but there was no breeze, so he found the cold bearable. He put one foot in front of the other without giving much thought to where he was going. Arkady's new safe house, where they had moved after the first one was compromised, was in Sarajevo's Stari Grad, or Old City. The streets were narrow, and buildings crowded the sidewalk. A few hardy tourists strolled about, admiring the store windows decorated for Christmas.

Adam was busy thinking about the books, running through possibilities in his mind. He didn't understand how he was supposed to "work faster." He was no closer to solving the clues to the whereabouts of the medallion than when he has started. And yet he had to wonder if he had missed something. A simple golden trinket couldn't have caused so much death.

Lost in thought, Adam wandered from the shopping district and onto a residential street lined with trees. The sun went behind the clouds, and the temperature dropped. On the other side of the street, a couple walked. Something seemed odd about them, but Adam couldn't place his finger on it.

As they drew closer, Adam slowed, trying to get a better look. They were huddled against the cold. The man covered his chin and mouth with a scarf. Only his eyes remained visible. The woman's blond hair peeked from underneath her fur hat. She wore a scarf as well, but left her mouth and nose exposed. As they passed, she turned her head to look at him.

Adam held his breath. He flashed back to the beautiful Russian agent who had saved his life months earlier. Her name had been Anya, and she was dead, a fact that still gnawed at him.

After the couple passed, Adam craned his neck to watch them retreat. When they were some distance away, the sun came out again from behind the clouds, and the air warmed, at least a little. The woman didn't show any signs of recognizing him. Still something unsettled Adam. He decided to return to the safe house.

FIVE

———ᴍ———

Sarajevo, Bosnia and Herzegovina
3 December 1999

W IND BLEW THROUGH THE TREES outside the
bedroom, causing the shadows to dance. Adam
glanced bleary-eyed at the clock on the nightstand. The angry red numbers blared. It was three o'clock
in the morning. Bored with staring at the ceiling, he threw
the covers off, climbed out of bed, and crept to his door.
He stepped out into the silent hallway. Adam hesitated for
a moment outside Clara's room before he pushed the door
open.

Nothing had been touched. In a chair beside the bed,
Clara's clothes for the next day were folded neatly. The
bedspread was turned down, and a glass of water rested on
the nightstand. Adam wasn't sure what he was doing. He
told himself there might be something in the room he
could use to find her, but he knew better.

A desk stood against one wall, a few books and some
papers stacked on top. Not wanting to stand aside while

the others did all the work, Clara had asked for everything Arkady and Nikola could give her related to vampires. She had wanted to test her theory that vampires were nothing more than super-sociopaths. She thought maybe if she studied their behavior she could help predict it. Unfortunately for her and everyone else, they had proved unpredictable.

Adam reached for the book on top of the stack when he noticed a picture propped up on the desk, slightly bent, as if it had spent time in a wallet. It was a picture of him, a few years younger. He was smiling at the camera. He remembered when Clara had taken it. They had ditched the retirement reception for one of Adam's colleagues, a man Adam couldn't stand, and they had found themselves at a midnight diner—Adam in a suit and Clara in an evening gown—eating burgers and drinking chocolate shakes. Adam almost forgot about Nadiye that night.

Almost.

Adam set the photograph down, surprised Clara had held onto it. He picked up the book he had reached for and leafed through it.

"Can't sleep either?" Arkady stood in the doorway.

"What are you doing here?" Adam asked.

"I could ask you the same thing."

Adam sighed. "To be honest, I don't know. I have no idea what to do, where to go from here. All I have are random circled letters in five books and no idea how to make sense of any of them." He scanned the desktop. "Clara thought she'd found something interesting, but she never had the chance to tell me. Maybe she wrote something down somewhere."

Arkady scratched his beard. "It's possible, I suppose, but I can tell you everything we gave her has been analyzed by people who have devoted their lives to fighting monsters like vampires. What could she discover that they haven't?"

Adam chuckled. "You haven't known Clara as long as I have. You'd be surprised what she can do when she puts her mind to something. There's no stopping her."

Arkady smirked. "I'd noticed."

"She was reading about all the old vampire panics in the Austrian empire," Adam said, returning his attention to the book in his hand, "Arnold Pavle, Petar Blaglojević, and the like."

"Didn't Yasamin turn Arnold Pavle?"

Adam nodded. "There was a letter about him in the book that led us to Dubrovnik, but I'm not sure how that is going to help."

"Where did he meet with Yasamin?"

Adam shook his head. "No one really knows. He was a soldier in the army at the time. They were constantly moving, though there is some suggestion they were somewhere in Kosovo."

"And where was Elena from?" Arkady asked.

"Gračanica, in Kosovo," Adam replied.

Arkady raised an eyebrow. "Do you think that's a coincidence?"

"No such thing."

"No, not in this line of work," Arkady agreed with a chuckle.

Adam flashed back to earlier when he had gone out for a walk and seen the woman who looked like Anya. Not without some difficulty, he pushed the image from his mind. "No, no, it's something to look into, at least."

"But tomorrow, don't you think?" Arkady yawned. "Nothing good can come from getting anything started now."

"I can't sleep." Adam picked up another book. "Might as well do something useful."

Arkady stepped back into the hallway. "As you wish. *I'm* going to get some sleep."

Adam grunted a good night, already focused on other things.

"Adam. Adam, look at me." Arkady waited until Adam met his gaze. "We have people all over the place looking for her. If she shows her face in public anywhere in Europe, we'll find her, you can bet."

Adam frowned. "*If.* I get the feeling we're dealing with someone too cunning to make that mistake."

"You forget Inspector Gavrilović and his people. They don't have the resources we do, but they have ways of getting people into places we can't go. Perhaps one of them will find a lead."

"Did you just give Nikola a compliment?"

Arkady grinned. "Don't tell him or I'll have to kill you."

Adam crossed his heart. "Not a word I promise."

Arkady's smile faded. "You're going to have to sleep sometime, or you won't be of use to anyone."

"I'll sleep when I'm dead."

Arkady shot him a dirty look. "That's what I'm afraid of."

"I can take care of myself, Arkady."

Arkady nodded. "Fine, I just want it on the record that I said something. Good night, Adam."

Adam didn't reply.

SIX

—꘎꘎꘎—

Near Cluj, Romania
3 December 1999

MOST OF THE BOOKS ON the shelf were in French. A few were in German, and still others in Romanian, with a smattering of other languages thrown in. Clara struggled her way through a thick French tome for the better part of an hour before she realized it was a horticultural treatise on the gardens of the Palace at Versailles.

At the jangle of the key in the door, her heart jumped. The shadows had grown long, crawling across the floor. A quick glance outside confirmed dusk had arrived. She expected the old caretaker with her dinner, but a small part of her hoped and feared in equal measure that her host had come calling again.

When the caretaker opened the door. Clara's shoulders slumped in disappointment. Not only was he not her mysterious host; he was also empty-handed. Until that moment she hadn't realized how hungry she was.

27

The caretaker waved for Clara to come with him. Darker thoughts filled her head. She glanced around the room, searching for something she could use as a weapon. The old man looked feeble enough. She could probably overpower him.

But where exactly would she go then? They were in the middle of the woods, and it was winter. She had a good chance of freezing to death before she found help.

The old man glared at her and beckoned again. This time she followed. At least, she thought, she'd get a better look at the rest of the house. Gas lamps lit the corridor outside at intervals, their low hiss audible in the otherwise silent hallway. Dark wood paneling covered the lower portion of the walls while damask wallpaper covered the rest. Clara made sure to count the number of doors they passed. When they came to a set of stairs, the caretaker began to descend.

Clara followed him down two floors, where he led her through a set of doors and into a sitting room filled with high-backed, overstuffed chairs and elaborately carved tables. A fire roared in the fireplace, though no one occupied the room. They passed through to the next room.

Clara stopped just inside the door. She found herself in the dining room. On the long, dark wood table was one place setting. Seated next to it, at the head of the table, her host waited with a patient smile.

"I'm glad you found a dress to your liking," he said. "The green is very becoming."

Clara's face grew hot. She had found a closet full of clothes that fit her. The styles were all from the last century—high collars and full sleeves—but given the drafty room, she didn't mind so much. "Thank you."

He pulled out a chair for her. "Please, have a seat."

As soon as she sat, a woman emerged through one of the several other doors. Behind her Clara caught a glimpse of the kitchen. The woman placed a covered dish in front of Clara. She pulled the cover away to reveal a roasted pheasant with potatoes and leeks. The savory aroma filled the room. The woman left and returned with a wine glass and a bottle of red wine. She poured a glass for Clara, whose eyes grew wide at the vintage printed on the label.

"You won't be joining me?" Clara asked her host when the woman was gone.

"I've already eaten," he replied, "but I'm more than happy to keep you company. Now please eat, before your food gets cold."

The meat was so tender, it fell off the bone, and the wine, while a little sweeter than she preferred, complemented the pheasant perfectly. It was one of the best meals she had ever had.

"I'd like to apologize to you," the man said.

"Apologize? For what?" Clara asked.

"For frightening you last night."

Alarms should have been sounding in her head. She had written her doctoral thesis on psychological warfare. She knew all the tricks a person could use to break another down—gaslighting, intimidation, positive reinforcement. And yet she took him at his word.

"You didn't frighten me."

"I feel we got off to a bad start, though. I truly don't want your stay here to be an unpleasant one. Have you been able to occupy your time?"

"I've been trying to read," Clara replied. "You wouldn't happen to have any books in English, would you?"

A wry smile spread across his face. "I might. What do you fancy?"

She wanted to respond that she liked books about picking locks, or rappelling down buildings, or warding off vampires. "History mainly. Biographies too."

He nodded. "I'll see what I can find."

"You said this house used to belong to Hungarian nobles. How long have you lived here?"

"The estate fell into disuse after the end of the Second World War. It was purchased a few years ago. We are working to bring back its original splendor."

Clara raised an eyebrow. "We?"

"There are a few others, like me, who believe that the world has gone off course. We do what we can to bring up reminders of how things used to be, a simpler time, a more ordered time. Now everywhere you look there is chaos. It wasn't always so."

"A time when everyone knew their station."

If he caught the slight sarcasm in her voice, he didn't show it. "Exactly."

"Your accent, it's … difficult to place. Where are you originally from?" she asked.

"A few different places," he replied.

"Your English is perfect."

"I lived in England for … a time."

His lean features seemed even more striking in the gaslight. The shock of white hair stood out among the black. A memory stirred at the back of her head. There was something familiar about the way he looked, but she couldn't place it.

"I'm not afraid of you," she said suddenly, "even though I should be. Why is that? Especially since this whole dinner feels like a scene from *Dracula*."

His expression darkened immediately, and his lips curled into a snarl. "A word of advice. You'll do well to remember not to mention his name in this house again."

They passed the rest of the meal in silence. The hour was late when the caretaker returned Clara to her room.

OUTSIDE, SHADOWS DANCED ACROSS THE snow, and wolves howled in the woods. Clara sat in the chair by the fireplace, trying to stay awake, not wanting to sleep, not wanting to let her guard down, but eventually her eyelids grew heavy, and she couldn't stop herself from nodding off. As soon as her eyes shut she slipped into another dream.

SEVEN

—◆—

Berlin, Germany
12 June 1878

I T IS SAID THAT EMPIRES, *like men, must eventually die.*
Like men, however, they often linger near death before the
end, and like men, their heirs often squabble over their pos-
sessions long before the life has left them.

In Istanbul, gone were the days when great barges glided
down the Bosporus, gaily colored flags waving in the breeze. The
wealthy Ottoman families had long since abandoned their summer homes on the water, leaving fire and flood to claim them.
The walls of the medieval Byzantine city crumbled, even as the
poor built their shacks on the moldering remains.

The Sultan did not even dwell in Istanbul proper anymore,
preferring a rambling Western palace far away from the city's
heart. Despite it all, the empire lingered, while the Great Powers
of Europe nipped at its borders and waited greedily for its de-
mise.

"IT'S WHAT WE'RE HERE TO do, you know," Alfred told her, "to pick the bones of the Turkish Empire."

Elizabeth adjusted her husband's tie. "You make it sound so ghastly."

"It is ghastly, dear, and believe me, I'm being polite. It's nothing compared to what I could say. At this, the most enlightened time in history, the Great Powers send their greatest statesmen here to Berlin to do what? Pledge to work together to eradicate illness? End poverty? Fight injustice? No. To paw over pieces of land that don't even belong to them in the first place."

Apparently it was time for her to talk Alfred down from the ceiling again. "I thought you said the purpose of the Congress was to undo some treaty. What was it? San..."

"Stefano," Alfred supplied, "And of course, it is. The Russians all but dictated the treaty to the Turks at the end of the recent hostilities. Now they have the Kingdom of Bulgaria as a giant puppet state in the heart of the Balkans. The treaty can't be allowed to stand, but don't think for a minute this Congress is about restoring the status quo ante bellum."

"Trust me, dear, I never thought such a thing."

"I just hope things don't get too terribly out of hand. The Russians are ... unpredictable."

"Lords Beaconsfield, Salisbury, and Russell seem more than capable of handling anything. And, of course they have a brilliant attaché to aid them."

"You mean me?" Alfred asked.

Elizabeth laughed. "Yes, you, dear. Who else?"

Alfred's face flushed. "And I have a beautiful wife to aid me."

"That, you do. Now tell me again why I can't go with you tonight?"

"Diplomats' wives aren't invited to the social gatherings. It's German custom."

"It's odd is what it is."

"Nonetheless, we have to play by their rules while we're here."

Elizabeth tried not to let her disappointment show. "And how long do you suppose that will be?"

Alfred shrugged. "The Congress is supposed to last about a month. After that, who knows? I don't plan to be an attaché forever. This is a huge opportunity for me, Elizabeth. If we play our cards right, I'll get a promotion, and we'll be back in London in the very near future." He gave his wife a peck on the cheek. "It will probably be quite late when I return. I'll try to be quiet."

ALFRED HADN'T RETURNED FROM THE reception by the time Elizabeth fell asleep, and when she woke in the morning, he had already left again. In what had become her routine since her arrival in Berlin a week earlier, she ate her breakfast sitting by the open window in her bedroom, looking out over the street below. She watched the branches of the linden trees lining the Wilhelmstraße sway in the gentle summer breeze.

In Vienna, Alfred's previous post, their mornings had always been frenzied as Alfred rushed about, preparing for his day, but at least she had a chance to say a few words to him. In Berlin, he was usually gone before the sunrise.

Elizabeth spotted Lady Russell, the wife of the British ambassador, passing by on her daily morning walk. The townhouse rented for them was only a block away from the Palais Strousberg, the new home of the British embassy. Lady Russell never missed her morning walk for any reason. Neither did she ever miss her afternoon tea or her evening walk. It was rumored she had once sent the wife of an undersecretary running from the room in tears with a mere disapproving glance, and the consensus among the embassy staff was that Lord Russell had to get Lady Russell's approval before he made any decision. Elizabeth smiled to herself. If she were ever to find out what others said about her, she suspected Lady Russell herself might laugh.

Elizabeth turned away from the window at the sound of the front door opening and closing. She hadn't heard the bell ring, nor had she heard Sarah, the maid, answer it. It would have been odd for Alfred to be home at that hour, and if he had come home, she expected he would have announced himself.

"Sarah?" she called, "Is someone at the door?"

The maid didn't respond. Elizabeth walked out to the landing at the top of the stairs and looked down onto the empty foyer below. She called for Sarah again as she descended. Still the maid didn't answer. To her left off the foyer was the parlor. She peered into the darkened room to find it unoccupied. To her right, opposite the parlor, the door to Alfred's office stood, closed as always. She hesitated before placing her hand on the doorknob.

In all the places they had lived, she always felt Alfred's office was not a place she was welcome. Still, in this instance, she told herself she needed to at least peek, to see if anyone was there. She turned the knob quickly and pushed the door open. Alfred's desk sat in the center of the room, its surface covered in papers and books stacked haphazardly. No one was there.

She backed out of the room and closed the door. As she did, she glanced down to see a white calling card resting on the table in the entryway. She picked it up. On it was a single name in black embossed type—Dr. Theodore Tolliver.

She froze.

Sarah entered from the kitchen just then. "Apologies, milady. Did you call for me?"

"Sarah, did someone come by and leave this card?"

"No, milady. No one has stopped by."

"Was it here earlier this morning?"

"No, milady, it wasn't. I've never seen it before."

"Where could it have come from?"

"I'm sure I don't know, milady."

Theodore Tolliver was her father. She hadn't seen him in ten years.

FRIEDRICH SMILED AT ELIZABETH AS he helped her into the carriage. "Pleasant day, milady, is it not? Perfect for an outing."

"Oh, yes, quite pleasant," she said absently.

Friedrich cocked his head to one side. "Is something the matter, milady?"

"No, nothing at all."

In truth, every time she closed her eyes, she saw the card with her father's name on it. Each letter tore open an old wound. He had been gone for so long she almost succeeded in forgetting what he looked like. She would have rather not been reminded of him at all.

"Are you sure there is nothing I can help you with, milady?" Friedrich asked. "I am, after all, here to serve."

Most of the embassy staff were English, but Friedrich was a special case. His full name, he told Elizabeth, was Friedrich Wilhelm Henry Stanton, the first two names bestowed by his Prussian mother and the last two by his English father. He had spent most of his life in Berlin, though, and like all the Germans Elizabeth had met, he tended to be upfront almost to the point of brusqueness. Elizabeth was not quite used to it.

"No, thank you, Friedrich. Just drive me to the Neues Palais, please."

The Crown Princess had invited her and the other British wives to the Neues Palais for tea. She and Alfred had been formally introduced to the Crown Prince shortly after their arrival. He had taken over state functions for his ailing father the Kaiser.

His wife, the Crown Princess, was in fact England's own Princess Royal, the oldest daughter of Queen Victoria. She had been incredibly gracious and seemed genuinely interested in Elizabeth and any news from abroad, but Elizabeth detected something in her eyes— melancholy almost. Elizabeth wondered.

She had heard the Princess Royal insisted on having English maids and English nannies for her children. Did she miss England? Was she happy in her marriage? Or was it something else? Elizabeth often thought about the kings and the queens, the princes and the princesses, the dukes and the duchesses. Did they ever tire of the duties, the protocols, the obligations?

The carriage ride afforded Elizabeth the first opportunity to really see the city. While Berlin was not as beautiful as Paris or Vienna, she had to admit to herself it was much cleaner than London, and it was a growing, vibrant city with new construction everywhere. In less than ten years, Berlin had gone from being the capital of a backwater state to the center of an empire sprawling across the middle of Europe.

People crowded the streets—women walking to the markets, workers going to the construction sites, couriers, shopkeepers, businessmen in their tailored suits. She studied their faces as the carriage made its way. Elizabeth had never seen people so industrious, so engrossed in their daily routines, so seemingly content with their lives. She wondered if they were truly happy, or if they simply didn't know enough to be unhappy.

A face among those on the street interrupted her thoughts. It appeared only for a second, so fleeting a glimpse she couldn't even be sure she saw it at all. A man with piercing green eyes and coal black hair stood on the sidewalk among the passing throngs of people. Their eyes met, and Elizabeth thought the corners of his mouth turned up, just slightly. He looked familiar.

She still thought about the way the man's eyes seemed to bore into her as Friedrich opened the door for her to exit the carriage. She didn't even notice they had arrived at the Neues Palais. The Crown Prince's summer palace was not, again, as impressive as the Hofburg or Schönbrunn Palaces in Vienna, or even Buckingham in London, but it was imposing and grand nonetheless—Teutonic was the word that came to mind.

She took Friedrich's hand while she stepped down and felt something, a slip of paper. She met the driver's gaze, puzzled.

He grinned and offered a slight bow. "As I said, milady, I'm here to help."

She unfolded the piece of paper. Written on it was an address.

EIGHT

—ᮀ—

Berlin, Germany
16 June 1878

ELIZABETH CLUTCHED THE PIECE OF paper in her
hand as she made her way down Unter den Linden. The day was warm, despite the early hour.
The address on the piece of paper was only a few blocks
from where she'd asked Friedrich to stop the carriage for
her, but that made the cobblestones no less difficult to
negotiate. At last, on a small side street lined with row
houses, she found the address she was looking for: No. 5.
In this supposedly well-to-do area, she expected more than
the neglected residence she stood facing.

Nonetheless, Elizabeth ascended the stairs and pulled
the rope hanging beside the door. Inside a tiny bell jingled.
She didn't wait long before footsteps echoed from within.
A girl, perhaps no older than ten, opened the door. Dark
eyes looked up at Lady James. The girl's black hair hung in
long, loose braids. She wore a simple dress and an apron.

"Hullo," Elizabeth said, a little uncertain, "I do hope

you speak English. My German is so atrocious. I'm looking for Mme. Kárpáthy."

The child stared.

Elizabeth made another attempt. "I was given this address—"

Just then a voice called from inside the house in a language Elizabeth didn't recognize. It certainly wasn't German. The girl replied in the same language. Moments later, a woman appeared in the doorway. Her red hair hung down almost to her waist, but her complexion was not like any redhead Elizabeth had ever seen. Her skin was a deep olive color, just like the girl's. She also wore a simple dress similar to the girl's, but her bearing, poise, and grace made it seem like a grand ball gown.

"Good morning," Elizabeth said. "Mme. Kárpáthy?"

The woman nodded. She was much younger than Elizabeth expected. She said something else to the girl, and the child ran back into the house.

"Good morning," the woman replied. "May I help you?" Her English was barely accented.

Elizabeth shook her head. "I ... I'm not sure."

Mme. Kárpáthy smiled. "A great many people are nervous the first time they have their fortunes read, Lady James, but really there's nothing to fear."

"How do you know my name?"

She laughed. It was a musical sound, like chimes. "You knew my name didn't you? Besides I advertise my ability to see the future. Surely it occurred to you I may have been expecting you."

The woman's familiarity put Elizabeth off. She didn't know what she had been expecting, but it wasn't this. "I ... I think maybe I've changed my mind. I don't think I want my fortune read. I'm sorry to have taken your time.

Please excuse me."

She turned to leave.

"Something compelled you to come here," Mme. Kárpáthy called after her, "even if you don't know what it is.
Wouldn't you like to find out?"

Elizabeth hesitated for a moment and then turned
back around.

The woman smiled at her again. "It won't take very
long. And my fees are reasonable. Please, come inside."

Once inside, Mme. Kárpáthy led Elizabeth to a small
drawing room. It, like the house's exterior, seemed old and
worn. The fabric on the chairs was faded and frayed in
places. Moth holes in the heavy curtains let in tiny pin-
points of light. Yet Elizabeth couldn't imagine the room
ever looked new. Mme. Kárpáthy invited her to sit and
took a chair opposite her. Between them stood a table that
held a beautiful box covered with inlaid wood.

Mme. Kárpáthy opened the lid of the box. From inside,
she pulled a deck of cards. "Shall we begin, then, Lady
James?"

At Elizabeth's nod, Mme. Kárpáthy closed her eyes.
Her hands rested in her lap, cradling the deck of cards.
She sat for a long time, saying nothing. Her breathing grew
more and more rhythmic. At one point, Elizabeth thought
she might have fallen asleep. She was about to say something when Mme. Kárpáthy suddenly opened her eyes
again. The fortuneteller placed the cards one by one face
up on the table in front of her.

On several occasions, Elizabeth had watched cards
used to tell a person's fortune, but these cards were unlike
any Elizabeth had ever seen. They bore elaborate draw-
ings, and the names written on them were in a language
Elizabeth couldn't read, not English, or German, or

French, or even Latin. Elizabeth wondered if it was the same language Mme. Kárpáthy had spoken earlier. The images offered no comfort. Among the cards the woman placed on the table was a dancing skeleton, a man hanging from a tree, and a demonic creature.

Elizabeth tried to find some sort of clue to the cards' meanings by watching Mme. Kárpáthy, but the fortune-teller's expression remained inscrutable. Elizabeth had seen a reading performed with as few as three cards. Mme. Kárpáthy drew over twenty. When she finished placing the cards on the table, she stared at them without speaking, without moving. Elizabeth felt the smallness of the room. The stale air made it difficult for her to breathe. She wanted to push back the curtains and throw open the window.

Instead, she watched as Mme. Kárpáthy picked up each card in reverse order. She shuffled the deck and began the process again. She turned the cards over three times.

After the third time, Mme. Kárpáthy looked at Elizabeth. "Your father has a message for you."

Elizabeth felt her face flush. "My father? That's impossible. He's— I think he's dead. He must be. How can he have a message for me?"

"Death is no barrier here. I can speak with those who have passed on as easily as I can speak with you. But your father is not dead. He needs to tell you something, but he can't. There is an obstacle in his way."

The bile rose in Elizabeth's throat. "But he disappeared when I was a child. One day he simply never came home. No one, to my knowledge, has seen him since. Why does he want to contact me now?"

Mme. Kárpáthy shook her head. "The cards don't tell

me, but there is more here. I see another man, one with dark features, of noble birth. He is very close, but far away at the same time."

"You must be speaking about my husband. He's an attaché to Lord Russell, the ambassador. His father is an earl, though he's not likely to inherit the title because he has two older brothers. This Congress is taking up all of his time. I've barely spoken to him in more than a week."

"No, not your husband."

"Not Alfred? I can't imagine who it could be, then."

"He is a man you have recently met, and you want to know whether you will see him again. This man, he is a wanderer."

"A wanderer? A Gypsy?"

"So there is another man."

Elizabeth struggled to remember. "There was a carriage accident, but that part wasn't real. I had a dream. That's all. Friedrich tended to the cut on my head and flagged down another carriage that came by that morning. The wolves and the Gypsy—it was a dream. How can I see him again? He isn't real."

"The cards say you will meet him again."

A chill flowed through Elizabeth, and the tiny hairs on the back of her neck stood on end. If she looked behind her chair, would she see the Gypsy there?

"When?" Elizabeth asked.

Mme. Kárpáthy didn't answer. She grew pale and clutched the arm of her chair. "I'm sorry. We must end our visit. I don't intend to be rude, but reading the cards has taken most of my energy. I need to lie down and rest."

"What about your payment?"

Mme. Kárpáthy opened the lid of the box and replaced the deck of cards. "There will be no fee for this session. My daughter will show you out."

"Lady James," Friedrich waited for her with the carriage where she had disembarked. He offered his hand to help her inside. "I trust you found your outing satisfactory?"

"Yes, Friedrich, thank you," Elizabeth replied, wanting nothing more than to rid herself of the memory of that stifling room.

"I'm pleased to hear it, milady."

NINE

—ллл—

Bucharest, Romania
4 December 1999

A ROUGH HAND NUDGED ADAM AWAKE.
"Pack your things," Arkady said as Adam sat up
and blinked the sleep from his eyes. "We're leaving."

"What time is it?" Adam asked.

"About three in the morning," Arkady replied.

Adam rolled out of bed, trying to shake the cobwebs
from his head. "Where are we going?"

But Arkady had already left the room.

Four hours later, they entered the suburbs of Bucharest, after flying on a plane Adam was convinced used rubber bands to turn the propellers. Arkady drove the nice silver BMW that had awaited them at the airport. Adam, in the passenger seat, hugged the satchel that rarely left his side anymore, the one containing all his books and notes pertaining to the search for Dracula's medallion.

"Did you look into what we talked about before, about

Kosovo?" Arkady shot him a sideways glance. He still hadn't told Adam why they were in Bucharest.

Adam rummaged through his satchel until he pulled out an old leather-bound volume. "I didn't realize it at the time, but there's actually a reference to Kosovo in *Dracula*." The book practically fell open to the page he wanted. "It's in the Count's speech to Jonathan Harker not long after he arrived at Dracula's castle. He references 'the shame of Cassova' when the Turks defeated the Christians and gained a toe-hold in Europe."

Arkady grunted. "So that can't be a coincidence."

Adam shook his head, "No, but that doesn't get us much of anywhere. Does that mean the medallion is in Kosovo? And if so, where?"

"Gračanica seems like a logical place, given past experience."

Adam stuffed *Dracula* back into his satchel. "Then why the books? Why the underlined passages, the circled letters, the random numbers? Why the wild goose chase across Eastern Europe that's nearly gotten me murdered several dozen times?"

Arkady slowed the car and turned onto a side street. "I wish I could tell you what we're here to see will clear it all up for you, but I'd be lying."

Adam glanced out the window. To his surprise, they were not pulling up to yet another nondescript townhouse in another forgettable neighborhood. Instead they approached a long building with a neoclassical façade. "Wait, this is the University of Bucharest. Why are we here? How is this little jaunt getting us closer to finding Clara?"

Arkady wedged the Mercedes between two police cars, directly in front of the building's main entrance. "Just come. You'll see."

THE MAN LAY AMID THE stacks on the third floor of the library, in the history section. His throat was slit, but Adam was not focused on the thin red line across the man's neck. Rather he stared at the man's right hand. Someone had painted it green.

"He's back," Adam whispered.

A grim smile played across Arkady's face. "And luckily for you, you were nowhere near here."

"Do you know who he was?"

"Lucian Borescu." The reply came from a lanky man with a pencil mustache and a tailored grey suit who stood at the end of the row. "One of ours. Might as well be an open declaration of war."

Arkady gestured toward the newcomer. "Dr. Mire this is Inspector Traian Stoenescu of the Bucharest Police, Special Inquiries."

Adam raised an eyebrow. "Special Inquiries? Inspector Gavrilović's Bucharest counterpart, I presume then. Anything in particular Mr. Borescu was investigating?"

The inspector shrugged. "He was looking into several things. A student went missing a few weeks ago under unusual circumstances. Also there have been reports of missing books and documents from the library. The subject matter of many of them is ... disconcerting. As you can imagine, it's a monumental task to keep track of all the collections with renovations still ongoing at the Central Library and everything in temporary locations like this one."

Adam nodded. In 1989, during the revolution, someone set fire to the building that housed the university's Central Library, destroying over 500,000 documents. The repairs had not yet been completed.

"And on top of that," the inspector continued, "there

has been some agitation among the more radical student groups."

Adam's gaze went back to the green hand. "What sort of agitation?"

Political organizations at European universities fascinated Adam. American students were rank amateurs compared to their European counterparts. Being captain of your high school debate team didn't compare to running an underground newspaper ... or knowing how to mix a Molotov cocktail.

"There's a group calling itself The Committee. They've become vocal recently demanding the removal of several professors they consider too far to the right politically."

"Are they?"

The Inspector chuckled. "Hardly. If you haven't guessed by the name, the members are all Communist to one extent or another, though they aren't calling themselves that of course. They came to our attention when they dredged up the old rumor that Nicolae Ceauşescu didn't die ten years ago, that an imposter is buried in his grave and he's going to come back when the country needs him most."

Adam grunted. "Like some twisted King Arthur. Did your man Lucian infiltrate them?"

"He had discussions with a few of their leaders," Inspector Stoenescu replied. "He was trying."

"The green hand, though, that's the symbol of the Iron Guard, the fascists."

Arkady frowned. "So the question becomes, did this Committee kill him and paint his hand green to label *him* as a fascist, or are we looking at some other organization using the green hand to claim responsibility, thinking Lucian was a secret Communist? And why kill him here?"

The inspector shrugged. "His last report indicated he had a lead on someone who might have helped smuggle documents out of the library. It's possible he was following someone and that person got the better of him."

"When was the body found?" Adam asked.

"Overnight," answered the inspector.

Adam took a breath and let it out slowly. "There's another possibility then."

The inspector shook his head. "He had too much of his blood in him for that."

"I've known them to resist drinking when they want to hide their true nature, and that's easier to do when they're already fed," Adam tried to focus for a moment on all that Inspector Stoenescu had told them. "You said there was a missing student."

"But that was last week," Inspector Stoenescu protested. "I can't imagine a vampire resisting the bloodlust without having fed more recently than that."

"Maybe there's another missing student," Adam suggested. "If it happened last night maybe they haven't been reported missing yet."

The inspector sighed. "I suppose it's a possibility, but for all our sakes, I hope you're wrong. A human killer would be much easier to deal with."

"Agreed," Arkady said.

Inspector Stoenescu's gaze slipped past Adam and Arkady to the body on the floor. The corner of his mouth twitched, the first time he let any emotion show. "I have someone looking through his apartment. We might know more after we see what's there."

Adam glanced around at the books on the shelves, skimming briefly over the titles on the spines. They were all books on Western European history, beginning with the

United Kingdom and moving on to France, then Germany. Among the volumes, however, one stood out. It was a book about Michael the Brave, the Romanian hero who united the three parts of the country for the first time in the sixteenth century, and it was misshelved. Adam also had a book about Michael the Brave, one given to him by Anya that she had "borrowed" from the Kunsthistorische Museum in Vienna.

"We might know more now." Adam reached for the book.

Arkady and the inspector joined him and peered over his shoulder as he opened it. On page after page, random letters were circled or underlined, sometimes in blue or black or red ink. Some of the ink was old and faded. Some looked new.

Arkady huffed. "More codes."

As Adam leafed through the book, a yellowed piece of paper popped up. He unfolded it carefully and began to read. The story transcribed in spidery handwriting made Adam wonder about a different motive for Lucian's murder.

TEN

—⟋⟍—

From the Journal of Heinrich Bayer

Timişoara, Austrian Banat
24 June 1788

IN FEBRUARY OF 1788, THE *Austrian Empire declared war on the Turks. Much of the initial fighting was centered on the region of the Banat, to the west of Transylvania. At first, the conflict did not go the way of the Austrians. They were forced to rely on their notoriously unreliable Russian allies for support. That winter a disease plagued the Austrian army, one that that appeared suddenly and mysteriously and disappeared just as suddenly and mysteriously.*

THEY SAY IT IS AN illness. They say modern medicine can explain what superstition cannot, but they are wrong. I've seen what they call superstition rise from its grave and stalk the night. It creeps like a fog over the ground toward the encampment of the German soldiers, and there it feeds. First the soldiers weaken and grow pale, then they stop eating, and then they die. The cause is as evident as the nose on the face of the doctor they sent from Vienna, but they all refuse to see it.

The creature that preys on these foreigners will not stop once there are no more German soldiers, either. Then it will turn its attention to us, and it will sustain itself with our blood.

My grandmother once told me they called Dracula a hero of the people for standing up against the Turks, but what they conveniently forgot is that he fed off his own people, even when he was alive. When he fought against the Turks, he was not defending them as children of God. He was protecting his hunting grounds.

I went to the graveyard as dusk approached. Dangerous I know, but it was the only way to discover which grave the creature sleeps in during the day. There I stood vigil among the stone monuments, black against the deepening indigo sky, waiting for the creature to emerge.

As the last rays of the sun died, the air grew cold, and my unease grew. The pale moonlight illuminated the graveyard, and I suddenly sensed I was not alone. As I scanned the tombstones the shadows began to move all at once, though no wind blew the branches of the trees. They all flowed to one place, one gravesite, swirling and turning faster and faster until a form emerged, planting its feet onto the wet ground.

A wretched sight, lean and pale and wearing nothing but tattered grave clothes, it slouched over its grave for a moment before it turned in the direction of the cemetery gate. I leaned forward, trying to get a better look in the gloom.

I shouldn't have.

It stopped and turned around, fixing me with two rheumy eyes. The shadows at its feet churned and roiled. Its lips parted, revealing a mouth full of sharp teeth, and then, to my surprise, it spoke.

"You should not have come here." Its gravelly voice filled me with dread.

I reached into my coat and pulled out a stake made of hawthorn wood and a silver knotted chain. "I did not come without defenses, vampire." I hoped I sounded more confident than I felt.

He let out a low gurgle I realized was a laugh, and then charged at me. I barely had time to raise my arms before a clawed hand raked across my sleeve. The vampire withdrew screaming as its skin sizzled and burned from the silver bracelets around my forearm. Hatred overtook its expression as it lunged again. Backed up against a gravestone, I had nowhere to go.

I gripped the stake and thrust it forward as the monster attacked, but with one swipe, it knocked the stake from my hand. It raised its other clawed hand to tear out my throat, but the killing blow never came. Instead the vampire reared up and let out an ear-piercing shriek. Flailing its arms, it frantically grasped at its back, and as it thrashed, the reason why became clear. The hilt of a knife jutted from between its shoulder blades. Not a normal knife either. The way the skin around the wound sizzled and smoked, the blade could have been made of nothing but silver.

A hand grasped my arm and pulled me away from the monster. I whipped my head around to come face-to-face with the Viennese doctor I had earlier dismissed.

He motioned for me to follow. "This way."

Together we made our way among the gravestones

while the monster struggled to free itself from the torment of the silver knife. We scaled the fence surrounding the cemetery and ran through the woods until we came to the road. The doctor had a carriage waiting. He untied the horse, and we both leapt aboard. He prodded the horse, urging it to a gallop. I glanced behind us to watch the shadows sliding down through the trees toward us. I made the sign of the cross and muttered a prayer.

The rolling black shapes pursued until we neared the town. The doctor did not drive the horse any less once we reached the cobblestone streets. He finally brought the carriage to a stop in front of an inn and handed the reins of the exhausted horse to a boy, along with a few silver coins. I followed him inside, past the curious stares of the inn's other denizens, and up a set of stairs to a room on the second floor.

The doctor shut the door behind him and lit a lamp. "Who are you? What were you doing in the cemetery?"

"My name is Heinrich," I replied, "and I was doing what I was brought up to do."

The doctor frowned. "Don't be absurd. No one was brought up to skulk around cemeteries looking for vampires."

"I was," I said. "My grandmother came from a village in Serbia. Her husband, my grandfather, was attacked by one of those creatures when he was a soldier in the army. He died a few years later in a farm accident, but he came back. He tormented his former friends and family until those same people who had been his neighbors dug up his body and burned it."

"And so you thought you'd go hunting them, because of her story?"

"She taught me how to hunt them. After what happened, she left the village with my father, who was still a small child at the time. She found her way to Sibiu where she has distant relations. She married a cobbler who raised my father as his own. She tried to start a new life for herself, but the monsters came back. They attacked my father one night. They would have killed him were it not for the silver necklace of St. Jude my mother had given him. After that she learned how to fight them. She killed several herself, in fact.

"She taught my father, and when I was old enough, she trained me." I studied the doctor in the stark light of the lamp. He was younger than I expected, but his pale eyes spoke of experience beyond his age. "I've told you about me. Now for you."

He crossed the room and knelt down to retrieve a box from underneath the bed. He set it down on the small table with his washbasin and opened it. "My name is Heinz Krause," he said, his back still to me. "A few years ago, I had the misfortune of examining a body of a soldier, a young man in perfect health who contracted a peculiar wasting disease." When he stepped aside I could see the contents of the box. It contained several carved wooden stakes, a bottle of holy water, a rosary, a silver chain similar to mine, and a silver crucifix. "Both times he died."

"Why not call the most recent attacks what they are? Why have you let this 'wasting disease' as you call it claim the lives of your own countrymen?"

"Because I'm a man of science. I have no choice. I have to call it a disease." Krause retrieved a stake from the box. "But just like you I have been preparing to hunt down the source and end it."

I nodded. "I know which grave belongs to it. Tomorrow we'll return."

After sunrise the next day we did just that, and I brought others with me, men I trusted, who understood the dangers we faced. I found the grave from the previous night after some searching. The graveyard did not look the same in the light of day, and there was no disturbed earth.

I knelt and read the marker as the others dug. The man buried there was young, the son of a farmer. He had died only the previous winter. When we opened the coffin, the corpse was there, looking every bit as if it were asleep rather than dead. Gone was the demonic visage from the night before. Here was a man in his twenties with tousled brown hair and boyish features. His hands were folded over his heart, and his eyes were closed, perfectly at peace.

When I drove the stake through the corpse's heart though, its eyes flew open, and a scream escaped its lungs. Most of the others scrambled to get away. Even the doctor took a few steps back. Fresh red blood gushed from the wound as the body convulsed, but after only a few moments, all was still again. We decapitated the body and burned the head for good measure, and then we returned the rest of the corpse to the grave.

The German soldiers moved their camp the following day. There were no more unexplained deaths from illness, and soon afterwards, I left as well. I know, however, that there will be other graves, other monsters lurking in the shadows, until the root of the evil is found and destroyed.

My father and my grandmother passed more than their knowledge to me. I have their tools for fighting the monsters, and I have other things; artifacts, relics, objects that hold power. One day before my own death, I pray I will come face to face with the Son of the Dragon, and on that day I will use that power to send him to Hell.

ELEVEN

—ᴍᴍ—

Near Cluj, Romania
4 December 1999

ALL DAY LONG THE SNOW fell, giant wet flakes drifting gently down from the steel grey sky. Sometimes flurries whipped by the wind created fanciful shapes, like apparitions dancing on the lawn, or so it seemed to Clara. She hoped they were merely figments of her overactive imagination.

As the darkness fell, the snowfall dwindled and finally stopped. The silver-white world outside Clara's window gleamed in the moonlight. No footprints marred the snow on the lawn. Beyond, the black shadows of the trees rose up to the clear dark sky that seemed so brittle it might break if she placed a hand on the glass.

"Beautiful, isn't it?"

Clara spun around at the voice, drawing her thin nightshirt around her. Her host stood in front of the fire. She hadn't heard the door open or close.

"The snow hides so much," he continued. "It makes

57

everything looks so clean and pure. Of course, we all know better, but it's nice sometimes to believe in the illusion. You were very quiet at dinner tonight. Is something the matter?"

As during his previous visit, he wasn't wearing a jacket, only a waistcoat. His shirt was open at the collar, and his sleeves were rolled to his elbows. She caught herself gazing at his physique and tried to look away. "What do you think?"

He motioned to the writing desk by the door. "I brought you more books. These are in English." Clara didn't reply. He adopted a hurt expression, but his words contained an edge. "I've gone out of my way to make you comfortable, haven't I?"

She turned to the scene through the window. "I'm still a prisoner."

When she looked back, he was standing next to her. The scent of sage and cinnamon filled her nostrils again. "You're only a prisoner if you view yourself that way. You don't have to be."

She found herself tracing the line of his collarbone, imagining one more button on his shirt undone. Reluctantly, she pushed the thought from her head. "There are people looking for me. They're not going to give up until they find me."

"Who? Your boyfriend the professor?"

Her face grew hot. "He's not my—"

"No? Well then maybe you mean the Russian agent. You grew close to him, didn't you?"

She shook her head. "No. It's not that way at all. I don't have feelings for him either."

He grinned. "I'm glad to hear it. Maybe you'll consider my proposal after all."

Clara frowned. "You didn't make a proposal."

"Didn't I?"

Clara fought against the fog in her head. "This is absurd. I've read about people who chose to live like Victorians, never mind they have the benefit of modern medicine or ideas like equal rights. It's fun to play dress-up, to wear a corset and carry around a parasol as long as you know you're not going to die of cholera or be denied the right to vote. But for you it goes beyond that. You're holding on to something. It's like you're trying to will the world to stop changing."

His smile faded. "There is truth in what you say."

"What do you want?" she asked.

"Merely the pleasure of your company."

"Besides that."

The corners of his mouth turned up again, but the smile was subdued, wistful. He backed away. "I am expecting you for dinner again tomorrow. I will try to pick topics of conversation more to your liking."

Clara glanced out the window for only a moment, but when she turned her attention to the room again, he was gone, vanished as if made of smoke.

As she prepared for bed, her thoughts inevitably went to the dreams she was having, the other life she was experiencing. She found she didn't dread it so much as she had the night before. She was beginning to sympathize with Elizabeth, thrust into a situation she didn't understand, more a prop in a stage play than anything else.

TWELVE

Berlin, Germany
18 June 1878

I F ELIZABETH DIDN'T KNOW BETTER she would have
thought someone intended for her to find the body.
Standing over the dead man lying on the floor in the
basement of the Palais Strousberg, she could not remove
her horrified gaze from his blood-caked hands and face.
Friedrich had not died quietly. She backed away and
turned to run, but someone blocked her path.

IT WAS STILL EARLY IN the morning when Elizabeth
emerged from her bedroom and descended the stairs. Alfred was already gone, and the banging of pots told her
Sarah was in the kitchen.

Another small white card lay on the table in the foyer.
Elizabeth didn't want to touch it, but she forced herself to
do so. She had to make sure Alfred didn't find it or any of
the cards that had been left over the past two days. Mme.

Kárpáthy had said her father was trying to reach her, but none of the cards bore anything but his name, and none of the housekeeping staff ever saw anyone place them there.

She hid the card in her bodice. Elizabeth had long since come to terms with the fact she would never know exactly what happened to her father, but with every new calling card, her desire to discover the reason for his disappearance grew.

She had arranged to see Mme. Kárpáthy again. Friedrich was to take her, but he was uncharacteristically late, and every minute Elizabeth waited fed her anxiety. She paced the foyer and fidgeted with her hands. Sarah emerged from the kitchen, but one look from Elizabeth sent her scurrying back.

When she couldn't take any more, she threw the front door open and stepped out onto the stoop. Alexej the Gypsy stood across the street. There was no mistaking his brilliant green eyes, but he wasn't dressed as a Gypsy, wearing instead a crisp, white military uniform. He looked at her and smiled.

She opened her mouth to call to him, but he took a step back, farther into the long early morning shadows cast by the buildings. He placed an index finger over his lips. Elizabeth turned at the sound of a carriage approaching, expecting Friedrich, but she didn't recognize the driver. The carriage passed on the street between the two of them, and Alexej was gone.

Elizabeth ran across the street to the spot where he had been standing, but he was nowhere to be found in any direction she looked. As she turned to go back across to the townhouse, she saw Lady Russell, out on her morning walk, coming toward her.

"Lady James," the ambassador's wife called as she

neared, "what a pleasant surprise. Such a lovely day for a stroll."

Elizabeth forced a smile. "Yes, Lady Russell, it's a beautiful day. Perfect for a walk."

Lady Russell beamed back, her sapphire blue eyes alight with amusement. Auburn ringlets escaped from underneath her bonnet. She was a good fifteen years older than Elizabeth, but it was impossible to tell. "Well, I see no reason why each of us should walk alone this morning. Would you care to join me?"

Elizabeth could think of nothing she'd rather do less. "I'd be delighted, Lady Russell."

Elizabeth struggled to keep up with Lady Russell as they walked. She mostly listened while the ambassador's wife talked, interjecting sympathetic murmurs whenever appropriate. The whole time, she looked in vain for Alexej. As they neared the Palais Strousberg, Lady Russell stopped abruptly.

A man exited the British Embassy and strode toward them. Dressed in a charcoal grey frock coat and a matching top hat, he boasted a large mustache greased into two points and an impressive set of muttonchops. He tipped his hat and gave them each a smile and a nod as he passed, but Elizabeth saw a storm raging in his dark eyes.

"Do you know who that was?" Lady Russell asked.

Elizabeth shook her head. "I'm afraid not."

"That was Jovan Ristić, the Serbian foreign minister. I'm aware of what people say about Lord Russell, Lady James, but the truth is that he rarely listens to my opinion on matters of his work. A shame really. A woman's opinion ought to be given equal weight. After all, women must be experts at diplomacy practically from the time they can speak. I'm sure you would agree."

"Of course, Lady Russell." Elizabeth was only half listening. She caught a blur of motion out of the corner of her eye, near the entrance of an alley, but when she looked, nothing was there.

"I suggested to Lord Russell that he make an effort to befriend Mr. Ristić. He's in Berlin for the Congress as Serbia's representative, though not officially. None of the new Balkan states were invited. A mistake, I'm certain, but again, no one seems to care about what I think. I liked Mr. Ristić very much when I met him a few years ago. He spoke calmly, and every word he said was deliberate. He was never unreasonable, and he always listened to others. Those qualities make him dangerous, especially to the Ottomans. Radicals, the Turks can execute and assassinate with impunity. Careful men like Mr. Ristić prove much harder to remove. I've wanted Lord Russell to realize he makes a far better ally than an enemy. Maybe he actually listened."

"I've never really tried to offer an opinion on Lord James' work," Elizabeth said. "In any event, when I ask about it, he tells me it's nothing I should worry over."

Lady Russell cocked her head to one side and made a noise deep in her throat. Elizabeth wasn't sure if she was expressing sympathy or disapproval. "You know I generally have a cup of tea after my morning walk. It would be delightful to have company. I'll have one of the maids bring us biscuits as well."

Again, Elizabeth forced a smile. "I'd love to, Lady Russell."

Every effort had been put forth to make the Palais Strousberg an extension of the British Empire. The former city residence of a railroad magnate, the urban palace had only been the home of the British embassy for a little over a year. Elizabeth and Lady Russell ascended the stairs and passed through the portico into the grand vestibule, which extended vertically two stories. From the vestibule, two marble staircases led upward. Beyond, a small drawing room connected the vestibule with the new stateroom in the process of being constructed.

Elizabeth felt immediately more at ease. The sumptuous interior of the Palais contrasted with the simple, almost sparse, and very German décor of the townhouse, and to her surprise, Elizabeth found herself looking forward to tea with Lady Russell. She didn't want to think about Friedrich or Mme. Kárpáthy. She didn't want to think about her father. She didn't even want to think about Alexej.

As Lady Russell led the way across the vestibule, however, a scent assaulted Elizabeth's nose, one she couldn't at first identify. It was rich and heady, with hints of cinnamon, cloves, and pine.

Images entered Elizabeth's mind—the drawing room of her family's home in Oxford, her mother and father sitting in high-backed chairs by the fire, her mother doing needlepoint, her father smoking his pipe. His pipe. Elizabeth smelled the smoke of her father's pipe. She was so distracted by the realization she didn't notice Lady Russell had stopped walking and nearly ran into her back.

One of the maids spoke to Lady Russell in hushed tones. When she finished, Lady Russell turned to Elizabeth. "I'm terribly sorry. I have to step away for a moment. I shouldn't be long though. Please excuse me."

Lady Russell hurried away with the maid, leaving Elizabeth alone. The smell of pipe smoke returned, even stronger. Elizabeth knew she should stay and wait for Lady Russell, but she couldn't help but take a few tentative steps in the direction of the smell. Those few steps led to a few more. As the smell grew more intense, Elizabeth grew bolder.

On one side of the vestibule, Elizabeth discovered a short hallway. At the end of the hallway, a staircase led downward. Elizabeth could almost see the smoke wafting up from the basement. With one final glance over her shoulder, she descended the stairs.

About a quarter of the way down, she placed a hand on the stair railing. As soon as she did, she jerked away. Something sticky clung to her fingers. A small dark smudge mirrored the deep, red smear on the wooden railing. Carefully, she brought her hand to her nose. The caustic, metallic smell told her everything she needed to know. It was blood, and it had not been there for very long.

She found another blood drop a few more steps down, and a third blood drop several steps after that. The trail of blood continued down the stairs. At the bottom she discovered another hallway, and more blood. She was near the kitchen, judging by he sounds of pots and dishes. She followed the drops of blood to the body of Friedrich Wilhelm Henry Stanton lying in a dark crimson pool on the floor.

"THERE YOU ARE," LADY RUSSELL said. "My sincerest apologies. I had to attend to a household matter. It seems one of the stable hands has disappeared."

Elizabeth stood frozen. Behind her lay Friedrich's body, blocked from Lady Russell's view. She didn't know how to respond.

Lady Russell's smile faded. "Something the matter,

dear? Why in Heaven's name are you down here?" Elizabeth stepped aside. Lady Russell's eyes grew wide. As the color drained from her face, a single syllable escaped her lips. "Oh."

"I … I heard a noise," Elizabeth said. "There are drops of blood on the stairs."

Lady Russell hurried past Elizabeth but stopped just short of the pool of blood, careful not to drag her dress through it. "Well, that answers one question at least. It's Friedrich, the missing stable hand."

"Yes," Elizabeth said. "I knew him. He was the one who brought me to Berlin from Vienna. How horrible. He must have tried to climb up the stairs after he was…"

Lady Russell shook her head. "No, dear, I'm afraid not. With this much blood, there would be great smears of it all over. Single drops could only have come from someone else, most likely his killer."

Elizabeth shuddered. She was about to ask Lady Russell what they should do when she noticed the other woman looking past Friedrich's body. About halfway down the hallway, one of the doors was ajar. A red streak marred the doorframe. Lady Russell hiked up her dress and stepped over Friedrich. Elizabeth had no choice but to follow. As she neared the body, she couldn't help but look again. As soon as she did, she wished she hadn't. His face was a twisted mask of rage and hatred, his lips drawn back into a snarl, his glare seemingly directed at her. She hurried to join Lady Russell.

It occurred to Elizabeth as the two women stood in front of the door that no one knew where they were, should something happen. She opened her mouth to suggest they go to get help, but Lady Russell chose a different course of action. Without any more hesitation, she pushed the door open. The two women peered into the room.

"This is truly monstrous," Lady Russell exclaimed.

The room was filled with table linens. No one was there, but someone had been there recently. A tablecloth lay in a pile on the floor, its edge ragged where a piece had been torn off. Lady Russell picked it up.

"This is Egyptian linen, a gift from the Khedive himself. It's irreplaceable. I supposed whoever killed poor Friedrich used it to make a bandage."

Underneath the tablecloth, the killer had left something else behind. While Lady Russell assessed the damage to the delicate fabric, Elizabeth retrieved the object, a large piece of wood, one end of which had been sharpened into a point with a knife. The sharpened tip was stained red with blood.

THIRTEEN

———ɱ———

Berlin, Germany
19 June 1878

"Really, Elizabeth," Alfred said, "if you want to go and stay with my brother and his family, you can. I've already cabled him to make arrangements."

Elizabeth sat on the bed, watching Alfred get ready for yet another state dinner. "Is that what you want me to do?"

"I want you to do what makes you feel the safest."

"Do you think it isn't safe here?"

"Of course it's safe, dear. That man was half German, probably up to no good anyway. He shouldn't even have been employed at the embassy. I don't understand why a proper Englishman couldn't be found to do his job. But I know it was a terrible shock. I'm sorry you had to see that. I'm simply telling you that if you don't want to be here anymore, I'll understand."

Elizabeth sighed. "I want to be with you. Do you have

to go this evening? Can't you stay home, just this once?"

Alfred finished tying his tie and then stepped over to the bed. He leaned down and kissed Elizabeth on the forehead. "You know the answer to that question, but I promise you it won't be for much longer. Another few weeks at the most. Then, who knows? We might be going back to England together."

"What's so important about tonight?"

Alfred's expression clouded over. "You don't understand the amount of pressure I'm under."

"All I'm asking for is one night. Please, Alfred, tell me why you have to go."

"Elizabeth, this isn't the time."

"It never is."

Alfred's shoulders slumped. "Fine, if you really have to know, I made a mistake."

"What sort of mistake?"

"Yesterday I met with Jovan Ristić, the Serbian foreign minister."

"I know who he is."

Alfred frowned. "How?"

"Lady Russell pointed him out to me as he was leaving the Palais yesterday. He must have been coming from his meeting with you. He didn't look happy."

"He wasn't. Mr. Ristić came to the embassy yesterday hoping to meet with Lord Russell and Lord Beaconsfield. Of course, they were too busy to see him, but rather than send him away, I convinced them to let me meet with him instead. The meeting didn't go as I had planned."

"How so?"

"Mr. Ristić is here to appeal for Serbia, but he wasn't invited to the Congress. He needs someone to advocate for him. No doubt, he's approaching all the delegates. I apologized on behalf of Lords Russell and Beaconsfield, but I told him that if he addressed his concerns to me, I would relay them. He told me he didn't feel comfortable speaking about it with an attaché. I interjected that I could be of great service to him. The entire reason Lord Russell selected me to be his attaché here during this Congress is because I'm an expert on the Balkan situation. No one here understands it better than I do."

"I don't doubt it," Elizabeth said.

"I told him I've taken it upon myself to know all I can about the Balkans and the problems of the people there. I told him I thought the Kingdom of Serbia and the Kingdom of Great Britain have much in common."

"What did he say to that?" asked Elizabeth.

"He asked me how many times I have visited Serbia. I told him I have been there once. He glared at me and asked me how I could possibly understand his country based only on one visit."

Elizabeth was used to her husband's moods, but she'd never seen him this agitated. "How did you answer him?"

"I said I've also read a great deal about his country, hoping that would convince him, but it didn't. He asked if a Serb had actually written any of the books I'd read. When I tried to explain that books by Serbian authors are difficult to come by in translation he stood and said he would be going if Lord Russell or Lord Beaconsfield couldn't meet with him. It was uncalled for, really. I was there to help him. He should have recognized that. The one person I could have used to make a name for myself here, and I've turned him against me." He looked at Elizabeth, his mouth twisted into a sullen smirk. "There, are you happy now?"

Normally Elizabeth would have let the matter drop,

but perhaps some of Lady Russell's tenacity had rubbed off on her. "I don't understand. If this Mr. Ristić wasn't invited to the Congress, how will going tonight help? Am I wrong in assuming he won't be there?"

Alfred let out an exasperated sigh. "He won't, but that's beside the point. Didn't I just say Mr. Ristić is likely approaching everyone? Did it not occur to you he might tell others about what happened, and that they might find a way to use it to their advantage? I have to go, to make sure no damage has been done. You can understand that, can't you?"

Elizabeth pursed her lips. "Well, when can I expect you back?"

"Fairly late."

"I suppose I won't wait for you then."

"Please, Elizabeth, it's all for the best."

She nodded weakly. "I know."

An odd chuckle escaped Alfred's lips. "It's absurd. All this trouble over a man who used to dedicate his time to monster hunting."

Elizabeth looked up at him sharply. "Monster hunting?"

"Oh, yes," he replied. "Serbia has a government office dedicated to monster hunting. Jovan Ristić headed it for a while. From what I gather, they spent a great deal of effort tracking down wolfmen and vampires. I wonder if they ever caught any."

He laughed at his own joke. Elizabeth didn't join him. Her thoughts were already elsewhere.

ELIZABETH LISTENED FOR THE FRONT door to close behind Alfred before retrieving one of her books from its hiding place. She drew the drapes and fumbled back to the center of the bedroom in the dark. She sat down on the floor in the middle of the circle of candles she had arranged and proceeded to light them in the order prescribed in the book. There were five of them, each spaced equally.

She took one of her embroidery needles and very carefully stuck her index finger. A tiny drop of red emerged. She was more fortunate this time. The time before, it had taken several tries to draw enough blood. Perhaps her efforts had been for naught for that reason. Quickly, before the blood had a chance to run off of her finger, she turned to the first candle and drew a symbol from the book in the bare floor. Then she pricked another finger and moved on to the next candle. After she had drawn all five symbols, she blew out each candle in turn.

She had just enough time to put everything away and cover up the markings on the floor with a rug before the maid came in to ready the room for the evening.

FOURTEEN

—⟋⟋⟍—

Bucharest, Romania
5 December 1999

IT WAS NOT THE FIRST time Adam had been stalked in a library. That morning he returned to the place where they found Lucian's body. The body itself had been removed, but the blood still stained the floor. Adam wasn't interested in examining the crime scene again, though. He stood several rows over, perusing the titles on Romanian history. In his hand he held the volume Lucian had apparently stashed away before he died, the history of Michael the Brave.

Unlike the biography Adam already possessed, *The Life and Death of Michael the Brave* by Ioan Nicolescu, this book contained no mention of the mysterious Alexandru, the advisor Michael himself credited with all his victories. What the prince never knew, at least not until the end, was the source of Alexandru's tactical genius. He was in fact Dracula. Michael paid with his life for his ambitions, but he almost paid with his soul as well. In the intervening years, Dracula had gone to great lengths to erase himself from the story of Michael the Brave, which made Nicolescu's biography all the more remarkable, and all the more dangerous.

Adam had just found the hole from where the book was taken when he caught a flicker of movement out of the corner of his eye. He tensed for a moment, but then forced himself to relax. He was far from alone. Dozens of police patrolled the floor.

After Adam replaced the book, he ran his hand down the spines of the others on the shelf. Several more dealt with the life of Michael the Brave. On a whim he picked up one and opened it only to discover more cryptic marks, letters underlined or circled with different colors of ink. He put the book back and grabbed another from a different shelf, a book about the Romanian principalities under the rule of the Phanariot Greeks in the eighteenth century. It didn't contain any marks.

He caught movement again in his peripheral vision, closer this time. His heart pounding, Adam discretely slipped the rosary out of his pocket and wrapped the string of beads around his wrist.

Adam forced himself to remain calm. He moved down the row, scanning the shelves until he found the book he was looking for. He pulled down a thick biography of Vlad the Impaler. Vlad, like Michael, was a hero to the Romanian people because he stood against invaders, both Muslim and Christian, and was martyred for it. He was not the monster the West made of him, though the Romanians weren't above capitalizing on the Western image of Dracula after Communism's fall.

When he opened the book, he found what he expected, more circled letters. By then he was all but certain they signified some form of code, maybe used to circumvent the prying eyes of the Securitate, the Communist Romanian secret police. Books about Michael the Brave and Vlad the Impaler would have been allowed under the Communist government, and possession of them wouldn't have been deemed suspicious.

Mihai Iliescu attended the University of Bucharest. It was not outside the realm of possibility he was acquainted with the group that used these secret messages. If Adam figured out the code, maybe he could use it to solve the riddle Mihai had left for him, find the medallion, and save Clara.

Adam had just replaced the book when a man brandishing a knife burst around the corner of the stack and lunged at him. When Adam dodged, the man careened past him into the bookshelf. He was young, barely out of his teens, probably a student. He pivoted to face Adam again, and held the knife out in front of him. He was sweating. The hand that held the knife shook.

"You don't want to do this," Adam said in Romanian.

"I have to," the boy replied.

He lunged again. Adam caught his arm and slammed it into the shelf with enough force that the whole thing rocked. He followed with a jab to the boy's nose with his elbow. The boy cried out and dropped the knife. He dabbed at the blood running from his nostrils. Panic in his eyes, he turned and fled.

The boy tried to lose Adam in the stacks, but all Adam had to do was follow his clumsy footfalls. He then tried flinging books off the shelves, but Adam managed to dodge the flying volumes. At the end of one row, Adam leapt and tackled the boy to the floor. He struggled to break free, but Adam put him in a chokehold until he went limp.

ADAM AND ARKADY WAITED ACROSS a table from the boy as he came to. University security had been kind enough to let them use a room in the basement. Old books and boxes lined the walls. A single overhead light illuminated the space. Adam hoped the scene proved appropriately intimidating.

The boy awoke with a jerk. His eyes grew wide when he found he was tied to a chair. He pulled against the restraints.

"Don't bother," Adam said. "Those knots are solid. My colleague here was a Boy Scout, or whatever the Russian equivalent of that is. What's your name?"

The boy remained silent.

Adam leaned across the table. "We're not with the university or the police."

"Whether that's good or bad for you remains to be seen," Arkady added in fairly fluent Romanian.

Adam glanced sideways at him.

Arkady grinned. "Jealous that you're not the only one?"

Adam turned his attention to the boy again. "Did you kill the man they found in the library yesterday, Lucian Borescu?"

He still didn't answer.

"If you don't tell us anything, we're going to assume that you did." Arkady held up the knife the man had used to attack Adam. "Who knows? The police may very conveniently find a connection between this knife and that murdered man."

"Please," the boy whispered. "Please I was just trying to scare you. I wasn't going to hurt you."

"Why did you want to scare me?"

The boy didn't say anything. He just started to sob.

Arkady slammed his hand down on the table. "Answer

the questions."

"My name is Paul. I ... I didn't kill him, I swear. I didn't know him. I had just seen him at some of our meetings."

Arkady popped an eyebrow. "Meetings?"

Paul bit his lip, perhaps realizing his mistake.

"You're a member of the Committee, aren't you?" Adam asked.

"I ... I shouldn't say anything else." Arkady simply held the knife in front of his face. Paul looked away and sighed. "Some of the others, they thought you might be government agents when you arrived yesterday. They wanted me to follow you, to try to see where you would go, if you would try to question any of us. I didn't expect you to come back to the library. When you went to the section on Romanian history I was afraid you'd find something."

"How did you get past the police?" Arkady asked.

Paul rolled his eyes. "It's an old building. There are many ways in. Not all of them are obvious."

"You were afraid I'd find something in the books?" Adam placed the page from the journal of Heinrich Bayer on the table in front of him. "You mean like a stolen manuscript that talks about staking vampires? Is the Committee smuggling manuscripts out of the University? And why would they be interested in this one?"

Sweat ran down his face. He pulled against the ropes again. "Look, I just wanted to scare you off. We didn't have anything to do with the murder. Why would we kill him? He was just another student who believed the same as we do." His gaze darted from Adam to Arkady as his eyes widened. "Oh, God. He wasn't was he?"

Arkady ignored the question. "Do you even remember what it was like under Ceaușescu?"

"A little," Paul answered.

Arkady threw up his hands. "And you want to go back to that?"

Paul glared. "*That* wasn't true Communism. Ceaușescu was corrupted by other forces."

"Corrupted by power like every other goddamn Communist dictator," Arkady sneered.

"That's not the kind of corruption I mean."

The two continued to stare at one another for several more seconds until Adam broke the silence. He dropped the book they'd found near Lucian's body in front of Paul. "Look, we can argue the merits of Nicolae Ceaușescu's brutal totalitarian dictatorship another day. I really don't care about your little student group right now. You're using these books to pass coded messages. Tell me how the code works."

FIFTEEN

—— ⚍ ——

Near Cluj, Romania
5 December 1999

CLARA DIDN'T WANT TO ADMIT to herself that she was enjoying the conversation, that she found this man who was holding her against her will to be charming and attractive, that she took pleasure in sparring with him over opinions on English Romantic poets and Dutch Renaissance painters.

That he reminded her of Adam.

Dinner that evening was a thick Hungarian goulash, bright red from the paprika. It left a pleasant burn in her mouth, which she doused with a glass of sweet red wine. When he brushed her hand across the dining room table, a jolt of electricity ran up her arm. She pulled her arm away, and her cheeks grew hot. After dinner, he led her back to her room himself.

"I hope you have pleasant dreams tonight," he said.

"So do I," Clara replied.

"Thank you for the conversation. It's not often that I

get to chat with a woman as intelligent as you. I forget how invigorating that can be."

Clara felt her cheeks go hot again. He took her hand and brought it up to his lips. He kissed it gently and, smiling, shut the door. With the clink of the key in the lock, the spell was broken. Alone in the chilly, dim room, Clara let her thoughts wander to darker places. She went to the window. The black shape of the forest loomed on the other side. She began to doubt whether Adam and Arkady could find her, if they were looking. No, not *if*. They *were* looking. How could they not be? But her nameless host's words echoed in her head. *They may have other worries at the moment.* What did that mean?

She crossed the room to the stack of books on the desk. They were an odd assortment—a treatise on indigenous plants of Southeast Asia, various biographies of minor nineteenth-century English public figures, even a few "penny dreadful" novels from the 1920s—but as promised, they were all in English. She picked out a book on Irish folklore.

CLARA SAT IN ONE OF the chairs next to the fire, reading. As the words on the page began to blend together and her head grew heavy, a low hum invaded her consciousness, a noise so subtle she couldn't remember when she had first noticed it. The sound was music. Someone in the house played a violin. For a moment she listened to the instrument's lonesome cries.

She tried to continue reading but found her attention drifting back to the soft and mournful melody. A sense of loss overcame her. She closed the book and set it down, then moved to the door and leaned her ear to the cool surface. The sound resonated through the heavy wood and the rhythm of the music seemed to synchronize with her heartbeat.

She placed a hand on the doorknob, and to her surprise, it turned. Clara frowned. She was certain the door had been locked. Before she even realized what she was doing, she pushed the door open and peered into the empty hallway. She stole down the corridor until she came to the stairs where she paused to listen.

The music came from above. She ascended slowly, careful not to make a sound. At the top, she found another hallway much like the one she had left, though no gas lamps illuminated the long space. At the end of the corridor, a warm yellow glow spilled out through an open door. The room was directly above Clara's and was the source of the violin's doleful song.

She crept toward the room. The music's tempo increased as if it knew she was there. Sudden staccato notes gave the melody a biting edge and drew her nearer. She hesitated when she came to the door, letting her hand hover near it before she worked up enough courage to push it open. At her touch, the gap in the doorway widened, and she gasped.

Dozens of candles illuminated the room. Bookshelves lined every wall, full of leather-bound volumes. An assortment of couches and chairs, all antique, filled the rest of the space. In the center of the room her host stood, the violin cradled under his chin as he drew the bow across the strings. He had shed his waistcoat. His eyes were closed, an expression of quiet bliss on his face. He played for a minute more before bringing the song to an end. The last few notes haunted the room as he lowered the violin.

He turned toward her, his mouth twisted into a knowing smile. "You don't have to stand in the doorway. Please come in."

She should have refused. She should have run, but instead, she crossed the threshold. "That was beautiful."

"It's an old Romanian folk tune." He placed the violin in its case. "There are lyrics, actually. It's a bittersweet story about a young man who leaves home to find his fortune. His mother, heartbroken, makes him promise to return someday, but he's killed before he can. His promise is so strong, however, that he returns even after death."

Clara shivered. "That doesn't sound bittersweet as much as it sounds frightening."

"Have you ever lost someone dear to you?"

Clara thought of her father. "Of course."

"What would you give to speak with that person again, just once?"

"Almost anything," she whispered.

"If you had the chance you wouldn't really consider it frightening then, would you? No matter what the circumstances."

"I suppose not, not when you put it that way."

He extended a hand. "Come, sit down. I'm having trouble sleeping. I enjoyed our conversation at dinner. I don't see any reason not to continue it. Do you?"

She took a seat in one of the high-backed chairs. It occurred to her she should ask about the lock on her door, or why he wasn't surprised to see her outside of her room, but those questions somehow didn't seem very important anymore. He took a seat in a chair next to her. His pale eyes shone in the candlelight, two points of cold fire. His shock of white hair fell rakishly across the bridge of his nose. He seemed content at the moment to stare at her when a sound caused them both to look toward the door.

The caretaker stood in the doorway. His gaze passed between the two of them. As he locked eyes with Clara, he frowned. "Sir, please forgive the intrusion, but we've received word that some of the roads are closed due to the snow. It might be difficult to make any excursion from the house tomorrow."

Her host sighed with a hint of annoyance. "Thank you, I'll keep that in mind."

The caretaker nodded. He made eye contact with Clara again, a peculiar look on his face. Sadness? Or pity? Without saying another word, he turned and left.

"What is his name?" Clara asked.

"Iosif," the man replied.

"How long as he been with you?"

"He was here when we acquired the house."

We again.

She let her gaze wander around the candlelit room. "Who else lives here?"

"The cook, Dorina."

"And no one else?"

"Not at the moment ... except for you." As he placed his hand atop hers a breeze stirred in the room, and all the candles guttered. He stood, drawing her out of the chair toward him. "Why dwell on the help, though? Why so focused on everyone else? When was the last time you did something because *you* wanted to?"

"That's a good question," she said. "I honestly don't know."

"Perhaps you ought to start making choices about your own life."

She closed her eyes. Again the scents of cinnamon and sage met her nostrils, but they were mingled with another aroma, something more primitive, like freshly turned earth. "It's really hard to think around you."

"Maybe you should let your heart make the choices then, instead of your head."

He cupped her head in his other hand and leaned down to kiss her. In her mind, the violin made its plaintive call again. She placed her hand on his chest, maybe to push him away, but the thought quickly faded as he continued to kiss her. Her fingers found their way to the buttons of his shirt. She unbuttoned them one by one, and soon his shirt lay discarded on the floor.

The candlelight threw the lines of his muscles into sharp relief, and she was delighted to find that reality did nothing to spoil her imagination. She ran both hands through the hair of his chest as he undid the clasps and buttons of her dress. It, too, fell to the floor, and together they tumbled onto one of the couches.

They quickly shed the rest of their clothes. He kissed her again, playfully biting her lip before his mouth and his tongue moved to her neck, her collarbone, and then lower. The music swelled, pushing everything else out of her head. She intertwined her legs with his, he wrapped his powerful arms around her, and they moved together to the rhythm. Images came to her as well. A village at the edge of a primeval forest. A horse-drawn carriage rumbling through the night. A high mountain pass during a raging thunderstorm.

The violin became more and more frantic, faster, wilder, louder. The tune seemed to take on a slight air of insanity, but Clara didn't care. When the frenzied finale came she lost herself completely.

Afterward, they lay on the couch, her head resting on his chest.

"What's your name?" she asked. "I think you at least

owe that much to me."

"The truth?"

"Yes."

He was silent for a moment. "I suppose you deserve to know. My name, at one point, was Jonathan Harking, but you know me better by a slightly different moniker, the one Bram Stoker gave to me—Jonathan Harker. The only difference is that Mr. Harker survived the end of the novel."

For Clara, the entire world went reeling.

A vampire.

He was a vampire using a glamour. She struggled to push him away but couldn't. Part of her still wanted to be near him, still craved the touch of his skin. She screamed as her whole world went black.

SIXTEEN

—⚬—

Berlin, Germany
20 June 1878

LADY RUSSELL SIPPED HER TEA from a china cup covered in tiny hand-painted pomegranate blossoms. "Chaos. It's the only word I can use to describe the last two days. It has simply been utter chaos. In all my life, I have never had to deal with such a situation, and it's about to put Lord Russell past the brink of insanity."

Elizabeth had yet to touch her own matching cup. "I'm sorry to hear that."

She sat with Lady Russell at an isolated table at Tallmadge's, the only English tearoom in Berlin. White linen covered the tables. Rose-colored damask wallpaper contrasted with deep walnut wainscoting. No doubt Lady Russell expected the visit to lift Elizabeth's spirits.

"I told him he needs to rest. It won't do any good having him collapse in front of everyone, but he tells me he can't. Lord Beaconsfield and Lord Salisbury are demanding answers, fearing for their own safety. I can't say I blame them. They're our guests, but this ... occurrence represents a potential danger to everyone. What concerns me is that no one wants to take the blame for letting it happen. Everyone is focused on the 'how' rather than the 'who' and the 'why.'"

Elizabeth stared at the biscuit in her hand. "A problem, indeed."

Lady Russell glanced down at Elizabeth's rapidly cooling tea. "I'm sorry dear. I've completely forgotten my manners. I invited you to tea today because I wanted to make sure you were all right. How are you doing?"

Elizabeth smiled weakly. "Everything is perfectly fine, Lady Russell, really."

"Dear, please, you don't have to keep up appearances with me. We're a family here, and I can tell you're still troubled. Perhaps you should consider leaving Berlin for a while. I assume you have relations in England you could stay with?"

"Lord James suggested I leave to stay with his brother's family."

"Why don't you?"

"I can't."

"But why not? I can't imagine Lord James' brother would be anything but hospitable."

Elizabeth shook her head. "No, he would be more than welcoming."

"Then what is it?"

Elizabeth sighed. She told Lady Russell about the calling cards and explained how the scent of her father's pipe smoke had led her to Friedrich's body. She left out her visit to the spiritualist and her encounter with the imaginary Gypsy.

"I was going to tell Lord James to make arrangements for my passage back to England, but when I descended the stairs this morning, I knew I couldn't leave. I expected to see another calling card. I didn't expect to see this." She reached into her purse and retrieved the calling card she found that morning. Like all the others, it bore her father's name in black type. Unlike the others, it exhibited a reddish-brown smear across the white paper. "I feel what happened to Friedrich has something to do with my father. I need to discover what that is."

Lady Russell took the card from Elizabeth and frowned as she examined it. "Someone is playing a horrid joke. I would agree you have to get to the bottom of this." She placed her hand on Elizabeth's. "And know you're not alone, my dear. I will do whatever it takes to protect Lord Russell's reputation. His hands are tied in the inquiries he can make. Mine are not."

"What sort of inquiries do you mean?" Elizabeth asked.

Lady Russell paused to take another sip of tea. "I think, Lady James, it might be prudent to learn about wooden stakes."

Elizabeth gazed into the depths of her now cold cup. "I may know someone who can help."

JOVAN RISTIĆ COCKED AN EYEBROW as he rounded the corner, no doubt surprised to find only the two women sitting on the bench. Still, he bowed and removed his hat and smiled as he took each woman's hand. Elizabeth's eyes met his as Lady Russell introduced them. The intensity of his gaze reminded her of the Gypsy's. Berliners of all classes were taking advantage of the warm weather to stroll through the Tiergarten. Elizabeth and Lady Russell had been careful to choose a secluded area, hidden from general view by a row of poplars.

"I'm very pleased to have a chance to speak with you again, Mr. Ristić," Lady Russell said.

"The pleasure is mine, Lady Russell," Ristić replied, "but I must admit I am somewhat perplexed. The note I received simply stated that representatives of the British government wished to meet with me. I did not know the representatives would be two such esteemed ladies. Pardon me for being so direct, but this is slightly out of the ordinary."

"You are, of course, absolutely correct, Mr. Ristić. It is out of the ordinary, and I do apologize for deceiving you, but it involves an extraordinary and unfortunate situation, and we're in desperate need of your counsel. You have no doubt heard of the recent unpleasantness at the Palais Strousberg?"

He nodded. "The accident with the German stable hand? I have."

"I'd like to show you something." Lady Russell reached into the small cloth bag she held and pulled out the wooden stake.

Ristić all but gasped. "Where did you find that?"

Lady Russell leaned forward. "Then you know what it is?"

His gaze did not leave the crude weapon. "I do."

"It was near the stairs where Friedrich's body was found," the ambassador's wife answered. "Circumstances lead us to believe it's the murder weapon."

His brow furrowed. "Murder? Then it wasn't an accident?"

Lady Russell pursed her lips. "No, unfortunately, it wasn't."

"My lady," Ristić said, "if what you say is true, shouldn't you hand it over to the officials in charge of the investigation and tell them where you found it?"

Lady Russell shook her head. "I don't think they would appreciate the significance of it."

His eyes narrowed. "Are you telling me you and Lady James do?"

"I am," Lady Russell replied.

He cocked his head to one side. "How, Lady Russell?"

"Quite by accident, actually," she answered, putting the stake away before it attracted unwanted attention. "One day, just after Lord Russell and I came here to Berlin, I was out looking around some of the shops when in one of them, one crammed with odds and ends and knick-knacks, I came across a peculiar box. It was very pretty on the outside. The wood had carvings of flowers and vines. The detail was very fine, but when I lifted the lid, I gasped. Inside was a Bible, a vial of water, a rosary with a crucifix, and a wooden stake much like this one. The entire box also smelled vaguely of garlic. The store's proprietor explained it was a vampire hunting kit. Of course, I had never heard of such a thing. He asked me if I was interested in purchasing it. I assured him I was not."

"I'm familiar with the kits you talk about," Ristić said.

"Pardon me for being forward, now, but how familiar are you, Mr. Ristić?" Lady Russell asked.

Ristić stiffened. "I'm afraid I don't understand the question."

Elizabeth and Lady Russell exchanged glances. The older woman nodded.

"I was talking to my husband," Elizabeth said, "and he told me the most peculiar thing, that you used to be the head of a Serbian government office in charge of hunting monsters, including vampires. Of course, it seemed quite ridiculous to me. You, sir, strike me as an immensely pragmatic person who would not believe such things or indulge those who do."

Ristić closed his eyes for a moment. The corners of his mouth turned up in a pained smile. "My admiration of the British intelligence service ever grows. Yes, for a time we had a small office in our government dedicated to dealing with strange occurrences, and I was the head of this office, but your husband is mistaken, Lady James. We didn't hunt monsters. You have stories in your own country, I'm certain, legends of forces unable to be seen, of creatures hostile to mankind. We have stories in my country as well, of creatures that prey on hapless travelers or others who are unfortunate enough to meet them. These creatures you call vampires."

"What did you do, then, if you didn't hunt monsters," Lady Russell asked.

His expression darkened. "For some, they are more than just legends. Occasionally, especially in the remoter areas, there will be a hysteria. Unexplained deaths. Sightings of those who supposedly have died walking outside of their graves. People believe, even people who ought to know better. Our goal was to disprove and suppress these incidents. You understand, Serbia wants to be perceived as a modern state, not the backwater many of your fellow countrymen think it is. We saw the perpetuation of these superstitions as a hindrance to our acceptance as a legitimate, sovereign nation. It pains me to know that our efforts backfired so severely."

"I apologize, Mr. Ristić, if we've offended you," Lady Russell said.

Ristić shook his head. "There is no need to apologize,

but I'm afraid I cannot help you. I urge you again to give what you hold in your hand over to the authorities. Let them deal with such base matters. Two beautiful women such as yourselves shouldn't be concerned with something so horrible."

Elizabeth glanced at Lady Russell, whose expression didn't betray her feelings, whatever they were. Elizabeth was certain she failed at hiding her own disappointment.

"I'm sorry we've troubled you, Mr. Ristić," the ambassador's wife said, "but thank you for your time."

Ristić nodded to them both and replaced his hat on his head, "Now, please excuse me. I have another appointment, and I must be going or else I'll be late. Good day to you both."

But as he turned to leave, Elizabeth spoke up. "Oh, but won't you reconsider, Mr. Ristić. It's important."

Ristić paused. The look he gave Elizabeth made her regret saying anything. "I don't doubt you, but please, leave it to the authorities. What you are involving yourselves in—murder, I mean—it is dangerous. It would be a terrible shame if anything should happen to either of you."

SEVENTEEN

—ᴍ—

Berlin, Germany
12 June 1878

ELIZABETH EXPECTED LADY RUSSELL TO give up altogether on the idea of looking into Friedrich's death after the failed meeting with Jovan Ristić. She returned to the Palais Strousberg the next day with a mixture of relief and trepidation. She had not, thankfully, received another bloody calling card, but the notion something terrible would happen if she didn't discover who murdered Friedrich gnawed at her, despite Ristić's last warning.

Lady Russell awaited her in an antechamber off of the main vestibule. She stood as Elizabeth entered. "So very good to see you, Lady James. Come now, we haven't a moment to lose. They'll be here shortly."

"Who?" Elizabeth asked as Lady Russell moved past her toward the door.

The ambassador's wife didn't stop. "There's no time. I'll explain when we get there."

She led Elizabeth across the vestibule to the stairs leading to the corridor where she had found Friedrich's body. The two women wound their way through the basement, around the kitchen, past the spot where Friedrich's body had lain. Elizabeth couldn't help but notice the bloodstains.

"A futile act, I'm afraid, cleaning the carpets," Lady Russell said over her shoulder, "and counterproductive. The embassy officers weren't very careful. I'm certain they trampled over more evidence than they uncovered, and whatever they didn't destroy, the maids did."

She led Elizabeth beyond the kitchen and the storerooms, down another long hallway. She stopped in front of a door near the end.

"This was Friedrich's room," she explained. "As far as anyone knows, he has no surviving family, and so his belongings are all still in there. The officers have already been through everything. It seems they found nothing helpful, but I believe they ought to have been more observant. I overheard the housekeeper say this morning that all of his things are going to be thrown out. I intend to look them over first."

She tried to open the door. It didn't budge.

"It appears to be locked," Elizabeth said.

"So it does. That's unfortunate. I wonder who would have the gall to do such a thing."

"Perhaps I can offer some assistance?"

Startled, the two women turned to find Jovan Ristić standing in the hallway.

"Mr. Ristić," Lady Russell said, "how did you get in here?"

His mouth twisted into a wry grin. "As recent events have demonstrated, I'm sorry to say, your security is some-

somewhat lax. There is an unattended door on the other side of the kitchen, granting access from an alleyway off of the Wilhelmstraße through the stables. It is probably how whoever killed your stable hand entered and subsequently escaped. I also bribed one of your servants. I told him I was a relative of this Friedrich, and I had come to collect his belongings."

Lady Russell made a clicking sound with her tongue. "Useful information, Mr. Ristić. Thank you, but why are you here now? When we spoke before, you advised us to leave well enough alone. Have you changed your mind?"

Ristić's face flushed red. "When we met before, Lady Russell, you struck me as a woman of great resolve. I had to make the effort, but I knew I would not dissuade you, just as I know your motives for wanting to solve this mystery are beyond reproach. I meant what I said before. What you are doing is dangerous, but I realized I couldn't live with myself if either of you were hurt and I could have prevented it."

"So you thought you'd take it upon yourself to see what you could find out by examining Friedrich's things," Lady Russell said. "We apparently had the same idea, but unfortunately, the door is locked."

"It that all?" Ristić reached into the pocked of his coat and pulled out what appeared to be a small metal file. "May I?"

Lady Russell and Elizabeth stood to the side while Ristić knelt in front of the door. He inserted the file into the keyhole. After a few adjustments, the tumblers fell into place with a click.

Lady Russell raised an eyebrow. "Mr. Ristić, I had no idea you were adept at picking locks."

Ristić smiled. "It's a useful skill sometimes."

He pushed the door open. Lady Russell led the way, and Ristić followed Elizabeth. There was barely enough room for the three of them, though the only furniture consisted of a cot, a small dresser, and a table with a washbasin. Only the light streaming in from the high window kept the space from being suffocating.

Lady Russell scanned the room. "Well, I suppose there wasn't much for the officers to search. They probably didn't spend more than five minutes in here. It all seems pretty straightforward. I suppose we should start with the contents of the dresser."

Mr. Ristić, though, turned his attention to the table. After a few moments of study, he reached underneath and wrapped it with his knuckles in several places. He settled on a spot he seemed to like, and Elizabeth heard a sound of metal scraping against metal. Suddenly, a hidden drawer popped open.

Mr. Ristić pulled it out as far as it would go. "The table has a false bottom. It is something I've seen before."

The three of them peered inside. The drawer held a small leather-bound journal. Lady Russell picked it up and began to look through it. "It's in English, rather poor English, but English nonetheless."

"Practice, perhaps?" Ristić asked.

"I don't believe so." Lady Russell turned the journal so Ristić and Elizabeth could see the page she had been reading. "There are date and time entries. I could be mistaken, but I think he was following someone. There are quite a few mentions of a Count von Brunn and an address not terribly far from here. His home, maybe? Also several other places around the city are mentioned over several days. And a woman's name. Charlotte. His wife?"

Ristić shook his head. "No, I have met the Count von

Brunn. He's from Bavaria. And his wife's name is not Charlotte."

"Interesting." Lady Russell returned to perusing the journal. She flipped forward several pages. "There is another set of entries about a man named Amsel."

"Jakob Amsel?" Ristić asked.

"Yes. Do you know him as well?"

"I know of him. He's an industrialist. He has several ventures in Eastern Europe, including Serbia. He makes it a point to be friendly with my government."

"There are a lot of references to Sophia Amsel, his daughter."

Ristić placed a hand over his heart. "That is a very sad story, I'm afraid. Sophia was Amsel's only child. Last winter, she became ill. Of course, Amsel took her to the best doctors in Berlin, but she never recovered. She died just short of her seventh birthday."

"How awful," Lady Russell said, "but it makes these entries even more curious, because they're all recent. Why would Friedrich have information about this man's deceased daughter?"

"That is a question I cannot answer, Lady Russell."

Lady Russell continued to leaf through the journal for a while longer, until she turned a page and stopped abruptly. She stared at it silently.

"What's the matter?" Elizabeth asked.

Lady Russell looked up at her, her brow furrowed in concern. "Lady James, there are entries about you."

A chill came over Elizabeth. "Me? Why would there be entries about me? What did he write?"

Lady Russell handed the journal to Elizabeth. "Perhaps you should read it yourself, Lady James. We can step outside, if you would like some privacy."

Elizabeth shook her head. "No, that won't be necessary. Thank you, though."

She peered down at the page the open journal. The more she read, the more she wished she hadn't. The words written in the journal cut into her, knives reopening old wounds until the blood flowed. It was all there. Every place she had visited since arriving in Berlin, every shopping trip, every social call, her visit to Mme. Kárpáthy, everything up to the morning she had found Friedrich's body.

There was more, though. Friedrich had notes about her entire life: her childhood as the daughter of an Oxford professor, the disappearance of her father after the violent murder of their chambermaid, the suspicions, the rumors, the aspersions, the death of her mother shortly thereafter, how she had gone to stay with an aunt in North Yorkshire, her engagement to her first husband Stanley, and his illness and death only months after they were married.

Elizabeth didn't know how to react. She felt the eyes of Lady Russell and Ristić boring into her. She opened her mouth to say something, but no sound came out. She couldn't breathe. The edges of her vision darkened. The room began to spin ...

She next remembered lying on the cot with Lady Russell standing and Ristić kneeling over her. Ristić held her head.

"Are you all right, dear?" Lady Russell asked.

She wasn't, not at all. "Yes, I'm fine. I'm so sorry. It was—It was a shock to see all the things Friedrich wrote about me."

Lady Russell cocked her head to the side. "Apologize? Lady James, I would defy anyone to have such poise after reading what you read."

While Mr. Ristić helped her to her feet, she noticed Lady Russell had the journal tucked neatly under her arm. "But why would Friedrich keep such a journal. How did he even discover about ... everything?"

"I promise you, Lady James, we'll figure it all out," Lady Russell said. "Right now, though, you should rest. I'll have a carriage take you home at once. But please, until we know more, do be careful."

AS ELIZABETH CROSSED THE TOWNHOUSE'S foyer, she heard voices and occasional laughter coming from inside the study. Alfred's meeting was running late. She had just reached the stairs when the study door opened. Alfred stepped out followed by another man. Elizabeth froze. Alexej the Gypsy stood before her, dressed as he had been on the street a few days earlier, the same half-smile on his face.

Alfred failed to notice her shock. "Elizabeth, you're back, I see. I trust you had a pleasant visit."

She wasn't looking at him. She was looking at his guest. "Yes, yes, it was quite pleasant."

Alfred picked up on the cue. "Oh, I'm terribly sorry. Aleksandr Vladimirovich, this is my wife, Lady Elizabeth James. Elizabeth, this is Aleksandr Vladimirovich Chernov, attaché to Prince Gorchakov, of the Russian embassy."

He took the hand she offered and bowed to kiss it. He did not take his eyes off of her face. "A pleasure to meet you, Lady James."

For her part, Elizabeth couldn't help but stare into his brilliant green eyes. "And you as well, Aleksandr Vladimirovich."

"Lord James, you have a beautiful wife. I would love to stay longer and visit with you both, but I'm afraid I must be going. There is a lot of work to do."

Alfred laughed. "Isn't there always? Here, allow me to show you out."

"Don't trouble yourself, my friend. I can show myself out."

He smiled at Elizabeth once more before turning to go. When he opened the door, a gust of wind swirled into the foyer. What had been a sunny day just minutes earlier had become threatening and overcast.

"It's amazing how quickly these summer thunderstorms can come up, isn't it?" Alfred said once the Russian stepped out. "Please tell Sarah I'll take my dinner in the study again tonight, dear. I'll be working late."

EIGHTEEN

Bucharest, Romania
6 December 1999

GIBBERISH. AGAIN. NOT FOR THE first time, Adam fought the urge to hurl the book across the room. As Paul the student subversive explained, the Committee employed something called a Baconian Cipher to pass their messages.

It worked by assigning every letter of the alphabet a five-digit binary number. Within the books the Committee used for their messages, the pattern of underlined or circled letters represented these binary numbers. Paul and his fellow agents provocateurs had another elaborate verbal code worked out to communicate what book contained a new message as well as the page and place it started.

Unfortunately, Mihai Iliescu had neglected to provide any guidance on that detail. The copy of *Dracula* he had given Adam seemed like the most logical place, but the effort drove him to fits.

Adam was lighting another cigarette when Arkady appeared at the door of the room he had claimed as his office. The most recent safe house was located in a posh neighborhood of Bucharest with tree-lines streets and a Mercedes in every driveway.

"I thought Clara made you quit smoking," Arkady said.

"I had a back-up supply." Adam surveyed the wreckage on the desk. "And I've almost burned through it already."

"So no luck, then."

Adam took a drag from his cigarette. "None at all. I was just getting ready to call it quits for another day."

As he stood his hand rested on the copy of *The Giaour* Clara had gotten in Mostar from the unfortunate police officer Danilo Grubelić. He picked it up and opened to the first page.

"Having a thought?" Arkady asked.

Adam held up the slender volume. "This book is the last one Mihai wanted me to find."

"So you think it might hold the key?"

Adam shrugged. "I don't know. It might. It's as good a guess as any. But there are five other books here. We need to do better than guess. We're running out of time. We have to find Clara, and we won't be able to do that until we find the medallion." He tossed the book down on the desk. "What page? What line?"

Arkady scratched his beard and focused on a point on the wall somewhere behind Adam. Then he smiled. "Start with the vampires."

Adam waved his hand across the book-strewn desk. "You can't be serious."

"As Dracula's empty grave, my friend. Think about it. If *The Giaour* is the key, wouldn't it make sense to look at the one very specific passage about a vampire?"

Adam eyed Arkady dubiously, but he picked up the

book again and turned to the page that contained the section about how the infidel Westerner, because of his transgressions, would be cursed to die and return as a vampire, to drink the blood of his own kin:

> *But first, on earth as Vampire sent,*
> *Thy corpse shall from its tomb be rent:*
> *Then ghastly haunt thy native place,*
> *And suck the blood of all thy race;*

Making note of which letters were circled, Adam applied the Baconian Cipher, one block at a time. This time the message on his notepad was clear:

SIGHISOARA

"Sighişoara," Adam whispered. "Dracula's birthplace."

Arkady grunted. "Makes perfect sense when you think about it. Everything goes back to Dracula it seems."

Adam stared at the word on the notepad. "The medallion still could be anywhere in the city."

"We'll figure it out when we get there. Who knows? Those books may yet hide other secrets." Arkady stretched. "Let's get some sleep. We should leave first thing in the morning."

AN HOUR LATER ADAM STILL lay wide awake, his mind racing. Every time he closed his eyes, Lucian Borescu's green hand reached for him out of the darkness. He hoped whatever they found in Sighişoara would help him put an end to the nightmares.

The sound of breaking glass sent Adam leaping out of

bed. He scooped up his Glock in one hand and his rosary in the other. When he pushed open his door he found Arkady already in the hallway, similarly armed. He gestured toward the stairs. At Adam's nod, Arkady took the lead, and together they stole down the hallway. A few feet from the stairs, they stopped again when a crash shook the walls of the townhouse. The knot of dread in Adam's stomach cinched tighter when he realized the noise came from his study.

Arkady sprinted down the stairs with Adam close behind. As they neared the door to the study, a man burst from the room clutching something to his chest.

"Stop!" Arkady called.

Without turning around the intruder sprinted for the door and ran out into the night. Arkady and Adam ran after him. After a few blocks, the thief showed no signs of tiring. Adam was giving out of breath. Beside him Arkady was huffing as well. Adam feared the thief would escape if they lost sight of him. At the next intersection the man hesitated. Again Arkady shouted for him to stop.

When the thief darted to the left, Arkady motioned for Adam to keep following. Arkady veered off, down an alley. Adam did as he was told, but he was losing ground quickly. One side street, and Adam would likely lose him.

Just as Adam felt he couldn't run any more, Arkady emerged from one of those side streets. He lunged for the man and tackled him to the ground. The package the thief clutched flew from his grip and skidded across the asphalt. Arkady struggled to subdue the man, grabbing him by his shaggy black hair. As Adam caught up, he spotted another detail—a pair of marks on the thief's neck, two tiny puncture wounds that had healed over.

Adam tried to pin one of the thief's arms behind his

back, but he shoved Adam away and then threw Arkady off with a well-placed elbow jab. As soon as he was free he jumped to his feet and took off. Adam turned to follow, but Arkady clutched his shoulder.

"Let him go." Arkady gestured toward his own neck. "You saw the same thing I did. We'd never get any information from him."

Adam walked over to the parcel the man had carried. As he suspected, it was a book, but not the one Adam thought it might be. He picked up *The Life and Death of Michael the Brave*, brushing off the street grime as best he could. Anya told him the book had been stolen from the Kunsthistorische Museum in Vienna, but Anya, or agents like her, recovered it. They just neglected to return it. According to her, the original thieves were not in a position to explain why they found the book so interesting, and at the time, Adam had not asked for more details. Now he considered that he ought to rectify that oversight.

Adam first noticed the shifting shadows about halfway back to the townhouse. A low mist rose up, and the night noises died. He glanced sideways at Arkady, whose hand tightened around the grip of his gun. Unlike Adam's pistol, which was loaded with regular ammunition, Arkady's fired silver bullets. The night became darker as they walked, the streetlamps dimming, as if shining through murky water. Then the stars overhead blinked out of existence, and the moon faded away.

Arkady swore, his eyes darting back and forth. He swept his hand in front of him, as if trying to clear away cobwebs. Adam mumbled a prayer to himself as he considered the possibility that the entire burglary had been an elaborate trap to lure them out of the safe house, one they had been more than happy to walk into.

As the townhouse came into view, a screech tore open the night, a sound that froze Adam's blood, a sound the ancestors of humanity learned to fear while huddled in caves clinging to the firelight. Adam and Arkady broke into a run. Just as they reached the door to the safe house, something brushed against Adam's back, nearly sending him to the pavement. Mocking laughter assaulted his ears as he and Arkady both stumbled inside. Arkady slammed the door behind them, and despite his terror, Adam peered out through the window.

A figure stood across the street.

A woman.

Her blond hair glistened in the newly returned moonlight.

As Adam watched, she dissolved into the fog.

NINETEEN

Near Cluj, Romania
6 December 1999

CLARA SLAMMED THE CHAIR AGAINST the floor until it shattered, feeling only slightly guilty for destroying the authentic Chippendale. She took one of the splintered legs and fashioned it into a crude stake.

When the key slid into the keyhole with a chink and the bolt of the lock turned, she was prepared. The door swung open, and Clara lunged at the dark figure in the doorway, stopping just short of impaling the caretaker, Iosif. She drew back her makeshift stake at the last possible second, but her momentum sent her stumbling into Iosif's arms. Once he steadied her, he motioned for her to come with him.

Dinner wasn't for another hour. Confused, she stepped into the hallway. Iosif took her hand in his and pressed something cold into her palm. When she opened her fingers she discovered a medal like the one Adam had given her. Its purpose was to ward off any evil, but it worked particularly well against vampires.

An image of Saint Benedict holding a cross adorned the front of the medal. The reverse bore a cross with letters arranged inside it:

VRSNSMV SMQLIVB

The letters stood for the words in the incantation *Vade retro satana*, the one Adam and others had used to drive vampires back.

Clara met the caretaker's solemn gaze. "Why are you doing this?"

Iosif held a finger to his lips. He took a few steps and beckoned her again. Together they slipped through the strangely dark and quite corridors and down the stairs. The fireplace in the sitting room was dark and cold. They crossed the dining room and passed through the door that led to the kitchen.

A heavy wooden table stood in the center. Above it hung a rack with assorted copper pots and pans. Off to one side stood an antique oven and range. Dishes sat on open shelves that ran the length of one wall, and a massive sink dominated the place underneath the room's only window. It was perfect, and like the rest of the house the kitchen exuded the same parts Victorian charm and menace. The cook, Dorina, waited by a door in the back. She wore a heavy coat and held another out for Clara.

Clara had become used to the chilly drafts in the house, but Clara was not prepared for the blast of cold air that assaulted her when Iosif opened the door. The sunlight blinded her as well, accustomed as she was to gas lamps and firelight. The trio trudged toward an outbuilding that appeared to be an old carriage house. When Iosif opened the garage door, Clara half expected a coach pulled by a pair of horses, but instead the garage housed an old black Peugeot. Iosif climbed into the driver's seat. Dorina climbed in next to him and motioned for Clara to get in the back.

Iosif had to try several times before the car's engine turned over. Once it did the car pulled out of the garage with a lurch Clara didn't know to attribute to the care-taker's inexperience or the car's disuse.

It was Clara's first chance to see the manor house from the outside. A rectangular building of stacked stone, it rose up four stories from the snow-covered lawn. Dark brown against the pale blue sky, its profile reminded Clara of a gravestone.

Snow covered most of the road with only two narrow tracks to mark its winding course. As they entered the woods, the road continued to twist and turn, but it seemed Iosif was finally getting a handle on the car.

"We are taking you into town," Dorina said in halting English. "There is someone there who can help you get home."

She didn't want to go home. She wanted to get back to Adam and Arkady, but she didn't tell them that. "Why are you doing this? Why now?"

"Because he is away and the day is clear and sunny," Dorina replied. "This has been our first opportunity. You do not deserve to be caught up in all of this."

"What about you?" Clara asked. "How did the two of you come to be caught up in it?"

Dorina and Iosif traded glances. Their expressions con-veyed some silent understanding between them. A sad-ness, but also a tenderness. Dorina placed a hand on his shoulder. "We have not had many choices in life. We have lived here our entire lives under the shadow of Ceaușescu. We do what we can, and we have spent most of our time learning not to see things. That is what a good servant does."

"So you've been taking care of the house for most of your lives?"

Dorina nodded. "Until now, we have had no good reason to intervene, but we cannot be complicit in holding you here against your will."

"Do you know why I'm here?"

She shook her head. "Unfortunately no. We just know that Mr. Harking grows more and more tense with each day, as if impatient for something to happen. He left yesterday evening in a hurry. He didn't announce when he would be returning."

"This person you know. Who are they? How can they help?"

"They will be able to protect you," Iosif said.

Clara felt a pang of guilt. "What about you? What are you going to do now?"

"You shouldn't worry about us. We have our own plan, and our own ways of protecting ourselves."

As they ventured deeper into the forest, the sunlight struggled to reach the ground, despite the leafless canopy. The bare trees also took on odd shapes, with trunks bent at unnatural angles. Clara lost all sense of direction staring at the looming black forms crowding the road, and as clouds moved in to obscure the sun, the road grew even darker.

Iosif pushed the tiny car to move faster. Dorina pasted a smile on her face, but Clara could see the concern in her eyes.

Clara caught movement in the woods, a shadow moving parallel to the car. On the other side of the road, another shadow disappeared behind a tree. Her mind flashed to Elizabeth's accident on the way to Berlin. Still, while a pack of wolves might be able to keep up with a horse-drawn carriage, keeping pace with an automobile was another matter entirely. And yet, the shadows continued to move through the snowy underbrush in tandem with the car. Iosif and Dorina must have seen them, too, and with a look of renewed determination on his face Iosif stepped on the accelerator.

They couldn't leave the shadows behind. Around the next bend, the dark forms emerged from the underbrush onto the edge of the road—close to a dozen large black animals. Clara had never seen wolves so large. They ran along with the car, yapping and barking and somehow keeping up no matter how fast the caretaker drove.

The car slipped, but Iosif managed to bring it back under control. Then with a loud thump, the car lurched, as one of the wolves threw its body against the rear right fender. Again and again, the members of the pack slammed into the car as Iosif struggled to stay on the road. As they rounded another corner, though, a giant wolf, larger than all the others, stood in their path. Iosif swerved to avoid hitting the massive beast, but lost control of the car on the snow-slick road.

The Peugeot spun around and slid off the road and down into a ditch, stopping only when it hit a tree. Clara was thrown forward into the dashboard. She gasped, trying to pull air back into her lungs. Her body screamed with pain. Just lifting her head became a Herculean effort. Iosif sat slumped over the steering wheel with blood covering his face. Dorina lay next to him, unmoving.

As Clara fought to climb free, a shadow passed over the car. A beautiful blond woman wearing a red dress opened the driver's side door. She peered inside, her mouth twisted into a malicious grin as she reached for Clara.

TWENTY

Berlin, Germany
23 June 1878

ELIZABETH STOOD ON THE BOAT'S upper deck gripping the railing so hard her hands hurt. All around her, the delegates and their wives mingled as a band played nearby.

She ignored all of it.

Sunlight danced on the water, as ducks and swans glided over its surface. Only a few wispy clouds dotted the deep azure sky. A breeze kept the oppressive heat away. People strolled along the wooded lakeshore. A little boy ran ahead of his parents. He stopped to wave at the people on the boat as it passed. Elizabeth smiled and waved back. Plenty of other boats sailed on the Wannsee that day, but none of them were the Kaiser's personal yacht.

Alfred joined her. "Are you enjoying yourself, my dear?"

"I'm trying. You know how much I hate boats."

He chuckled. "Well, as long as no one else knows that."

"Don't you worry. I'm a very good actress." She mustered a smile.

"I knew you wouldn't let me down." He kissed her on the cheek. "Now, if you'll excuse me, I've got to track down Aleksandr Vladimirovich. I haven't spotted him yet."

Alone again, Elizabeth maintained her grip on the railing. The yacht moved through the water almost silently, save for the low hum of the engines far below. The lakeshore gradually became more rugged, and the forest grew denser. The strolling Berliners disappeared. Elizabeth was reminded of the forest during the carriage ride to Berlin.

As she gazed across the water, she suddenly wished she could transport herself there, to the forest, away from the boat, away from people who knew anything about her or the things she had worked so hard to forget. To see everything written out so plainly in Friedrich's book had been awful, but to know that Lady Russell and Mr. Ristić—perfect strangers for all intents and purposes—had read it as well was even worse. If other people knew, she couldn't pretend none of it was real.

She didn't notice Lady Russell standing next to her until the other woman spoke. "It's a beautiful day for a sail, isn't it?"

Elizabeth jumped and let go of the rail. Though she immediately grabbed hold again, she feared for a moment she would tumble over into the water.

"Yes," she replied, as naturally as she could manage. "It's quite a lovely day."

Lady Russell smiled and pat her hand. "Dear, you really shouldn't try to lie. You're not very good at it."

Elizabeth sighed. "My apologies, Lady Russell. I just keep dwelling on what I read in Friedrich's journal. It's hard to think of anything else."

"I hope you don't think I'm judging you. I'm not. How

could what happened be your fault? You were just a child. And believe me, it was the last thing we were expecting to find in that journal." Lady Russell leaned in closer and lowered her voice. "On that score, I've heard from the captain of the embassy guard. He believes they've solved the case. He says Friedrich was murdered outside the embassy by someone trying to rob him, and that he stumbled wounded into the Palais. Rubbish, of course, but don't worry. Mr. Ristić and I are devising with a plan."

Elizabeth closed her eyes. In her mind, she saw another summer day and the little house within view of the Oxford spires. The chambermaid lay on the floor of her parent's bedroom, a crimson gash across her neck. Her father stood over the body, his hands covered in blood. He looked at her, the most peculiar expression on his face. No one saw him again after that day.

"There's a storm coming," Elizabeth said when she opened her eyes again.

Lady Russell looked up at the nearly cloudless sky.

ALMOST AN HOUR LATER, ELIZABETH stood in the same spot. A waiter carrying a tray of drinks approached her. He smiled and offered her a glass. She smiled back, shook her head, and turned away. The waiter didn't leave.

Thinking he must have misunderstood, she tried again. "I'm sorry. No, thank you."

Still the waiter remained. Elizabeth glanced around for someone to help her. Alfred was nowhere to be seen. Across the boat Lady Russell was deep in conversation with Mr. Ristić.

The waiter leaned forward. "They don't have your best interests at heart, you know."

For the second time, Elizabeth thought she might fall overboard. "Excuse me?"

"Lady Russell and Jovan Ristić. They don't have your best interests at heart."

"You're not a waiter. Your accent—you're not German either. Who are you? And how do you know what my best interests are?"

The man bowed. "Thomas Parson, from Tennessee, the finest of the United States, at your service."

"How did you get on the Kaiser's yacht?"

Mr. Parson smiled wryly. "No one ever notices the servants. I learned a long time ago I could hide in plain sight as a butler, or a carriage driver, or a waiter. The uniform is a little snug, but it'll do. The man whose place I've taken will probably come to in a few hours with a nasty headache, wondering why his clothes are missing. I feel slightly bad about that, but I needed to get on this boat."

"Why?"

"To speak to you."

"Me? Whatever for?"

He arched an eyebrow. "You need to know you're in danger, Lady James."

Elizabeth, trying her hardest not to show her growing disquiet, straightened herself and gave him her best withering glare. "I assure you, Mr. Parson, I don't know what you're talking about."

"I think you do. Friedrich Wilhelm Henry Stanton didn't have the luxury of any forewarning. You ought to at least listen to what I have to say."

"I have people to watch out for me."

He shook his head. "They can't protect you from the danger I mean. Look around at the people here. They all have proper manners and wear the proper clothes. They have proper educations, make the proper greetings and the proper introductions, and engage in the proper topics of conversation. These are the people deciding the future of Europe and the world, yet they don't even know what the world is really like. For their sakes, I hope they never find out. As for your friends, Lady Russell only wants to protect her husband's reputation. Jovan Ristić...well let's just say he has his own motivations."

"You never answered my earlier question, Mr. Parson. How do you know what my best interests are?"

With his free hand he reached into his coat and pulled out a small rectangular piece of paper, a calling card. He handed it to Elizabeth. "Because we have the same interests. We both want to find your father."

Elizabeth's hand trembled. She didn't have to read the card. Though a dark red smear obscured the name, she knew to whom it belonged. "Where did you get this? Have you been the one leaving them at our townhouse?"

Parson took a step back. "Lady James, I'm too much of a gentleman to ever do such a thing. I didn't know you were getting them, too. Interesting. Mine was slipped underneath my door yesterday morning at the boarding house where I'm staying."

"Mr. Parson, what do you know about my father?"

"I know enough, and I can explain everything, if you'll give me a chance."

Elizabeth kept her voice even, her tone as cold as ice. "Mr. Parson, I've met others like you before, people who think they know what happened. People like you sent my mother to an early grave with their outlandish theories and allegations. I don't pretend to know what's happening, and I don't know who slipped that card under your door, but please don't involve yourself in this. I can do without the kind of 'help' you're offering."

"Lady James—"

"Mr. Parson, I can have the Kaiser's guards toss you overboard, if you'd prefer. Our conversation is over. Good day, sir."

Parson didn't protest anymore. With a curt nod, he backed away and melted into the crowd. Elizabeth looked back over the water.

A few minutes later the first peal of thunder sounded.

Elizabeth couldn't say how she knew a storm was coming. She just did. The few white, wispy clouds in the sky grew and multiplied, first turning grey, and then black. The wind gusted. The boat rocked back and forth, gently at first, then more violently. The first mate called for everyone to go below deck. Elizabeth searched through the crowd for Alfred, but she didn't see him anywhere. She thought for sure he would come find her.

Just as she was about to join everyone else, the rain began to fall, and the boat pitched hard to one side. She lost her footing and fell. When the boat righted itself, she slid and would have gone overboard, had it not been for the railing itself. The rain and the rocking of the boat made it impossible for her to return to her feet.

As waves reached the deck, she looked around and realized she was alone. When she finally managed to pull herself upright the boat pitched again. The railing passed underneath her, and she knew she was going into the water. She desperately grabbed for anything she could, but there was nothing to hold onto.

As a wave reached up from the lake to claim her, a hand grabbed hers, and she felt herself being pulled firmly back onto the boat. When both of her feet were on the deck again, she discovered not her husband, but the

Gypsy, or rather, the Russian, Aleksandr Vladimirovich.

"Everything is well, now, madam," he said. "I have you."

He meant what he said in the most literal way possible. Despite the wind, the rain, and the waves, everything was well, because he was holding onto her, and as long as he did, nothing could harm her.

Moments later, the rain stopped, the wind died, and the storm subsided as suddenly as it had begun. Everyone came up from below deck. Elizabeth ran her hands over her drenched clothes, certain she was a spectacle to behold. She heard someone calling her name and turned in time to see Alfred pushing through the crowd.

"Elizabeth!" he said, "I couldn't find you. My God, what happened? Are you all right?"

She nodded. Rays of sun peeked through the clouds. Elizabeth turned to express her gratitude to Aleksandr Vladimirovich, but he was gone.

TWENTY-ONE

Berlin, Germany
25 June 1878

ELIZABETH PAUSED AT THE EDGE of one of the Tiergarten's wide lawns. Kept in an almost natural state, it reminded her of the English meadows she wandered through as a girl. She didn't even think it unusual to see a man reclining against the trunk of a wide oak tree nearby. He looked so much like one of her father's students in his ill-fitting suit, his lanky frame lackadaisically sprawled across the grass.

She also wasn't surprised to discover the man was Thomas Parson. He smiled and tipped his hat. Curls of unkempt brown hair fell in front of his eyes. Elizabeth didn't return his salutation but waited for him to join her on the path.

"I suspect you're here to talk to me," she said.

"Can't a fellow enjoy a warm, sunny day out among the trees and flowers without any ulterior motives?"

"Oh, I suspect any number of fellows could, Mr. Parson, but not you. In fact, I would go even further to say you never do anything without an ulterior motive."

Parson feigned a hurt expression. "Well, that's a bit harsh, don't you think?"

"Am I wrong?"

"You know, I could say the same about you."

Elizabeth glanced sideways at the American. "What do you mean?"

"Your choice to take a walk, today here in the Tiergarten."

"Can't a lady enjoy a warm, sunny day out among the trees and flowers?"

"She could, but she isn't. You're here to meet Lady Russell and Mr. Ristić."

"What if I am? You seem to know all about my business with them. I have a legitimate reason for meeting them here. And I have no reason to hide anything from them."

He grinned. "Then why haven't you told them about me?"

She stiffened. "How do you know I haven't?"

"If you had, this conversation with you would be infinitely more difficult."

"Why is that?" Elizabeth asked.

"If my friend Jovan knew I was in Berlin, I would have already received a visit from him."

"Then the two of you have a history."

Mr. Parson chuckled. "That's one word for it."

"If that's so, why did you run the risk of talking to me?"

"Because I trust you."

Elizabeth looked away, at the water lilies growing in the blue-green pond at the edge of the path. "Maybe you shouldn't."

"Still, I'm willing to take that chance. I'd hate to see

anything happen to you."

"What is it you want to speak to me about, Mr. Parson?" Elizabeth was growing tired of the games, and did little to hide her exasperation.

"The topic of your meeting with Lady Russell and Mr. Ristić." Mr. Parson replied.

Elizabeth laughed. "Honestly, do you think I'm going to tell you?"

"But I already know. Mr. Ristić went to meet Count Augustus von Brunn this afternoon. I followed him to the count's townhouse."

"And did you find a way to listen in on their conversation as well? Perhaps you passed yourself off as the count's butler?"

"I didn't have to listen in on their conversation."

"Why not?"

The seemingly permanent grin on Mr. Parson's face melted. "Because they didn't have one. When Ristić arrived at the townhouse, he discovered the count was dead. He apparently committed suicide. Of course, I shouldn't have been surprised. This morning, I found another bloody calling card under my door. I assume one was left at your townhouse as well."

"No, actually."

Parson raised an eyebrow. "Interesting."

Elizabeth stopped in the middle of the path. "Mr. Parson, this changes nothing. My decision remains. I don't have any wish to speak with you about this matter. If you try to contact me again, you can trust I will tell Lady Russell and Mr. Ristić about you."

His smile returned, the same lopsided grin he had greeted her with. Elizabeth admitted to herself it was not unappealing. "When you're ready, Lady James, you can find me here. I'll leave you to your meeting. Have a pleasant day."

"THE POLICE IN THIS COUNTRY don't treat those from my part of the world very well." Ristić said of his call upon the count as the three of them strolled along one of the park's more secluded paths. "They were already there when I arrived. They shunted me into a sitting room and left me there for more than an hour. I explained that I had an appointment with the count to discuss a matter of business. It didn't seem to satisfy them. They wouldn't at first tell me what had happened. It was only after I finally convinced one of them of who I was that he informed me the count had taken his own life. Even then, it was only with a fraction more respect. They dismissed me not soon after that."

Elizabeth silently cursed Mr. Parson. "I'm sorry, Mr. Ristić. Were you able to find nothing helpful?"

Ristić shook his head. "I did not say that. I was left alone for a considerable amount of time in the sitting room, enough to study its contents in great detail, including the writing desk."

"But how does that help?" Elizabeth asked.

"I'll tell you." A curious smile spread across his face. "I have asked questions discretely, but no one has heard of a woman named Charlotte associated with the count. I believe it was a pseudonym he invented. I also believe that theirs was no ordinary affair, no dalliance with a servant or a member of the working class." He reached into the pocket of his coat and pulled out a piece of paper folded in half, which he handed to Lady Russell. "This piece of paper was on top of the desk."

Lady Russell unfolded it. "It's blank."

Ristić's curious smile returned. "Look closer."

Elizabeth examined the piece of paper along with Lady Russell, and she discovered it wasn't blank at all. Someone had skimmed over the entire surface with a pencil. Faint writing appeared in the negative space the pencil's graphite missed.

"The count wrote a letter," Ristić explained. "This piece of paper was underneath the one he used. The pressure of his writing left indentations."

Elizabeth squinted in a vain effort to read the cramped German script. "What does it say?"

"It's a letter to Charlotte," Ristić said, "an apology."

Lady Russell held the piece of paper closer, struggling herself to read the count's handwriting. "An apology? For killing himself?"

Ristić wrinkled his nose. "Not exactly. In fact, I'm not sure what he was apologizing for. He tells Charlotte he still loves her, that he wishes she would come back to him, but he understands her reasons and knows it will never be the case. He then expresses condolences at the recent death of her husband after a bout with illness. Here is his apology. The letter becomes difficult to read, but it seems as if he feels the death of Charlotte's husband was somehow his doing."

Lady Russell glanced up from the paper. "Maybe it was."

Ristić shrugged. "Perhaps, but I hardly think it likely. There would have been nothing gained from it. The count, after all, still has a wife."

"We still don't have a connection to Friedrich, though." Elizabeth said.

"Not yet," Lady Russell replied. "This 'Charlotte' appears to be a woman of a somewhat high station. This letter could help us discover her identity. If the count doesn't have a direct link to Friedrich, perhaps she does."

Ristić nodded as she handed the letter back to him. "Precisely what I was thinking."

WHEN ELIZABETH RETURNED TO THE townhouse, she again heard voices coming from the study. She paused in the foyer hoping maybe Alfred would emerge again with Aleksandr Vladimirovich. She hadn't had the opportunity to thank him for coming to her rescue on the Kaiser's yacht. After several minutes, however, it soon became apparent the meeting would last a while longer, and she climbed the stairs to her bedroom. She retrieved one of her books, opening it to the place where she had left off. A piece of paper fluttered to the floor, another bloodstained calling card.

TWENTY-TWO

—✺—

Sighișoara, Romania
7 December 1999

ONLY A SMALL PLAQUE MARKED the ochre-colored house as the birthplace of Vlad the Impaler. However, as he and Arkady entered, Adam's gaze went to the more ostentatious sign hanging above the door—a wrought iron dragon.

The building contained a museum dedicated to the historical Dracula, as well as a bar.

They took seats at a table in the back. Arkady went to retrieve drinks for them and returned with two small glasses filled with a golden liquid.

Adam examined his glass. "Palincă?"

Arkady raised his own. "What's your saying? 'When in Rome...'"

Adam returned the salute and took a sip of the fiery apricot brandy. It burned his throat going down. A pleasant numbness followed.

"What do you know about *The Life and Death of Michael*

126

the Brave?" Adam asked. "Why does everyone want the get their hands on it?"

Arkady downed the rest of his drink and paused for a moment. "I don't know very much. Ioan Nicolescu never revealed his sources, and pretty much everyone thought he made it all up. The letters Michael the Brave supposedly sent to his cousin have never been found. Most people who've heard of the book don't believe they exist."

"But they do, or they did at some point. Where did Nicolescu get them? And why is he the only one to record the existence of Dracula's involvement in Michael the Brave's military victories?"

Like every other biography the book chronicled the rise to power of Prince Michael the Brave in the Romanian principality of Wallachia, his campaign to unite all three of the Romanian lands—Wallachia, Transylvania, and Moldavia—and his eventual and swift downfall. His united Romania lasted for only one summer.

Nowhere else, though was there a mention of Alexandru Balaurescu, a soldier Michael apparently grew to rely upon greatly and who was actually responsible for much of Michael's success. He may have even been the driving force behind Michael's ambitions.

Alexandru, of course, was Dracula.

"And why this particular copy?" Adam continued. "Why go to the trouble of breaking into the archives of a world-class museum? Surely other copies exist."

Arkady shook his head. "Not that we know of."

Adam narrowed his eyes. "How can that be? It was printed by a real publishing house, one I've never heard of, but it has an imprint."

"The main print shop of the publishing company burned down in 1856. Everything was destroyed. As you can imagine, in a warehouse full of books a fire spreads quickly."

"Surely Nicolescu would have had more copies."

Arkady shrugged. "He died a pauper after everyone rejected the book. He was disgraced, forced to leave the university. If he had any copies, they weren't found after his death."

Adam persisted. "But the universities—"

Arkady held up two fingers. "Two world wars, Adam. Lots of things get lost and destroyed."

Adam frowned and stared at his empty glass. "Is there anything you know about who stole it?"

Arkady shrugged. "They were professionals. We do know that, but as for who hired them, we were never able to trace the money. They didn't know who their client was or why they wanted the book. Whoever it was, they went to great lengths to hide their identity."

On the wall behind Arkady hung a picture of Vlad the Impaler, one very similar to his most famous portrait. Adam pointed to it. "Do you think it was him? Trying to destroy the last reference to his role in bringing Michael the Brave to power?"

"Why go to the trouble? The book wasn't on display. The archivists didn't even know it existed beyond a line in a catalogue. Besides, as you say, Nicolescu had to get his resources from somewhere. What if Dracula came to him? What if he wanted Nicolescu to write his story?"

Adam pinched the bridge of his nose. "So much speculation. I'm sick of all the questions. I'm tired of feeling like we're one step behind. I just wish we could find some answers."

"Well, this is as good a place to start as any, don't you think?" Arkady stood and threw some money on the table.

Adam pushed his chair back as well. "I just wish we had a few more clues. It's not like we can pick apart the bricks or take up the boards from the floor."

"We don't even know the medallion is here," Arkady said. "It could be anywhere in the city. Or we could be completely wrong and it's a thousand miles away."

"That's what I love about Russians." Adam chuckled. "Ever the optimists."

Arkady merely grimaced. "Give us one reason why we should be optimistic."

Emerging from the dim interior into the daylight, Adam paused to give his eyes time to adjust. He glanced around the square, and his gaze rested on a small shop tucked away into a corner.

"You want a reason to be optimistic? I'll give you one." Adam pointed to the shop. Books were stacked high in the window, and a small overloaded bookshelf stood next to the open door. "A bookstore. Mihai liked nothing more than used books."

"Could be a coincidence."

"Not likely. I guarantee you Mihai has visited this bookstore." Adam started across the square.

Arkady placed a hand on his shoulder. "Wait."

"What is it?" Adam asked.

Arkady glanced to his left. "We've attracted some notice."

Without turning his head, Adam followed Arkady's gaze. Two men dressed in black stood in the shadow of an archway at the entrance of an alley. "What are you suggesting we do?"

"We're still going to visit your bookstore, but we're going to walk slowly there, and browse in a few other shops first."

The several minutes walking around the square were some of the longest of Adam's life. Not many people had dared to venture out on the cold December day, but there were enough onlookers that anyone who wished them harm would attract attention. Adam hoped that was enough of a deterrent. When they finally reached the threshold of the bookstore, he risked a glance back at the archway. The men were gone.

A small space heater stood near the door of the bookstore, but it did little good. Adam rubbed his hands together to keep warm. A maze of bookshelves twisted through the small space, empty, or so Adam thought. A noise from the back raised the hairs on Adam's neck, and Arkady's hand immediately went to the gun concealed in his coat. Both relaxed when a short, balding man emerged from behind a shelf carrying a stack of books. He seemed just as startled to see the two of them as they were to see him.

"Can I help you?" he asked in Romanian as he set the books down on a table.

Adam tilted his head to read some of the titles. They were all old, from the early part of the century mostly, and many of them were history books. He tried a long shot. "You wouldn't happen to have any books on Michael the Brave, would you?"

A corner of the shopkeeper's mouth twitched, but otherwise his face remained impassive. "I have a few of those in the corner over there. You're welcome to look."

Adam nodded. "Thank you. I'm also interested in a historian from the 1800s. His name was Ioan Nicolescu. You wouldn't happen to have any of his works as well?"

The man's eyes narrowed. "Sorry, I've never heard of him."

Adam smiled apologetically. "Not many have."

He and Arkady wandered to the section the shopkeeper had indicated. Adam found a few books about Michael the Brave. He picked them up and flipped through them in turn.

"Any secret codes?" Arkady watched the shopkeeper out of the corner of his eye.

Adam kept scanning. "Not a stray mark in any of them."

"I don't see much more we can do here, then," Arkady said.

Adam replaced the last book on the shelf. "Agreed. Still I get the sense there's something off. You?"

"Absolutely, but we won't accomplish anything by asking any more questions."

Adam and Arkady made their way back to the front of the store. "Thank you," Adam called with a wave on his way out the door. The shopkeeper didn't respond.

After they exited the bookstore, Adam glanced over his shoulder to see the shopkeeper standing in the window. He took one of the books displayed there and turned it around so the back cover faced out. It was a strange thing to do. He couldn't think of a reason for the shopkeeper to turn the book around ... unless it was a signal.

Adam shouted as a man pounced on Arkady. He moved to help, but a vice-like hand seized Adam's shoulder and spun him around. Adam threw up an arm to block the blow aimed at his face. Adam had fought with knives, with guns, with wooden stakes. They all made him nervous, but when it came to a good, old-fashioned fistfight, he was right at home.

Adam and his assailant danced in a circle, their breaths coming out in small puffs. Adam's heart raced. The man was one of the two who had been watching them earlier. He was older than Adam, with a pug nose and a thick face but a muscular frame, probably from a lifetime of working in a factory.

The man tried for a right hook. Adam blocked it but didn't see the left jab that followed, and the man's fist slammed into his right eye. Adam staggered backwards. Something warm ran down his cheek. A probing finger revealed a gash over his eyebrow. He wiped the blood away with his sleeve and put up his arm just in time to deflect another punch.

The man let out a frustrated cry, and Adam went on the offensive. He made a few feints that forced the man back, and then connected with an uppercut to the man's pug nose. Blood streamed out of both nostrils. Drops stained the snow. The man cursed, but didn't fall. As he glared, Adam held up his fists in preparation for another round. He didn't want to know how many more bruises he'd find later.

If he didn't get killed first.

The man took another swing. Adam dodged, and his right fist connected with the man's chin, sending him sprawling. He struggled to his feet, but couldn't get his arms up in time. Adam's fist met his jaw again. The man staggered and then fell for a second time. He didn't try to get back up.

Adam fought to catch his breath. Nearby Arkady stood over his attacker, who lay face-up on the cobblestone pavement of the citadel square, but as Adam glanced around, a circle of angry glares confronted him from those he had assumed were mere bystanders.

No one was going to come to their aid.

As the circle of hostile faces closed in, Adam spun

around, only to be met with the shopkeeper's meaty fist against his nose. The world tilted, and his feet flew out from underneath him. His shoulder, the one he had dislocated only a few months earlier, slammed into the pavement. Pain shot through his arm and into his chest. He lay on the ground, struggling to stop his head from swimming.

"If you think you're going to finish what you started, you're sadly mistaken," The shopkeeper growled.

Arkady stepped over and offered Adam a hand. Adam reached to clasp it, and Arkady pulled him up.

"What are you talking about?" Arkady asked, wiping blood from the corner of his mouth.

"You're not welcome here," the shopkeeper replied. "If you value your lives, you'll leave now."

Arkady's hand went to his gun again, but several of the men closing in around them already had weapons in hand. There was no way he could take them all out.

"I don't know who you think we are," Adam said, "but we didn't come here to do anyone harm. My name is Adam Mire." He gestured toward Arkady. "This is Arkady Danilovich Markov."

The shopkeeper grinned. "I don't care what your names are. Do you honestly think you can come into my store asking about Michael the Brave and Ioan Nicolescu without giving yourselves away?" He spat at Adam's feet. "Damned Iron Guard pigs."

Adam stared at him stunned. "What? No, we're not—"

He smacked Adam across the face. "Shut up! I've heard enough. Maybe if we make an example of you two, the rest of your kind will learn to stay away."

By then, the others were only an arm's length away. Adam and Arkady stood back to back.

"Any ideas?" Adam asked, rubbing his jaw.

"Pray," Arkady said.

In the distance a whistle blew. A second later, several men in police uniforms ran into the square. One in particular shouted for the crowd of men to disperse. They all glanced nervously at one another until one-by-one, they walked away, though several threw one last hateful glower at Adam and Arkady.

The policeman who shouted strode toward the shopkeeper. "What do you think you're doing, Serghei?"

The shopkeeper glanced toward Adam and Arkady. "These men—"

"These men are not a reason to incite a mob," the officer said.

The shopkeeper raised an eyebrow. "They should know better than to ask the questions they asked."

"They also should have informed someone they were paying a visit." The officer shot Arkady a sardonic glance. "That still isn't a reason to beat them up."

"Sorry, Felix," Arkady said. "It was a surprise trip."

The officer saluted Arkady. "I just think you enjoy making a dramatic entrance, Arkady Danilovich."

Adam looked from Arkady to the officer. "Could we possibly go somewhere else to discuss all of this, maybe out of the cold?"

The officer nodded toward the bookstore. "I can think of a private place to talk."

The shopkeeper scowled.

Once inside the bookstore, they took some time to address Adam's and Arkady's cuts and bruises. Adam felt like he'd been given a full-body massage with a meat tenderizer. He could only guess Arkady felt the same way.

The shopkeeper, whose name was Serghei Martinescu, glared at them, his arms crossed in front of his chest. "So what are you doing here? What is it you want?"

Adam stroked his right temple, hoping the throbbing would stop. "Did you know a man named Mihai Iliescu?"

The man nodded. "I did, but I haven't talked to him in a very long time. He used to buy books from me."

"He's dead," Adam told him.

Serghei hesitated before he spoke again. "I thought as much. The last time he was here, it seemed as if he didn't expect to see me again."

Adam pulled a book from his satchel, the copy of *Dracula*. "He sent this to me. Did you sell it to him?"

The man took the book from Adam. His hand trembled. As he leafed through it, his expression became grimmer. "A shame it has been defaced so. It would be worth quite a bit if it were in better condition." He shut the book and handed it back to Adam.

Adam returned the book to his satchel. "He led us here for a reason."

Serghei shook his head. "I don't know what that might be."

"But you have an idea," Arkady said. "Has anything unusual or strange happened lately?"

"Not in the sense you mean," Serghei answered.

"Tell them," the inspector said. Arkady had introduced him as Felix Rudeanu.

Serghei sighed, his expression a little sheepish. "There have been several ... attacks about the city, people being beaten up, intimidated. Locals. Good people. And then just last week there was a murder. Someone who worked for the mayor. He was found with his throat slit and his right hand painted green."

"The Iron Guard," Adam whispered.

"You see why I drew the conclusions I did when you

came in earlier," Serghei said.

"Could it be a group pretending to be the Iron Guard?" Adam offered. "Do you honestly think they could return after all these years?"

"The Chetniks did," Arkady replied.

"The Chetniks were led by a—" Adam glanced at Serghei. "The Chetniks had charismatic leadership."

The Chetniks were led by a vampire, he was going to say.

Arkady's mouth twisted into a smirk. "That doesn't mean the Iron Guard doesn't also have 'charismatic leadership'."

Adam turned back to Serghei. "Thank you for your help."

"Mihai was a good friend, actually," Serghei went behind the counter and retrieved a book, which he held out to Adam. "Take this. I was saving it for him the next time I saw him. It isn't much, but he would have appreciated it."

Adam made a slight bow and took the book. It was a small, leather-bound book of poetry, with an illustration of an oak tree on the cover. The three men left the shopkeeper alone in his store. Once outside, Adam turned to Inspector Rudeanu. "What more can you tell us about this man who was murdered? Where was he found?"

The inspector pointed upward toward the spire of a church that loomed over the citadel square. "In the library at the School on the Hill."

Arkady and Adam traded glances.

"Why exactly are you two here, anyway?" Inspector Rudeanu asked. "Your questions to Serghei didn't make a lot of sense."

"We may have a lead on the whereabouts of Dracula's medallion," Arkady said.

The inspector's eyes grew wide. "Dracula's medallion? Here?"

Adam's gaze wandered back to the Vlad Dracul house. "We think so."

The inspector frowned. "And you couldn't have shown up two days ago?"

TWENTY-THREE

Satu Mare, Romania
7 December 1999

C LARA'S FOOTSTEPS ECHOED ON THE stone floor of
the sanctuary. The Saints Michael and Gabriel
Cathedral was a modest affair, at least as cathe-
drals went. Lamplight banished the shadows and illuminated the murals on the walls. No one else was in the
sanctuary. The hour was late, and soon it would be dark.

She could stay there. She would be safe.

The trouble is that no one else would be.

Her footsteps continued to reverberate throughout the
space, but as she proceeded toward the iconostasis, she
realized something was off. Clara stopped, and for just a
second too long her footfalls still echoed. Someone else was
there. She turned and scanned the sanctuary, but the
cathedral was still empty.

"May I help you?"

Clara jumped at the voice. She spun around to find a
man in a black priest's cassock standing near the iconosta-

sis. He was thickset and balding. A pair of round glasses rested on his nose.

"Dr. MacIntosh?" he continued before Clara could manage a response. "I'm Father Remus. We spoke on the telephone."

Clara forced a smile, though her heart still pounded. "Oh, yes, of course. I'm sorry. I thought I was alone."

The priest held up a hand. "I should be the one to apologize. I didn't mean to startle you. I was behind the iconostasis, preparing for tomorrow's service."

An awkward silence followed. Clara searched for something to say while she fought to hide her panic. "Thank you for taking the time to meet with me on such short notice," she finally stammered.

Father Remus smiled faintly. "Well, I admit your request was a little out of the ordinary, but we're always happy to accommodate scholars. And this time of year we tend to have a bit more time on our hands." He motioned to a side door near the altar. "Please, follow me."

The priest pushed the door open and ushered Clara into a narrow corridor on the other side. As she stepped across the threshold, she glanced over her shoulder. A shadow moved across the iconostasis. She quickened her pace and let the heavy door close. She didn't want to take a second look.

After only a few feet, the corridor ended at a set of wooden stairs illuminated by electric lights. At the bottom was another, wider hallway.

Clara wondered if there was some sort of signal she could give the priest to let him know of the predicament she was in, but all of her ideas led back to one conclusion. If she didn't do as she was instructed, Arkady would die.

CLARA WOKE AFTER THE CAR accident in a familiar bed. Shadows, cast by the flames of candles, danced on the ceiling of her room at the manor house. Immediately she knew she wasn't alone. She turned her head to find them both there, Jonathan and the woman she had seen standing in the snow. The woman wore a black corseted dress with a plunging neckline and black gloves. Her golden hair fell in waves past her shoulders. Her pale blue eyes held nothing but malice. Her red lips promised poison.

"Elizabeth," Clara whispered.

The woman nodded. "A pleasure to finally meet you, Clara."

Clara tried to sit up, but her pounding head forced her to lie down again. "Iosif and Dorina. Where—"

Jonathan grasped her hand. His touch was warm. "They aren't your concern right now. You should get some more rest. We can talk in the morning."

Clara tried to say something else, but as soon as she opened her mouth, the words escaped her. She wanted to get out of the bed. She wanted to run, but her body betrayed her. She couldn't move. Her head sank back into her pillow, and soon she was asleep. At least she didn't dream.

In the morning Jonathan returned to explain what they wanted her to do. "We'd do it ourselves, but you understand we can't exactly enter the church."

Clara gazed out the window at the grey-and-white day. She refused to look at him. "What makes you think I won't just run?"

"What makes you think we can't find you again?"

"I could stay in the church," Clara suggested.

"There are others you care about here in this part of the world." A sharp edge entered his voice, one Clara had never heard before.

"You won't hurt Adam. You need him, just like you need me. He's no good to you dead."

Jonathan stepped close enough for her to breathe in his all too alluring scent. "He's not the only one you care about."

She glanced sideways at him. "You mean Arkady?"

"We don't need him. He's a bit of a nuisance actually."

"Are you saying you'd kill him if I don't do what you say?"

"I'm saying we don't need him."

Her heart sank.

Jonathan let out a chuckle. "Does Adam know you have feelings for the Russian?"

Her face grew hot, but not for the same reasons as before. She balled her hands into fists. "It's not like that."

"If you say. We'll be leaving in an hour." He left her staring out at the cold, harsh day.

FATHER REMUS CAME TO A door and pushed it open to reveal a large room. Clara didn't know what she had expected. Maybe mahogany shelves and rows of dusty books, wood paneling everywhere, soft lights in wall sconces. Instead metal shelves gleamed under the fluorescent lights overhead.

"Welcome to our humble library," the priest said. "I believe the books you want are over here."

As he led her through the stacks, Clara attempted to make note of the books on the shelves they passed. Many of the titles were in Romanian. Some were in Greek, others in languages that used the Cyrillic alphabet, but she occasionally caught words and phrases in English.

Father Remus stopped in front of a set of shelved at the far end of the room. "Usually we get requests to look at the medieval manuscripts. We have one of the largest collections in the world of Romanian-language works from the Middle Ages. Few people want to look at the twentieth-century additions to our collection."

Clara did her best to channel Adam. "I won't know exactly what I'm looking for until I find it, but as I explained, I'm looking into the relationship between the Order of the Archangel Michael and the Church."

Father Remus' brow furrowed, and his face grew a deeper shade of pink.

"Please," Clara continued, "I don't mean offense. I just think it might be important to know how such relationships form. Maybe in the future, we can prevent the tragedies that happened."

Father Remus seemed to accept that explanation. He nodded. "I'll check on you later, to see if you need anything."

Clara smiled. "Thank you."

As soon as he left, Clara began pulling down books. She couldn't read Romanian, but Jonathan had told her what to look for. A name. Petru Romanescu. He was a partisan during the Second World War, someone opposed to the fascist government. Most of the books were collections of journals and pictures from soldiers during the war. As Clara scanned through them, her hands began to shake.

Some of the pictures just showed people staring at the camera, but most were not so benign. She saw ruined buildings—office buildings, stores, churches, houses. She saw wounded soldiers, dead soldiers, dead civilians. Jews and Gypsies, others deemed unfit. The Romanians were almost as fanatical as the Germans about ridding their country of undesirables.

She pulled down a thin volume bound in faded green fabric. Inside were more soldiers' stories. Clara sighed and started scanning the pages, wanting to move on to the next book as quickly as possible, but about half way through, her gaze fell on the name she had been looking for, Petru Romanescu. The pictures accompanying his spidery handwriting were not like the rest. More dead bodies confronted Clara, but the people, mostly in uniform, all had their throats ripped out, as if mauled by a wild animal. A wild animal had not killed them, though.

There were also inscriptions in Latin and a language Clara again failed to recognize, but when she turned the page her blood froze. Sketched in pencil was a dragon with its tail wrapped around its neck, a cross on its leathery wings. She knew the symbol well. She had seen it drawn in blood.

Out of the corner of her eye Clara caught movement again. She looked up, expecting the priest had returned, but no one was there. Her heart pounded as she placed the book inside her coat. She arranged the other books on the shelf so the gap hopefully wouldn't be noticed. Clara had almost made it to the stairs leading up to the sanctuary when Father Remus called out from behind her.

"Dr. MacIntosh, are you leaving?"

She spun around. "Yes. I lost track of time. I have another appointment."

He raised an eyebrow. "Did you find what you were looking for?"

Clara smiled apologetically. "Unfortunately, no. Thank you anyway for your help."

Father Remus moved closer. "Maybe you'll find your answers someplace else." He held out his hand. When

Clara reached to take it, he placed a crucifix in her palm and closed her fingers over it. "It's always good to have a higher power watching over you. May God be with you."

She nodded and turned around abruptly so he wouldn't see the tears welling up in her eyes. She climbed the stairs two at a time, and it was all she could do to keep from running through the sanctuary. The shadows churned all around the edges. Clara pushed open the door and stepped outside into the frigid air. Overhead the sky was grey and heavy with clouds. Jonathan waited across the street in the snow. There were no footprints around him. She took a deep breath and said a short prayer before walking toward him.

"YOU THINK YOU'RE ON THE side for good here don't you?" Jonathan asked.

They had returned to the manor house. On the way Clara tried to memorize every detail she could about the route they took, but once they entered the strange forest surrounding the property, she again found herself confused. Landmarks seemed to shift in the inconsistent light, and the trees' odd angles unnerved her once more.

She stood near the window, shivering from the chill, well away from the fire in the fireplace where Jonathan sprawled himself across one of the chairs. "I'm not on the side of widespread death and destruction."

"Is that all you think we want?" He adopted a feigned hurt tone. "Do you honestly think so little of us?"

"Isn't it what you want, though?" She asked.

He made a clicking noise with his tongue. "A certain amount of death and destruction can't be helped of course, but we really don't have grand plans. All we really want to do is rid the world of the plague that is Dracula."

"You're telling me you want to destroy Dracula?"

"Is that so hard to understand? Wouldn't you, given the chance?"

"We're not talking about me," she spat. "Why do you want to destroy him?"

"His time has come. He has manipulated history for long enough."

Something in his voice led Clara to conclude Jonathan wasn't telling her everything. "Who exactly was Petru Romanescu? Why so eager to get your hands on his journal?"

"We hope to find a clue as to how to destroy Dracula."

"I take it he doesn't respond to the normal methods."

"He was not created by the normal methods."

"How was he created?" she asked.

"No one knows," he replied.

"Did he participate in World War II?"

"Many of us participated in the Second World War." Jonathan's baritone voice continued to resonate through the room, as dark and rich as a fine cognac. "It was a plentiful time."

"And you don't want to return to that? The chaos? The carnage? Drinking your fill must have been so easy for you." She did nothing to mask the spite in her voice.

He didn't react, that she could tell. "The war had its challenges. We experienced more than a few close calls." The grandfather clock in the hallway struck midnight. "It's getting late," he said as the last peal faded away. "I should let you sleep."

She spun around as he stood from his chair. "Wait."

He paused. "Yes?"

"I still want to know Petru Romanescu's story."

He smiled as he sat back down and motioned to the empty chair opposite him. "Have a seat. The fire is nice and warm. Please make yourself comfortable."

She hated herself for asking him to stay, even as she sat. She needed to know more about Elizabeth's plans, but she also knew she couldn't trust herself. She didn't think Jonathan had used a glamour on her since the night he told her his name, but a small part of her still just longed for his company.

TWENTY-FOUR

From the Journal of Petru Romanescu

Ploiești, Romania
8 August 1943

URING THE SECOND WORLD WAR, *Romania was the largest producer of petroleum for the Axis Powers. As the tide of the war turned in favor of the Allies, Romania's refineries became targets for the United States Army Air Force. At the beginning of August 1943, the Allies unleashed Operation Tidal Wave, bombing the refineries around the city of Ploiești in an effort to deliver a crippling blow to the Axis oil supply.*

They failed at that objective, but rumors abounded that the refineries were not the primary target, that the Allies had other reasons for targeting Ploiești, and for years afterward the bombings were the subject of conspiracy theories, until the stories faded in the harsh reality of Nicolae Ceaușescu's rule.

Something has remained.

The fires are still burning. Great black clouds block the sun, creating almost perpetual night. Amidst the chaos something stayed, though, something that thrives on the disorder, something that relishes the darkness. I stumbled upon the first body in the rubble of a building on the edge of the city after the third day of bombing, but the unfortunate soldier did not die there. His throat had been ripped out, the jagged wound suggestive of a wild animal. The body had been drained of blood.

That night turned out to be the last night of bombing. When the sun set the following evening, we listened for the hum of engines again, but the American planes never came.

The dead bodies, however, continued.

I counted three more over the next three nights, all with their throats ripped out, all left with considerably less blood than they should've had. The bodies were all scattered, one in the village of Câmpina, one near the Astra Română Refinery, and one near the Columbia Aquila Refinery. Together, though, they gave me a rough radius with which to work.

Near the periphery of the Concordia Vesta Refinery, a warehouse just so happened to survive the bombings. The building also just so happened to be in the center of where the bodies were found.

The wind blew from the south the day I chose to pay a visit, sending the smoke away. Still, my lungs burned, and I couldn't imagine anything surviving there long. Anything natural at any rate.

I found a door with a broken lock and slipped inside. The darkness covered everything like a blanket. It was also cold, colder than it should have been given the fires and the summer heat, and quieter than it had any business being. A few pieces of derelict machinery lay about. They cast odd shadows in the beam of my flashlight. Then one of the shadows moved, and a long lean figure rose up. It looked like a person, but something about it was off. Its proportions were not quite ... human.

It looked directly at me, the irises of its eyes a brilliant red, even in the darkness. It smiled, showing a mouth full of fangs. It also wore an army uniform, either one it had pieced together from its victims, or its own.

Some of them, over time, lose their humanity entirely and become nothing more than animals, driven entirely by the bloodlust. This one was on its way, but it still retained enough of its personality to speak. "You're a fool to come here."

"And yet you're not attacking." I pulled the silver crucifix that hung around my neck out into the air. He winced and pulled back. "Does this bother you?"

He growled, but despite the pain he must have been feeling, he held his ground. "I can outlast you. All it takes is one little lapse in your concentration, and my fingers are around your throat."

He reached out with a clawed hand toward me. He was right. I had very little chance of outlasting him.

"I'm not trying to outlast you," I said.

"Are you here to die, then?"

"Not exactly. I'd like just a sample of your blood."

He laughed out loud. "My blood? Whatever for?"

"That shouldn't concern you."

His eyes narrowed. "But it does."

"Do you even know what you are?" I asked. "Where you came from, why you were made?"

"I have no use for philosophy," he snarled.

An explosion at the refinery shook the warehouse. In a flash he was on me. He couldn't have known about the silver threaded through my clothes. He screamed when his hands touched me but he didn't recoil. As he promised his claws dug into my neck. I kicked and flailed until I managed to reach the knife at my side. I sunk the silver blade into his stomach. His shriek echoed through the empty space. He let me go and retreated.

He clutched his stomach as black liquid oozed between his fingers. "This? This is what you want? Is it because you think you want to become like me? You're a bigger fool if you do."

I pointed the knife blade at him. "No, thank you. I have no desire for that."

"Then I can only offer you death."

Already the wound in his stomach had healed. He lunged at me again, but I had one more trick up my sleeve, literally. I let a small pouch slide out and flung it into the air. A cloud of fine particles shimmered the beam of my flashlight. When the vampire came in contact with the silver dust, he screeched in agony. I had to cover my ears. His skin sizzled and blistered all over. He clawed at his clothes, ripping them off and raking gashes in his already raw chest before collapsing to the floor, writhing.

I stepped over to him and slashed open his throat. I took a vial and filled it with the thick ebony liquid that poured out. His eyes no longer focused on me.

"You could have cooperated," I said as I stood.

I was halfway to the door when the shadows again moved. I spun around to discover the now hideous, malformed creature was almost on top of me. I used the last weapon in my arsenal. The wooden bolt from the handheld crossbow slammed into his chest. He staggered backwards and fell to his knees before supernatural flames reduced him to so much ash.

As I was leaving, my flashlight passed over something written on the walls. After glancing back at the pile of ash on the floor, I went for a closer look. He had written in all he had—blood. Scraps of paper littered the floor, pages ripped from books. I made an effort to collect them all and reproduce the writing here. I don't know what any of it means. Much of what is written isn't in Romanian, though it appears to be a collection of verses or incantations.

I can only guess the creature was trying to piece things together as well. I suppose he lied when he said he had no use for philosophy.

Maybe I should have asked him his name.

TWENTY-FIVE

—∿∿—

Berlin, Germany
26 June 1878

A S LADY RUSSELL HASTILY USHERED Elizabeth
and Ristić into one of the several small antecham-
bers off the Palais Strousberg's main vestibule, the
cold lump of unease in Elizabeth's stomach grew. "I'm not
sure I'm entirely comfortable with this plan. If word gets
to Alfred—"

Lady Russell held up a hand. "It has already been han-
dled. If your husband finds out about the meeting we've
set up between Jakob Amsel and Mr. Ristić, Lord Russell
will intervene with a plausible story involving 'delicate
sensibilities' and 'fragile agreements' or some such nonsense, but we needed to use Lord James' name to get Mr.
Amsel to agree to a meeting at all."

Elizabeth sighed. "I understand, although I'm not sure
what you're going to say to him once he arrives, Mr.
Ristić."

"I plan on simply speaking to him in the language he

understands," Ristić replied. "Business. I am going to propose a joint venture with the government of Serbia."

"But what if he agrees to such a venture?" Elizabeth asked. "How would you back out of it, without letting on that it was a ruse?"

Ristić smiled. "It isn't a ruse, Lady James. There is a real plan I have discussed with my government, and I have all the authority I need to negotiate an agreement to go forward with it."

"Clever," said Lady Russell.

"I am Serbian." He tapped his forehead. "I can't afford not to be clever."

Elizabeth suddenly remembered Alfred's distress after his meeting with the Serbian ambassador. "Mr. Ristić, pardon me for being so forward, but I must ask you a question. Did my husband say something to offend you when he met with you? If he did, I assure you it was unintentional."

Ristić shook his head. "He did no such thing, my dear. He merely made the same mistake many make, thinking they know what is best for my country without asking me or my countrymen if we agree. You cannot understand what it is like to have your country under the yoke of a foreign power for five hundred years, and not just any foreign power, but one that is not even Christian. Until you experience it, you don't know what it is like to fear the death of your culture, to have to fight to protect the tiny scraps you have managed to save. And you cannot know what it's like to realize you will have no help at all in winning your freedom, and that once you *have* fought for your freedom and shed blood for it, no one respects your achievement. Some may even resent you for it."

"I see," said Elizabeth, somewhat dejected.

153

The Serbian ambassador's smile took on a paternal cast. "He is young. He will make a great statesman one day. He made a mistake. He simply needs to understand that he cannot lead in every situation. Sometimes you need to see where events take you. And if he is worried about his reputation, I would never be so gauche to repeat our conversation outside these walls."

Lady Russell cleared her throat. "Speaking of, it's almost time for your meeting with Mr. Amsel, Mr. Ristić. Perhaps we should all take our places."

"As you say, Lady Russell." He nodded to the two women and left. The meeting was to take place in the room next door.

"What will we do while Mr. Ristić meets with Mr. Amsel?" Elizabeth asked.

"We'll listen." Lady Russell smiled knowingly.

Elizabeth was taken aback. "Listen? But how?"

Lady Russell chuckled. "You forget, the Crown leases the Palais from the estate of a bankrupt railroad magnate. The building was never designed to house an embassy, and there are some … quirks in the construction. Isn't that right, Mr. Ristić?"

"You are indeed correct, Lady Russell," Ristić replied from the other room, as clearly as if he were standing next to them.

Lady Russell cocked an eyebrow. "Of course, we aren't above using such quirks to our advantage."

A few minutes later, the door to the other room opened and closed again. Ristić exchanged pleasantries with Jakob Amsel, who had a high-pitched, nasal accent. They spoke in German, and Elizabeth did her best to follow.

"I beg your pardon, Mr. Ristić, but where is Lord Alfred James?" Amsel asked once they were beyond their initial greetings. "I understood him to be the one who arranged this meeting."

"Lord James sends his apologies," Ristić replied. "He was called away unexpectedly, but he has assured me that what we discuss today has the full backing of the British Crown."

Elizabeth frowned and looked at Lady Russell, who smiled and silently nodded.

"And what exactly are we discussing?" Amsel inquired.

"A proposal," answered Ristić. "Hundreds of years of misrule by the Turks have left my people at a disadvantage as we struggle to make Serbia a modern state. Still today, many of our cities and towns are not connected by roads that are passable year-round."

Amsel grunted. "I'm well aware. In fact, I've just returned from a trip touring several of my factories in Serbia, and I was forced to wait several days in Paraćin while the road back to Belgrade was repaired after being washed out in a storm."

Did you know that? Elizabeth mouthed silently to Lady Russell. The ambassador's wife shook her head.

"Paraćin is an unassuming village. I was unaware of any industry there."

"There is none," Amsel said. "A business opportunity was brought to my attention."

"What sort of business opportunity?"

Amsel let out a chuckle. "You ought to know better than anyone that you never play all your cards up front. You always save something for later, when you need it. A business opportunity brought me there, Mr. Ristić. Let's just leave it at that."

"A beautiful area of the country at least." Ristić said. "Did you perhaps pass through Kisiljevo? There is a tavern there that serves the most superb *šljivovica*. Or Medveđa? You can take in the whole valley from one of the hills above the village."

"I have visited both," Amsel answered.

Elizabeth let out a small gasp. Lady Russell placed a hand on her arm.

"Did you hear that?" the industrialist asked.

"Hear what?" Ristić replied.

"I just heard a noise. It sounded like … someone breathing. Are you sure you didn't hear it?" A hint of suspicion entered Amsel's voice.

"I'm certain."

Silence followed. Elizabeth and Lady Russell exchanged panicked glances.

"It's an old building. Old buildings make odd noises," Ristić added hastily. "You know, it's quite refreshing to speak to someone who knows my country so well. I think you'll be especially interested in what I have to say. On behalf of the Kingdom of Serbia, I am proposing a joint venture to build a rail line from Berlin to Belgrade."

Another pause.

Another moment of panic.

Finally Amsel spoke. "That is a very interesting proposal, Mr. Ristić, but I immediately see a great many problems. The success of such a venture is highly unlikely."

"Mr. Amsel, we are all determined to bring Serbia into the modern era, no matter what the challenges. If you'll simply consider—"

Amsel broke in. "I said unlikely. I did not say impossible. I believe the idea has merit, but I need time to think about it, to study the figures, say a week. I will send a message to your hotel when I'm ready to talk again. Now I must be going, I've been away from my office for too long."

Once Amsel had left, Ristić rejoined Elizabeth and Lady Russell.

"That was a tad disappointing," Lady Russell said. "I'm not sure we found out anything useful."

"Jakob Amsel is nothing if not cagey about his own affairs," Ristić conceded, "but I wouldn't say our meeting was all for naught. We now know that he recently visited Paraćin, Kisiljevo, and Medveđa. That's very curious."

"How so, Mr. Ristić?" Lady Russell asked.

He leaned forward and lowered his voice. "The three villages were the locations of vampire panics in the last century."

Elizabeth's knuckles were white from clutching the arms of the chair where she sat. She forced her voice to work. "There is something else." Both Ristić and Lady Russell looked at her. "My father went to all three villages on his last visit to the Continent, just before he disappeared."

TWENTY-SIX

—m—

Berlin, Germany
27 June 1878

"HERE, MILADY?" THE CARRIAGE DRIVER asked as he opened the door for Elizabeth. "Are you certain?"

Elizabeth wrinkled her nose. The odor of alcohol mixed with human sweat, garbage, and burning coal hit her as she exited the carriage. A fine layer of soot covered the street, the cobblestones, and the buildings.

"Yes, I'm certain," she said.

The driver bowed. "As you wish, milady. I shall wait for you."

Elizabeth had ordered the driver to bring her to a tavern among the tenements of Wedding. This was Jakob Amsel's Berlin. The city's new working class lived here, on top of one another, always pushing and jostling for space, crowded into shacks in the shadows of the factories, shrines to Germany's new industrial might.

Steps led downward into the darkened interior of the

tavern. Elizabeth paused to give her eyes time to adjust. The shouting and the laughter, the clinking of glasses, the scuff of chairs on wooden floors overwhelmed her almost as much as the smell. Elizabeth counted no less than five different games of chance being played—cards, dice, dominoes. She wondered which was Friedrich's choice when she spotted a woman approaching through the crowd. Elizabeth couldn't help but notice the deep V of the woman's neckline.

"Milady," the woman said, "I have to tell you you're drawing quite a bit of attention to yourself."

Elizabeth peered around the dim room. The din had lessened considerably since her entrance and more than a few pairs of eyes were upon her. She fingered the old cloak she had worn in the hopes it would hide her status. Obviously her ploy had not worked.

"A lady like you should be careful." The woman clutched her arm. "Pickpockets, you know, and worse. Come with me. You'll be less noticeable if you aren't standing in the middle of the room."

She led Elizabeth through the crowd to a table in a corner. Nearby, some men played dice. They glanced up briefly as the two women took seats but then returned to their game, apparently more interested in the money exchanging hands.

"My name is Brigitte," the woman said as soon as they were seated. "What brings you to this part of town?"

"I'm looking for someone," Elizabeth replied. "His name is Friedrich, Friedrich Wilhelm Henry Stanton. I hear he frequents this ... place."

Elizabeth had asked her maid if she knew the kinds of places Friedrich liked to go in his free time. Sarah had been reluctant to say at first, but after some prodding, she told Elizabeth, in a hushed voice, about the tavern.

Brigitte laughed. "Freddie! Oh, of course I know him, but I haven't seen him in a few days. I'm afraid I don't know where he is. Why do you need to talk with him?"

"It's a personal matter."

Brigitte winked at her. "Aren't they all?"

She made a subtle gesture to the men playing dice. A giant redheaded man came over to the table and slammed his beer down so hard some of it sloshed out and very nearly landed on Elizabeth's dress.

"This is Max," Brigitte explained. "He and Freddie are good pals. Maybe he knows where Freddie might be."

"Why are you looking for him?" Max asked. "He doesn't owe you money, too, does he?"

"It's a personal matter," Brigitte answered for Elizabeth.

Max grunted. "No, haven't seen him in a few days. It's not like him to go so long without stopping by for a few games. Funny, too, because just last week, he said he had come into some money, good money, and he'd be able to pay me everything he owes me—and everyone else."

Elizabeth leaned in. "Did he say where the money came from?"

"No, he didn't, other than saying someone hired him to do a job. He said he'd never owe anyone anything again. We all laughed at him. Freddie always owes someone money."

As Max talked, he inched closer and closer to Elizabeth until he almost had her pinned in her chair. She peered over at Brigitte, whose smile did nothing to comfort her. Elizabeth shifted her gaze to the tavern's exit, noting the distance and the crush of boisterous bar patrons in the way.

"I'm so sorry to have troubled you all." She tried to stand. "If you'll excuse me now, I think I'll be going."

Max didn't move. Elizabeth fell back into her chair.

"Why so soon, milady?" Max's foot brushed hers.

Brigitte reached across the table and ran her fingers across the silver and jet brooch on Elizabeth's dress. "That's very pretty. Family heirloom?"

Elizabeth tried to pull away, but Max left her little room, so close she could smell the alcohol on his breath. "No, my husband gave it to me."

"I wish I had a gentleman to give me such nice things."

Brigitte glanced at Max who chuckled and leaned in toward Elizabeth. She tried to stand again. "Really, I should be going. My husband will be expecting me. He'll worry if I'm gone too long."

Max placed a hand on her shoulder to keep her in her chair. "He can wait a while longer."

"I think the lady wishes to leave."

Max spun around at the new voice. Thomas Parson stood facing him, arms folded across his chest. He wore the same suit he had worn the last time Elizabeth saw him, but his crooked grin was absent, and there was no playfulness in his chestnut eyes.

He stepped to the table and offered his hand to Elizabeth. "Are you all right?"

Elizabeth nodded, but before she could take Parson's hand, Max shoved him aside.

"I wouldn't do that again," Parson said.

Max drew himself up to his full height, which was several inches taller than Parson. "Is that so?"

Parson ignored him and offered his hand to Elizabeth again. Max shoved him harder, forcing him backwards into another table. He steadied himself, took a swig of beer from the stein on the table, and marched back toward the giant German. Without a warning, Parson punched him in the jaw.

Max stood dazed for a few seconds before the rage spread across his face. He charged at Parson with a feral growl. The American ducked the German's swing. Max spun and swung at him again, but Parson managed to evade him a second time, barely. The scene reminded Elizabeth of a bullfight she had seen once in Spain. Over and over Parson avoided Max's blows by hair's breadth, but Parson couldn't touch him either, until the German stumbled and Parson snuck in a right hook that twisted the big man around.

Parson leapt onto his back and tried to place Max in a headlock, but Max stooped and flipped Parson over, slamming him into the floor. As easily as someone would lift a sack of potatoes, Max picked him up and threw him against the wall. He caught Parson on the rebound and wrenched his arm behind his back. Parson struggled to break free, but Max's grip was too strong.

Elizabeth watched the wheels turning in Parson's head as he tried to find a way out. When his eyes came to rest on the beer glass on the table in front of her, a grin spread across his face. With his free hand, he pointed at the glass, his gesturing becoming more frantic as Max ratcheted up the pressure, threatening to pull his shoulder out of its socket. Parson winced and cried out, and made a broad motion with his arm as if throwing something over his shoulder. Elizabeth, finally realizing what he wanted, snatched up the beer glass and slammed it against Max's head.

Max yelled and let Parson go as he staggered backwards, blinded by the mixture of beer and blood flowing down his face. Parson ducked Max's wild swings and punched him squarely in the stomach. The German doubled over and crumpled to the floor. Parson took Elizabeth by the hand and, over Brigitte's shrieking protests, ran for the door.

The late afternoon sun dazzled Elizabeth as they emerged onto the street. Parson pulled her along, dodging people, carts, and carriages, and leaving a trail of German curses in their wake. Elizabeth glanced over her shoulder to see Max exit the tavern, the blood flowing freely from the gash over his left eye. It only took a second for him to spot them and start running in their direction.

Not paying attention to where she was going Elizabeth barreled into Parson's back. She turned to find a large carriage blocking their way. She panicked at the thought of Max catching up to them, but to her surprise, the carriage door flew open and Mr. Ristić leaned out.

"Inside, quickly," he said.

Elizabeth took Ristić's offered hand, and he pulled her inside. Parson climbed in after and slammed the door shut just as Max reached it. The carriage took off.

"Lady James, I'm terribly sorry for whatever happened just now, are you all right?" Ristić asked.

Elizabeth took in a deep breath. "Yes, Mr. Ristić, I'm fine."

Ristić turned his attention to Parson. "I can't say I'm at all shocked to find you in Berlin, as much as I'd like to say otherwise. What have you done now?"

Parson's eyes narrowed. "What have I done? I just risked my life to save the lovely lady here. That's what I've done."

Elizabeth intervened. "Really, Mr. Ristić, Mr. Parson is right. This isn't his fault. It's mine. I came to Wedding because ... because I had information on Friedrich. It was a stupid thing to do. I'm not sure what I was thinking. I should have told you."

Ristić continued to glare at Parson. "Information? What sort of information?"

"I learned from some of the staff that Friedrich apparently had a number of vices," Elizabeth replied, "among them drinking and gambling. Because of them he owed money to quite a few people. But today I learned that he claimed to have found a way to pay back everyone he owed. He bragged about a job offer, one that would pay very well."

"Interesting," Parson said.

"Mr. Parson, this affair isn't any of your concern," Ristić snapped.

Parson set his jaw. "It's as much my concern as it is yours."

"My assistance was requested." Ristić jabbed a finger at Parson. "Yours was not."

Parson shook his head. "Don't be such a fool, Jovan. You remember what happened the last time—"

Elizabeth thought Ristić might come across the cab at Parson. "How dare you attempt to lecture me! I remember what happened. You, in your own recklessness, endangered innocent lives. I won't let you do that again."

They turned a corner. Ristić rapped on the wall behind him and the driver brought the carriage to a halt.

"You're getting off here." Ristić opened the carriage door. "And as soon as you can, you're leaving Berlin."

Parson smirked. "I'm sorry. I must have missed your coronation as Emperor of All the Germanies. My apologies, your Majesty."

"Get out." Ristić said through clinched teeth.

Parson turned to Elizabeth and tipped his hat. "Milady." But before he jumped out, he glanced at Ristić again, cocked his head to the side, and asked, "How do you know who's innocent, Jovan?"

TWENTY-SEVEN

—〰—

Sighișoara, Romania
7 December 1999

O NE HUNDRED SEVENTY-SIX WOODEN steps led up
the slope to where the Church on the Hill loomed
over Sighișoara's medieval citadel. Known at the
Scholars' Steps, the covered stairway was built in the
1600s for use by students attending the school adjacent to
the church.

One by one Arkady, Adam, and Inspector Rudeanu entered the gloom. The wooden boards creaked with each
step, echoing along the corridor. Weak daylight pushed
through the slats in the boards making up the walls but
failed to dispel the shadows entirely. Adam imagined
things in the dark, keeping just out of reach of the shafts of
sunlight. He squeezed the rosary beads in his pocket until
the attached crucifix threatened to cut into his hand.

They emerged at the top of the hill onto the grounds of
the school, aptly named the School on the Hill. The main
building, surrounded by bare trees, had been renovated

and restored more than once since the school's founding, but it retained its Gothic façade and distinctive red-tiled roof so common in places where the Transylvanian Saxons settled.

"Where did you find him?" Arkady said.

Inspector Rudeanu pointed to a window on one of the upper stories. "On the third floor, in the library."

"Perhaps the least shocking news of the day," Adam said. "Can you show us exactly where?"

"That's why I brought you here. Maybe you'll notice something we overlooked." He gestured toward the school. "If you'll follow me."

The policeman standing guard at the door tipped his hat to the inspector as they passed. He was the only other human being they encountered. Inside the building the silence nearly overwhelmed Adam. The halls were dark and the air still.

"All the students are on winter break," the inspector explained. "No one should have been in the building at all."

"And yet someone made it inside," Arkady remarked.

As soon as they entered the stairwell, an acute sense of *wrongness* struck Adam, leaving a greasy stain in the air that only grew stronger as they climbed. By the time they reached the third floor, Adam had to fight to keep from retching. The feeling eased up when they entered the library, but Adam still had to steady himself on a bookshelf while Inspector Rudeanu showed him where the body had been found. As Adam expected, they stood in the history section.

Inspector Rudeanu indicated a bloodstain on the carpet. "He was found here by the caretaker. His throat had been slit, and his right hand was painted green." He shot a knowing glance at Adam.

"Just like Lucian Borescu." Adam muttered. "What was his name?"

"Gheorghe Romanescu."

Adam's gaze went from the red stain on the carpet, to the surrounding books, to Inspector Rudeanu leaning forward, eyes wide and eager. Something clicked into place. "He wasn't one of yours, was he?"

The inspector shook his head. "No, he wasn't."

"And that's why you're baffled."

Inspector Rudeanu frowned. "We prefer to think of it as having insufficient evidence at this time, but yes, we're baffled."

"Wrong place, wrong time?" Arkady knelt over the bloodstained carpet.

"That's what we suspect," said the inspector. "It doesn't explain what he was doing here, but he may have come across someone else doing something they weren't supposed to."

"Like stealing documents from the library," Arkady said, "or putting hidden codes into the books?"

Adam scanned the shelves until he found the section on Romanian history. He pulled down several of the books on Vlad the Impaler and Michael the Brave. None of them had even a stray mark. "No hidden messages here. Do you know if any of the library staff have reported anything missing?"

Inspector Rudeanu shook his head. "There have been no reports of such."

Arkady threw up his hands. "None of this makes any sense."

Adam scratched his chin as his gaze swept the library one more time. "Maybe it doesn't have anything to do with manuscripts or books this time."

Arkady narrowed his eyes. "Are you suggesting the medallion is here?"

Adam shrugged. "What if he came upon someone else looking for it?"

"No." Arkady frowned. "If that were the case why would the killer advertise? Why not dispose of his body quietly?"

"It's a diversion, then." Adam threw up his hands. "This is all a diversion. It always has been. Doesn't the green paint strike you as somewhat theatrical?"

"And bloody dragons on the wall aren't?" Arkady asked with a dry laugh.

Adam persisted. "This killer is more premeditated. You have to plan ahead to have green paint with you."

Arkady crossed his arms in front of his chest. "Okay, so what are we being distracted from?"

"Have you dug into Gheorghe Romanescu's background?" Adam asked the inspector. "Any unusual acquaintances?"

"He had a few run-ins with some radical political groups in college, but nothing since then," the inspector answered. "His father is something of a local celebrity though."

Arkady raised an eyebrow. "How so?"

"He's an old eccentric. Does tour groups for foreigners wanting the Dracula experience." Inspector Rudeanu's mouth twisted into a lopsided grin. "Dresses up in a cape and everything."

Something nagged at the very edge of Adam's consciousness. Something important. The name Romanescu. From his satchel he pulled the book of poetry the shopkeeper had given him. Nothing stood out about it. No letters were hidden inside. No notes were scrawled in the margins. But the bookplate contained a name: *Ex Libris* Petru Romanescu.

"I think we need to talk to Gheorghe Romanescu's father," he said.

PETRU ROMANESCU, A GAUNT MAN with a mane of grey hair, lived in a second-story apartment not far from the ochre house where Dracula was born. He sat opposite Adam and Arkady, in a chair facing the room's sole window.

When he spoke, he didn't look at either of them, but rather out the window, at the medieval city set against the dull grey sky. "My son never believed. I dress up and pretend because the truth is not something most can handle. Sometimes the best place to hide things is in plain sight."

Arkady fidgeted in the threadbare chair. "And the truth is?"

Romanescu eyed him. "You know what I'm talking about, or you wouldn't be here."

"Do you have any idea why your son would have been in the library of the School on the Hill?" Adam asked.

Romanescu's attention returned to the scene outside the window. "He was trying to put something back."

Arkady huffed. "What was he trying to put back?"

"A document," Romanescu replied.

"What sort of document?" Arkady asked, grinding his jaw.

"And why was he trying to put it back?" added Adam.

Romanescu let his gaze slide over Adam. "He was trying to put it back because I stole it. He decided to pay me a visit last week. We hadn't talked in some time, and the guilt probably became too much for him. He found the document, and when I told him what I did, he started yelling. He didn't understand. He never did. He must have taken it with him when he left. I only noticed it missing later. That is really all there is to say."

"Except you didn't answer my question," Arkady mumbled.

Adam shot him a reproachful glance "Mr. Romanescu, you were a fairly active member of the Romanian Communist Party, so I've been told. You wouldn't happen to know anything about a group known as the Committee, would you?"

Romanescu pursed his lips. "They're a bunch of children playing make-believe, but they have proven useful."

Adam leaned forward. "You're not alone, are you? There are others doing the same thing. Old guard Communists like you if I had to guess. You're stealing documents from libraries. Why?"

"To keep them out of the hands of the Iron Guard," Romanescu answered with a sigh.

"Do you honestly think they're back?" Arkady asked.

Romanescu narrowed his eyes. "You know they are. The green fist is all you need as proof. And we all know the current government of this country is completely incapable of stopping them."

Arkady barked a laugh. "And you can? You and the rest of your geriatric spymasters are all in hopelessly over your heads."

Romanescu's mouth twisted into a sneer. "Typical of the Russians to think that."

"You don't know what you've gotten yourself into." Arkady jabbed a finger in the Romanian's direction. "You don't—"

Eyes aflame and lips pulled back in a snarl, Romanescu rose from his chair, the veil of years melting away. He was tall, and in his youth Adam guessed he would have been all lean and wiry muscle. "You don't think I know? Where were you when the Russians came over the border and announced they were annexing part of our country? Where were you when the Hungarians took another part? Where were you over the decades while Ceaușescu drained our country dry? And where were you while I fought the vampires operating in the shadows, influencing things for their own agenda? I've killed dozens. How many have you killed?"

Arkady frowned. "Are you implying vampires infiltrated Ceaușescu's regime?"

"Ceaușescu ransomed this nation's soul for his own power." Romanescu took his seat again. "I will not let history repeat itself."

Adam shook his head. "Neither will we. We're on the same side."

Romanescu fixed him with a glare. "You can tell yourself that, Professor. But the Russian, he's on no one's side but his own."

Adam tried to ignore the remark and prayed Arkady would as well. "Whatever document your son took wasn't found with him. Presumably the Iron Guard has it. Can you tell us what it said?"

"I can do better." For the first time, Romanescu smiled. "I kept a copy."

TWENTY-EIGHT

From the Journal of Alexander Sift

Near Cluj, Romania
9 August 1968

SOME SAY THE FOREST IS haunted by the angry ghosts of murdered peasants, victims of some long-forgotten massacre who exact their revenge on those who enter. Glowing green eyes glower at trespassers, and dark forms lumber in the mist. Others see strange lights in the sky and claim they are alien visitors from outer space. Still others believe there is a hidden portal leading to another dimension, that if you pass through you could lose days or even weeks. Nearly everyone who comes here reports feeling disoriented, unsettled, anxious.

For all the speculation, though, no one has come close to the truth.

I came to the Hoia-Baciu Forest as a botanist. There are plant species here that exist nowhere else. My purpose is to study them, but I would be lying if I said I was not curious about the rest. Bent and twisted trees loom over-head, misshapen for no apparent reason, and I cannot trust my equipment here. My camera malfunctions constantly. I see shadows moving and flickers of light. When the wind blows, I hear voices.

Yesterday as night was falling, I set up camp in an area not far from the place everyone calls the Round Meadow, a circular clearing near the center of the forest where nothing except the hardiest grass will grow. As I set about starting a fire to cook my dinner, a fog rolled in, but as tendrils of black mist snaked through the trees I quickly realized it was not a normal fog. Soon I couldn't see any-thing at all beyond my small encampment. The night noises ceased, although as eerie as it was, I wish the si-lence had lasted.

The voices began again, but gone were the harsh whis-pers, the barely intelligible murmurs. These voices, clear and seductive, urged me to join them. I wish I could say I had the resolve to resist, that I fought against the pull and won, but I did not. I followed the voices.

The fog churned around me, and the shadows swirled. I could hear nothing but the voices. Though I stalked through the thick underbrush, my boots didn't make a sound. Minutes or hours later, I couldn't tell, the voices stopped. I didn't know where I was, or how to get back to my campsite.

But I knew I wasn't alone.

A sudden chill climbed up my legs. I glanced down, and to my shock discovered the ground covered in snow. The fog dissipated, and I found myself at the edge of the Round Meadow. The trees were bare. My breath came out in white puffs.

Winter had replaced summer.

A silver crescent moon hung low in the clear indigo sky. Two men stood in the center of the clearing, facing one another. The older of the two was dressed as one of the Roma. The other wore medieval armor. I knew immediately who he was. He looked very much like the pictures I had seen. Flowing black hair, a hawkish nose, an intense gaze.

Vlad Dracula.

He handed something to the Roma. It glinted in the pale moonlight, a medal perhaps. The Roma examined the object. He smiled and said a few unintelligible words before handing back what I could see now was some sort of medallion. Dracula hung it around his neck by a chain. As the Roma began to chant in his own language, Vlad Dracula removed his gloves and unsheathed a dagger from his belt. He poised the blade over his bare forearm, and after a moment's hesitation, slashed the dagger across his skin.

Again and again, Vlad Dracula cut into his arm, until the snow around him was stained red. He dropped the dagger, and, gritting his teeth, seized the medallion in his bloody hands. As soon as he touched it, he cried out and fell to his knees. With his anguished wails the forest itself shuddered. An overwhelming sense of *wrongness* radiated out from the clearing, tainting everything it touched.

Seemingly oblivious to the spectacle, the Roma continued to chant. Vlad Dracula, still clutching the medallion, heaved and collapsed. His black cloak covered his prostrate form in the snow. There was no way he could have survived losing so much blood.

The Roma ended his chant and turned away from the body of Vlad Dracula. He trudged across the clearing to the tree line where he picked up a sack. Only a few seconds later, I could see it wasn't a sack at all, but a boy, maybe in his teens. His hands and feet were tied. He had no cloak or gloves of any kind, and his feet were bare. The Roma dragged him across the snowy clearing and forced him to his knees in front of the motionless Vlad Dracula.

The boy didn't try to fight. He seemed dazed, disoriented, as if he were drugged. The Roma took out his own dagger. He seized a shock of the boy's hair and jerked back, exposing the boy's neck. The Roma sliced open the boys throat just as one would slaughter a pig. His blood mingled with the blood of Vlad Dracula on the snowy ground.

Only then did Vlad Dracula stir.

He rose off the ground, his hair wild, his face stained red from the boy's blood. No human should have been able to survive so much blood loss. But he wasn't human anymore. His canine teeth, grown into sharp fangs, protruded from his mouth, and his eyes burned with a hellish light all their own.

He pounced on the boy, lapping up the blood pouring from his throat, emitting sounds an animal might make after a kill. There was no intelligence there, only bloodlust. The Roma, an odd smile on his face, turned and walked away from the gruesome scene.

No sooner did he look away than Dracula's eyes narrowed. He dropped the boy's body, reached for his own dagger lying in the crimson snow, and threw it through the air. The dagger whistled as it flew, and the blade buried itself to the hilt in the Roma's back.

The old man lurched forward and fell to the ground. Dracula covered the distance in a blink. He pulled the Roma's body up from where he lay and dug into his throat, ripping flesh and crushing bone. When he was finished, he wiped the blood off his face with his arm, no trace of his wounds on his skin.

A small book was attached to the Roma's coat with a leather strap. Dracula tore the book free and tucked it under his belt. Then he stood.

And he looked directly at me.

In that moment I knew I was dead.

Do you know who I am?

His lips didn't move, but I still heard his words in my head. I nodded.

Tell them to stop looking for me.

"Who?" I asked, my voice nothing more than a dry rasp.

The men who lead this country now. The ones who refuse the old titles but who act like nobles and princes nonetheless. They will not find me.

"How do I tell them?"

Find a way.

My next question died on my tongue as Dracula dissolved into a black mist that rushed toward me. Before I could even take a step, the mist surrounded me. It squeezed on my chest forcing the air from my lungs. Then it relented, and I breathed in foul air that tasted of dirt and decay. I gagged and gasped for breath, but I could only choke on the black mist until I crumpled to the ground. Then everything went dark.

I woke up with the sun beating down on me. I lay on the ground at the edge of the Round Meadow. The snow was gone. It was summer again, and judging by the angle of the sun in the sky, it was early afternoon.

As I struggled to sit up, a sharp pain radiated from my neck. Thinking it was just cramped from lying on the ground for so long, I reached up to massage the muscles, only to feel the two small wounds near my throat about three centimeters apart, the same distance that separates human canine teeth.

TWENTY-NINE

—⁂—

Near Cluj, Romania
8 December 1999

OUTSIDE CLARA'S ROOM, THE SHADOWS flit around the grounds of the manor like flocking birds, angry and agitated. Raised voices reverberated from the floor above. She couldn't make out the words, but she felt something had changed. Perhaps they didn't need her anymore. Perhaps they were arguing about how to get rid of her.

As Clara paced the room, she caught a flicker of movement out of the corner of her eye. Without Iosif to start a fire in the fireplace, she'd had to make do with the two oil lamps. At first she simply assumed one of the lamps sputtered, but the shadows didn't return to their former places. The air moved, even though the door and the windows were closed.

The dust in the air swirled.

Light and shadow mingled.

Clara clutched a post of the bed to steady herself. As

the shadows churned, she remembered the house in Thessaloniki and the malevolent watcher. She was fairly certain Jonathan had stalked her and Arkady that day.

The doorknob moved, slowly at first, then faster, rattling and twisting back and forth. Clara was so intently focused on the door and the thought Jonathan might be on the other side that she didn't notice someone standing in the room until the other woman spoke.

"Clara."

Clara jerked around with a start. The woman stood by the window in the spot Clara usually occupied. Her raven hair hung in a braid almost to her waist. Her olive skin contrasted with the pale moonlight.

"Who are you?" Clara asked.

The woman stepped toward her. "You may call me Yasamin."

At the name Clara's heart skipped a beat. "You're the one Adam came to look for."

The woman continued to regard Clara with impassive eyes. "Perhaps."

Every instinct told Clara to run, but there was nowhere to go. "Perhaps?"

"Dr. Adam Mire came searching for a number of things."

Clara struggled to control her breathing. "Are you here to kill me?"

Yasamin twisted her mouth into a wry smile. "Far from it, I assure you."

"Then why are you here?"

The vampire reached a hand toward her. "To take you from this place."

Clara raised an eyebrow. "You're here to rescue me?"

"Unless you want to stay."

Clara's thoughts went to Jonathan, his powerful arms embracing her, the earthy scent of his skin, his lips on her neck. "No," she said. "I don't want to stay."

Yasamin reached her hand out again. "Then you'll come with me."

She opened the door as if it had been unlocked all along and led Clara through the house, following the same route as Iosif. In the kitchen, she paused to let Clara put on a coat but didn't don one herself. When Yasamin opened the door, the cold struck Clara in the face. She wrapped the coat around her as tightly as she could as they trudged through the snow. A car, a shiny silver Mercedes, rested beside the carriage house.

About halfway there, Clara realized she couldn't hear anything, nothing at all. The night noises were simply missing. And as they neared the garage, she realized something else was missing as well.

There were no shadows.

Even in the weak light of the moon there should have been shadows. Before she could say anything to Yasamin a blast of cold air nearly knocked her back. The snow swirled up from the ground, obscuring her vision. A horrible scream emanated from the night sky, and a great cloud of bats descended. In the woods the wolves howled. Yasamin grabbed her arm and pulled her toward the car. Even if she had wanted, she couldn't have broken free of the vampire's grip.

"Get in," Yasamin yelled to Clara when they reached the car.

Clara hesitated.

"Do you want to survive the night?" Yasamin hissed. "Get in the car."

Clara shoved down her fear and did as she was told.

Yasamin climbed into the driver's side and started the engine. The car surged forward into the night. Already the cloud of bats obscured the windshield. Clara screamed as the small animals hit the glass, their eyes wide with rage, teeth and claws gnashing at the car. Heedless of the onslaught, Yasamin drove onward.

As soon as they entered the woods, the familiar shapes of the wolves joined the chase. Unlike the old caretaker, Yasamin didn't slow the car. Her driving seemed to defy physics as she wound her way through the woods, and soon the wolves fell behind, unable to keep pace. Only the looming shapes of the black trees against the almost-black sky remained.

"Why are you doing this?" Clara asked.

"I have my reasons," Yasamin replied.

"That's not an answer."

Yasamin shot her a sideways glance. "I can see why Adam liked you."

"He won't give up finding me."

"I hope he won't."

Clara shook her head. "All of this over a silly piece of jewelry."

"You know it's more than that."

"So I'm still just a bargaining chip then?"

Yasamin drew her lips into a thin line. "As I said. I have my reasons."

Eventually the trees thinned out, and rolling pastureland replaced the forest. A little over an hour later they came upon a small village.

Yasamin parked the car in front of a two-story house on the edge of the town. "When you get out, move quickly. We are still not completely safe." Once they were inside. Yasamin made no delay in shutting and locking the door.

"Welcome to my home. Make yourself comfortable, Dr. MacIntosh. You'll probably be here a while."

Clara nodded, too exhausted to argue. Later, after a hot shower that made her realize how desperately she had missed modern plumbing, she lay in bed, exhausted and relieved she would finally be free of the dreams about Elizabeth.

Her relief was short-lived.

THIRTY

Berlin, Germany
28 June 1878

T HOMAS PARSON SAT UNDERNEATH THE willow tree on the bank of one of the Tiergarten's ponds, skipping stones across the water. Elizabeth watched as the flat, smooth pebbles skimmed the surface of the water, disturbing the glassy reflection of the azure sky before destroying it altogether with a splash.

"You could have asked for my help," Parson said without turning around. "All you had to do was come here. I would have found you."

"Learning more about Friedrich wasn't my only reason for going to Wedding."

"What was your other?"

"I wanted to see it for myself, Wedding, the people, the way they lived, what they did."

He turned to face her, a smirk planted on his face. "Was it everything you thought it would be?"

"Why do you mock me? I didn't mean it like that. I just

wanted to see where Friedrich came from, if there was some connection I could find. I thought it would help."

Parson stood, wincing and clutching his side as he did. "You shouldn't have gone on your own."

"I'm sorry about Max."

"So that was the ogre's name?"

Elizabeth smiled. "Thank you for coming to my aid, Mr. Parson."

"I was only doing what any gentleman would." By this time, he had joined her on the path.

"I came to tell you, I found another card."

Parson grinned. "I was right, then."

"What do you know about what's happening?"

"I know who killed Friedrich."

Elizabeth stopped cold. She could do nothing but stare in shock. "Why haven't you said anything before now?"

Parson held up his hands. "To be fair, you haven't given me a chance."

"Did you kill him?"

Parson set his jaw. "Not directly."

Elizabeth narrowed her eyes. "What does that mean?"

"He was more or less already dead. I guess the fine officers in her Majesty's service failed to notice the strange bite mark on his neck."

"Mr. Parson—"

"I'm telling you the truth. I wouldn't lie, not to you."

"You would have me believe vampires are real, and that they're in Berlin?"

Parson nodded.

Elizabeth shook her head. "I don't. I won't. I can't."

Parson touched his neck. Elizabeth could see a faint mark, what looked like an upper set of human teeth plus two small puncture wounds. "Suit yourself. It doesn't make them any less real."

"Where did you get that scar?" Elizabeth asked.

"Ragusa, about ten years ago. It's a fascinating story. I'll tell it to you sometime."

"So you're saying one of those things attacked Friedrich?"

"I am. I was following him that night."

Elizabeth frowned. "Why?"

"You left out one of Friedrich's vices. He apparently enjoyed dabbling in blackmail. I was following him as a favor to a friend. It's why I came to Berlin in the first place. It was near midnight when he left the tavern you visited yesterday. He stumbled down the street until he found a cab to take him back to the Palais Strousberg. I flagged down the next cab. When he disembarked, so did I. He continued to stagger down the Wilhelmstraße until he came to the opening of an alley.

"The monster waited for him there. Suddenly Friedrich was yanked into the darkness. I heard him scream and ran as fast as I could. The light from the streetlamps barely penetrated into the alley, but as far as I could see, no one was there. Friedrich had vanished, and so had the thing. I retrieved the stake from my coat and crept farther in, watching for the shadows to move. I found a door, which led to the basement of the Palais."

"So that was your wooden stake we found," Elizabeth said.

Parson raised an eyebrow. "You found it? I'd like it returned, if at all possible."

"Lady Russell has it. I'll see what I can do. Please, Mr. Parson, continue your story."

Parson cleared his throat. "As I said, I found myself in a hallway in the basement of the Palais. Friedrich, the wound on his neck still bleeding, attacked me just as I rounded a corner. He had a knife, and my hand was cut trying to fight him off. I managed to push him away, and when he came at me again, I stabbed him with the stake. I would have moved him, but I had to take care of my hand. Luckily, I found a room they use to store linens. I tore off a piece of a tablecloth to use as a bandage."

"Lady Russell's Egyptian linen."

The expression on Parson's face made it abundantly clear what he thought of Lady Russell's tablecloth. "Add it to my tab. In any event, I was afraid to stay any longer. I knew I wouldn't be able to explain what happened to anyone I came across. I really am sorry for the trouble I caused in that regard. The next day, I found the bloody calling card with your father's name on it, which led me to you."

"And the calling cards led me to Friedrich's body, in a round-about way."

Parson grinned. "Full circle, so to speak."

Something nagged at Elizabeth, though. "You said Friedrich was all but dead, yet you survived a vampire attack. What made Friedrich different?"

His smile faded. "You didn't see his eyes. When one of those monsters attacks, it's not just a physical attack. It's an attack on the psyche, too. Some people are strong enough to resist. Others aren't. There wasn't enough of Friedrich's humanity left. He would have succumbed, sooner or later."

Elizabeth's next question was the one she really wanted to ask all along. "How do you know about my father, Mr. Parson?"

Parson paused before he answered. "After my encounter in Ragusa, I devoted myself to finding out as much as I could about what happened to me. I became an expert on the creatures in question—vampires, what they want, how they kill, how they can be killed. I started to pay attention to the stories I heard. Many of them I investigated myself. I heard about your father while I was staying in Amsterdam, from an Englishman who had just arrived there. The poor man probably thought I was a bit of a ghoul myself the way I hounded him for details. Vampire scares may be common in certain parts of Europe, but southern England is not one of those places."

"My father is not a vampire."

"Several young girls disappeared in the villages around Oxford in the months before and after the murder of the Tolliver family's chambermaid. She herself was found with a bloody gash across her neck. Your father's area of study was the Balkans. He had recently returned from a trip there."

Elizabeth's face grew hot. She balled her hands into fists. "His rivals encouraged those stories. They never understood his work. They saw it as useless, almost blasphemous, to devote so much to a land ruled by nonbelievers—the same hypocrites who worshipped Plato and Cicero."

"But the calling cards—"

"My father is not a vampire," Elizabeth repeated, "and he isn't here in Berlin now. He didn't kill Friedrich."

"Are you saying that to convince me, or yourself?"

The branches of the willow swayed in the warm breeze. A few birds darted back and forth across the sky. Elizabeth gazed back over the pond. "I don't know."

THIRTY-ONE

—〰—

Berlin, Germany
29 June 1878

THE OLD WOMAN WAS SNORING again. On some
nights the noise was so loud it woke Elizabeth. She
missed her mother the most on those nights. Elizabeth was sixteen years old. Her mother had been gone for
over two years. More than two years of living under her
aunt's roof.

If the snoring was particularly bad, she climbed out of
bed, slipped out of her room, and snuck out of the house,
which rested on a bluff overlooking the sea. Below, the
town of Whitby spread out along the shallow crescent bay.
The ruins of the eleventh-century abbey loomed nearby.

Her aunt had caught her sneaking out once and had
punished her by locking her in her room for a day. She was
allowed to leave only after she promised to ask God to forgive her of her moral failings. After all, it wasn't proper for
a young woman to be out by herself after dark. What
would the neighbors think if they looked out their windows

and saw her in her nightclothes?

Elizabeth didn't care what the neighbors thought. The house was dark and cold, even in the summer. It smelled of decaying wallpaper, rotting wood, and moldy fabric. Sometimes she thought she would lose her mind if she spent one more day there under the constant watch of her aunt. Night was her only refuge. The only peace she ever felt was when she sat on the hill, looking up at the moon and the stars with the breeze off the water blowing through her hair.

That night was different. There was no moon. The darkness filled Elizabeth's room to the point she could almost touch it. She opened her door just enough to slip out, and she felt her way along the hall, down the stairs, and into the kitchen. There she found a lantern. When she lit it the yellow light immediately repelled the darkness, but as she tried to pick the lantern up, it slipped from her hands. It hit the floor and broke, and the burning oil spilled out, catching the wooden floor on fire. The flame grew angry and red as the fire raced through the house. Elizabeth barely escaped. Her aunt didn't.

THE SOUND OF THE FRONT door opening downstairs brought Elizabeth back to the present. Alfred was at another one of his "accursed" dinners. She was certain he added the pejorative for her sake. Elizabeth frowned. He wasn't due back for a few more hours, yet he had to be the one who opened the door. Elizabeth hadn't heard either the door chime or Sarah speaking with a visitor. She ran out to the landing to try to catch him before he shut himself up in his study.

Aleksandr Vladimirovich stood in the foyer. Elizabeth

inhaled sharply.

He looked up at her and smiled. "Good evening, Lady James," he said, bowing slightly.

"Mr. Chernov, good evening to you as well," Elizabeth tried to will herself from blushing. "If you're looking for Lord James, I'm afraid he isn't here. I don't expect him back until late."

His face fell. "Then I'm sorry to have disturbed you. I'll just take my leave. Please, if you'd be so kind, let him know that I stopped by." He turned and walked toward the door, but as he reached for the handle, he hesitated. He dropped his hand and turned back around. "I hope you're well, Lady James, after your mishap on the boat, I mean."

Elizabeth nodded. "I am. Thank you for asking."

"It would have been a tragedy had anything happened to someone as beautiful as you. Forgive me for being so forward, but it's true."

Elizabeth felt her cheeks flush despite her best efforts. "You're welcome to wait for Lord James in the sitting room, if you'd like. I know it's late, but I can have Sarah make you tea."

"No, that won't be necessary."

"Mr. Chernov, I should thank you for more than asking about me. You saved me. I didn't have the chance to tell you before, but I am truly grateful."

"I meant everything I said to you. If you need anything, you only have to ask."

"Then will you join me in the sitting room, Mr. Chernov, just for a little while? I won't keep you if you have someplace else to be."

He smiled again. "The only place I have to be is here."

Elizabeth descended the stairs and showed Aleksandr

into the sitting room opposite Alfred's study. Once they were seated in the high-backed chairs, awkward silence followed. Elizabeth looked down at her hands folded in her lap. They trembled.

After several aborted attempts to say something she finally managed to get her voice to work. "May I ask you an odd question, Mr. Chernov?"

"Of course, Lady James, though, whatever it is I'm sure it's not as odd as you think."

"You ... you don't look like the other Russians. They all have blond or red hair and pale blue eyes, not your black hair or your green eyes. You're not really are you? Russian, I mean."

Aleksandr laughed. "I assure you I am as Russian as the tsar, but your are correct in a way. My mother was a Gypsy. Apparently, I resemble her."

"Apparently? Then she's—"

"No longer, I'm afraid. I never really knew her."

"I'm sorry to hear that."

He waved his hand in the air, as if to banish some painful memory. "It's all in the past. All that matters is what is happening now. I am curious, though. Why ask me such a question?"

"I don't want to tell you. You'll think me insane."

"Nothing you say could make me think that, I swear."

Elizabeth took a deep breath and told him about her dreamlike encounter on the journey to Berlin, about the Gypsy who had saved her from the wolves, and about how startled she was when she met him because the two of them looked almost exactly alike. Even their names were similar—Alexej and Aleksandr.

He didn't reply immediately. He held her gaze, a strange half-smile lingering on his face. She began to fear he did think her insane, despite what he had said.

"I shouldn't have told you," she burst out. "I knew it. It's ridiculous."

He shook his head. "No, not ridiculous, not at all. In fact, it makes perfect sense. You see, a little over a month ago, I had a dream as well."

"You're just lying to make me feel better."

"I promise you I'm not. In this dream, it was night, and I was in some ancient, primeval forest. The trees overhead completely blocked out the sky. I had a lantern, but even with its light, I couldn't see more than a few feet in front of me. I walked along a sort of path, occasionally stumbling over the giant roots of the old trees. All around me, I could hear sounds of animals foraging and hunting. Soon, though, I heard a different sound, the sound of running water. I increased my pace. The trail began to slope downward. I saw light up ahead of me, and it was not long before I came upon a clearing in the woods. A stream ran through it. Moonlight danced across the water, and on the other bank, you were there. I wanted you then, but I couldn't cross the stream."

Elizabeth gazed into his green eyes, greener than the meadows from her childhood. She thought she could easily lose herself in those eyes. *We're both here now. There's no stream separating us.*

The clock in the corner of the dim room chimed. They both turned their heads toward it.

"I should be going now." Aleksandr Vladimirovich rose from his chair.

"Alfred will be back soon. If you need to talk to him, you might as well stay."

But it was no use. The spell was broken.

"I can speak with him another time," Aleksandr said.

"Nothing I have to tell him is urgent. Thank you for the lovely evening, Lady James." She offered her hand. He took it and leaned down to gently kiss it. "I do hope there are other evenings."

About an hour later, Elizabeth heard the front door open again. She listened as Alfred entered his study and shut himself up inside as expected. She returned to reading her book.

THIRTY-TWO

Sighişoara, Romania
9 December 1999

ADAM SHOVED THE LAST OF the books aside when the words began to bleed together. Stacks surrounded him from libraries, churches, even a few from Serghei's bookshop, everything from historical treatises on the religious beliefs of the Transylvanian Saxons to schematics for the city's sewage system. Anything he could think of to try to pinpoint the hiding place of Dracula's medallion.

And he'd found nothing.

Outside the sun was setting. Another day wasted. Another day he'd failed Clara.

"Is this how all academic progress is made? You bang your head against a wall until something gets jogged loose?" Arkady stood in the doorway.

Adam glanced up. "You'd be surprised how close to the truth that is. I don't get it. Why would Mihai go to all the trouble to lead us here and then not provide at least some clue where the medallion is?"

"Maybe you should take a break? Perhaps come downstairs?"

Rather than putting them up in one of the normal Russian safe houses this time, Arkady had procured a furnished row house near the citadel square. Whether the reason was because there was no safe house in Sighişoara or because none of their previous hiding places had proven very "safe," Adam didn't know.

Adam glanced out the window at the rapidly darkening sky. "What time is it?"

"Time for dinner. I let you skip lunch, but you really ought to eat something."

Adam shook his head. "I'm not hungry."

Arkady grunted. "Suit yourself. I'll leave you some takeout in the kitchen."

After Arkady left, Adam picked up another book and opened it. About an hour later he found himself nodding off and decided finally he needed to get up and stretch his legs a bit.

His head full of figures and dates, he trudged down the stairs. He found Arkady standing in the entryway, a bag of food in one hand—Greek, judging from the aroma—and an envelope in the other.

Arkady held the envelope toward him. "This was on the doorstep. It's for you."

Adam's hand trembled as he took it and opened it. Inside was a slip of paper with an address. His mind flashed to Elena and the abandoned building in Sarajevo she had directed him to. His visits there had almost ended in his death. Twice.

Adam handed the piece of paper back to Arkady. The Russian studied it for a moment. "Could be a trap."

Adam nodded. "That's a possibility."

Arkady frowned. "But you're going anyway, aren't you?"

"Do you have a better idea?"

"Yes. Send Inspector Rudeanu's men in."

Adam snatched the piece of paper back. "And if a vampire like Yasamin happened to send this note? Do you want all those deaths on you conscience?"

"Do you think Yasamin sent it?" Arkady asked.

Adam shrugged. "She's looking for the medallion, too."

"What about Elena?"

"She never wanted to be involved. She just didn't want the Chetniks to have the medallion."

Arkady crossed his arms. "Did she really want to keep them from getting it? Or did she just use you to get to her ex-boyfriend?"

Adam grimaced. "The thought had crossed my mind."

Arkady pointed to the scrap of paper. "It could be from Yasamin. It could be from Elena. It could be from the Iron Guard or the Chetniks or Süleyman's Blade even. We don't know. We should consider our plan."

"I'm going to see what's at this address." Adam scrutinized the vaguely familiar handwriting. "All you have to consider is whether you're coming with me."

THE ADDRESS TURNED OUT TO be a house in the newer part of Sighişoara, outside the citadel. The warm glow of lamplights filtered through the curtains in the windows, but when Adam knocked on the door, no one answered.

"I knew this was a bad idea," Arkady said. "What are we supposed to find here? Another book with cryptic clues?"

Adam smirked. "At this point I'd be overjoyed with

that."

Arkady scowled. "Or another nest of vampires."

Adam rolled his eyes. "Don't be ridiculous. You know they don't have nests. Besides, one is enough to kill us both."

Just then the door opened. Arkady tensed, his hand hovering over the gun at his hip. A gaunt young man stood in the doorway. Adam didn't recognize him, but he did recognize the expression on the man's face, the sunken eyes, the disheveled hair, the look of disdain.

The man nodded at Adam. "Come in."

Adam stepped over the threshold. Arkady moved to follow.

The man held up a hand. "Not you, just him."

Arkady glared. "What do you mean—"

"It's okay, Arkady. I'll be fine. If I'm gone more than fifteen minutes, you can break down the door and come in guns blazing." Adam glanced back at the man. "Fair enough?"

Without answering, he stepped back to let Adam in, and then shut the door behind him. He led Adam deeper into the house. The sunlight didn't penetrate very far, and none of the rooms beyond those facing the street were furnished. The man directed Adam into a room containing only a high-backed chair in front of a fireplace that obviously hadn't been used in quite some time. The room appeared unoccupied, but Adam knew better. The shadows around the legs of the chair swirled in tiny eddies.

"You've made a bit of a fool of me," Adam said. "I just finished telling Arkady you didn't have a reason to be involved, seeing as how you didn't care about any of this."

Elena laughed as she stood up from the chair and turned to face Adam. The last time he'd seen her, she had been disguised as a man, her jet-black hair cut short. In only a few months it had grown out again, long and lustrous. Adam found himself gazing into her mesmerizing green eyes as her full red lips curved into a wry smile.

"There you go making assumptions again," she said.

"Why are you here?" Adam asked.

"I want to help."

"Why?"

She stepped around the chair, pulling the shadows with her, her shoes echoing on the bare floor. "Do you remember what I told you about what would happen if the Chetniks gained possession of the medallion?"

"You used the word *chaos*."

"Exactly." She stopped directly in front of Adam. "You're close to finding it yourself."

"The medallion? It's here in Sighișoara?"

She raised an eyebrow. "That I don't know, but Sighișoara is the key. You'll figure it out. You're a clever boy remember? Just be careful. There are still those who would cause chaos."

"Like the Iron Guard," he said.

"If there is such an organization."

"If the Chetniks could survive, why not?"

She leaned in closer. Her perfume smelled of lilacs, just as he remembered. "Sometimes the simplest explanation is the correct one. Sometimes it isn't."

He took a step back. "That's enough. I thought you said you wanted to help."

Her smile faded, though a hint remained. "Fine. What would you like to know?"

"What am I supposed to do with the medallion once I find it?"

"Use it to save your love, but be careful. You read the

botanist's account of his encounter in the woods. You know how the medallion made Dracula. That is powerful knowledge. Be mindful what you do with it."

Something at the edge of Adam's consciousness nagged at him again. He couldn't help but think he was missing something important. "How do you know about Alexander Sift?"

"We all know about Alexander Sift."

"Then you know all his manuscripts disappeared shortly after he died six years ago."

"Except for the ones he left here in Sighișoara."

A realization sent a chill up Adam's spine. "There's another vampire involved in the green fist murders, isn't there? That's how the Iron Guard knew to look here."

Elena's smile returned. Her gaze lingered on him as she circled the chair again. "I'd say that's an interesting theory."

"There's something else you could do to help," he said as she sat again. "You could find Clara. You could get her back. I may not understand your code of ethics, but I don't believe you'd intentionally cause her harm."

"Miroslav," she called.

The man appeared again almost immediately, wearing the same expression of contempt Adam remembered on Bogdan's face. Adam wondered what he had done to earn Elena's attention.

"Please show Dr. Mire out," Elena ordered.

Miroslav nodded and motioned for Adam to follow him. Arkady was waiting outside on the stoop.

"What went on in there?" he asked.

"Not sure," Adam replied. "Either we just gained an ally or a new threat."

THIRTY-THREE

—〜—

Huedin, Romania
10 December 1999

I N THE HOUSE YASAMIN HAD chosen to call her own, there were no forced dinners, no innuendo-filled conversations, no conversation of any kind really. Clara never heard her hostess, and only rarely saw her. There was always food for her, and unlike the manor, this house had more modern amenities, like heating and plumbing. Clara took to wandering from room to room, marveling at the wealth on display, wondering what Yasamin had done to acquire each piece.

In one room, she found a work by Rodin. In another she found a Picasso. She was studying a painting by Vincent van Gogh when the shadows shifted and Yasamin appeared beside her.

"Did you know him?" Clara asked.

She laughed. "You mean van Gogh? Oh, no. This painting belonged to one of my husbands. It came to me when he passed away."

"When was that?"

"1895. The winter was harsh that year."

Clara's head was full of questions she was afraid to ask. She wanted to know his name. She wanted to know if Yasamin loved him. How many husbands had she had before? How many came after?

Instead she asked a different question. "What is going to happen to Adam?"

She pursed her lips. "That depends on what he does."

"You want him to hand this medallion to you."

"It would be the prudent choice," Yasamin said.

"But if he does Elizabeth will kill him."

Yasamin sighed. "And if he gives the medallion to her, it won't matter. Death will be the least of his worries at that point."

"Can you protect him?"

"Perhaps."

Clara allowed her anger to bubble over. "Perhaps? It seems like the least you could do. He'd be risking his life for you."

Yasamin's silence made Clara immediately regret what she had said. The stony stillness provided a stark reminder her host wasn't entirely human. When she spoke, each word hit Clara with physical force. "Dr. MacIntosh, he involved himself in this affair voluntarily. No one forced him to stay. He could have walked away at any time."

"If you think he could have walked away, you don't know him very well," Clara replied in a small voice.

"There are forces at work here beyond just me. If I had my way Elizabeth would be destroyed, and the medallion would be restored to its rightful owner."

"Why does Elizabeth even want it?" Clara asked.

Yasamin hesitated before she answered, and when she

did, her voice contained a fine thread of fear. "She wants to use it to kill Dracula."

CLARA PULLED THE CURTAINS BACK from the window in her bedroom. It was well after midnight, but she couldn't sleep. Outside shafts of silver moonlight pierced the canopy of the trees. The snow on the ground shimmered. As she watched, a figure emerged from the house. The shadows bent to follow Yasamin, and she made no tracks in the snow. When she reached the edge of the property she paused and glanced over her shoulder. Clara retreated from the window. When she looked out again, Yasamin had vanished.

Clara went to her door and opened it slowly. She peered into the dark hallway before slipping from her room. As far as Clara could tell Yasamin did not have a bedroom, though she spent a great deal of time in a room near the end of the hall. When she tried the doorknob she was mildly surprised to find it unlocked.

In contrast to the rest of the house the room was austere. There was only a desk and a bookcase full of books and binders. She pulled one of the books off its shelf. It was not in English, nor were any of the next four she looked at. Eventually she came to a binder stuffed with papers. It was in Romanian. At least she knew that much. Judging from what little she could glean using her college Italian, they were government documents from the early 1980s.

She was still in the room when she heard the door to the house open. Clara's heart leapt into her throat, terrified of what would happen if Yasamin caught her. The heavy boots tramping up the stairs didn't belong to Yasamin, though. She never made a sound. Clara frantically searched for a place to hide, but all she could do was crouch into the shadows by the desk. The footsteps, at least two sets, came closer.

Whoever had entered the house was looking for something. Moving furniture reverberated through the floor, and occasionally a loud crash shook the walls. The noises grew louder as the intruders approached. Something banged into the wall hard enough to make Clara jump. They were in the room next door.

The doorknob turned. Clara had locked it behind her. She breathed a sigh of relief until the door burst open, splintering the doorjamb. A man dressed in a black paramilitary uniform and built like an Olympic wrestler stood in the ruined doorway. His pale eyes scanned the room. He didn't seem to notice her. When his gaze came to rest on the bookshelf, his mouth curled up into a smile.

He took a step into the room. Clara balled herself up as small as she could, but it was no use. Their eyes met. All she could think to do was dart for the door, but he caught her arm. She thrashed her other arm around trying to break free and managed to rake her fingernails across his face. He yelped and let her go. She tried to make another run for the door, but he lunged for her. This time he grabbed hold of both arms. His face just inches from her own, he sneered and said something in what sounded like Russian.

He didn't count on her knee in his groin. He released her again and crumpled to the floor. Clara dashed out the door, but in the hallway, she ran square into another man, similar build and similar dress, who grabbed her by the wrist and squeezed until she cried out. A smile spread across his face, a smile that melted away a moment later as his face went pale. He uttered a quiet groan and let go of her hand. Clara leapt back to avoid being trapped beneath his falling body.

The hilt of a knife protruded from his back.

Clara stood facing Yasamin.

The first man staggered out of the study, freezing when he saw Yasamin. The vampire glared, her eyes burning crimson, and faster than Clara could see, she pounced on him. He only screamed once before Yasamin ripped out his throat with her teeth. She rose from the man's mauled corpse, blood still on her hands and face. "Get your things together. We have to go."

Clara ran to her room to gather up her handful of possessions. When she came back out, Yasamin waited with a suitcase of her own. Yasamin clenched her jaw as they moved through the house, navigating around the broken furniture and other antiques. The painting Clara had studied earlier rested on the floor, its frame busted.

"What were they looking for?" Clara asked.

"The books," Yasamin replied.

"Why? What's in them?"

Yasamin paused with a hand on the front door, askew on its hinges. "Secrets some would rather not be known. Secrets of how to make a vampire."

THIRTY-FOUR

—✺—

Berlin, Germany
4 July 1878

ELIZABETH HAD GIVEN UP ON Alfred ever coming home at a decent hour. He had apparently taken to finding some unused room in the embassy where he could sleep, just so he could work longer.

Meanwhile sleep eluded Elizabeth. Every time she closed her eyes, the faces of Thomas, Aleksandr, Friedrich, and her father loomed. Her father's face disturbed her the most, pale, gaunt, with hollowed eyes and a trickle of blood from the corner of his mouth. His lips moved, as if he was trying to tell her something, but he made no sound.

She toyed briefly with the idea of telling Alfred everything that had happened, but that plan immediately hit obstacles. She'd first have to find the time to speak with him, and even then, she didn't know if he'd dismiss it all as flights of fantasy.

Besides, she could never tell Alfred about Aleksandr.

She had almost managed to drift off when a creak from

a floorboard jolted her awake. The noise was close, inside her room. Elizabeth listened. There was a faint rustle of fabric. Something disturbed the air. An odd odor assaulted her nose, a mixture of anise and cardamom and alcohol. Someone was lurking in the room. She sat up to discover a figure at the foot of her bed, hidden in the shadows.

"Wh-Who are you?" she asked, unable to control the tremor in her voice. "What are you doing here?"

The blade of a knife glinted in response. The figure lunged for her. A meaty hand wrapped around her arm and pulled her from the bed. She tried to fight, but the intruder's grip was too tight, and the knife blade hovered dangerously close.

"Where is it?" His accent told Elizabeth he was not German, but from somewhere farther east.

She was afraid even to swallow. "Where is what?"

He squeezed hard enough to hurt. "Don't be stupid. The book. Where is the book?"

"We have lots of books," she protested as tears welled up in her eyes. Her heart threatened to pound out of her chest. She wished Alfred were there. If he had been there, he could have protected her.

"You know exactly what book I mean," the man snarled as he yanked her closer.

Suddenly the temperature dropped until their breaths came out in white puffs. The man opened his mouth to say something more when his grip vanished and Elizabeth was thrown across the room. The shadows churned and rose up around the intruder, but in the darkness, Elizabeth couldn't see everything that happened. The man began to yell, angrily spitting out curses in a language she couldn't identify as he swung at some imagined assailant. Soon, though, his shouts turned into terrified screams. He jerked from side to side and flailed his arms at the shadows before he slammed against the fireplace and crashed to the floor. A heavy gold candlestick fell from the mantle and came to rest next to his body.

Elizabeth jumped to her feet and ran to where he lay. She discovered his neck bent at an odd angle. Blood ran from the side of his head where it had bashed into the stone hearth. As she picked up the candlestick and put it back in its place, she realized they had been standing in the magic circle she drew on the floor and hid underneath the rug.

Minutes later Elizabeth was dressed and outside in front of the townhouse. The cab she had sent for picked her up soon thereafter and made its way through the darkened city streets. She clutched the crucifix on the silver chain around her neck, a hasty purchase days earlier, and one that would have earned a beating from her God-fearing aunt for partaking in idolatry. She wondered what her aunt would have done if confronted with a vampire, or if a vampire would have even bothered with her.

After a short while the carriage pulled up in front of a tenement building in the district of Prenzlauer Berg, not far from Wedding's factories. Elizabeth climbed to the third floor and knocked on the second door on the left after she entered the hallway. Then she waited.

She was about to knock again when a bleary-eyed Thomas Parson opened the door, still in his trousers and shirt-tails.

"I'm sorry, Mr. Parson," she said. "I know it's a completely inappropriate hour to come calling, but would you be willing to help me move a dead body?"

He raised an eyebrow. "Are you all right, Lady James?"

"Yes," she replied. "And you?" she added after a moment's hesitation.

A smile crept across his face. "For one o'clock in the morning, I'm just dandy." The smile faded, replaced by a frown. "How did you know where I've been staying?"

Elizabeth responded with her own wry grin. "Mr. Ristić's intelligence gathering is startlingly efficient. I've been meaning to alert Alfred about it."

"And so you should." Parson stepped aside from the door. "Please come in. Give me a few minutes to get dressed. As you can see, there's nowhere to go really. I'll just have to trust you to avert your eyes."

The room was small, smaller than Elizabeth expected. There was barely enough space for the bed and a tiny dresser. Elizabeth did her best to maintain decorum, but couldn't help the several times she and Parson brushed against one another. He apologized every time, though Elizabeth, blushing, murmured no apologies were necessary.

They rode back to the Wilhelmstraße in silence, Parson not wanting to risk their conversation being overheard. He didn't say anything until he was kneeling over the body of Elizabeth's attacker.

"Where is Lord James?"

"At the embassy," Elizabeth answered, "probably."

Parson's gaze wandered over the body, stopping briefly at the bloody divot in the side of the man's head. "So you're the only one who knows about this … problem?"

Elizabeth nodded. "I checked on Sarah. She's sound asleep. Why do you ask?"

"It makes it easier, that's all. I can carry him down the back stairs past the kitchen and then out into the mews. If I leave his body in a sewage ditch a few blocks from here, the authorities will think he was robbed and left for dead.

We can use rags from the kitchen to wipe up the blood. The bricks on the hearth are dark. You shouldn't be able to see any stain." He turned to look at her. "But that doesn't resolve everything."

"Why not?" she asked.

"Well first off, what the hell happened here?"

"I tried to fight him off," Elizabeth explained. "He tripped and hit his head."

"How fortunate for you."

"He may have had help in the tripping."

Parson chuckled. "I'm sure. Now our next question is why a Turk would break into your home and attack you."

"He's a Turk?"

Parson pointed to the long, thin knife lying on the floor next to the body. "See that? That's a *yatagan*. It's used by Ottoman soldiers."

"He demanded a book. I said I didn't know what he was talking about. Alfred's study is full of books. He could have been after any one of them."

"But he came to you," Parson said as he cocked his head to one side.

"Perhaps he figured out that the study was locked and assumed I would have a key?"

Parson's gaze fell again to the expression of shock frozen on the unfortunate Turk's face. "Perhaps."

THIRTY-FIVE

Berlin, Germany
5 July 1878

ELIZABETH WAITED FOR THE SUN to set before she slipped down the stairs and outside to the tiny garden behind the townhouse. Aleksandr was already there. He smiled when he saw her, the same charming smile he had given her the day he met her, the same one he gave her every time he saw her, as if to reassure her the delight he took in her company would never fade. He took her hand and led her to a small bench. They had spent several nights there, talking in whispers.

Aleksandr told her stories of the places he had been—Romania, Greece, Albania, Turkey. His stories were full of noble bandits, wily Gypsies, treacherous monks, stupid bureaucrats, and earnest farmers. Elizabeth had her doubts about whether any of the stories were true, but he made them seem so real it really didn't matter. She wanted him to take her to all of the places he had been. That night, he told her a tale about the time he had spent in the mountains among the Albanian insurgents. It was finally one tale too far.

"You're lying." Her tone was more teasing than accusatory, though. "You can't possibly be old enough to have done all of the things you've talked about."

"How old do you think I am?"

"You must be about the same age as Alfred. I can't imagine you're any older."

Alfred had continued his habit of staying at the embassy until the very early morning hours, if he came home at all. Elizabeth felt a pang of guilt upon mentioning his name. Why couldn't they spend time together the way she and Aleksandr did?

Aleksandr chuckled. "It's not the years. It's what you do with them."

"What is it you and Alfred discuss when you're holed up in his office?" she asked.

Aleksandr's eyes grew wide in surprise. "You mean he hasn't told you?"

Elizabeth pursed her lips. "No, I've asked, but he always says it's nothing that should worry me."

Aleksandr shook his head. "That is a shame. Someone as intelligent as you? He should realize how fortunate he is. You could be his secret weapon, if he'd let you."

"I've tried that argument."

"Well, I suppose if you're persistent enough, he'll eventually realize the truth. If you want something, you do whatever it takes to get it. I see that in you, as I'm the same way."

Elizabeth blushed. Apparently, he could see that, too, despite the darkness.

"Don't be modest, now," he continued. "What I've said, it's true. You have a strength few do. Your husband will see it someday. You could be a great help in promoting him. You've befriended the other diplomats' wives, including the wife of the ambassador himself. He wouldn't have to work half as hard if he understood exactly how much influence some women have over their husbands. Also, what we do is not as complicated as he makes it out to be."

"Tell me about it."

"We are in Berlin now because there is perhaps no other more important place on the planet right now than Constantinople. The Turks consider it the navel of the world, as did the Byzantines before them. Until the collapse of Turkey-in-Europe, it seemed as if the city would always be in the hands of the Turks. Now it is not so certain, but one thing is. Whichever nation controls the Balkans has the upper hand in eventually flying its flag from the Maiden's Tower in the middle of the Bosporus. It is the reason for Russia's recent war with Turkey."

"Alfred explained that much to me," Elizabeth said. "This Congress is meant to undo the treaty that ended the war."

"The other Powers want to conjure up a different outcome for the war we fought all by ourselves." He paused and knit his brow. "It's all completely unnecessary. Russia isn't a threat to anyone right now. We don't see the need for another war for quite some time, but what can we do with everyone else arrayed against us? So we agreed to the Congress, and what has been the result? Almost a month of bickering and arguing. Not one thing has been accomplished. Lord James could change that."

Elizabeth studied Aleksandr's face for any sign he was less than serious. "Alfred? Really?"

"He has put forth a very simple solution, to create a confederation of the smaller states as a buffer against the

Turks and a fail-safe against the ambitions of the Great Powers. It is all very clever."

"So you think it would work?" Elizabeth asked.

Aleksandr nodded. "If the right people hear about it."

Possibilities Elizabeth had never considered unfolded in front of her. "It would make his career. He'd likely get an appointment to the Foreign Secretary's staff. We'd go back to London."

"Isn't that what you want?"

"England is my home."

"That is not what I asked," Aleksandr said.

Elizabeth sighed. "I think it's what I want."

Aleksandr leaned closer. The smell of the crisp linen of his uniform mingled with cinnamon and sage. "When this Congress is over, I will miss you."

Elizabeth hadn't expected to start crying.

Aleksandr reached up to brush the tears from her cheeks. "There, now, you shouldn't be crying on a warm summer night such as this. With the moon and the stars overhead and the rustle of the wind in the trees, it is perfect. There is nothing to cry about."

Elizabeth shook her head. "It's not because of tonight. I'm crying because of what you said. Everyone leaves me eventually—my parents, my first husband Stanley, everyone."

"Your first husband? What was he like?"

Elizabeth smiled at the memory of him. "Stanley was a solicitor. Not the most exciting career choice, I suppose, but a stable one. He was a sweet, quiet man. He rarely smiled in public, but there was warmth in his brown eyes, and anyone fortunate enough to hear him laugh never forgot it. Only a few months after we were married, he fell ill. It was gradual at first. He complained of being tired. He seemed a little pale. He and I both blamed it on his work, which was going quite well, but kept him busy. Then suddenly it got worse. His hands began to shake uncontrollably, and he would retch violently. None of the doctors knew what was wrong with him. Eventually, be became so weak he couldn't get out of bed, and then one day he just died."

Aleksandr took her hand in his. "I can't promise I won't go away someday as well, but I'm here right now, and I'll stay here with you until the sun comes up if you'd like me to. We have all the time in the world to enjoy the night."

THIRTY-SIX

Sighişoara, Romania
11 December 1999

A CRUCIFIX HUNG ON THE wall over Adam's bed.
He wondered as he lay staring at the ceiling if the
owner of the townhouse meant the placement of
the crucifix as a sincere gesture, or if he was trying to be
ironic.

He closed his eyes to pray, but found himself doubting
whether God was listening. The doubt was new. He'd
been at odds for quite some time with God's plan for his
life, but he'd never doubted God was there. Now he was
just lost. Adrift. Grasping for a lifeline and finding nothing.

And because of his doubt Clara was going to die.

By all rights, he should be the one six feet under. He
had faced down anarchists, extremists, terrorists, not to
mention vampires, and yet he survived. Everything he had
done, though, had been his choice. Clara didn't know what
she was walking into. None of what had happened was her

fault, but she was still going to pay the price.

Sighișoara was the key, or so Elena said, but Adam had no idea where in the city the medallion could be and no obvious way to find it. The supposedly lost papers of Alexander Sift, as astounding as they were, didn't provide anything useful on that front.

He just wanted to talk to Clara again, to hear her voice one more time. He ran their last conversation over in his head as he had done countless other times, hanging on her words, as mundane as they were.

This time, though, he focused on something he hadn't before. He talked to her about the Vigenère diagram he had drawn. At its heart, a Vigenère cipher was a simple substitution cipher. It worked just like the codes kids used to send secret messages, by substituting one letter of the alphabet for another, but unlike those codes, the substitution in a Vigenère cipher changed for every letter. It couldn't be broken without a diagram, or the right key.

Sighișoara was the key.

That's what Mihai had been trying to tell him. The medallion wasn't in the city of Sighișoara. The word *Sighișoara* was the key to solving the real code. His mind racing, Adam jumped out of bed, just as all the lights went out. For an eerie second he stood in the darkness, allowing his eyes to adjust to the faint moonlight.

He knew he'd have no more time than that.

He lunged for the crucifix and pivoted for the door when something crashed through the bedroom window. Amid the flying glass and wood splinters, a clawed hand scraped his back. Adam stumbled down the hallway, hoping he'd run into Arkady. Instead, he tumbled down the stairs. The thing was on top of him immediately, but as soon as it touched the crucifix it shrieked and fell back.

Adam staggered to his feet and sprinted out the front door of the townhouse.

Every other house on the street had power. The streetlights gave Adam a small measure of confidence, but he did not stop running. He could hear the creature chasing him, inhuman footfalls echoing on the cobblestones, hissing whispers, scraping claws. In the maze of narrow streets Adam took left and right turns at random, hoping to throw off the vampire, but he knew everything he did was in vain. It smelled his blood, and it came for him still.

He rounded another corner, and the sight before him compelled him to stop. He stood in the citadel square, Dracula's birthplace looming out of the darkness. The vampire had driven him there, he realized. Unlike in the daytime, the building pulsed with malevolence. Adam couldn't help but drop the crucifix and walk toward it.

Had anyone known what evil they had unleashed into the world the day Vlad Dracula was born? Did they care? For them, the goal was the same as for everyone in power—to stay in power. Just to survive, the Romanians had to perform a complicated dance with the Hungarians, the Turks, the Germans, the Poles, the Russians. Notions of good and evil had little place in the thoughts of the people. From time to time Adam wondered if the vampire curse predated Vlad Dracula, or if he himself had brought it about.

As he reached for the handle on the door of the building, hands like an iron vice grabbed him from behind and held him motionless. "That was a good chase," a rough voice said in his ear. "I haven't had one like that in a long time."

Adam didn't reply. He shut his eyes and waited for the end.

"Let him go, Grigor."

Adam's eyes flew open. That voice. Adam couldn't see the woman who spoke, but he knew her voice, even if the accent was different.

"I don't work for you," the vampire growled. "Not anymore."

"True," said the woman, "but you ought not involve yourself in things you don't understand."

Adam turned his head as much as he could, scanning the courtyard for the woman. All he could see were moving shadows.

"I understand enough," Grigor said. "The American knows an awful lot about us. Too much. And yet you let him live. Why are you so interested in him? Why is he important?"

"I don't have to explain myself to you, Grigor." The voice was closer. Adam's heart pounded. He longed to see her and yet at the same time, he was utterly terrified.

Grigor laughed. It was not a pleasant sound. "Maybe you will, though. I could snap his neck or draw a nail across his throat and let his blood spill right here on the doorstep of Vlad Dracul's house."

The shadows around the edges of the square began to swirl. When the woman spoke again, her voice was hard and cold as steel. "If you don't let go of him right now, I assure you I will not stop until I destroy you."

Grigor let out another low growl, but his grip on Adam loosened. "You're no better than the rest of us, Elizabeth. You'd best be careful—"

He screamed and flailed, raking his claws across Adam's back. Adam stumbled and toppled headlong into the door of Vlad Dracul's house. He pushed himself to his feet in time to see Grigor combust in a brilliant white flash. When Adam's eyes adjusted to the night again, the vampire was nothing more than a heap of ash.

Anya stood in front of him smiling demurely, hands on her hips, though she looked nothing like he remembered. Her hair, cascading in waves past her shoulders, was golden blond instead of brilliant red. The low-cut, corseted bodice of her black Victorian-style dress accentuated the curves of her body. Long black gloves reached to her elbows. Around her neck she wore a black choker necklace with a small onyx cameo. The malevolence in her icy blue eyes would have made the pope doubt the existence of God, but all Adam longed to do was kiss her cherry lips again. He shuddered at the thought of touching her milky-white skin once more.

"Hello, Adam," she said.

Adam could barely catch his breath. "Anya, but you're—"

"Dead? It's difficult to kill someone who's already dead."

"But how—"

She held a finger to his lips. "No questions right now."

He recalled the strange woman he had seen in Sarajevo the day after Clara was abducted and the woman who had been watching the house in Bucharest the night the burglar tried to steal Ioan Nicolescu's book. "You're the third Bride. The fair one." Adam glanced at the pile of white ash that had once been Grigor. "He called you Elizabeth."

"Lady Elizabeth James," she said as she curtseyed.

"Why did you save me?"

She shook her head. "I said no questions."

Footsteps echoed across the square.

Her demure smile returned. "Until we meet again, Adam."

She vanished, dissolving into the shadows. Adam's knees buckled underneath him. He felt hollowed out. Inside of him there was nothing but a gnawing hunger, a bottomless longing. He was tumbling in the void again.

"Adam. Adam, are you okay?" Arkady's voice sounded like he was underwater.

Adam remained huddled in the doorway. "No, I'm not. Not at all."

Hours later Adam couldn't stop shaking. "How could I not have seen it? How could I not have known?"

He paced the room while Arkady watched. They had gone to the home of Felix Rudeanu, much to the annoyance of his wife, but once the inspector saw Adam's haggard form, he didn't hesitate to invite them in.

"She used a glamour," Arkady said. "She had us all fooled."

"But I've seen through glamours before."

Arkady held up a finger. "When you knew the other person was a vampire. You didn't know."

Adam closed his eyes. All he could think of was the night he and Anya shared in Dubrovnik. That night had meant more to him than he wanted to admit. For at least a short time, he wasn't alone, unmoored in the world. He had bared his soul to her, and she had healed a portion of it, or so he thought. Apparently she was simply playing a long con.

"But I saw her during the day," he protested.

Arkady raised an eyebrow. "Was it ever sunny?"

Adam stopped to think, and in every memory of Anya during the day, the sky was overcast. "No, no it wasn't."

"The idea that sunlight kills vampires is only partly

true. It hurts them. It weakens them, and it can kill them given time, but they don't die immediately, not to mention the fact that particularly strong vampires can manipulate the atmosphere."

Adam shook his head. "She's not that old, though. She can't be."

Arkady drew his mouth into a grim line. "There are other ways for a vampire to become strong. Come to think of it, the few times I ever encountered Anya were never on sunny days. Of course, in St. Petersburg sunny days are a rarity."

"This changes things entirely."

Arkady let out a humorless chuckle. "You think?"

Adam glared. "She has Clara. I know she does."

Arkady threw up his hands. "What can we do besides what we've already been doing? We don't know where to find Anya."

Adam toyed with the buckle on his satchel. They had gone to retrieve their things from the townhouse accompanied by a police escort. That same escort found the owner of the townhouse dead in his own apartments, his throat torn open. "Her real name is Elizabeth, and that's more than we knew before. Maybe the inspector's men can find something."

"They've been looking since Clara disappeared, Adam. Here, Bucharest, Sarajevo, Thessaloniki, Dubrovnik, Banja Luka, everywhere." Arkady exhaled slowly. "I don't think we're going to find Anya or Elizabeth or whatever her name is until she wants us to."

"What about the murders here and in Bucharest? Maybe there's something we overlooked."

Arkady frowned. "You think she's the one manipulating the Iron Guard as well?"

Adam met his questioning gaze. "I don't think. I know."

"What makes you so certain?"

Adam pulled the journal of Mihai Iliescu's father from his satchel. "Because of this." He handed it to Arkady. "Read the very last entry."

THIRTY-SEVEN

—∿—

From the Journal of Andras Iliescu

Near Bucharest, Romania
24 June 1943

I PRAY THIS JOURNAL REACHES YOU, my son.

I am convinced this war will never end. I have traveled from Sarajevo to Athens to Sofia, and nowhere have I found quarter. Now I find myself in Bucharest again. At least in the warmer weather the traveling is easier, and the longer days have given me more time to be active before I've had to find a secure place for the night.

The monsters have followed me ever since I left Sarajevo. They thrive on the disorder and the chaos ruling our everyday lives now. I have destroyed a few of them, but the last encounter put me on my present path.

About three weeks ago, I found an abandoned farmhouse to sleep in a few hundred miles from Sofia. The house had only one entrance, and there was a loft built over the main room. From up there, I could see anyone coming and going, but it would have been difficult for any-one entering to see me.

The sun had just set, and the light was quickly failing. I settled into the loft and was drifting off to sleep when I heard something below. I peered down to spot two of the monsters coming through the front door. I was puzzled. I had placed a holy wafer above the door. They shouldn't have been able to enter the house that way, even if it was abandoned. Then I noticed the wafer was missing. No doubt some small animal had come along and taken it for food.

They were looking for something, and it didn't take long for me to realize they were looking for me. I don't pre-tend to understand the motivations of these monsters. They don't have any sort of organization. At most they ex-ist in small groups, but they have hounded our family for generations. I thought their obsession had to do with our family's role as bearers of the medallion.

But I came to understand on that night that the me-dallion is not the only thing connecting us to them. Our tainted blood does as well. They must sense that a small part of their disease flows down our bloodline, that an ancestor of ours fathered a child after having been bitten by one of them. I'm afraid, my son, that I have left you with this horrible legacy. You will always have a con-nection to these monsters. Every generation of our family willAt that point there was no use hiding from them. They already knew I was there, so I stood up with my bow and arrow ready. They both looked up at the loft, their red eyes burning. I destroyed one of them before they had time to react. The other one was faster than I expected. He rushed up the stairs before I could pull back another ar-row, though I did manage to bring the crucifix around my neck between us before he attacked. For several moments, we stood, facing one another.

"Why do you even bother?" he asked, taking a step forward.

I stepped back. "Ridding the world of the evil you represent is my duty."

"You'll never win. You can't kill us all. There will always be more, and one day, your luck is going to run out."

"Maybe, but as long as I'm alive, it's what I'll do."

The monster took a different line. "And what kind of life is it, really? Is it one worth living? You're homeless, living in a war zone. Do you have any hope that your life will get better?"

"Perhaps not for me, but for the generations to come, yes."

He laughed. "Not likely. This war isn't our work. It's the work of men. We didn't cause this misery and suffering. And if there ever is an end to this war, something like it will happen again. You don't need us to destroy you. You're already doing a good job of that yourselves. So you see, eradicating our kind is pointless."

By this time, we had almost made a full circle of the loft. I had my back to the opening below. My quiver was within arms' length. I made a move for another arrow, but I wasn't really trying for it. As I hoped, he lunged at me. At the last second I dodged him. He flew past me and crashed through the railing, but he managed to catch my arm as he fell. He would have pulled me over, had I not grabbed hold of one of the wooden columns supporting the roof.

He clawed at my arm, trying his best to climb back up. They can't die, but they can still be injured. The fall would have no doubt broken his legs, making it easy for me to finish him. I tried to shake him off, but I barely held on myself. Finally, he used his own body weight to swing up and gain a handhold on the loft. His mistake. Without his full weight pulling on me, I freed my hand to grab an arrow, and I stabbed him in the neck. With a scream, he let go and fell to the floor below.

I hadn't destroyed him. His red eyes glared up at me from the floor. I descended the stairs and stood over him.

"Perhaps you're right." I spun the arrow in my fingers. "Perhaps it is pointless to try to eliminate all of you, but the one thing I do know beyond a shadow of a doubt, is that this world will be just slightly better after I've sent you back to hell."

And with that, I drove the arrow into his chest.

As I left the old house that night, I thought about what the monster said. To an extent he was right. I would never make a difference, not the way I could have, given the horrible things I had done, and day by day, my hope faded in seeing you again. The war does seem like it will go on forever, but at least I know you were safe.

I decided to return to Bucharest, to confront the one evil I ran away from, the evil I had been a part of. Even if I could not rid the world of monsters, I could do my part to rid the world of that evil. Little did I know how closely the two were intertwined.

It took me the better part of a week to reach Bucharest again. The city is not how I remember it. A desperation has settled in and discolored everything. Grey has washed over the bright city. Grey and red. I attempted to contact a few of my old compatriots in the Iron Guard. There are scarcely any left, but a few lurk here and there, unnoticed by the powers that be. Most of them did not want to talk to me at all for fear of attracting attention, but there was one who would.

His name is Constantin Dalca. He is older that I am by about ten years and was acquainted with many in the leadership of the Iron Guard. I'm amazed he has escaped death. We met in a coffee shop frequented mostly by drug addicts and prostitutes. When I saw him, he looked much older than I remembered. We sat back-to-back at adjoining tables.

He spoke first. "So, I see you have a death wish. I never thought you had much sense."

"You didn't have to come here," I replied. "The fact that you have means my note made sense to you on some level."

"Still, you'll be lucky if you get out alive."

I took a sip of my tea and grimaced. It tasted like cigarette ash. "Let me worry about that. Just give me the information I asked for."

"I don't have it."

I almost cried out loud, forgetting for a moment how foolish that would have been. Who knows where the ears of the government might be. "Then why did you agree to meet me here?"

"You misunderstand my motives, my friend. I don't have the information you want because no one has it. The Iron Guard is not the same organization. Things are different now that it's an underground society. Maybe I shouldn't say 'different.' There was always something there. You know, something dark lurking just below the surface. It has come to the surface now."

"What are you trying to say?"

"There have been strange rumors going around of odd rituals. Not the ceremonies we were used to, not the special church services, but something else. Something decidedly more violent. One by one, I've seen the people we used to know just disappear. Some of them don't come back. The ones that do seem … changed somehow. No one knows where these rituals are taking place. They're not in any of our old places."

"Do you know what they do at these rituals?"

"Nothing I want to say out loud. They involve blood, and … other things."

I finished my tea and threw some money on the table. "Thank you."

"Wait," he said, a little too forcefully.

One of the other patrons looked up from his coffee, but if he worked for the government, we would never know. He just as quickly returned to his drink, seemingly uncaring about two old men at the opposite end of the café. I waited.

"Have you listened to anything I said?" His voice was pained.

"I have," I replied, "and I know what I have to do now. We have both been fools, my friend. We have been tools for an evil without a name. I am going to make sure there is an end to that evil."

"How can you be so certain?"

"I have to be."

I walked out of the café into the rapidly fading twilight. I didn't know yet where to go, but everything was becoming clearer. The monsters thrive in chaos. Wherever there is death and violence, they will be. The one I had killed at the farmhouse was right in that regard as well. Men are capable of killing each other without help, but in this case, they had it. The monsters sparked our hatred and pushed our country into this awful war through the Iron Guard—through me. I was determined to end their influence.

All the old places were off-limits to the monsters. They were churches and monasteries—consecrated ground. After all, our patron was the archangel Michael himself. There was one place, however, the monsters would be able to go, a clearing in the forest just north of the city. I had heard rumors of rituals performed there did not involve a priest. They were more primitive than that, and I often wondered what their purpose could be. Now I know. The masses, the taking of communion, the prayer, it was all for show. None of the angels in heaven condoned what we did. The real ritual in the woods honored an evil older than the church itself.

I would find them there.

I reached the clearing while the sun was still high in the sky, and I waited. At dusk, they came, wearing their dress uniforms. None of them spoke as they set about building the fire. Once the fire grew into a blaze, they circled, and the chanted, not the old prayers, not the petitions to our patron saint. They chanted in a language I barely understood, words of hatred, words of violence, words of death. When they stopped, so did the world.

Then she appeared.

Even the harsh and inconstant light of the fire failed to diminish her beauty. She too wore a dress uniform, but it did nothing to hide her figure. Her golden blond hair fell in waves. Her skin was so pale it was almost translucent. Her cold blue eyes fixed on every one of the men assembled there, and her red lips spread in a wicked grin.

Her features changed. Her eyes turned the color of blood. Her eyeteeth grew into fangs. She picked one of the men in the front row and kissed him violently on the mouth before plunging her fangs into his neck. She ripped the man's shirt off and licked the blood off his bare chest as it ran down. He moaned in bliss.

She stripped off her own clothes and smeared his blood on her body. As the two of them writhed together, she continued to drink. Their howls and cries echoed through the trees, and the wolves in the forest responded to their screams of ecstasy.

When she was done with him, he collapsed to the ground. The other men never said a word. Two of them stood and threw the lifeless body into the fire. They chanted and marched until the fire almost burned out, the woman standing in the middle of the circle all the while, smiling, laughing.

I will tell you something now, something I should have told you sooner. You, my son, are the last in a line of vampire hunters, descended all the way from Arnold Pavle, a Serbian farmer and soldier from the 1700s. While fighting for the Austrian army, he encountered a vampire and somehow came to possess Dracula's most prized possession, a medallion representing the Order of the Dragon, the thing that gave Dracula his name.

He eventually succumbed to the wretched creatures. Tragically, he didn't survive to witness the birth of his son, but the medallion passed to his widow. She took an oath to protect her son at all costs from the sickness that had taken her husband. She left the village where they lived, and settled in Sibiu, among the Germans there.

She became a vampire hunter in her own right, and because of that, her son grew to manhood. Ever since then, fighting the monsters has been a duty passed down from father to son, mother to daughter. My life has brought me full circle, and now I must act like I am part of the noble lineage I hesitate to claim.

I will give Constantin this journal to send to you. Tomorrow, I will return to the clearing, and I will be prepared. This evil prolongs the war. Without her, I am convinced the suffering our country has endured will end, and perhaps I can make up for my part in bringing that suffering about. Perhaps one day, you will be able to say you are proud of the man your father was.

THIRTY-EIGHT

—〜〜—

Bucharest, Romania
11 December 1999

YASAMIN DIDN'T STOP AT THE hotel's front desk, instead leading Clara directly to an elevator away from the others. The staff didn't seem to notice either of them. Clara wondered if they were trained to turn a blind eye or if Yasamin cast a glamour. Once in the elevator Yasamin flashed an electronic key before pressing the button for the top floor.

They stepped off directly into a suite, the kind Clara knew only from movies about rich Hollywood executives or mob bosses. A wall of windows showcased the entire city. The expansive room contained a number of couches and chairs, some arranged in front of a giant television, others arrayed near a fully stocked bar standing along one wall. A door on each side led to what Clara assumed were the bedrooms.

"I apologize for the accommodations," Yasamin said, "but given the short notice, this will have to do."

Clara gaped. "You're apologizing for this?"

Yasamin pursed her lips as she ran her fingers along one of the leather couches. "It's not to my taste. I find it a little … what's the English word … tacky? Everything is too new. I distrust it."

Clara cocked an eyebrow. "You distrust furniture?"

"I distrust the mentality that created this furniture, that says this is what indulgence is, that this is what living without care is like. It's so … limited. But as I said, it will have to do, for tonight."

"Who were they, the ones who broke in?" Clara asked. "What did they want?"

Yasamin stepped to the floor-to-ceiling windows. The lights of Bucharest glowed below, making obvious why the city was called "Little Paris." Clara caught her breath. Yasamin didn't cast a reflection in the glass.

"They were Russians," the vampire answered.

Clara's heart pounded. Maybe Arkady would be able to find her after all. Maybe she shouldn't have fought off the man who discovered her in the study.

"And as I said," Yasamin continued, "they were looking for the books you discovered."

Clara froze.

Yasamin turned to face her. "Really, Dr. MacIntosh, I would have been shocked if you hadn't found them. There was nothing in that house I wouldn't have wanted you to see. Otherwise I wouldn't have brought you there."

"You said the books contained secrets some don't want out, secrets that have to do with how to make a vampire."

Yasamin stood silent for a moment before she responded. "Tell me, what would you do if you could live forever?"

Clara shook her head, "I wouldn't want that."

Yasamin chuckled. "Are you certain?"

"I'm positive. I wouldn't want to watch all my friends, my family, everyone I've ever known grow old and die, or the places I knew in life change until they were unrecognizable."

"I'm sure there are some circumstances that would lead you to make the choice. For instance, what if you were diagnosed with a terminal illness tomorrow. Faced with the prospect of your life cut short, wouldn't you look for ways prolong it?"

Clara frowned. "I'm still not sure."

"Then the life of someone else, someone you love?"

Clara hesitated.

Yasamin's smile widened. "See that is where the difference is. You would do it. We all have something that would make us decide."

"What made you decide?" Clara asked.

Yasamin's gaze wandered to the window again. "I was dying. He saved me. He showed me another way."

"Another way than what?"

"Than the society I lived in. The role determined for me. He showed me an escape. But there are others who might decide for different reasons. Power. Wealth. Some have been foolish enough to think they can achieve immortality without the consequences, and some have even tried."

Clara joined her at the window. "Why haven't they sought Dracula out?"

"What makes you think they haven't?"

"I suspect he's not interested in cooperating."

"He has his own plans."

"What happened to him?" Clara asked. "Where is he?"

Yasamin shook her head. "I don't know, but I know he

is waiting."

"For what?"

Yasamin stared out the window. Far below automobile lights traced a complicated dance in the illuminated streets. People going about their business, unaware of the extraordinary things in their midst. "For when he is needed."

She turned her back to the window and walked away, making it clear to Clara that the conversation was over.

CLARA COULDN'T SLEEP. THE MASSIVE bed, with all its blankets and pillows, proved to be too soft. Generally she preferred to sleep on something closer to a wooden plank, and she briefly considered relocating to the floor. Yasamin's words came back to her, about people who would consider the penthouse suite in a five-star hotel the literal pinnacle of success. They had no idea how meaningless their lives were. As she finally drifted into a fitful slumber, Clara worried she could so easily identify with the vampire's point of view.

THIRTY-NINE

—◦◦◦—

Berlin, Germany
6 July 1878

E LIZABETH FOUGHT DOWN THE WAVE of panic
when she opened the door to find Thomas standing
on the threshold.

He tipped his hat to her. "Good evening, Lady
James. I hope I'm not intruding."

Aleksandr. It was nearing dusk. He would be waiting
soon in the courtyard.

Elizabeth forced a smile. "Not at all. Please, come in.
What is it that brings you here?"

He stepped past her into the foyer of the townhouse. "I
thought we'd take the opportunity to go through your husband's books."

Elizabeth frowned. "What? We can't do that."

Thomas cocked his head to the side. "Why not?"

Elizabeth glanced toward the hallway that led past the
kitchen to the courtyard. The thought of keeping Aleksandr waiting terrified her. "Because Alfred always keeps

his office locked."

Thomas produced a set of odd metal instruments. "That is no obstacle, I assure you."

"But what if he comes back?"

The corners of Thomas' mouth turned up in a wry grin. "Has he any night this week?"

Elizabeth sighed. "No, he's been staying at the embassy more and more. I've barely seen him."

"Must be important work, then."

"Apparently it is."

He raised an eyebrow. "How do you know?"

"He tells me as much," Elizabeth lied.

"So chances are he won't be back for a while, if at all. Shall we get started?" Thomas moved toward the study.

Elizabeth placed a hand on his arm. "Wait. We don't even know what we're looking for."

His gaze went to Elizabeth's hand. "I'm hoping we'll know it when we see it."

The sun was setting. Already the surrounding buildings had thrown the townhouse into shadow. "But he has hundreds of books."

Thomas took her hand in his and gently squeezed before letting it drop. "Lady James, if I didn't know any better, I'd say you were completely against this plan."

When he started toward the study again Elizabeth remained where she was. "I am. I can't let you do this."

Thomas again stopped and faced her. The lopsided smile was gone. "Do you want to find out what's going on or not?"

Elizabeth let her gaze fall to the floor. "Of course I do."

"So what's the problem?"

Aleksandr was waiting for her. She couldn't think of anything else. Aleksandr was waiting. "I ... I haven't spoken to Lady Russell or Mr. Ristić about what happened yet. Perhaps they can think of another plan."

Thomas crossed his arms. "There's a reason you haven't gone running to them. You know good and well a dead Turk in your bedroom isn't exactly going to help your husband's career."

She shook her head. "I didn't kill him."

Thomas held up a chiding finger. "But you helped. And I disposed of the body for you. I'd rather not get any more entangled with Jovan Ristić than I have to."

"What happened between the two of you?"

"That's not my story to tell. Ask him."

Something tugged at Elizabeth's consciousness, like a passing shadow, a fleeting memory triggered by a familiar aroma, a long forgotten tune. Aleksandr, if he had been there at all, was gone. She wouldn't see him that night. Her heart sank.

She bit her lip to keep Thomas from seeing it tremble. "Fine, Mr. Parson. Tonight we shall do things your way, but if we don't find anything, I'm going to tell the others what happened."

He nodded. "Fair enough."

Thomas spent less than a minute picking the lock on the door to Alfred's study. The hinges creaked as he pushed the door open. Elizabeth followed him inside. She turned a dial on the wall, and the gas lamps hissed to life, forcing the darkness to the corners. A mahogany wood desk dominated the center of the room, its surface covered in maps, notes, and letters. Shelves covered three of the walls, all overstuffed with books.

"Did you bring all these to Berlin?" Thomas asked, gazing at the collection.

"Most of them," Elizabeth answered. "Some of them he

bought here."

Thomas went to the nearest shelf and scanned the titles. "Any chance he has a system for organizing them all?"

Elizabeth surveyed the contents of the desk. "If he does, it would be one that makes sense only to him."

"I'm not surprised." He picked a book off the shelf and opened it to the middle. "How exactly *did* you come to be Lady James?"

She glanced sidelong at him. "That's a rather forward question, Mr. Parson."

He shrugged. "I'm American."

She sighed. "There is not much of a story to tell. Alfred's father was a client of the law firm where my first husband Stanley was a solicitor. He would often send Alfred to our house to discuss legal matters with Stanley."

Thomas looked up from the book. "Your first husband?"

"He died, Mr. Parson."

"I'm sorry."

"No, it's fine. It happened several years ago. I've moved on."

Silence settled over them. Thomas examined one book after another, skimming the pages and then replacing each one on the shelf. Elizabeth did the same, but she couldn't bring herself to take the task seriously. She couldn't imagine Alfred owning anything incendiary enough for the Turks to send an assassin.

"Do all these books belong to Lord James?" Thomas asked after a while. "There's nothing here that would have belonged to your father, for example?"

Elizabeth shook her head. "My mother donated his personal library to the university after he … once it became evident he wasn't returning."

Thomas frowned. "I was afraid of that. You know Lord

James has quite the body of work on the history of Transylvania. Here's *Description of the Székely Lands* by Bálazs Orbán, and a few others I recognize."

"One of his passions is the history of that part of the world," Elizabeth said.

"Interesting," Thomas muttered as he put the book back and moved on to the next.

"You never told me why all this matters to you. What happened that put you on this path?"

He flashed his crooked grin. "Isn't that rather forward of you?"

She shrugged. "You're American. I didn't think you'd be offended."

He paused and closed the book he was holding. "I can tell you what I remember, in any event. It started with a card game in Sarajevo about ten years ago, one I probably shouldn't have agreed to join. I know I shouldn't have agreed to the bottle of *šljivovica* I was offered. I woke up the next morning being beaten with a broom by an old lady. All my money was gone."

"You have just confirmed many of my suspicions about you, Mr. Parson."

He adopted a feigned hurt expression. "A man can change. Look at the company I choose to keep now."

She laughed. "That's a bit of a left-handed compliment, but thank you. I thought you said it happened in Ragusa, though."

"It did," Thomas replied. "Luckily for me, I had some money hidden away at the boarding house where I was staying, just enough for a coach ride to Ragusa, and maybe a night's stay. I had heard there was work there at the docks, so I found a ride and tried to ignore the fact that I felt like someone was trying to drive a railway spike through my head. I swear I think the driver tried to hit every rock and rut he could, just to kill me."

"You do have an effect on people."

Thomas glared, but his smile remained. "Now you're just trying to be mean. I'll have you know I make friends wherever I go. Even Ragusa, unfortunately. We arrived as the sun was setting. I recommend a visit. It's a beautiful city, though at the time I was too preoccupied with finding a place to stay to take in the scenery. At the first boardinghouse I tried, I didn't even get a word out before the old woman who answered the door screamed 'No room!' in my face and slammed the door so hard it made my teeth vibrate."

"Quite friendly," Elizabeth remarked.

Thomas cleared his throat. "Patience. I'm getting there. The same thing happened over and over until I was on the verge of giving up and just finding a tavern. That's when someone ran up behind me, knocked me down and stole my satchel. I chased the thief, but he was like a rabbit in his home warren. I didn't have a chance. I lost him and got myself lost in the process."

"That sounds like a particularly bad day."

"It got worse. Remember I told you I make friends wherever I go. By then it was dark, and all the houses were shuttered. It was the oddest thing. No one else was about. But at the time I didn't think too deeply about it. I was so tired and sore that when I rounded a corner and saw a light coming from an unshuttered window, I practically ran toward it. I may have thanked the heavens when I discovered it was a boardinghouse. A woman answered the door, more beautiful than I had ever seen. Her olive skin glistened in the warm light that spilled through the open doorway, and her raven black hair shimmered as she moved. When I asked if she had a vacancy, she smiled and stepped aside so I could enter."

Elizabeth put down the book she was holding. Something about the description of the woman seemed familiar, another whisper of a memory she couldn't place. "Something tells me you shouldn't have been thanking the heavens."

"Not at that moment, no. She asked me if I wanted anything to eat or drink. Frankly at the time I just wanted to collapse, and I told her I was only looking for a place to sleep for the night. I'd figure out how to pay her in the morning, I told myself. At that moment another woman entered the room. She was just as beautiful as the first. She also had jet-black hair, but her eyes were a brilliant green. They might have been sisters. I don't remember. I don't even remember their names, though I'm sure they told me."

A small knot of dread formed in Elizabeth's stomach. She didn't know why.

"The second sister led me upstairs to a small room," Thomas continued. "It was nice, far nicer than any other place I'd stayed. I began to panic, but at that point it was just about the price. I asked how much. She laughed and told me not to worry about it. We could discuss payment later. Her voice was mesmerizing. I wanted her to stay, but she turned and left before I could say anything else. I undressed and got into the bed. I was asleep as soon as my head hit the pillow."

"But you had dark dreams, didn't you?"

Thomas looked at her, mouth agape. "How did you know?"

"My father spoke of them sometimes," she said quickly.

"I was somewhere dark, lost. It could have been in the

forest. I remember trees. Maybe there was a structure ahead of me I was trying to get to. There were voices carried on the wind and shadows that followed me."

Elizabeth shivered.

"When I woke up, the sun hadn't risen yet. They were standing in my room. I could see their faces in the tiny sliver of moonlight coming through the gap in the shutters. I didn't even have time to scream before they were on top of me, pinning me to the bed. Their hands and lips were cold as ice. Their nails dug into my skin, and then their teeth drew blood. At that moment images flooded my mind. A cold high mountain pass. A ship cutting through the water on a moonlit night. Icons in a candlelit sanctuary. A crumbling mosque. A stone bridge lined with looming statues. A battlefield strewn with bodies, quiet save for the calls of the blackbirds."

"How did you escape?" Elizabeth asked almost in a whisper. It seemed as if there was nothing outside the room, no one in the world but the two of them.

Thomas slowly exhaled. "I'd like to think I fought back, but I really didn't. Whatever was happening to me, I wanted it. I wanted their cold hands and their sharp fangs. But maybe I had an angel watching over me, because the next image in my head was my Annie from back home. I called her name, and immediately the two sisters leapt off me, shrieking. I didn't hesitate. I jumped out of the bed, grabbed my clothes and ran out of the room. I found a ship the next morning that would take me to Venice in return for work. I've never gone back."

They had begun their conversation on opposite sides of the desk, but now they stood next to one another. Thomas' breathing was heavy. His face was red. His hands were balled into fists.

"Who's Annie?" Elizabeth asked.

"She was my girl. A lifetime ago. We were going to get married."

"What happened?"

He laughed, but there was no mirth in his voice. "The war you may have heard about. I went to fight, and when I came back, my family's farm was gone. It just wasn't there anymore. Burned to the ground. My parents. My sisters. I don't even know where they're buried."

"Annie, too?"

Tears welled in Thomas' eyes. "Gone, too, with her family's farm. I still can't tell you which side did it."

"But you still love her."

"With everything I have." His hand brushed against hers. "But that's not to say life doesn't go on. I've tried, as much as I can."

Warmth rose in Elizabeth's cheeks. She looked away, though she let his touch linger a while longer. "We should keep looking through these books. There are more here than I remember."

Thomas nodded and turned his back to her, presumably to continue examining Alfred's collection, but his shoulders shuddered as he fought down sobs. Time passed in silence once again. After a while, the books all seemed to be the same to Elizabeth. Treatises on history and diplomacy covering everything from ancient Greece to the present, she had seen most of them before, and it wasn't long before she found herself nodding off.

She started awake when Thomas said her name. "Lady James, I thought you said your mother donated all of your father's books."

"She did," Elizabeth said, fighting back the fog of sleep. Thomas held a book toward her. "Then why would

Lord James have something like this?"

Elizabeth took the book from him. Her hands trembling, she opened the worn cover. She had seen this book before, but not since she was a child. It was her father's book on the folklore of the Balkan region, not just a copy of the book he had written, but *his own* personal copy. She leafed through the worn pages in terrified fascination. His faded notes were still visible in the margins of some of the pages.

"I doubt this is the book the Turk was looking for, but it *is* curious, don't you think? Where would Lord James have gotten this?"

"I don't know," Elizabeth said. "He's never expressed an interest before. Given his family, what happened to my father was never discussed."

"Perhaps you ought to discuss it with him now."

Elizabeth stared at the book. The air about it seemed disturbed, as if the residue of something foul clung to it. She brushed her fingers over her father's lingering handwriting.

FORTY

—⁓—

ELIZABETH DIDN'T SEE ALFRED UNTIL tea the next day, and even then he only spent a few minutes at the townhouse. He greeted her with a smile and a peck on the cheek before accepting a cup of tea from Sarah and drinking it down in an entirely improper amount of time. She held her breath when he went into his office to retrieve some papers, but he never gave an indication he noticed anything amiss. He also never gave her a chance to bring up her father's book.

She hadn't had the courage to remove it from his office, but she could feel it there every time she walked by the locked door. She could almost hear it whispering in her father's voice. Alfred had not changed. He was the same person as he had been the day before, but everything was different. Elizabeth found herself watching him as he ate a biscuit, as he put on his jacket, as he walked out the door, wondering if she really knew him at all.

At around five o'clock, a carriage came from the embassy to retrieve her. Lady Russell met her in the vestibule and rushed her to another side room. "I'm sorry for asking you to come on such short notice, but we've had a development, and I thought you'd want to be here."

"What's happened?" Elizabeth asked.

"We found Charlotte."

The name meant nothing to Elizabeth.

"The mistress of Count von Brunn." Lady Russell clarified.

Elizabeth frowned. She had forgotten all about the count's marital troubles as scribbled out in Friedrich's notebook, especially in light of more recent events. "What does she have to do with all this? Now that we know about Friedrich's penchant for blackmail, can't we assume he was blackmailing the count with the knowledge of his affair? I'm not so sure the count or this Charlotte had anything to do with whatever Friedrich's plans were for Jakob Amsel or me.

Lady Russell pursed her lips. "Apparently there's a little more to the matter, my dear, but we can let Charlotte explain herself."

Elizabeth regarded the ambassador's wife with incredulity. "You brought her here?"

"It was the only safe place."

Elizabeth could make sense of none of it. "Safe? From whom? Where is Mr. Ristić?"

"With Charlotte currently," Lady Russell replied, "watching her to make sure she doesn't go anywhere."

"Why would he have to do that?"

Lady Russell motioned for Elizabeth to follow her. "As I said, I think it's best to hear the story from her."

They entered a room on the second floor Elizabeth had

never seen before. The room's décor—clean lines and little in the way of ornamentation—seemed out of step with the rest of the embassy and told Elizabeth this room was not normally used to entertain guests. Mr. Ristić stood by a tall window. The only other occupant of the room, a woman, sat in a straight-backed chair nearby. Her expression was one of utter disgust. She had deep chestnut hair, a delicate upturned nose, and a finely sculpted jaw line. She was beautiful, but not in a memorable way. Elizabeth had the impression she preferred it that way.

When the woman saw Lady Russell, she turned to Mr. Ristić. "You said you would not be involving the Germans. How is this any better?" She spoke French.

"Mlle. Lefeuvre, Lady Russell is not here in any sort of official capacity," said Mr. Ristić.

"Yet," Lady Russell added. "Whether that changes has everything to do with what you say today, Mlle. Lefeuvre."

The woman glared. "What am I to say, Lady Russell? And who is this with you?" She flashed a venomous smile. "We have not been properly introduced."

Lady Russell's smile was equally as venomous. "This is Lady Elizabeth James." She turned to Elizabeth. "Lady James, allow me to introduce Viviane Lefeuvre."

Elizabeth offered the woman a halfhearted nod. "But where is Charlotte?" she asked.

Mlle. Lefeuvre barked a laugh.

"She is here," said Mr. Ristić. "But her name isn't Charlotte. In fact we're not sure if Viviane Lefeuvre is her real name either, but she won't give us another."

Elizabeth shook her head. "Mr. Ristić, I'm sorry, but I don't understand."

Ristić nodded toward the Frenchwoman. "Mlle. Lefeuvre is a French spy."

"As if you are any better, M. Ristić," Mlle. Lefeuvre spat. "You were not invited to participate in the Congress here, and yet you have come representing your government. Why are you here, if not to gather information you can use to exploit other nations on behalf of your own?"

Ristić set his jaw. "I do not lie or toy with the lives of others."

They stared at one another for several seconds, until Mlle. Lefeuvre looked away. "We all lie, M. Ristić, even if it is only to ourselves."

Ristić turned toward Elizabeth and Lady Russell. "I began asking questions discretely after the Count von Brunn's apparent suicide. Good servants are loyal, but only so far, and in this case, their loyalty did not extend beyond the count's death. They seemed more concerned with the well being of the recently widowed countess. I received a fairly good description of the woman who regularly visited the count while he resided in Berlin. The carriage driver who retrieved her kindly provided an address. I visited the address yesterday, a small townhouse on the Charlotten-straße actually. I did not expect to see her, but as I stood across the street, she exited the townhouse. I decided to follow her."

Mlle. Lefeuvre snorted derisively. "There was nothing wrong about my friendship with the count."

Mr. Ristić shot her a dubious glance before continuing. "She walked to a small café nearby and sat down at a table. I took a table not far from her. She ordered a cup of tea, and she sat there, by herself, while she watched the crowds walk by on the street."

Mlle. Lefeuvre continued to protest. "That is something many Berliners do every day."

"But what you did next, Mlle. Lefeuvre, is not so typical," Mr. Ristić chided. "You finished your tea and left your payment, but you left something else as well. A small slip of paper. Your waiter took it up, and before he went inside again, he passed it to another man."

The color rushed to Mlle. Lefeuvre's face. If she could have killed Mr. Ristić, Elizabeth was certain the Frenchwoman would have. "You cannot possibly have seen all of that."

Mr. Ristić grinned. "I may not be a spy now, but that doesn't mean I wasn't one in the past." He turned his attention to Elizabeth and Lady Russell once more. "Quickly I decided it would be best to follow the other man, whose final destination, after a few detours, was the French embassy. As it turns out, the café is about halfway between the embassy and Mlle. Lefeuvre's townhouse. Today, I went back to the café and I watched the scenario play out again. Except this time, before Mlle. Lefeuvre left, I introduced myself, and I told her that if she did not come with me, I would alert the German authorities."

Mlle. Lefeuvre jutted out her chin in defiance. "You have no proof I did anything wrong."

"And yet you are here," said Lady Russell. "The Count von Brunn, many believe, had the ear of the Crown Prince. Undoubtedly he knew a great many things that would be of interest to the French government."

The Frenchwoman threw up her hands. "What would you have me do? Confess? What good will it do anyone now? The count is dead."

"Did you kill him?" Ristić asked.

Her eyes grew wide. She drew herself up in her chair. "Absolutely not! He committed suicide."

There was ice in Lady Russell's voice when she spoke. "It might be difficult to convince the Germans of that, especially given that the count's suicide note mentioned your recently deceased husband. But you have no husband, deceased or otherwise, do you, Mlle. Lefeuvre?"

For the first time Mlle. Lefeuvre's composure broke. She jumped to her feet, her eyes filled with angry tears. "I did not kill him. I would never— You cannot do this to me!"

Lady Russell stepped forward. For a moment Elizabeth thought she was going to physically restrain the Frenchwoman. "We won't, if you tell us about Friedrich Wilhelm Henry Stanton."

At the name, the color drained from her face. "I'd be better off taking my chances with the Germans."

Mr. Ristić cocked his head to one side. "Why is that, Mlle. Lefeuvre?"

"M. Stanton is dangerous in a way the Germans never could be," she replied.

"Mr. Stanton is dead, Mlle. Lefeuvre," said Lady Russell.

Elizabeth had never seen the ambassador's wife like this. With the embassy staff she adopted such a motherly persona. Elizabeth had trouble believing she could be so cold.

Mlle Lefeuvre's face became a mask again. She sat in her chair once more. "I'm not surprised. I was certain one day he would trifle with the wrong person."

"Do you know who that 'wrong person' might be?" questioned Mr. Ristić.

She shook her head. "No, I don't."

Mr. Ristić continued his interrogation. "What was the nature of your interaction with him?"

Mlle. Lefeuvre sighed, apparently resigned. "He was ... useful. He was connected to a great many in the city's lower classes. He was always very good at finding out things."

"And had you used him to find anything out for you recently?" Just as with Lady Russell, Elizabeth silently marveled at the change that had come over the man. He was not at all the amiable statesman he had presented himself to be. What secrets did his past hold?

"He came to me," Mlle. Lefeuvre said. "He said he had something that would interest my government very much—some kind of ancient book containing secrets that would upend the current balance of power in Europe forever."

Elizabeth held her breath. *A book.*

Mr. Ristić made a clicking sound with his tongue. "Sounds overly dramatic. Did you believe him?"

Mlle. Lefeuvre met his gaze. "I did."

Lady Russell and Mr. Ristić exchanged glances. The Serb statesman leaned in closer. "What made you believe him?"

She continued to look him in the eye. "M. Ristić, I have seen many things in my life that cannot be explained using logic or reason. There are planes of existence other than our own. M. Stanton would not say where exactly this book was located or whether he even had it in his possession, but he seemed to indicate some spiritual help in finding it."

"Why did he choose to offer it to you?" Ristić asked.

"I was not the only one. M. Stanton implied he had approached other governments."

"Which ones?"

Her mouth spread into a sly smile. "He wouldn't say, of course, but I have my suspicions."

"Tell us."

She pointed a reproving finger. "Not without some assurances, M. Ristić."

Ristić glowered. "What do you want?"

"I want to leave here freely."

"Impossible." Ristić spat.

Lady Russell held up a hand. "We can agree to that." Mlle Lefeuvre and Mr. Ristić both opened their mouths to say something, but she cut them off. "Provided you leave Berlin and never come back."

Mlle. Lefeuvre's smile melted. "Leave? Where will I go?"

"That is none of our concern," replied Lady Russell.

"This is outrageous," Mlle. Lefeuvre hissed.

Lady Russell lowered her voice almost to a whisper. "I can have my husband contact Chancellor Bismarck if you'd prefer."

Mlle. Lefeuvre sat in her chair, looking daggers at the ambassador's wife. When she spoke her words dripped with acid. "I have heard rumors that there is a woman in Berlin, a Hungarian, who is a spy for the Austrians. I would not be shocked if M. Stanton had approached her."

"What about the Turks?" The question escaped Elizabeth's lips before she could stop it.

Mlle. Lefeuvre regarded her coolly. "Yes, the Turks, perhaps. The Russians, too, from what I've heard, have someone specifically working at this Congress to obtain secrets."

Mr. Ristić's eyes grew wide. "At the Congress? You mean part of their delegation?"

Mlle. Lefeuvre waved a hand in the air. "I don't know for certain, but that is a safe guess."

Elizabeth, however, did know.

Aleksandr.

The late meetings. The reports and letters strewn across Alfred's desk, all of them exposed to prying eyes. What if Aleksandr was using Alfred to steal Crown secrets? What if he was using her? Elizabeth suddenly felt sick. She placed a hand on the chair next to her to steady herself.

"Lady James, is everything all right?" Ristić asked.

She shook her head. "No, I'm sorry. I'm suddenly feeling a little faint."

Lady Russell placed a hand on her arm. "We can arrange a cab back to your townhouse for you. Mr. Ristić and I can handle things from here."

Elizabeth nodded. "Thank you."

She needed to find Alfred, to tell him what she knew. On the short ride back to the townhouse, her head swam with doubts about everything she had experienced since coming to Berlin. Valiant Gypsies. Alfred's inattention. Her father's calling cards. Thomas. Aleksandr. The Turk. Vampires. Just when she thought she had made sense of it all, everything fell apart again. She barely noticed when the carriage arrived at its destination. Still in a fog, she exited the cab and made her way up the steps to the door.

Alfred stood with Aleksandr in the foyer. Lord James smiled and came toward Elizabeth as she entered, his arms outstretched. He took her hands in his and kissed her on the cheek.

"There you are," he exclaimed. "I trust your afternoon with Lady Russell was enjoyable?"

Elizabeth never took her eyes off Aleksandr. "Yes, quite."

The Russian stared back at her, his green eyes gleaming.

Alfred followed Elizabeth's gaze. "Aleksandr Vladimirovich and I have a lot of work to do this evening."

"I'll have Sarah bring your dinner to your study," Elizabeth said.

Alfred smiled again. "Thank you." He turned toward Aleksandr. "Come along, my friend. I have some news to share about our progress."

Elizabeth watched the two men as they walked to Alfred's study. Just before the door closed, Aleksandr glanced over his shoulder. Their eyes met once more. The corners of his mouth turned up in an enigmatic grin, and he placed a finger over his lips. Then he disappeared into the study.

FORTY-ONE

—⁕—

Sighișoara, Romania
12 December 1999

ADAM GLANCED UP AS ARKADY walked into the room. The Russian's raised eyebrows effectively conveyed his belief Adam had finally gone insane. All the books Adam had collected were strewn across the floor, including the first edition of *Dracula*, *Description of the Székely Lands*, *The Land Beyond the Forest*, *Bulfinch's Mythology*, and *The Giaour*.

Arkady scanned the chaos. "What's all this?"

Adam concentrated on the notepad in his lap. "One technique for making a code less vulnerable to decryption is to break it up into pieces. Without all the pieces, you can't decipher any of it."

Arkady frowned. "I don't follow."

Adam sighed. "Like I said yesterday, I think Mihai used a Vigenère cipher. The circled letters in these books make up a coded message you need a key to decipher, but going through the books in turn didn't work. All I got was more nonsense, so now I'm going through them all together, taking one letter at a time from each book."

Arkady grunted. "Sounds tedious."

"I've been at it since this morning."

"Any luck?"

"I'm only just now finishing up the cipher's sequence. I still have to run it through the Vigenère grid using *Sighișoara* as the key."

"Well, I'd stay and watch, but ..."

"I know, it's a bit like watching paint dry. Where are you going?"

"To the police station with Felix to see if there are any leads on the whereabouts of our former colleague Anna Fyodorovna."

Adam merely nodded.

"Adam, if Clara's out there we'll find her."

Adam met Arkady's gaze. "She's out there."

After a moment Arkady turned and left without another word. Adam hunched over the books once more. Once he finished jotting down the last of the letters in the string of text, he reached for the Vigenère grid he had made and began the arduous process of deciphering the message. He didn't even know what language Mihai used.

English, as it turned out.

Word by word, a message formed from the jumble of letters, and as Adam continued to work, his heart pounded harder in his chest.

A time will come when
Shadow and Blood will overtake the World.
Look to the one who defends mankind.
Look to the Tower.
Look to where the Dragon sleeps.

When Arkady returned, Adam was waiting. Arkady had scarcely stepped through the door when Adam thrust his transcription in Arkady's face. "The Chindia Tower at the ruins of the Princely Court in Târgoviște. I think that's where the medallion is."

Arkady took the paper from Adam. "This is your decrypted message?" He scanned the page. "I see where it says, 'Look to the Tower,' but what is the rest of this? 'Look to the one who defends mankind.' 'Look to where the Dragon sleeps.' What does that mean?"

Adam shrugged. "It could all refer to the same place. They used to light a torch from the top of the tower each night at sunset to signal the closing of the city gates. The tower was integral to the city's defense. And the Princely Court was where Dracula slept when he was in power. Remember, too, Ceaușescu was fleeing to Târgoviște when he was captured. There has to be a reason."

Arkady scratched his beard. "Seems a little too convenient, though, don't you think? Something about this isn't right."

Adam snatched the paper back. "Do you have a better idea?"

Arkady sighed. "Not at the moment."

"Great. We can get going in the morning." Adam grabbed his coat from the hook next to the door.

"Where are you going now?" Arkady asked.

"Out," Adam replied.

Arkady crossed his arms. "Where?"

"The Vlad Dracul House."

"Do you want me to come with you? I could use a drink."

Adam shook his head. "I'd rather be alone."

"You know you never asked about Clara. I spent the

day trying to find her."

Adam paused with his hand on the doorknob. He choked down all the replies that immediately leapt to his tongue. "So did I."

"We followed up on every scrap of information we had. I'm sorry to say we didn't get very far."

Adam opened the door. Cold air assaulted them both. "I wasn't expecting you to."

"Adam, the sun is setting."

Adam peered out into the rapidly darkening evening. "I'll be careful. Nothing's going to happen to me."

Arkady scowled. "You get yourself killed, and I'm going to dig you up and kill you again, do you understand?"

"Absolutely." Adam closed the door behind him without looking back.

AS ADAM STOOD IN THE cold twilight underneath the wrought iron dragon adorning the Vlad Dracul House, the snow began to fall again. He didn't have to wait for very long. A sudden flurry kicked up, sending the snow swirling in a cyclone all around him and turning the world white for a moment. When the wind died down, a woman stood next to him.

He nodded. "Hello, Elena."

Her hands were thrust into the pockets of her full-length white fur coat. Even her cheeks were pink from the cold. Her act would have been completely convincing if she had been wearing a hat. "Good evening, Dr. Mire."

"I need to know something."

Elena chuckled. "Getting down to business quickly. I thought you'd at least ask me how I'm doing first."

Adam remained stone-faced. "I know how you're doing."

Her smile faded, and she sighed. "Must we go around and around about this again?"

For the second time that evening, Adam forced down the retort he wanted to make. "Do you want the medallion falling into the wrong hands? I just need some information."

Elena's bottom lip jutted out in an exquisite pout. "Fine, then. What do you want to know?"

"The Ceaușescus, are they really buried in their graves?"

"It says so on the markers."

Adam glared. "You know what I mean. Are they buried there or somewhere else? Are they buried at all?

Her eyes narrowed. "They are buried in the center of Bucharest, Dr. Mire, in the center of the devastation they orchestrated. They are dead, well and truly dead."

"But I'm asking the right questions, aren't I?"

Elena drew her mouth into a thin line. "There have been many throughout the years who have sought immortality without the consequences."

Adam glanced up and the iron dragon looming overhead, teeth bared, claws out, its tail wrapped around its neck. "Like Dracula?"

She followed his gaze. "He knew the consequences. He was willing to pay the price."

"He used blood magic to become a vampire."

She nodded. "Yes."

"So someone else could do the same thing."

"No, Dr. Mire. The spell has been lost to the ages."

Adam smirked. "I'm sure Dracula had a hand in making sure of that."

Elena used a long elegant finger to push a stray lock of

hair behind her ear. "As you say."

"But what if someone found a way?"

There was no joy in her smile, only pity and regret. "Then I'd say you'd best hurry and find the medallion, Dr. Mire."

The wind kicked up the snow again, and when it subsided, the vampire was gone.

FORTY-TWO

—⚬⚬⚬—

Târgoviște, Romania
13 December 1999

N O TOURISTS BRAVED THE COLD to visit the medieval stronghold of Vlad the Impaler on that
overcast day. Three figures crossed the empty
courtyard, leaving their tracks in the snow-covered
ground. Arkady walked in front, followed by Adam and
Inspector Stoenescu from the Bucharest Police, who had
joined them in case someone official was needed.

In one pocket Adam clutched his rosary, and in the
other he gripped the handle of his Glock pistol, but they
reached the door in the base of the Chindia Tower without incident. When Arkady pulled on the handle, though,
the door didn't budge. He tried again and gave the door a
violent shake when it still refused to open.

"That's unusual," Inspector Stoenescu said. "It's not
supposed to be locked during operating hours."

Adam's teeth chattered in the cold. "There's no one
here. Maybe all the staff went home."

The inspector shook his head. "Not likely. Even at night there's a guard." He started back across the courtyard. "I'll go find someone who can open this door."

"We should be careful," Arkady called after him. "I don't like this."

"What are you thinking?" Adam asked.

Arkady craned his neck looking up the stone face of the tower. "I don't know, but something's definitely off. Call it instincts."

Moments later, the inspector returned with an apologetic security guard. "I'm sorry, but we were ordered to lock the door. I can't let you up."

The inspector raised an eyebrow. "Ordered? Who order you?"

"I'm … I'm not sure. I didn't take the call. Victor did."

Arkady's eyes narrowed. "Did Victor say why you needed to lock the door?"

The guard eyed the three of them suspiciously. "No, he didn't."

"And you didn't bother to ask?" Arkady continued to glower at the guard.

He shrugged. "We haven't had any visitors today. I thought they'd decided to do some sort of maintenance work."

Arkady turned to Adam. "Now do you think I'm being paranoid?"

The guard continued to peer at Arkady warily. "What's going on here? Is something wrong?"

"That's what we're trying to determine," Inspector Stoenescu said. "Can you take us to your colleague? We need to speak to him."

After a moment's hesitation, the man nodded and motioned for the trio to follow him. A guardhouse stood on the other side of the courtyard. When they reached it, the guard called out, but no one answered.

"Victor?" he called again, but he was met only with silence.

The guard pushed on the door, but it wouldn't open. He put his whole weight against it. The door moved a few inches but wouldn't budge any more until Arkady and Adam joined the guard. Together they managed to shove aside whatever was in the way. The guard stepped inside and slipped in the puddle of blood on the floor. The obstacle turned out to be Victor.

His throat had been slit.

Arkady swore in Russian. "They beat us here."

Adam surveyed the bloody interior of the guardhouse. "How? I didn't figure out the code until last night."

The inspector knelt to examine the body. "Someone probably tailed us, figured out our destination, and then radioed ahead to others."

Adam suddenly felt exposed. He glanced over his shoulder, across the courtyard to the tower. "Do we even have any idea who *they* are at the moment? The Iron Guard, vampires, Chetniks?"

"Would someone just tell me what's going on?" The guard's face had gone pale, and sweat beaded on his forehead, despite the chill.

Inspector Stoenescu took him aside and sat him in a chair. "Don't worry. We're going to take care of this, okay?"

The guard nodded.

The inspector pat him on the shoulder. "Now why don't you take a deep breath and let it out slowly."

The guard did so, and Inspector Stoenescu put him in a chokehold until he passed out.

"Do you think that was necessary?" Adam asked as he

looked over the guard's slumped form.

"Yes," the Inspector and Arkady both said at the same time.

"We need to get to the top of that tower," Arkady added.

Adam's gaze went up to the parapets around the Chindia Tower's crown. "How do we make that happen?"

Arkady grinned. "We knock."

TEN MINUTES LATER THE THREE of them rushed out of the guardhouse and immediately came under fire. Adam kept his head down and ducked for cover behind a car parked nearby. Arkady and Inspector Stoenescu dashed forward, but they were forced to crouch behind a partially collapsed stone wall, originally part of the Princely Court's fortifications. Adam scanned the tops of the courtyard walls for a sign of the shooter but didn't see anyone. The gunfire had to come from the top of the tower. Getting there without being picked off would be impossible.

Adam couldn't get a good shot in from where he was, though his little Glock probably wouldn't have done much good anyway. Arkady and Inspector Stoenescu had heavier firepower, but even they wouldn't be any match for someone with a rifle. Adam watched as Arkady and the inspector discussed something, and from their hand gestures and facial expressions, Adam guessed they were having a minor disagreement. Finally, Arkady rose up on his haunches.

He was going to make a run for it.

Adam wanted to call out a warning, but he knew better. The gunman on the tower would shoot him as soon as he poked a hand out. Not knowing what else to do, Adam stood and took a shot. He immediately ducked back down as the bullets slammed into the car and threw up little puffs of snow around him. Arkady yelled something, but Adam lost it in the sound of the gunfire.

The distraction still wasn't enough for Arkady to make it.

Just then, the guard emerged from the guardhouse. Adam opened his mouth to shout for him to get back, but the guard had his own rifle. With a look of determination on his face, he raised it to his shoulder and fired. A choked scream came from the top of the tower, and then silence.

Slowly Adam stood. Arkady and the inspector did the same. They turned toward the guard, who nodded. They all raced toward the tower. When they converged on the door, the guard produced the key.

The inspector raised an eyebrow. "If I had known you could do that—"

"Sharpshooter in the Romanian army," the guard replied. "I'm sorry I panicked before. I've never seen a dead body up close."

On the other side of the door, they came upon a solidly build man holding a pistol. The report of Arkady's gun deafened Adam for a moment. They stepped over the man's body and rushed up the stairs. About halfway up, a bullet buried itself in the stone, inches from Adam's head. They all backed down. Someone hid behind the curve of the stairs.

Arkady motioned for the others to stay back. He crept up the stairs, back pressed to the inner wall. When he drew near to where the new gunman had positioned himself, he removed something from his pocket and threw it on the floor. When the gunman stuck his arm out to fire, Arkady grabbed him. They struggled for a few seconds before the gunman tumbled down the stairs, past the others, where he came to rest with his neck at an awkward angle.

At the next landing they came to, a ladder led to a trap door in the ceiling.

"Are there any more of them, or do you think we got them all?" Arkady asked.

Inspector Stoenescu motioned toward the ladder. "Do you want to be the one to open the door to find out?"

Adam sighed and started climbing. "Does it matter? We need to get up to the roof."

He pushed open the trap door and climbed into the frigid air. The rest joined him one by one. The dead shooter lay sprawled against the outer wall. No one else was on the roof.

Arkady glanced at Adam. "Well?"

"It's here. It has to be."

The snow had been cleared from half the roof. Adam started on the other half, uncovering the stones underneath. Arkady and the others followed suit until the roof was clear.

"Now what?" Inspector Stoenescu asked.

Adam scanned the roof again. Briefly his eyes fell on the gunman and the blood pooled beneath his body. It was starting to thicken, but Adam's gaze went to one particular crack where the blood appeared to seep in between the stones.

He strode toward the shooter's body "He was standing over it the whole time. Arkady, help me move our friend here."

After they heaved the body out of the way, Adam knelt down, and despite the blood he probed for a purchase with his fingers. After a few minutes he found a stone that moved, and with a little effort he was able to lift it. Underneath the stone was a cavity that held a wooden box.

Adam reached for it.

Arkady put a hand on his shoulder. "Wait, not here."

Adam's hand hovered over the lid. "We should at least see if this is the medallion, shouldn't we?"

"We'll take the box back to the guardhouse," Arkady said.

Adam could hardly contain himself as they all trudged down the stairs again. The medallion was there, so close, but Arkady was right. If such a thing as blood magic existed, exposing the medallion in the center of Dracula's stronghold might not be the most prudent course of action.

Adam practically ran into the room and set the box down on the desk. It had a lock, but an easy one to force. As the others crowed around, Adam pulled the lid off to reveal a small velvet bag. He picked it up. The weight was right, but when he untied the length of rope holding the bag closed and reached in, he pulled out yet another book.

Arkady swore in Russian again.

The book was small, with a hard, wooden cover wrapped in flaking leather. A tarnished silver clasp held it closed. Adam very carefully unfastened it. The pages were made of parchment each covered in writing and hand-drawn diagrams. Adam recognized at least half a dozen languages, including Greek, Latin, Aramaic, Romany, and Old Hungarian runes. In the back, though, he discovered a decidedly more modern slip of paper, and a name written in faded pen.

Gabriel Popescu

"That's a first," Inspector Stoenescu said, "a thief who leaves a calling card and doesn't steal anything."

FORTY-THREE

Bucharest, Romania
14 December 1999

A MAN STAGGERED DOWN THE SIDEWALK and passed out into the street, barely earning a glance from the three other men standing nearby, huddled against the cold. On every building iron bars covered the windows and graffiti covered the walls. Trash and debris filled in the spaces between. Yasamin eased the car to a stop in front of one particular crumbling brick edifice where garish neon lights shone through the windows.

Clara stared wide-eyed at the examples of humanity crowding the door. None of them she would have wanted to meet in a dark alley. "Tell me we're not spending the night here."

Yasamin eyed her coolly. "You have nothing to fear."

A sudden rush of anger warmed Clara's cheeks. "It seems to me I have a lot to fear. What are we doing here?"

"It's a necessary stop. We're not staying long."

"But what are we doing here?" Clara repeated, forgetting for a moment she sat in a car with a four-hundred-year-old vampire.

Yasamin's eyes flashed crimson, as if to remind her. "We're here for information." She opened the car door. "I can protect you inside. I can't if you stay here."

Reluctantly, Clara joined her. Few people looked in their direction as they entered the smoke-filled bar. The ones who did averted their gazes quickly as Yasamin and Clara made their way through the grey haze.

Yasamin approached a table in the back where a man sat. His girth pressed against the table's edge. A cigar hung from the corner of his mouth. A beer and a plate piled high with sausage links rested in front of him. Yasamin sat down across from him without saying a word and motioned for Clara to do the same.

Between puffs on his cigar, the man alternated between popping sausages into his mouth and taking swigs of his beer. He ignored them completely until the plate and the glass were both empty, and the cigar had been reduced to a stub.

"What do you want?" he asked without looking at them.

"I need information," Yasamin said.

The man pulled another cigar from his shirt pocket and used a table knife to cut off the end. "Then you should go find a library. They have lots of books that can help you there. As you can see, I'm not a librarian."

"No, Vasile, no you're not, but we both know that's not the kind of information I want."

Vasile glanced up for the first time, meeting Yasamin's gaze. If he was afraid of her, he didn't show it. "That kind of information comes with a price. Are you prepared to pay?"

Yasamin nodded. "I am."

Clara surveyed the bar. A number of patrons observed their meeting discretely, exchanging glances, whispering to their companions. One of them, a younger man in his twenties with a mop of curly black hair and a tattoo of a raven on his forearm, made eye contact with her and held her gaze. A smile spread slowly across his face.

"Who is she?" the fat man asked, bringing Clara's attention back to the table. "I'd be willing to part with quite a bit of information for her."

Clara knew the fear showed in her eyes. The fat man leered at her from across the table. He laughed, until Yasamin grabbed him by the chin and jerked him out of his chair.

"She is not your prize. Not tonight. Not ever. I am willing to pay you fairly for the information I need, but I will not play your petty games. Do I make myself clear?"

Those who hadn't been paying attention were doing so now. All other conversations stopped, and everyone stared in their direction. Clara searched for the man with the raven tattoo, but he was gone. With a wave of Yasamin's hand, though, everyone went back to their own business.

Vasile glared at her, but he nodded as he sat down again. "I know your kind. I'm not afraid of you."

"Then you're a fool."

His mouth twisted into an oily grin. "A fool you need. Now, about payment."

Yasamin reached into the bag she carried and placed a stack of German marks on the table. "There is an entire suitcase waiting for you."

The man reached across the table and snatched up the stack of currency. "What do you need to know?"

"I'm looking for some Russian agents."

The fat man chuckled. "Is that all? The easiest money ever. There are three Russian agents in this bar right now."

Yasamin's nostrils flared, but otherwise her face remained impassive. "Russian agents broke into my home and destroyed my property. Would any of these three know something about that?"

Vasile made a production of lighting his cigar, flicking the lighter open with an exaggerated gesture and taking several deep drags before he blew the smoke out slowly. "You'd have to ask them. It's no secret Ceaușescu left this country in tatters. The state of things has made the Russians ... nervous. They have a lot of secrets they would prefer remain hidden, things they did, people they disappeared, bargains they made. Only now, they have no way of ensuring those secrets don't escape to the West. The rumor is that they have sent in their people to tie up loose ends. Perhaps you know a thing or two about one of these loose ends?"

Yasamin narrowed her eyes. "If I did know anything, I wouldn't tell you."

Vasile's smarmy grin didn't diminish. "As you wish, but because I'm feeling magnanimous today, I'll give you a piece of advice for free."

Yasamin scoffed. "No doubt worth its price."

Vasile flicked the ash from his cigar. "That depends on whether you take it, now doesn't it? There is only one Russian you should be looking for. He can answer your questions, and you may not even have to pay him."

"And who is that?" Yasamin asked.

The fat man leaned across the table as best he could. "His name is Arkady Danilovich Markov."

Clara caught her breath. Vasile's gaze shifted to her. "Does that name mean something to you? Perhaps you have some information to barter, my dear?"

Yasamin smacked the table to direct his attention back to her. "Where do we find him?"

Vasile wagged a chubby finger at her. "Now that's a different question. Do you have another suitcase full of money for me?"

Yasamin crinkled her nose at the grinning fat man. "We'll find him ourselves."

Vasile shrugged. "Suit yourself."

Yasamin stood and signaled for Clara to do the same. "Thank you." She tossed a key toward Vasile. It hit the table and bounced, forcing him to scramble for it. "That is a key to locker three eighteen at the Piața Victoriei Metro station. You'll find your money there."

As she and Clara left, more eyes followed them. Outside Clara watched the shadows warily.

They had only taken a few steps toward the car when Yasamin held up a hand. "Wait."

A man, knife in hand, jumped out of the nearby alley and lunged at Yasamin. She sidestepped his attack and seized his arm, wrenching it backwards and breaking it with a sickening crack. He dropped the knife and tumbled into a heap. Yasamin picked him up as if he weighed nothing and snapped his neck.

She still clutched the body when another man leapt at her. She tossed the first man's lifeless form aside and backhanded her new attacker into a wall. He hit so hard he left a bloody streak as he slid down. When the third man emerged from behind a garbage dumpster, he wasn't so stupid. He kept his distance, the knife in his hand poised, a crucifix dangling in the other. Yasamin hissed. She tried to strike at him, but he drove her back with the crucifix while spitting out words Clara didn't understand.

Yasamin was still focused on the man when Vasile stormed out of the bar clutching a small handheld crossbow. Clara called out. Yasamin spun around, barely dodging the bolt. The other man took the opportunity to get a swipe in with his knife. The silver blade swept through her side. She cried out as the skin sizzled, but the man had made the mistake of getting too close. Yasamin shoved him between her and Vasile's next crossbow bolt. He let out a hoarse croak as he fell to the ground.

Eyes burning red with hellfire and fangs bared, Yasamin stared down Vasile, He fired the crossbow again, but the bolt went wide. Yasamin didn't give him a chance to fire again. She pounced.

He didn't have time to scream.

Watching Yasamin feed felt like some sort of violation. The act seemed so intimate, so personal, but Clara couldn't look away as much as she tried, as much as she wanted. When Yasamin finished, she let Vasile's body drop to the ground and turned to Clara. Her features had reverted to normal, but blood still dripped from her chin.

"Get in the car," she ordered.

Clara looked from her to Vasile's body. "What's happening?"

Yasamin's eyes narrowed. "Get in the car before you get killed."

This time Clara obeyed. Yasamin slid into the driver's seat, and they sped off into the Bucharest night as police sirens blared in the distance.

"What's happening?" Clara asked again.

Yasamin glanced at the rearview mirror. "I got more information out of Vasile than he intended. A price has been put on my head … and yours as well, though he probably would have kept you alive."

Clara shuddered at the thought. "Who would do that?"

Yasamin clenched her jaw. "Elizabeth."

FORTY-FOUR

Berlin, Germany
8 July 1878

ELIZABETH ASCENDED THE STAIRS TO the house
marked No. 5 for the second time, clutching the
invitation that had come by courier that morning.
As before, the girl with the olive skin and dark hair led
Elizabeth to the parlor where Mme. Kárpáthy had performed her reading previously.

Mme. Kárpáthy sat in the same threadbare chair, her
face illuminated in the candlelight, her hands folded in her
lap, and her cards displayed on the table before her. Jovan
Ristić occupied the chair opposite. Elizabeth tried to hide
her surprise underneath a smile as the two rose to greet
her.

Mme. Kárpáthy made a slight curtsey. "Lady James,
it's very good to see you again."

Ristić bent to kiss Elizabeth's hand. "Thank you for
coming on such short notice."

Elizabeth's gaze moved from Ristić to Mme. Kárpáthy,

to the cards lying face-up on the table. "I was unaware the two of you were acquainted, Mr. Ristić."

Had she just performed a reading for him?

Ristić glanced at the fortuneteller. His expression contained a great deal of affection. "We have known one another for ... a long time, but I promise to explain. We are waiting for one more to arrive."

The bell at the front door rang. The girl scurried to answer it, and moments later she led Lady Russell into the parlor. The ambassador's wife, too, seemed confused after appraising the scene. She looked to Elizabeth and Ristić, questioning each of them silently, but Elizabeth had no answers for her.

Mme. Kárpáthy curtseyed to Lady Russell, just slightly deeper than she had to Elizabeth. "Welcome to my home, Lady Russell. My apologies as I'm certain all of this is quite confusing for you." She turned to Elizabeth. "And I must apologize to you as well, Lady James, for cutting your reading short and for not being entirely truthful to you about what I saw."

Lady Russell cocked her head to one side. "Lady James asked you to ... read her fortune?"

"I'm afraid I don't understand." Elizabeth said.

"Nor do I, not entirely." Mme. Kárpáthy waved her hand over the cards on the table. "I've turned the cards over a number of times in the days since our meeting, and every time they point to something dark, like a shadow cast across the future."

"You can see the future?" Lady Russell frowned. Vampires she could accept, but genuine fortunetellers were apparently proving a strain on her credulity.

Ristić nodded. "Zsuzsana is quite good at it, actually."

"Jovan is exaggerating. I see what the spirits let me see.

With your leave, I want to perform one more reading, with all of you present. Jovan has told me some of what you have been dealing with, and I think having you all here will provide me with the energy I need to see more clearly."

"By all means," said Ristić.

Elizabeth looked to Lady Russell. "I would be lying if I told you I wasn't curious," the ambassador's wife said. "Go ahead, Mme. Kárpáthy."

Only Elizabeth, it seemed, felt a lump of dread in the pit of her stomach. Something inside her whispered a warning. She should say no. She should leave and never come back, but she couldn't do either. Reluctantly she nodded.

Without another word, Mme. Kárpáthy gathered up the cards in front of her and returned them to the deck. She closed her eyes and took several deep breaths before shuffling the deck and turning the cards over one-by-one, just as she had in the reading she gave Elizabeth. Elizabeth tried to make sense of the jumble of images—people, skeletons, devils, swords, pentacles—but she quickly gave up.

Lady Russell and Ristić watched intently as well, though it seemed they were just as confused by the unsettling illustrations. As Mme. Kárpáthy placed the cards one after another, an unnatural quiet settled over the room. No noises from the street, nor any ticking clock, not even Elizabeth's own breathing disturbed the silence. Outside a cloud passed in front of the sun. The room became dimmer, enough that Elizabeth had trouble seeing the cards.

The air grew colder, but the chill down her spine had nothing to do with the drop in temperature. A quick glance at Lady Russell and Ristić told her they were just as uneasy. Only Mme. Kárpáthy seemed oblivious to everything except for the cards in front of her.

She turned over a total of twenty-four, arranged in two interlocking circles. Her eyes open, but oddly unfocused, as if she were looking at something none of the rest of them could see, she placed the unused deck to one side and passed a hand over the cards. Several of them twitched, though Elizabeth told herself what she saw was just a trick of the weak candlelight.

"Four more will die before he is finished," Mme. Kárpáthy said.

Her voice contained an odd timbre, as if some other voice, deep and gravelly, spoke with her.

"Before who is finished?" Ristić asked.

Mme. Kárpáthy didn't acknowledge him. "Before the book is found four will die."

Lady Russell's eyes grew wide. "The book?"

Ristić leaned forward, reaching for the sleeve of Mme. Kárpáthy's dress, but he stopped himself at the last second. "Zsuzsana, what are you talking about?"

"The first will die of pride," Mme. Kárpáthy continued. "The second will die of greed. The third will die of vanity. The fourth will die of lust."

All the candles went out at once, though the air remained still, stale, oppressive.

Mme. Kárpáthy's voice echoed in the darkness. "The fourth will kill the third. The third will kill the second. The second will kill the first."

Elizabeth held her breath. *But who will kill the fourth?*

The cloud outside passed, and the sun shone again, filtering into the room through the curtains. Mme. Kárpáthy moaned and collapsed. Ristić rushed to catch her. He laid her gently on the floor, placing a pillow beneath her head.

He took her hand in his. "Zsuzsana, Zsuzsana, are you all right? Speak to me."

Her eyes fluttered open. "How … how did I get here?"

She tried to sit up, but Ristić placed a hand on her shoulder. "No, don't. Do you … do you remember anything?"

Mme. Kárpáthy shook her head weakly. "The last thing I remember clearly was placing the last card, the Hanged Man, and then nothing."

Elizabeth's gaze went to the table, to the last card Mme. Kárpáthy had turned over, a man hanging upside-down by his feet from a tree.

Lady Russell observed Ristić tending to Mme. Kárpáthy. "So you don't remember anything of what you said?"

Mme. Kárpáthy looked to Ristić, eyes wide in horror. "I spoke?"

Ristić nodded and proceeded to recite back to her what she had said. With every word, her expression became graver.

Elizabeth still stared at the strange upside-down man. "Do you know what any of it means?"

"I don't," Mme. Kárpáthy replied, "but I feel a darkness close by, one that I haven't felt since Vračar."

Lady Russell frowned. "What's Vračar?"

Ristić grimaced. "It's not important."

Mme. Kárpáthy clutched his arm. "Jovan, you don't have to protect me. They should know."

Ristić sighed. "Perhaps you're right. Perhaps I've been a fool. It is a story I had hoped to avoid telling, because it pains me to relive it. With your permission then, Zsuzsana?"

She smiled faintly. "You don't need my permission."

Ristić turned to Lady Russell and Elizabeth. "Vračar is

the name of a small neighborhood in Belgrade, near the center of the city. There is a hill there where nothing is built. It is covered in a thicket, allowed to grow wild. A humiliating event in our history happened on this hill three hundred years ago. The Turks disinterred the remains of St. Sava, our patron, and burned them. It has always been a place of foreboding."

He paused, took a breath, and glanced at Mme. Kárpáthy before continuing. "About eight years ago, when I was still in charge of the Bureau of Strange Occurrences, something happened in Vračar. The case took on great importance for us because what happened didn't occur in the countryside, but in Belgrade itself. Could you imagine if news that the fine citizens of our capital allowed their lives to be governed by superstition reached your Western press? We would have been a laughingstock."

"You weren't concerned just with appearances, though, were you?" Lady Russell asked. "Whatever happened was real."

Ristić nodded. "As much as I wish it weren't, I cannot deny what I saw. That summer was unusually hot, and over the course of several days in August, more than a handful of people died, most of them in Vračar. Of course, it was tragic, but we knew the cause was the heat. Such deaths are not unusual in the summer, especially among older people."

Lady Russell nodded. "We're not unfamiliar with deaths from the heat during the summer months, even in London."

Ristić's expression remained grim. "Rumors surfaced, though, that the deaths were not caused by the heat. Residents reported seeing unusual things on the hill, and dead animals were found at its base. It's impossible to say who

who first uttered the word 'vampire,' but once it was said, the panic set in. People refused to leave their homes after sunset. Vračar was a vibrant neighborhood, full of cafes, restaurants, and shops. Those places quickly became deserted, and as more people died, more extreme measures were taken, ones I hesitate to mention."

"Please, Mr. Ristić," Lady Russell said, "I assure you I've heard lots. You won't be upsetting me."

Ristić looked to Elizabeth, who nodded. He continued. "People mutilated the corpses, and despite threats of severe punishment, one night a mob invaded the cemetery of a church and exhumed several of the recently deceased. They claimed the bodies were not decayed at all. Though the people had been dead a few weeks, there were no signs of putrefaction. The hysteria spread. People said St. Sava was exacting his revenge. Because the Serbs had not honored their patron as they should, he brought a new plague onto the city."

Mme. Kárpáthy reached a hand toward him. "Jovan, please will you help me sit up?"

Ristić grasped her outstretched hand. "Are you sure?"

"Yes. I'm fine now."

"You don't have to stay and listen to the rest if you don't want to."

Mme. Kárpáthy shook her head. "No, it's all right, Jovan, but I appreciate your concern."

Once he had helped Mme. Kárpáthy to her chair, Ristić continued. "After the incident in the graveyard, the Bureau sent an agent to investigate, a young Hungarian by the name of Istvan Kárpáthy." He looked to Mme. Kárpáthy. "He was quite brilliant. In no time at all, he deduced that a number of the first victims were associated with a doctor at the hospital in the Dedinje neighborhood, not far from Vračar. Istvan concluded the doctor must have brought an infection from there, but the doctor himself was not sick, and when Istvan went to the hospital, he could find no signs of any infection. Unfortunately, the panic did not abate. Another person died, and soon there were protests to the city government demanding they do something about the 'vampire.'"

Elizabeth glanced at Mme. Kárpáthy, who stared at her hands folded in her lap. Her face remained impassive.

"They ordered soldiers stationed on Vračar Hill and more to patrol the neighborhood." Ristić explained. "They had the vagrants expelled, and any known petty criminals were apprehended. They thought that would be the end of it. They were wrong. On the very first night of the patrols, a soldier died. To hear the city leaders tell the story, it was simply an accident. Sometime during the night, he disappeared, and in the morning, they found his body at the bottom of an escarpment on one side of the hill. After that, the officials in the city hall couldn't order another patrol without risking a mutiny."

"I'm assuming no one truly believed it was an accident, then." Lady Russell watched Mme. Kárpáthy as well.

"Of course I knew there was no accident," Ristić replied, "but before I could act a man appeared calling himself a vampire hunter. Thomas Parson, our mutual acquaintance, Lady James. He said he would hunt down the creature and 'put a stop to its reign of terror.' We naturally assumed he was a charlatan. Istvan confronted him one evening. He swore he was serious. Hunting down the vampire was his 'duty' he said. Istvan ordered him out of the city before he could fan the hysteria any more. I also relayed the message that my agents would not be so kind to him if they saw him in Belgrade again."

"That must be what he meant," Elizabeth muttered.

"What he meant?" Ristić's brow furrowed.

Elizabeth's cheeks grew hot, remembering that afternoon in Wedding. "Mr. Parson wouldn't tell me what happened between the two of you, Mr. Ristić. He said it was your story."

Lady Russell raised an eyebrow. "Lady James, you've spoken with this Thomas Parson? Here, in Berlin?"

Elizabeth nodded. "He's a nuisance. He's constantly appearing at inopportune times, insisting he can help. He's done research on my father, it seems."

Lady Russell frowned. "Well, if he has knowledge pertinent to what is happening now, perhaps we should *all* be speaking with him."

"No," Ristić said quickly. "He has nothing of value to add."

Lady Russell narrowed her eyes, but she didn't push the matter. "Please, Mr. Ristić, continue your story, then."

Ristić and Elizabeth traded glances before he proceeded. "I vowed to put a stop to the panic, even if I had to go to Vračar Hill myself. In fact, Istvan and I planned to do just that when Parson again appeared at my office. I was in the process of having the guards throw him out when he said something I'll never forget. He called me ignorant. He said I was arrogant in attempting to root out superstitions, and that the deaths kept occurring because I refused to call it by its name. I don't know why I listened to him, perhaps because I didn't know what else to do, perhaps because I wanted to prove him wrong. He urged us to go to the hill with him to flush out the 'creature' in order to kill it."

Lady Russell pursed her lips. "But surely you had experience dealing with such ... matters."

"In the country, Lady Russell. Not in Belgrade itself. Politics tied my hands. My impossible task was to abate the panic and present a plausible explanation to the powers that be. That was how I found myself on Vračar Hill one sweltering afternoon. Parson, Istvan, and I arrived when the sun was still high in the sky. We fanned out to look for irregularities in the ground—loose earth and the like. We spent hours scouring every square inch of the hill. None of us found anything unusual, until Istvan spied something partway down the eastern slope—broken tree branches, too high to have been made by an animal. I stayed near the top of the ridge while he ventured down to look closer. I lost sight of him for a moment, and it occurred to me the trees were so dense that even during the day, a large part of the hill remained in complete shadow."

"Oh, no," Elizabeth whispered.

Ristić carried on, his jaw set. "When I spotted Istvan again a few minutes later, he was climbing back up the hill. He glanced up at me and shook his head. Apparently, he had not discovered anything. The creature chose that moment to attack. It could have been a bear, or a large cat as it pounced, growling and snarling. I tried to run toward Istvan, but a hand caught my arm, Mr. Parson's. He pointed up the hill. The sun had begun to sink below the ridgeline. Soon darkness would overtake the entire slope."

"He was your husband?" Lady Russell asked Mme. Kárpáthy.

She nodded. Her expression remained inscrutable. Elizabeth could only imagine her inner turmoil.

Ristić settled his gaze on the floor, unable, it seemed, to look at her at all. "As Istvan's screams faded away, a new sound took their place. The thing crashed through the underbrush, directly toward us. Parson dragged me up the hill, and we reached the ridgeline just ahead of the darkness. He didn't let me stop running until we were off the hill, into the neighborhood and safe, according to him, in a tavern. The next day I had Parson expelled from Belgrade again, and I returned to look for Istvan. There was no sign of him anywhere. After that, the deaths stopped, just as abruptly as they had begun. Life gradually returned to normal in Vračar, but everyone still believed there had been a vampire. The incident remains the greatest failure of my life."

"Mr. Ristić, it doesn't sound like you have anything to blame yourself for," Lady Russell said.

A melancholy reflected in Ristić's dark eyes. "I'm not finished. Late one evening a few months later, I saw someone as I stepped out onto the street to return home from my offices. I noticed him because of his odd gait. He approached me quickly, but he stopped when he was still some distance away. In the light of the gas lamps, I recognized him. It was Istvan. My heart stopped. He was dead. I just kept telling myself that. He was dead. Yet, we both stood there staring at one another. He never said a word. The moment seemed to last hours. I took my eyes off him, and when I looked back, he was gone. It wasn't really Istvan, I told myself. It was my grief and my guilt."

Silence pervaded the room, threatening to smother them all until Lady Russell at last spoke. "I'm terribly sorry, Mme. Kárpáthy."

Mme. Kárpáthy stroked the silver ring on the fourth finger of her right hand with her thumb. "Thank you, Lady Russell, but I am at peace, as is my husband."

Elizabeth did not like the implications of the last part of that sentence.

"I suppose the question now," Lady Russell said, "is

where do we go from here?"

"We find the book Mlle. Lefeuvre told us about. And the others Friedrich may have approached about buying it."

Elizabeth glanced at the Hanged Man again. The heavy black lines of the man's mouth were drawn into a twisted, mocking grin.

While we all try not to die.

FORTY-FIVE

Berlin, Germany
9 July 1878

THE SMELL OF ALEKSANDR'S STARCHED uniform lingered in the courtyard. He could only spare a few minutes to see her, he said. With the work of the Congress nearing completion, Prince Gorchakov required his assistance almost around the clock. Elizabeth wanted to ask him if he was spying for the Russians, if he was using her to stay close to Alfred, but he moment his fingers intertwined with hers and she rested her head on his chest, she no longer cared. When they parted, he left her with a kiss on her forehead and a promise to return as soon as he was able.

Elizabeth reentered the townhouse to discover all the lamps out. Only the one by the front door sputtered and struggled to stay alive. She crossed the foyer and turned the dial to allow for the gas to flow. The lamp blossomed, filling the room with yellow light and throwing stark shadows across the walls.

There on the table in the center of the foyer the calling card lay, a red-brown streak defiling its clean, white surface. She picked it up and read her father's name, which she had expected to see. She did not expect the words written underneath in elegant handwriting.

Death will wait no longer.

A shadow stirred near the door to Alfred's study. Elizabeth's heart pounded out of her chest. She had given Sarah the night off, and she hadn't seen Alfred in a few days. At that moment, however, she knew without a doubt that she was not alone in the townhouse. Another shadow moved and then more, detaching themselves from the walls, flowing like smoke around the foyer. She closed her eyes. She didn't want to look. She didn't want to see it, to acknowledge it was real.

"What do you want?" she asked. "Please just tell me what you want."

When she opened her eyes a black figure stood on the opposite side of the table, its face hidden in darkness, despite the lamplight. A scream stuck in Elizabeth's throat. The gas lamp went out with a pop.

For a moment nothing happened, and then a rushing wind swirled around the foyer, moaning with the voice of a thousand dead souls, past Elizabeth and through the front door. She turned and looked out into the night, beyond the open door swinging on its hinges.

The figure stood across the street, in the same place she saw Aleksandr on the morning shortly after she arrived in Berlin. It beckoned to her. The light of the streetlamps still failed to illuminate its face. Before she realized what she was doing Elizabeth stepped over the threshold into the balmy night. The dark figure pointed down the Wilhelmstraße toward the Palais Strousberg, and then it vanished.

Elizabeth strode across the street. There was no sign of the entity. She looked in the direction it had pointed. Something called to her, something she was meant to see. She started walking.

After a few blocks, the Palais came into view. Lights shown through many of the windows, despite the hour. Elizabeth wondered which room Alfred was in, whom he was with, if all his grand ideas would allow him to achieve his ambitions. After all, they were *his* ambitions. Elizabeth didn't share them. Maybe once she had, but Alfred refused to let her into his world, and too many empty nights had passed.

Elizabeth slowed her pace, unsure of what to do. She scanned the street, looking for the shadow figure, when a hand clasped her wrist. She let out a small yelp and spun around to find herself face-to-face with Thomas Parson.

Deep lines of worry creased his brow. "Lady James, what are you doing out here at night?"

Elizabeth jerked her hand away. "I could ask you the same, Mr. Parson."

He reached into his coat pocket and pulled out a small card. "I found this slipped under my door not even an hour ago. I've been chasing shadows ever since."

He gave it to Elizabeth to examine, but she already knew what it was, another bloodstained calling card emblazoned with her father's name and the same handwritten words. *Death will wait no longer.* "I found a card very much like this at our townhouse."

"What do you suppose it means?" Parson asked.

"It means what it says."

The new voice startled them both. The dark figure from before stood in the doorway of a nearby townhouse. Merely a human-shaped form in the foyer, the figure was now dressed in a gentleman's morning suit. A top hat obscured his face. The voice, though, while low and rough, did not seem like it belonged to a man.

Parson stepped between Elizabeth and the stranger. "Dr. Theodore Tolliver?"

The man strode forward. "Not quite, Mr. Parson. Consider me a harbinger, though in this particular case, I seem to be fulfilling the role of Cassandra. I have tried to warn you. Now death will no longer wait. Leave Berlin, before it comes to claim you both."

Elizabeth pushed aside Parson's arm, outstretched to protect her. "You left the calling cards for us?"

The stranger nodded. "Indeed, though I can't claim to have originated the idea. Friedrich Wilhelm Henry Stanton had them printed."

"The bloody ones only began appearing after he died," Parson said.

"What about my father's book?" Elizabeth asked. "Did you leave that as well?"

The man tilted his head to the side, and for just a second the streetlamp illuminated his eyes. They were a brilliant green, like Aleksandr's. "Yes, that as well."

"How did you get into the townhouse?"

The stranger's edges became indistinct, as if he were again preparing to evaporate into smoke. "I have means."

Elizabeth's anger flared. She took another step forward despite Parson's whispered warnings. "Why are you playing these games? Why bring up my father after all these years?"

The man laughed, a deep, raspy, and altogether unsettling chuckle. "Do you really need me to answer that question for you? It is because of your father's legacy that we are here now, after all."

Elizabeth shook her head. "I still don't understand."

The stranger stepped back into the shadow of the doorway. "The book of blood magic, Lady James. The one you kept. You should take it with you when you leave. Hide it. Make sure no one can find it." By the time the last sentence was finished, he had already vanished.

Parson looked sidelong at Elizabeth. "So the book everyone has been looking for, you've known about it. You've had it all along."

The anger still churned inside her. She balled her hands up into fists so tight her fingernails cut into her palms. She thought what had happened to her father was behind her. To have everything dredged up again, to have everyone reminded of where she had come from. She hated him, and yet, he was still her father. "Don't you understand? It's the only thing I have left of him."

"Lady James, there's more to this book than that if people are willing to kill for it. What's this about blood magic?"

Elizabeth turned away. "You wouldn't believe me."

Parson maneuvered around to face her again. "Trust me, I can believe in a lot. Let's not talk about it here, though." He held out his hand. "Your townhouse is closer than my room at the boarding house, and safer."

The corners of his mouth turned up in a reassuring smile, but the worry lines remained around his eyes. After a moment's hesitation, she placed her hand in his, and together they ran through the dark streets, though Elizabeth wasn't so certain the townhouse would be any safer.

"My father brought the book back from his last trip to

the Continent." Elizabeth explained after she ushered Parson into the sitting room and firmly locked the door behind them. "Mother wouldn't even touch it. She said there was something wrong with it. He told her she was overreacting. He said the book was quite a discovery, that they would name a chair after him at the university because of it. I was also forbidden to touch it, but of course that didn't stop me. I always snuck into his study to look at his books. That one, though. It seemed to call to me. I couldn't understand any of the writing, but I use to look at the pages for hours. When Mother gave away the rest of his books, I saved it."

"But if it's truly a book of blood magic—"

"I couldn't have known that, Mr. Parson." Elizabeth snapped.

"The mere fact that others think it is makes it dangerous," he said calmly. "You should get rid of it."

"Would that be wise, though?" Elizabeth asked. "It would be very easy for the wrong hands to get hold of it."

"But the wrong hands have already come for it once. There's no way of knowing who else besides your Turkish assassin is after it."

Elizabeth pursed her lips. "Actually we do know. Friedrich approached representatives of several governments. He was trying to sell it to the highest bidder."

Parson frowned. "What do you mean?"

As Parson listened, Elizabeth told him about the encounter with Lady Russell, Mr. Ristić, and Mlle. Lefeuvre. After she finished, he sat for several minutes, scratching his chin.

"Interesting. The question is, how did Friedrich know about the book?"

"He drove the carriage that brought me here from Vienna," Elizabeth replied. "He could have gone through my things when I wasn't looking."

Parson wrinkled his nose. "But how would he know the significance of it?"

"There are all kinds of rumors and legends about magical books." Elizabeth remembered the many folk tales her father told her, to the chagrin of her mother. "Maybe he didn't know. Maybe for him it was just another swindle."

Parson scratched his chin again. "Perhaps. Did you know Count von Brunn was left-handed?"

The question took Elizabeth aback. "What does that have to do with anything?"

"A friendly gendarme told me they found the gun he supposedly used to kill himself in his right hand," Parson said, "The gunshot wound couldn't have been made if he had been holding the gun in his left."

"Then you're suggesting he was murdered."

"Most likely, if not by Mlle. Lefeuvre herself then maybe by your Turkish assassin."

Elizabeth glared. "Stop calling him my Turkish assassin. You think the count was killed because of the book, and that's why Friedrich had information on him?"

"Absolutely, and I think your magical book is the reason Friedrich had information on Jakob Amsel as well. Over the past year, Amsel has conferred with several psychics and mediums to try to contact his daughter. He's even held his own séances. It's become something of an obsession with him."

Elizabeth gasped. "His business trip."

"What business trip?"

"He just recently came back from a trip to Serbia where he visited the villages of Paraćin, Kisiljevo and Medveđa, the same villages my father visited on his last tour of the Continent."

Parson's eyes grew wide. "And all places notorious for vampire panics. He was looking for the book, too."

"Maybe he still is."

"Where is the book now?" Parson asked.

Elizabeth had already decided what her answer to that question would be. "In a safe place."

He raised an eyebrow. "You're not going to tell me?"

She shook her head. "You'd try to make me give it to you."

"You don't trust me." He tried to hide his hurt pride, but she could see it, in the way he set his jaw, in the way his shoulders slumped.

"No, that's not the reason. I trust you more than anyone I've ever trusted." As she spoke she realized she was telling the truth.

"Then what is the reason?"

Elizabeth forced herself to look him in the eye. "You'll try to be the hero again, to stop the evil, to save the day. Mr. Ristić told me what happened in Belgrade. Maybe this isn't the time for heroes, Mr. Parson."

She expected him to get angry, to lecture her, to demand to know the whereabouts of the book, but he didn't. He stood and crossed over to her, and kissed her long and full on the lips. Just as she began to respond, he ended it and stepped back.

"Maybe you're right. Maybe this isn't the time for heroes, but I don't plan on letting that stop me. Evil will not take the day, not as long as I breathe." He walked out of the sitting room and across the foyer. At the front door he paused. "If you don't mind, I'll call on you tomorrow." He opened the door and stepped out into the dark.

Elizabeth crossed to the door and stood watching him

as he headed toward the Wilhelmplatz, where he would be likely to find a cab to take him back to his boarding house. From the opposite direction a man approached him. Something metal in the man's hand glinted in the light of the streetlamps. Before Elizabeth could call out, a flash of light erupted from the man's side, accompanied by a bang that echoed off the buildings. Parson lurched and crumpled to the ground. His attacker ran.

Elizabeth heard herself scream.

She rushed out to the street. Parson lay on the ground, his face ashen, his chestnut brown eyes glazing over. A bright crimson bloom spread across his chest. He tried to reach for her, tried to speak, but his breath only came out in ragged gurgles. She knelt and took his hand. He squeezed hers weakly and smiled.

"Annie," he whispered.

Then his fingers went limp, and one last breath left him.

Mme. Kárpáthy's words echoed in Elizabeth's head.

The first will die of pride.

The second will kill the first.

FORTY-SIX

—— ͣ̃ͣ̃ ——

Bucharest Romania
15 December 1999

ADAM AND INSPECTOR STOENESCU WAITED in a booth in the back of a dingy, crowded bar. Adam had done his best to contribute to the grey haze hovering over their heads. He had just lit another cigarette when a slight man with dark hair and a goatee slid into the seat across from them. The man nodded to the inspector.

The inspector greeted him in turn. "Thank you for meeting us, Gabriel."

Gabriel Popescu surveyed their surroundings, his mouth twisted in disgust. "Any reason in particular you chose this place?"

The inspector smiled wryly. "Less chance of an incident in a public place. Something the matter? You used to feel at home in places like this."

Popescu glared. "You know those days are long behind me."

Adam shifted in his seat. Whatever history the inspector and Popescu shared, he had little patience for delving into it.

"I'm sorry," Inspector Stoenescu said. "Gabriel, this is Dr. Adam Mire. Dr. Mire, Gabriel Popescu, reformed thief."

"Reformed *alleged* thief," Popescu corrected.

The inspector grunted. "Only because you were never convicted."

"And whose fault is that?" Popescu shot back. "In any event, I've worked at the National Archives for almost a decade now as a productive, law-abiding citizen. Speaking of which, I'm assuming this is about the missing documents."

The inspector raised an eyebrow. "Missing documents?"

Popescu frowned. "You mean you haven't heard?"

The inspector shook his head. "No. What went missing?"

Popescu leaned across the table and lowered his voice. "Everything we have about the Bucharest Vampire. You know the rumors. Secret military projects. Government experiments."

"Someone trying to erase the evidence?" the inspector asked.

"Or even worse, to recreate the results." Popescu reached into a coat pocket, pulled out a parcel wrapped in brown paper, and slid it across the table. "Fortunately, we keep copies."

Adam took the parcel and began to open it.

Popescu held out a hand. "No, not here. Incident or not, there are too many eyes."

Adam tucked the parcel into his coat. "Later then."

Popescu looked from Adam to Inspector Stoenescu. "So

why exactly are you here?"

"We found your name in a book at the top of the Chindia Tower," Adam replied.

Popescu made a pained expression and pounded a fist on the table. "I had hoped a day like this would not come, but given the state of the world I'm not surprised. Mihai is dead, isn't he?"

"Mihai Iliescu?" asked Adam. "How do you know him?"

"Mihai was a collector. He and I had a ... complicated business relationship. Sometimes we worked together. Sometimes we competed. I lost track of him after my change in careers. He's the one who put my name in the book, as insurance, so if something happened to him, his story could still be told. It's been almost ten years exactly since we were on top of that tower."

Inspector Stoenescu jabbed a finger at him. "You were there to steal the book."

"Yes, Inspector, I was going to steal it and anything else I could get my hands on from a dead dictator who spent decades stealing everything he could from the people of this country," Popescu snapped, face flushed red and nostrils flaring. "In truth I didn't know what I would find. All I knew was that Ceaușescu went to Târgoviște for a reason. He could have fled to Moscow, to Belgrade even, but he risked everything to get to Dracula's castle. Why?"

"Something I've often wondered myself," Adam said.

"Mihai knew what I was thinking. I was perhaps a little too forthcoming with my ideas of what Ceaușescu might be hiding after he and I shared a few bottles of wine on the evening of Ceaușescu's execution. He followed me the night I went to Târgoviște, and there, on top of the Chindia tower, he saved my life."

Inspector Stoenescu narrowed his eyes. "Saved your

life? How?"

"We weren't alone. There was ... something else there. I never really saw what it was, but I felt it. Claws and teeth." Popescu pointed to his head. "And I felt it inside here, too. I can't explain it, but I felt its hunger, its blood-lust. Mihai killed it. He shot it, and it fell off the tower. It almost took me with it, but Mihai caught me. He opened my eyes to a few things about our world that night."

A chill ran down Adam's spine, despite the bar's warmth. "Did he tell you anything about the book, or perhaps anything else about Dracula's legacy?"

Popescu shook his head. "Not that night, but he did contact me a few months ago. I suppose that would have been shortly before he died. He said he wanted me to keep something for him. A different book, a rare one that might be a valuable addition to the Archives. A book on Michael the Brave. I told him we already had countless books on Michael the Brave. He said I didn't have one like this, and if anyone came to ask me about the book from the Chindia Tower, I should give them this book as well. But I never received it. Now I know why."

THE MAN STANDING IN THE doorway of the townhouse where Adam and Arkady had taken up residence looked to be in his mid twenties. He had dark, curly hair and a sub-stantial five-o'clock shadow.

Adam glared as he approached. "Does everyone in the whole damned city know where we are?" he muttered.

Their eyes met, and the man reached into his coat. Adam tackled him before he could retrieve whatever it was, slamming his head into the hard wooden door. With his arm pinned across the startled man's throat, he leaned in inches from his face. "You're going to tell me who you are and who you're with, or I swear I'll kill you right here. I am not in any mood for games anymore."

"His name is Adrian, and he's with me," Inspector Stoenescu said. "You can stop choking him now."

Adam removed his arm. The man gasped for air. "You should tell him not to lurk in doorways."

The inspector sighed. "What is it, Adrian? Why couldn't you report to the station?"

"I tried. They told me you were away," Adrian said.

"And what's so important you had to come to me personally?" the inspector asked.

Adrian held up his hands. "You told us to report to you personally if any of us saw Clara MacIntosh. I saw her. Last night."

Adam grabbed Adrian's coat lapel again. "Where?"

"At a bar on the wrong side of town," Adrian replied, bracing for another assault. "She was with another woman."

Elizabeth, Adam presumed. "Blond hair, blue eyes, insanely gorgeous?"

"No, black hair, dark eyes, olive skin." A twisted grin spread across the police officer's face. "But insanely gorgeous."

Adam let him go and shoved him away. "Yasamin? What were they doing?"

Adrian straightened out his coat. "Talking to Vasile Cernat, a known money launderer and blackmailer. I couldn't tell what they were saying, but the conversation was intense."

Adam looked to Inspector Stoenescu. "Why don't we ask this Vasile Cernat what they talked about then?"

"We can't," Adrian said. "He's dead. He tried to orchestrate an attack on them outside the bar, and the woman you called Yasamin killed him and a few others. I couldn't help Clara. I tried, but there was no way to get to her. Yasamin was driving a silver Mercedes. I have the license number."

Adam stewed for a moment. He still wanted to punch Adrian for not doing anything to help Clara, even though he knew the police officer probably couldn't have without getting killed himself.

"This has to end." Adam pivoted and marched away from the townhouse.

"Where are you going?" Inspector Stoenescu asked.

"To ask for help," Adam replied.

ADAM WAITED IN THE COLD in the Ghencea Civil Cemetery, at the gravesite of the Ceaușescus. He was a fool for being there at dusk. If any of the vampires he had encountered so far decided they wanted him dead, he couldn't do much about it.

As if to punctuate his thought, Elena stepped out of the shadows and took a place beside him. "Come for more advice?"

Adam stared straight ahead at the two simple graves marked with crosses draped in the blue-yellow-red Romanian tricolor. "I need to know how to end this."

She laughed. "What makes you think you can? How do you know things aren't already too far gone?"

"*Look to the one who defends mankind. Look to the Tower. Look to where the Dragon sleeps.*" Adam recited. "Those are the riddles Mihai gave me to solve. So far I've only been able to decipher one, and I still don't understand how anything fits together."

"You understand more than you think you do."

"What do you mean?"

"You found something at the Chindia Tower, yes?"

He nodded, unsurprised she already knew about the excursion to Târgoviște. "A book."

"More than a book," she corrected. "A book of blood magic."

He risked a glance at her. As always she looked exquisite. This time she wore a hat to match her fur coat and a scarf that set off her green eyes. For a moment, he longed for the touch of her lips again. "There's no such thing as blood magic."

"A lie you tell yourself, Dr. Mire. There have been creatures like us since the dawn of humanity, but our blood is not the only way to transmit the 'curse' as you would call it. Dracula made himself."

Adam remembered the vision of the botanist in the forest. His blood froze at the realization. "It's the book the old Roma carried."

"That's your second riddle. Now about the first, who is the defender of mankind?"

"Alexander. Alexandru. Iskander. Lek," Adam replied. "All the names he took are variations of the same. They all mean 'defender of mankind.'"

"And if I'm not mistaken, you already have a book about a man named Alexander."

Again, Adam wasn't shocked Elena would know about the book by Ioan Nicolescu. "You mean *The Life and Death of Michael the Brave*? What's so special about it?"

She laughed again, a sound like silver bells ringing. "Maybe if you read the book of blood magic you'll find out."

"Maybe," Adam forced himself to focus. "What about

the last riddle. *Look to where the dragon sleeps.*"

"The simplest one of all, and interesting, given we're standing at a gravesite."

Adam shook his head. "The medallion is not here. You said so."

She stepped closer. "True, but where does the Dragon sleep, Dr. Mire?"

He frowned. "Nowhere. Dracula doesn't have a grave."

Elena sighed, a beautiful, perfect sound. "You and I know that, but what about everyone else, everyone who doesn't believe in vampires? What do your rational historians say?"

"They say Vlad the Impaler is buried at Snagov Monastery."

"Then that is your answer, Dr. Mire." She ran a bare finger across his frozen face. He shuddered at the touch. "I pray you haven't run out of time."

Smiling, she stepped back into the shadows and was gone.

FORTY-SEVEN

—⧟—

From the Journal of Ion Rimaru

Bucharest, Romania
5 March 1971

THEY CAME FOR ME AGAIN this morning, the men. I was sleeping. Everyone else was gone. One of the men put a gag in my mouth so I couldn't scream while the others held me down. They stabbed me in the arm with a syringe. I watched as the red liquid flowed into me. No matter how hard I struggle, they always win.

My roommates think I hurt myself. I told them the truth, that it wasn't me, but they didn't believe me, so I let them think what they want, let them think I'm odd, let them keep their distance. They don't want to share in my hell anyway.

Things are happening now like they always do. I feel the liquid moving through my body. It is all I can feel. Up my arms and down my legs. When it reaches my heart, the pain begins. I scream, or at least I think I do. I don't remember much after that usually.

When I wake up it's night. Thunder rumbles outside and flashes of lightning tear open the sky. I don't feel any pain anymore since my heart has stopped beating. It's exactly the same as all the other times. I can hear the rain beating on the roof of the dormitory. I can hear my neighbors. They are talking about a football match. I can hear my neighbors on the other side, too. They're having sex. In fact I can hear everyone in the entire dormitory. I know all their conversations. I know all their secrets.

I can smell them as well, the humanity all clustered together, inside the building and outside, in the other buildings, in the city. I walk across the room to the window. It's completely dark, save for the flashes of lightning, but I don't need any light. I can see as clearly as if it were day.

I open up the window, and even though we're on the fourth floor, I throw my leg over the sill. The rain is soaking into my clothes, but I don't care. I don't feel the cold. The rest of my body goes through. I land on the ground without breaking any bones. I stand and run away as fast as I can, faster than I should be able to run. I need to get away, in case someone saw me leave, and also because I need to find someone. I need to get to her.

The first time the men came I felt ecstasy I cannot describe, but it was short lived. One of my hallmates brought his girlfriend to visit. I could smell her the instant she entered the building. I couldn't help it. When they came up to the floor, I went out to see them. I watched them go to his room. She saw me staring at her. I recognized the look in her eyes because I had seen it in the mirror. It was fear. She grabbed hold of her boyfriend's arm and moved closer to him before they entered his room.

I prowled outside the room all night. I wanted to be in

there, with her. I wanted her, but there was nothing I could do about it. It was driving me insane, when suddenly the pain came back. I doubled over, and stumbled back to my room. I locked myself in the bathroom and stayed there until the pain passed, maybe a few hours I don't know. I went to bed, and when I woke up in the morning, my senses had returned to normal.

The second time the men came, I knew better. I knew I couldn't stay in my room. I would not be able to help myself. I left as soon as I could. I went out into the city. It was incredibly foggy that night, foggier than I ever remembered. And it didn't move like normal fog. It seemed to part around me wherever I went. It swirled and turned, casting shadows all around, seeming to direct me. I didn't know how far I had walked when I saw her, or rather smelled her. I smelled her blood. She was walking by herself, still in her waitress uniform. I assumed she was going to her house. All I knew was that I couldn't let her reach her destination. I made my move when she was walking by a park. I changed somehow. I couldn't describe it. I still can't. I moved into the shadows. I became part of them. I flowed through the fog until I was directly behind her. She never heard me.

I grabbed her arm and spun her around. She screamed and struggled to break free, but I was too strong for her. I pushed her against the fence. Even closer her smell was intoxicating, overwhelming. Something in my jaw hurt. I wanted her. I had to have her. All reason left me. I bit her neck, hard enough to break the skin, and as her blood flowed into my mouth, the feeling of euphoria came back. I had flashes, too, of her fear and her terror, which just made me more excited.

I felt her heart falter, but then I grabbed her arm. As

soon as I touched her bracelet, my skin burned. When I pulled my hand away it was blistered and red. She ran, but I couldn't follow her. I looked at my hand again. As I watched the blisters disappeared, and the skin went from red to pink. I suddenly felt so weak. I staggered back to the dormitory and collapsed into my bed.

Tonight, I don't feel like I will make the same mistake. The rain, like the fog, is not a normal rain. The drops seem to part around me. I hear the beating of every heart in the city. I find her as she walks on the street. Despite her umbrella she's getting soaked. I've learned my lesson from the last time. I disappear into the shadows, and I come up behind her. I seize her and don't give her a chance to struggle. My jaw hurts, and I feel my teeth move. I bite her in the neck, and that familiar feeling comes again. I hold her until her heart stops, and then I let her body slump to the ground. I kneel over her. I stroke her wet hair and run my hand over her cheek.

29 May 1971

I HAVE BEEN SITTING IN this cell for two days now. They caught me by tracing me through my doctor's note. I left it with one of the bodies. I did it on purpose. I want this to end. I couldn't turn myself in. I don't think they would have believed me, or worse, they would just turn me over to the people who have done this to me. I knew the only way was to give them no choice, was to let them catch me. I thought they'd kill me, but they didn't, and now I'm here.

My father came to visit me yesterday. He didn't say anything. He just looked at me, frowning. In his eyes I saw disappointment, but not in me. I saw disappointment in himself. He had failed. I knew he was involved in what is happening to me. All my life I have known he was tangled up in our corrupt government. Ever since the war. He let them turn me into this monster. I know he did.

I suspect they let me have a pen and paper because they want me to write down what I'm thinking, so they can read it later. Use it against me. Let them. It won't change anything. The place where they are keeping me has no windows, but I know when the night comes. What they did to me, it's changed me permanently. I can tell when the sun is setting. It drives me mad. I can't help the screaming, the ranting. Most of the time I don't even know what I'm saying. Maybe I'm hallucinating, I don't know. I see images from the past. I see armies and battles. I see blood and death, mountaintop fortresses. I scream about murder, betrayal, death, until the guards can't stand it.

During the day they try to question me, but I have a hard time putting my thoughts together when the sun is up. I try to focus on the words they're saying, but they don't always make sense. They scream. They yell, but I can't respond. I forget how to talk. Sometimes they hit me. They would never dare do that at night. It doesn't matter. None of it does. I know what is going to happen to me. I know I deserve it.

23 October 1971

THEY ARE COMING FOR ME. I'm not ready. My father should be here. He should see what has happened to me. He should see what they've done to me. I won't go without a fight. I will let everyone know what they have done. They will not be able to hide from it. They made me into a monster, just to see what would happen. They are coming. I hear their footsteps. I will not be silent. The world will know about the Vampire of Bucharest.

FORTY-EIGHT

—⁓—

Braşov, Romania
16 December 1999

YASAMIN DROVE THROUGH THE NIGHT. Clara watched the cold, dark countryside fly by in silence. She could have run when Vasile and his goons attacked Yasamin. She could have escaped, but she didn't. She stayed, willingly. She even helped, and now she couldn't shake the feeling she had made a mistake. Of course she didn't share her thoughts with Yasamin, though she wondered how much the vampire already knew.

She rested her head against the window and closed her eyes. When she opened them again, the car was stopped, and the sky was considerably lighter. They were parked in front of a house on a quiet, tree-lined street in the kind of neighborhood found in every city in Europe. No lights shone through any of the windows.

"Where are we?" Clara asked.

"Braşov. This is where the trail leads." Yasamin climbed out of the car without offering any further explanation.

After a moment's hesitation, Clara followed. For all her second-guessing, she'd still rather deal with the devil she knew than the one she didn't. Instead of going to the front door, Yasamin slipped around the house to the door in the back. She turned the knob and pushed it open. Creaking, it swung inward.

"There is no threshold here," she announced. "This is not someone's home anymore."

Clara peered into the dark house. "If I didn't know better, I'd say you expected the door to be unlocked."

"I did," Yasamin said as she stepped through the doorway.

They found themselves in the kitchen. To Clara, the house certainly looked like it was still someone's home. A bowl of apples rested on the table, none of them rotten. A teakettle sat on the stove, ready to use. In the adjacent living room, a copy of the newspaper from the day before lay folded neatly on a table next to the sofa.

As they neared the stairs, Yasamin tilted her head to the side, an odd look on her face, and then she simply dissolved into the shadows, leaving Clara alone. The stillness of the house seemed unnatural, menacing. Her heart pounded in her chest.

"Yasamin," she called up the stairs.

There was no answer.

Slowly, she climbed up to the second floor. At the very end of the hallway there, a door stood ajar. Light spilled out into the dark corridor.

"Yasamin," Clara called again, "are you in there?"

Still no answer.

She crept to the door and pushed it slowly open.

"Yasamin, are you in—"

The question died on Clara's tongue. A nightmare confronted her. While the rest of the house was neat and orderly, the bedroom where Clara found herself had been completely ransacked. As Clara stepped over an overturned nightstand, pieces of a shattered lamp crunched beneath her shoes. Her gaze, however, was fixed on the blood spatter that arced across the floral wallpaper and the older couple who lay on the bed, both of them with their throats torn open.

Yasamin stood at the foot of the bed. "I smelled the blood. It appears Elizabeth has already left."

"Who were they?" Clara asked, her mouth suddenly dry.

There was a desk in the corner. Yasamin went to it and opened a drawer. While she sifted through the papers she found, Clara looked at the photographs in frames on the dresser. In one of them the man and the woman smiled at the camera while sitting on a park bench, their arms around one another. In another picture, they each held a small child. Grandchildren, Clara guessed.

"Their names were Costin and Stela Florescu," Yasamin said. "She was a housewife. He was an accountant."

Clara forced herself to look at the bodies. "What do they have to do with anything?"

Yasamin shook her head. "Nothing. Elizabeth needed to feed."

Clara balled her hands into fists. Hot tears streamed down her cheeks. She ran out of the room and down the stairs, back to the relative normalcy of the living room. By then the dawn light filtered in through the closed blinds.

"They didn't do anything," she screamed when Yasamin appeared next to her seconds later. "Their only sin was being in the wrong place at the wrong time. This isn't right. It shouldn't be this way. I'm sick of this. I'm sick of the death."

A fire flared in Yasamin's usually impassive eyes. "Life is about death. You were in the wrong place at the wrong time as well. Do you believe you have been treated unfairly?"

"I do, as a matter of fact." Clara replied.

"Even though you made the choices that led you here?"

"I just wanted to make sure Adam was still alive. I didn't know about all this."

Yasamin pointed up to the second floor. "Neither did they. Right or wrong, this is the world. If you don't accept it, then you will end up like them much sooner than otherwise."

Clara took a deep breath and wiped her tears away. "How did you know Elizabeth was here?"

Yasamin hesitated before answering. "We share a ... connection. A weak one, but if I concentrate, I can follow her trail. It's easier when she's feeding."

"Then you knew what we were likely to find."

Yasamin nodded.

"You could have warned me."

"Would it have helped?"

Clara started to reply when a noise came from outside. Through a part in the blinds, Clara glimpsed another car pulled up in front of the house, an old junker from the days of the Communist Bloc, the kind that ran on a lawnmower engine. A man climbed out of the driver's side. He was thin, with shaggy blond hair and a wispy beard. He reminded Clara of the patrons of the hipster bar in Berlin she'd walked into accidentally once. He didn't approach the door. He just stood, staring at the house.

"He knows we're inside," Yasamin said.

"How?" Clara asked. "Who is he?"

"I don't know his name, but I know why he's here." She shot Clara a sideways glance. "You must go outside and speak to him."

Clara balked. "Me? What if he's armed?"

"He probably is, but he won't try to hurt you."

"How can you be so sure?" Clara studied the man, trying to note any place he could conceal a gun or a knife.

"No one told him to."

When it became evident she wouldn't get any more of an explanation, Clara sighed and went to the door. She opened it just a crack at first. The man didn't move. She made the gap wider, just enough for her to step through, and she pulled the door shut behind her. Still the man didn't acknowledge her.

Not until she spoke up. "Excuse me. Can I help you?"

He looked at her, and a strange grin spread across his face. "Good morning. My name is Miroslav. I'm here to deliver a message."

He spoke English with a heavy accent. Clara waited, but he stood silently again, the odd grin seemingly frozen in place.

It didn't take long for Clara to lose her patience. "Are you waiting for the secret password? 'The crow calls at midnight,' or something like that?"

"I'm supposed to deliver it to your mistress."

Clara scowled. "She's not my mistress, and in case you haven't noticed the sun is up. She's not coming out here, and trust me you don't want to go in there. So tell me your message."

He blinked once, then nodded. "They are going to Snagov."

Clara resisted the urge to choke him. "They? Who are

they? Is that supposed to mean something?"

"It will mean something to her." He made a move to get back in his car.

"Wait," Clara called. Miroslav paused. She took several steps toward him. "Take me with you, away from here. Please. You don't have to take me very far. You can drop me off at a police station."

The man grinned again. "I'm sorry. I can't do that."

"Why not?"

He gestured toward the house. "She's watching. She'd kill me."

Clara glanced over her shoulder. She couldn't see Yasamin at the window, but it didn't mean she wasn't watching somewhere.

"Besides," Miroslav added, "I was just sent here to deliver the message."

"Who sent you?"

Miroslav fixed her with his gaze. "You are safer remaining where you are."

He climbed back into the car, leaving Clara to watch him pull away as angry tears welled up in her eyes again.

FORTY-NINE

—◊—

Berlin, Germany
10 July 1878

THE GUARD AT THE PALAIS Strousberg looked dubiously at the bloody calling card Elizabeth passed
to him, but she had few options. It was the only
thing certain to get Lady Russell's attention. Mere minutes later, the ambassador's wife greeted her.

Elizabeth uttered the only two words she could at that
moment. "It's started."

She hadn't slept. Every time she closed her eyes, the
words burned, searing into her brain. *Death will wait no
longer.* She saw too, visions of Thomas dying in the street,
over and over, blood spreading across his chest, the life
leaving his eyes. Now she sat beneath the willow tree by
the pond in the Tiergarten where she had first met him.
Lady Russell sat with her. When Mr. Ristić approached,
they both stood and joined him on the path.

"Thank you for meeting us here this morning," Lady
Russell said.

Ristić merely nodded. Lady Russell had dispatched a courier to inform him of Thomas' death. She had told Elizabeth not to worry, that she would take care of everything. Elizabeth didn't doubt her capabilities, but she worried nonetheless.

"Mr. Parson and I had our differences," Ristić said. "I cannot say that I liked him, but he did not deserve to die the way he did. I'm sorry you were forced to witness such a horrible thing, Lady James."

On the pond the sunlight danced in the ripples made by the swimming swans. On any other day Elizabeth would have enjoyed the scene. "Thank you."

"Where is the … body?" The question seemed to pain Ristić.

"It's safe in a basement room in the Palais," Lady Russell answered.

"May I see it?" he asked.

Lady Russell frowned. "I suppose, if you wish."

"Yes, please. It's important."

Lady Russell merely nodded.

The room where Thomas' body lay was directly across from where Elizabeth and Lady Russell found Friedrich's body. Elizabeth couldn't help but look at the spot on the floor as they passed by. The events of that day seemed a lifetime ago.

Thomas had been placed on a table, still dressed in his bloody clothes. His hands were folded over his heart. His skin was an unnatural bluish tint, but more disturbing were his eyes. They were open. Once bright and clear, full of intelligence and humor, they were now cloudy and empty, seeing nothing. Elizabeth almost expected them to move as they approached. She could only imagine the stories Lady Russell must have concocted to convince members of the embassy guard to retrieve him from the street and put him there.

Ristić stooped over Thomas. He reached into the pocket of his waistcoat and pulled out a handkerchief. Using it to shield his hand, he probed the body, which was still stiff. He traced over the two marks on the side of Thomas' neck. They had turned a deep purple.

Ristić reached into his pocket again and produced three silver coins. Two he placed over Thomas' eyes. The third he placed in Thomas' mouth. He also placed a tiny silver cross in between his fingers.

"He must be buried this way," Ristić said after he finished, "soon preferably."

Elizabeth forced herself not to look away. "He didn't have any family left, or a home. It's not fair. He shouldn't be forgotten in some unmarked pauper's grave."

Lady Russell placed a reassuring hand on her arm. "He won't be forgotten. And his grave will have a marker."

"What do we do now?" Elizabeth asked. "What Mme. Kárpáthy prophesied, it's coming true. There are going to be three more deaths if we can't stop them somehow."

"I'm not sure what we can do." Lady Russell's expression was apologetic. "The things Mme. Kárpáthy said were too vague. If we had anything—a name, a place, a time—we might be able to put a stop to this madness, but we don't have any of those things."

Elizabeth struggled to remember everything she could about the reading. "What about the tarot cards themselves? Could they provide any clues?"

Ristić shook his head. "I don't remember any of them."

In her mind, Elizabeth went back to the candlelit parlor and Mme. Kárpáthy's long, elegant fingers peeling the cards from the deck one-by-one, turning them over, and placing them on the table. They were all a jumble of contorted images, all except for the last one. "I remember the Hanged Man. What does that card mean?"

"The Hanged Man represents in-between states." Ristić explained. "Neither light nor dark. Neither asleep nor awake. Neither dead nor alive."

"Like a vampire," Elizabeth whispered.

The word seemed to hang in the air, making the room seem darker, colder, damper. Elizabeth didn't risk another glance at Thomas' body, afraid of what she might see.

"Perhaps we should visit Mme. Kárpáthy again," Elizabeth suggested. "Maybe another reading would reveal more."

Ristić sighed. "That we cannot do, I'm afraid."

"Why not?" Elizabeth asked.

"Because she's gone," Ristić replied. "I received a letter from her this morning. She said it's not safe here in Berlin anymore for her and her daughter."

"I would imagine so, after the reading we witnessed," Lady Russell remarked.

Ristić expression remained grim. "There is more, though. It appears she was in Berlin as a spy for the Austrians."

Lady Russell's eyes grew wide. "Two female spies?"

Ristić shifted on his feet. "The situation was not entirely her choice. She apparently owed a debt to some Austrian government official who assisted her after Istvan's passing. As you can imagine, the world is not an easy place for a widow with a young child. Something disturbed her enough to risk reneging on the repayment of this debt."

"Perhaps Friedrich approached her about this mysterious book," Lady Russell offered.

Ristić stroked his beard. "That is possible."

Elizabeth didn't need to speculate, though. She was certain Friedrich had approached Mme. Kárpáthy, just as she was certain Friedrich had tried to scare her with the first few calling cards—the unbloodied ones—and referred her to Mme. Kárpáthy, in the hopes the psychic could discern more about the book. Only Mme. Kárpáthy had seen dark things when she tried to read Elizabeth, dark enough for her to leave the city entirely.

"But what do they all have in common?" she asked. "Count von Brunn wasn't a spy."

"His mistress was," Ristić pointed out.

Elizabeth struggled to hide her growing agitation. "Even so, Mr. Parson wasn't."

"Are you sure?" Ristić raised an eyebrow. "How much do we really know about Mr. Parson, other than what he told us all?"

Elizabeth risked another glance at the body. Thankfully it hadn't moved. "The scars on his neck are real."

Ristić's gaze wandered to the two marks on Thomas' neck. "Maybe so, but what about everything else?"

"Are you suggesting he could have been a spy as well? For the Americans?" Elizabeth didn't like the implications of Ristić's line of questioning.

Ristić shrugged. "Can we prove he wasn't?"

In her head Elizabeth thrashed about for a lifeline, something solid to hold onto, to keep her sanity. If she had told Thomas where she kept the book, he would have taken it from her, she was sure. She thought it was because he wanted to protect her, but what if he just wanted the book for himself, or for his employers? What if he didn't care for her the way she believed? What if none of them did? What if Aleksandr…

She wouldn't finish the thought.

"Maybe," she said, "we can continue our conversation elsewhere."

Upstairs in the vestibule of the Palais, Elizabeth asked another question. "If all this has to do with the spies Friedrich approached about this book, then why did he have information on me in his journal? I'm not a spy."

Ristić cocked his head to one side. "You're married to a diplomat. Isn't that close enough?"

"Mr. Ristić, Lord James is nothing if not doggedly devoted to the rules," Lady Russell said reproachfully. "He wouldn't even know where to begin if he were confronted with such a conspiracy as this."

"Lord James would have told me if Friedrich approached him." Elizabeth echoed. "I'm certain of it."

She wasn't so certain, though.

Ristić persisted. "There is your father to consider. He was a scholar with ... unusual interests. He was familiar with the folklore and legends of my region. He would have owned quite a few books on the subject, no?"

Elizabeth's cheeks turned hot. "I'll tell you what I told Mr. Parson. My mother got rid of all his books. I have nothing of his."

Ristić nodded. "As you say."

Elizabeth suddenly felt tired. "I believe I have had enough for one day." She turned to Lady Russell. "I'd like to take my leave, if you don't object."

WHEN THE KNOCK AT THE door came, Elizabeth expected Sarah to answer, but another knock followed, louder this time. After the third, even more insistent, Elizabeth set aside the latest batch of correspondence arrived from England—gossip mostly—and emerged from her bedroom. Still clutching the letter opener, she descended the stairs. She crossed the foyer and opened the door to find herself reflected in the spectacles of a short, balding gentleman.

He smiled at her. "Good afternoon, Lady James."

She smiled politely back. "Good afternoon. I'm sorry, but I don't believe we've been introduced."

"We haven't, Lady James, but you've no doubt heard about me." He presented a calling card. "My name is Jakob Amsel."

Elizabeth's heart leapt into her throat at the sight of the small white card. She took it from Amsel's outstretched hand, hoping he didn't notice the tremble in her own. It bore his name in thick Gothic letters, nothing more. "Mr. Amsel, we weren't expecting you, but I'm pleased to make your acquaintance. Please come in."

"Thank you," he said as he stepped over the threshold.

"I'm afraid Lord James isn't here right now."

"Oh, but I haven't come here to see him. I've come here to see you."

"Me?" Her voice rose in surprise. "Whatever for?"

Amsel's smile melted. He produced a gun, a derringer he had concealed in the sleeve of his coat. "Give me the book and I'll leave."

Elizabeth regarded the cold, metal weapon in Rosen's hand and then glanced down at the letter opener in her own.

"Careful now," Amsel said, as if reading her thoughts. "Let's not do anything rash."

She took a step back, toward the stairs. "I ... I don't know what book you're talking about."

He sneered. "Of course you do. It's a small book with parchment pages and a tarnished silver clasp. Your father stole it when he was traveling through Bosnia ten years ago."

"Mr. Amsel, my father was a distinguished scholar. He did not steal things."

Amsel laughed. "I have yet to meet a scholar who doesn't steal things. It's all they do. And your father did steal this book. An old man in the village of Kisiljevo told me so. It was kept in a church there. They discovered it missing after he left."

"Even if what you say is true, why do you think I have it now? As you said, that was ten years ago, and my father is dead."

"He disappeared," Amsel corrected. "You don't know he's dead."

"He's dead," Elizabeth insisted. "It's the only explanation."

Amsel's twisted grin grew wider. "No, it's not the only one. And you have the book. Friedrich Stanton told me so."

"Why would he tell you that?"

"I paid him to look for it," Amsel replied, "and he found it, but he got greedy. He double-crossed me and decided to sell it to the highest bidder. If he hadn't met his unfortunate end, I would have killed him myself."

Elizabeth shook her head. "He lied to you. He didn't find anything. It was all a scam to get money. And I still don't understand why you think I have it."

Amsel stepped forward. "Come now, Lady James. Your father disappears, your mother dies in a carriage accident, your aunt dies in a fire, and your first husband dies of an illness no doctor can cure. The book brings misfortune with it."

"Then why do you want it?"

A tear ran down his cheek. "I want to talk to my daughter again. When she was sick, I brought in doctors from Paris, London, even New York. No one could cure her either. After she passed, I tried different means of contacting her. Nothing worked."

If it weren't for the gun pointed at her, Elizabeth might have felt sympathy for him. "How will this book help you?"

"It's a book of magic, blood magic. It contains instructions on how to contact the other side, and perhaps even cheat death."

"But blood magic requires a sacrifice."

He chuckled. "Then you do know something about it after all."

"I am my father's daughter. I share his interest in folklore. Nothing more."

Amsel's smile disappeared again. "Enough of these games. Where is it, Lady James?"

"I won't tell you," she said.

"Then I'll kill you."

"And you won't get the book."

"It's here. I'll find it," he snarled. "You don't think I have the fortitude to pull the trigger? I killed Count von Brunn after Friedrich approached him about buying the book. I even made it look like a suicide. It seems he couldn't bear to live life without his mistress after realizing they could never truly be together. Very romantic."

"You killed the wrong person. Friedrich was trying to get to his mistress. She was spying for the French, feeding them information she learned from the count."

"Was she now? It doesn't matter. Count von Brunn and I have had business dealings. He knew about my daughter. I couldn't afford to risk him finding out about my interest in the book. He would have used it against me."

A cold chill passed through Elizabeth. "You killed Thomas, too. Why?"

"You mean Thomas Parson? The American. He asked too many questions about me. He was remarkably good at inserting himself in matters that were none of his business. By the way, I'm really interested in how the two of you became acquainted."

"He had an interest in my father's work."

Amsel's eyebrow inched upward. "Are you sure he didn't also have an interest in you?"

Elizabeth stood up as tall as she could. "That is not any of *your* business, Mr. Amsel."

"As you say." He licked his lips. "But it is perhaps you husband's business."

White-hot anger burned in her. If she could have clawed his eyes out she would have. "You wouldn't dare."

He thrust the barrel of the gun closer. "Where is the book, Lady James? It belongs to me. I will not be denied now. I always get what I want."

Before she could answer Alfred burst the door. His faced was flushed. He had been yelling. His face always turned red when he was angry. When he saw Amsel with a gun aimed at Elizabeth, his eyes widened in surprise, then narrowed in cold determination. His entrance threw Amsel off his guard. Alfred rushed at him and tackled him to the floor. He almost succeeded in wresting the gun from Amsel's hand, but Amsel, surprisingly strong for his age, fought back fiercely. They tumbled over one another.

And then the gun fired.

The noise left Elizabeth's ears ringing. For a moment her heart stopped. Alfred and Jakob Amsel both lay still on the floor, blood pooling underneath their bodies. Elizabeth screamed Alfred's name. He didn't respond right away, but then there was a groan. Alfred pushed Amsel's lifeless body off of him and sat up. Blood soaked the front of his shirt.

The second will die of greed.

The third will kill the second.

Elizabeth ran to him and knelt, paying no attention to the blood soaking into her dress. "Alfred. Alfred, are you all right?"

He looked at her and nodded. "Help me up please."

After he managed to get to his feet he glanced down at Amsel's body. "Who was that? Why was he pointing a gun at you?"

"A madman. He wanted something he said belonged to my father."

"And here I thought we were finally rid of his legacy." He rested his hands on the table and sighed. Elizabeth had never seen him look so ... broken.

"What's wrong, Alfred?"

"I'm through. I'm ruined. What are we going to do about this?" He waved his hand over the foyer. "I just shot and killed a man."

"We tell the truth," Elizabeth said. "Lord and Lady Russell will believe you. They'll take care of it."

"Will they?" he spat.

Elizabeth stepped back from him. "You don't think so?"

Alfred took a deep breath. "I think, that very shortly I will be returning to England, in disgrace at best. In shackles at worst."

"Alfred, what happened?"

"My plan, Elizabeth, the one I've been working on this entire time, the one that would have put me on the path to becoming Foreign Secretary one day. It was rejected."

"The plan, the one you were working on with Aleksandr Vladimirovich?"

"The same Aleksandr Vladimirovich who double-crossed me."

Elizabeth couldn't imagine such a thing, but then she remembered the look he gave her that day as he entered Alfred's study, the finger over his lips. "How did he double-cross you?"

"He promised me Russia would back my proposal. He assured me they all thought it was genius—a confederation of independent buffer states all along the border with Turkey. Multiple pawns for the Powers to maneuver against one another. The balance restored. No need for war, at least not in our generation."

"It's a brilliant idea." She meant it.

He scowled. "A shame no one else thought so. The Russians, the Austrians, even our own government, they all seem to want war. The treaty they've cobbled together accomplishes nothing. They even went out of their way to humiliate Jovan Ristić and the delegates from the other minor powers. Mark my words, because of this there will never be peace in Europe."

Elizabeth had never seen Alfred so impassioned. She wouldn't have guessed it possible. What he said also explained why Mr. Ristić had been so testy earlier.

A shadow appeared at the open door. They both turned their heads to find Aleksandr Vladimirovich struggling to take in the scene before him. The rage ignited in Alfred's eyes anew.

"You! How dare you come here after what you did. Get out! Get out now!" Alfred rushed toward the Russian, hands balled into fists, but just as Elizabeth thought Alfred might punch him in the face, Aleksandr grabbed him by his jacket and slammed him against the wall, as if he were nothing more than a rag doll. Alfred slid down to the floor, clutching his shoulder.

"Why did you do that?" Alfred asked through clinched teeth.

"You attacked me," the Russian growled. "Just like it was not my countryman who made an ultimatum, who slammed a list of demands down on the table and declared in front of everyone that a train was waiting to take the entire British delegation away from Berlin at that moment, if they were not agreed to."

Alfred's brow furrowed in confusion. "That was just for show. Lord Beaconsfield couldn't let everyone know we had a secret deal. That speech was for the sake of the other Powers and the smaller nations. All Prince Gorchakov had to do was bring up my proposal. Lord Beaconsfield and everyone else would have immediately agreed."

Aleksandr grunted. "No doubt they would have."

"Then why didn't Prince Gorchakov say anything? Why did he just agree to the British demands? The last time we spoke, you said the plan was in place."

"It was," Aleksandr replied. "My plan."

Alfred's brow knit in confusion. "What do you mean, your plan?"

"All I ever cared for was ensuring my country regained its sovereignty, able to command its own destiny, to recapture its greatness." His accent changed, losing its sharp Slavic qualities. "And I did. Under the new treaty Romania is free. Just know that you played your part perfectly. My useful idiot." He lifted Alfred up and pinned against the wall with his right hand. His left hand closed around Alfred's throat. "Of course, you aren't really useful anymore."

Alfred looked to Elizabeth. The hands that had been balled into fists now trembled. The eyes that had burned with rage were now wide with fear. "Please, Elizabeth, run and get help."

Elizabeth didn't run. She looked away.

"Elizabeth, please go for help. Why are you just standing there?"

Aleksandr laughed. "Perhaps she doesn't want to help you."

"That's absurd. Why wouldn't she help? Why? Elizabeth, tell him he's wrong. Please."

Elizabeth said nothing.

"Please, Elizabeth, tell him he's wrong."

Elizabeth still did not reply.

The tears welled up in Alfred's eyes. "Why, Elizabeth, why? I love you, Elizabeth. I always have. Everything I've done, it's been for you, to give you the life you deserve, the life you've always wanted."

"Have you ever asked her what kind of life she wanted?" Aleksandr asked.

"Elizabeth, please," Alfred whispered.

Aleksandr met Elizabeth's gaze. He released his grip, and Alfred tumbled to the floor. "It would appear the two of you have some things to discuss. I should let you." As abruptly as he appeared, he vanished.

Alfred looked at Elizabeth with the rage he had reserved for Aleksandr earlier. "How could you just stand there? He was trying to kill me."

Elizabeth watched him, but she couldn't bring herself to respond.

Alfred climbed to his feet. "Dammit, Elizabeth. Answer me."

She shook her head.

He rushed toward her and grabbed her by the shoulders. "Answer me!"

He started shaking her, but then suddenly stopped. An odd squeak escaped his lips, and his expression went from anger to shock. He released her and backed away. The letter opener protruded from between his ribs. Elizabeth had forgotten she still held onto it. Alfred looked down at it and slowly wrapped his fingers around it. He winced as he pulled. When the letter opener was free, he dropped it on the tile floor. His breathing had become uneven. He coughed and spat blood. Clutching his side, he fell to his knees. Blood oozed between his fingers.

He glared at her. Between pained breaths, he spoke. "I … always … loved … you."

He tried to return to his feet, and when that didn't work, he crawled toward her. His eyes losing focus and his breathing becoming more and more ragged, he only made it a few feet before he collapsed. He reached a bloody hand toward her, and with one last gasp he gave up and closed his eyes.

Elizabeth knelt and picked up the letter opener.

The third will die of vanity.
The fourth will kill the third.

FIFTY

—∿—

Berlin, Germany
11 July 1878

A GAIN, LADY RUSSELL TOOK CARE of everything.
Already rumors circulated through the city of Industrialist Jakob Amsel, who tragically lost his life
trying to save Lord Alfred James and his wife from a robber. Sadly, Lord James was killed as well, and the robber
escaped with a large part of Lady James' priceless jewelry.
Lady Russell had a room for Elizabeth arranged at the
Palais Strousberg. She reasoned, rightly, that Elizabeth
would not want to spend any more time in their townhouse. A wire had been sent to Alfred's oldest brother, and
he was already on his way to Berlin to retrieve Alfred's
body, and her as well.

Elizabeth lay in bed, staring at the ceiling, waiting. At
the insistence of Mr. Ristić a holy wafer rested above the
door.

She had torn it in two.

Just before midnight, Aleksandr appeared, though she

didn't hear him enter. The shadows shifted subtly, almost imperceptibly. The room became colder, stiller, darker. When he slipped his strong arms around her she wasn't startled. She pressed her body to his, wanting to be as close to him as possible.

She turned to face him and admired his compact, powerful build. She placed a hand on his bare chest and felt the beating of his heart. He radiated heat. When he kissed her, his warm breath set her skin aflame. Only, none of those things should have been. A spike of fear pierced her thoughts. What if she was wrong?

He seemed to sense her hesitation. "Let me give you what you never had with him," he whispered. "Please. Let me do this for you."

She nodded. He kissed her again, first on the lips, then on the neck. He knew all the places to touch her, his fingers following the curve of her breasts and her hips. She closed her eyes and let him take her.

When she opened her eyes again she was no longer in a room in the Palais Strousberg, or in Berlin at all. Firelight flickered dimly through the canvas walls of the tent. The smell of cloves, cinnamon, and paprika filled her nostrils, and underneath was the smell of horses and fresh straw and sweat. Rough woven blankets lay under her. Somewhere a violin played a frenzied tune, accompanied by an accordion and a guitar. Elizabeth looked up not into the face of Aleksandr the Russian attaché, but Alexej the Gypsy.

He smiled at her and took her in his arms. "Welcome back."

Their intertwined bodies moved together to the rhythm of the violin, growing slick with sweat as they tumbled together over the floor of the tent. Alexej's taut muscles gleamed. Back and forth they shifted as they each explored one another with their hands, their mouths, their teeth. Nothing else mattered. Nothing else existed except the two of them in the Gypsy camp on a night out of time, accompanied by the staccato notes of the violin. As the music rose to a crescendo, so did their exertion until the pleasure overwhelmed Elizabeth, and the world went away.

Some time later, Aleksandr stood up from the bed. His eyes burned crimson, and in faint moonlight, his long, sharp, white eyeteeth gleamed.

He offered his hand. "It's time."

Smiling, she placed her hand in his.

FIFTY-ONE

Braşov, Romania
17 December 1999

JONATHAN STUDIED ELIZABETH'S FORM AS she stood
by the window, her bare ivory-white skin luminous in
the silver moonlight. He came up behind her and
wrapped his arms around her waist. The red-tile rooftops
of the sleeping city spread out before them. The stone façade of the Black Church rose up in the distance, and behind it loomed the Transylvanian hills.

A naked man lay in the bed behind them, his body
smeared in blood. Jonathan hadn't enjoyed the feeding
much. The ones they had chosen, the ones they had duped
into helping them by telling lies about the resurrected Iron
Guard, did not possess the strongest minds. The memories
Jonathan drank up along with the man's blood were of
petty grievances and petulant entitlement. Nothing was
worth experiencing.

Except one thing.

The moment the man realized it was all a lie. The

shock and surprise at the betrayal. There was no Iron Guard anymore. There never would be again. There was Elizabeth, and there was Jonathan, and their scheme to finish what they had started ten years earlier. The man was a pawn. He had been used. And when he was no longer useful, he became a meal.

Jonathan put his lips to Elizabeth's ear. "Tell me, my dear, what lovely thoughts are you having right now?"

"We should have known all along to go to Dracula's grave."

The luckless man they had just shared came to deliver a message, that Adam Mire and his entourage were on the move again, headed in the direction of Lake Snagov and the monastery where legend had it Vlad the Impaler was finally laid to rest.

"The others have figured it out as well," she added, with a slight edge to her voice.

"What do we do if the medallion is on the monastery grounds?"

Elizabeth glanced over her shoulder at the body on the bed. "We have ways of getting around those rules, remember?"

He chuckled. "Of course. When do we leave?"

"Tomorrow night."

"Have you determined how to do it? How to actually end him?"

Elizabeth turned to face him. She traced a finger over his chest and down his stomach, sending a charge of electricity through him. "Why don't you just leave that to me? We almost destroyed him the last time. We just didn't have all the pieces. This time will be different, you'll see."

Jonathan combed his fingers through her golden hair. "Soon you'll have what you want."

Elizabeth nuzzled his chest. "Soon *we'll* have what *we* want. No more moving in the shadows. No more hiding. I'll make myself a queen, and you'll be my consort."

He kissed her, relishing the acrid, metallic taste of blood still lingering in her mouth. "Only you'll be a very different Queen Elizabeth."

FIFTY-TWO

Lake Snagov, Romania
18 December 1999

ACCORDING TO YASAMIN, THE LAKESIDE villas once provided a haven for Communist Party higher-ups, including Nicolae Ceaușescu. Now they could be rented by anyone with enough money.

Clara stood on a wide balcony overlooking the lake. Yasamin's words from the previous evening still echoed in her ears. She had made the mistake of telling her about her dreams of Elizabeth's life.

Yasamin's eyes widened. "You dreamt of her? What did she let you see?"

"Mostly a lonely and unhappy woman whose husband abandoned her for his work, who chafed at the role her society expected her to play, and who was swept up in events she couldn't control. I might have made the same decision she did."

Yasamin frowned. "You shouldn't empathize with her."

"Why not?" Clara asked. "Adam told me about you and

337

Elena, how you were trapped by your circumstances. Dracula offered you a way out. Elizabeth doesn't seem any different."

"She is," Yasamin said, a little too quickly.

Clara sensed something more. "How?"

Yasamin pulled the corners of her mouth up in a vicious grin. "Did she show you how she murdered her own father for having an affair with a chambermaid?"

Clara shook her head in disbelief. "But she would have only been eleven years old."

"Nonetheless it is the truth. She murdered her mother a few years later by pushing her in front of a carriage and making it look like a suicide. She burned her aunt's house to the ground, and she poisoned her first husband."

"How is that possible?" Clara asked.

"Think about what you saw. Did she ever say or do anything to contradict what I've told you?"

Clara suddenly felt like retching. Again everything she thought was true had been thrown into turmoil. It's what the vampires did. They made you question everything, including who you were.

"She used blood magic to call Dracula to her," Yasamin continued. "She wanted to use him for her own ends."

"What does she want now?"

Yasamin was silent for a moment before she answered. "To watch everything go up in flames."

NO LIGHTS SHONE ON THE lake. Across the water, the small island where the monastery stood was barely visible in the pre-dawn light. As quietly as she could, Clara opened the door to her bedroom. Yasamin had taken the bedroom on the other side of the villa's living area. The door was ajar, but the lights were off.

Of course Yasamin didn't need the lights.

Clara had to hold herself back from running. She merely willed one foot in front of the other. Only when she reached the front door and the daylight did she break into a sprint. Her shoes crunched in the light dusting of snow on the ground. She kept to the line of trees ringing the perimeter of the grounds, still feeling vulnerable and knowing not all of her enemies had a weakness to sunlight. Although when she reached the driveway that led to the main road, she had no choice but to step out into the open.

The urge to look behind her persisted, and she wondered if she'd ever be able to walk down a street without the overwhelming feeling of being stalked, hunted. Every time a shadow flickered, she jumped, exactly what she wanted to avoid when she made the decision to stay with Adam and help him finish his mission. Now she wasn't even sure she'd live to see another day.

In truth, she stayed for another reason as well. Adam himself. When she saw him for the first time, she couldn't deny the tiny ember that still burned with her feelings for him. She wanted for things to go back to the way they had been, but she realized that was only a foolish dream. Things would never be the same.

Clara should have paid more attention to where she was going. When she looked around, she didn't recognize anything. She thought the driveway would take her back to the main road, but of course they had arrived at night, and it was hard for her to see. Because the ground sloped down to her left, she assumed the lake was in that direction, but up ahead the road curved to the left as well. She was certain they had approached the lake from the other direction.

As she tried to decide which way to go, the sky darkened. The wind picked up and underneath the crisp smell of the snow she caught a whiff of something familiar, enticing—cinnamon and sage. The bottom of her stomach dropped out. She didn't want to look back. She knew what she would see. She had come all this way without looking back. She began walking again, slowly, one step at a time. She didn't make it very far.

"Clara, look behind you," Jonathan said.

She came to a halt. "No."

"Why not?" he asked.

"I can't."

"Of course you can. You can do anything."

Clara shook her head. "Not when you're involved, I can't."

"Clara—"

"Don't. Don't say my name. There is nothing between us. Nothing real."

"You know that's not true."

"I know what you are. I know what you do."

"I'm not going to apologize for what I am. I didn't ask for it."

Clara let out a mirthless chuckle. "Now who's lying?"

"I was not in a position to refuse what was offered."

"So are you giving me a choice? You should know better. I'd never—"

"What will you do otherwise? Go back to a man who has admitted that he was in love with a ghost the entire time he was sharing your bed? You were a mere comfort to him. Nothing more. He didn't love you. He couldn't."

Hot tears streamed down her face. "Stop it. He loved me. He still loves me."

"Then why didn't he fight for you?"

She turned around to face him. Jonathan stood in the middle of the road in his black suit, his gloved hands by his side, the shock of white standing out in his dark hair. His pale eyes reflected red for a second. He smiled at her.

Her voice echoed through the silent trees. "Stop it! Stop it!"

She could no longer see through the tears, and so at first she didn't recognize the second figure who joined him. The realization came a second too late. As hard as she tried, Clara couldn't move, couldn't run.

"You can't leave now," Elizabeth said. "The party won't be complete without you."

FIFTY-THREE

—∿—

Lake Snagov, Romania
19 December 1999

ALL THE LEGENDS SAID THAT when they attempted to take the body of Vlad Ţepeş across the
waters of Lake Snagov, to the island where the
tiny monastery stood, a storm blew in suddenly and with
such violence it threatened to capsize the boat.

There were no storms that day. The sun shone down
on the bleak wintry landscape as the boat ferried Adam
and Arkady across. The air was crisp and cold. The sky
was so pale and brittle it seemed it might shatter.

A small dock jutted out into the water near the
grounds of the monastery. As the local pilot tied the boat
up, Adam and Arkady jumped out. Three monks confronted them, all in black robes, all with long, grey beards.

The one in the middle, who appeared slightly more ancient than the others, stabbed a finger at the book in
Adam's hand. "That is not welcome on holy ground."

Adam frowned and held up the book of blood magic.

"This? Why?"

The monk scowled. "It is tainted. You must leave it here."

Adam glanced at Arkady, and then back at the monk's stern face. He returned the book to his satchel, which he then hoisted over his shoulder and set on the ground. "Fine. I won't carry it inside."

"You think that's wise?" Arkady asked in Russian.

"We need their cooperation," Adam replied, also in Russian. "What if we have to dig up part of the floor of the chapel to get to the medallion?"

Arkady nodded. "You have a point, though in my experience it's much easier to get forgiveness than permission."

"My name is Adam Mire, and this is my colleague Arkady Danilovich Markov," Adam said to the monk, switching back to Romanian and ignoring the last part of Arkady's comment. "I assume you know why we're here then."

The monk bowed. "I am Brother Teodor. And, yes, I know why you're here. You are here looking for that which belonged to Dracula, just like all the others who have come. You will not find it. Please turn around and go. Your search will be futile."

"We're not like the others," Adam argued.

Brother Teodor's mouth widened in a patronizing grin. "That's what all the others have said."

He turned and walked back toward the monastery. The two others followed suit.

"Wait," Adam called after them. "I know about Ceaușescu. I know about what he tried to do. I want to make sure no one is able to do that again. Isn't that worth letting us try? Isn't making sure the monsters don't come back important?"

Brother Teodor turned around again and regarded Adam with his deep-set, black eyes. "There is no way to keep the monsters from coming back." He motioned for Adam and Arkady to follow. "Come, this way if you must."

They trudged across the grounds toward the chapel. Brother Teodor stopped at the door and allowed Adam and Arkady to enter before him. Adam paused for his eyes to adjust to the dim light. The walls were covered in murals. Candles glowed in sconces and on candelabras near the altar. Adam shivered. The air in the chapel seemed even colder. Brother Teodor entered with them, but the other two monks stayed outside.

"Do you recall a visit recently by a man named Mihai Iliescu?" Adam asked.

Brother Teodor shook his head. "I do not know that name."

"Are you certain?" Arkady crossed himself as he stepped into the shadowy chapel. "Perhaps you were indisposed the day he visited."

"I know all the visitors who come to this island," Brother Teodor replied. "I have never heard of him. He would have had to come covertly, and that is impossible. It's a small island."

"Maybe he came at night," Arkady offered.

Brother Teodor made a clicking sound in his throat. "That is inadvisable."

"Why?" Adam asked.

"It is dangerous. There is not much light on the lake, and we are prone to sudden storms."

Adam didn't think the monk was being entirely truthful. "That wouldn't have stopped Mihai."

Arkady's gaze roamed around the chapel. "This is a big place. He could have hidden it anywhere."

"Whatever Mihai did, there would be a logic to it." Adam stepped toward the supposed grave of Vlad the Impaler. A portrait of the warlord stood over a slight dip in the floor just to the left of the altar. Candles burned around it, many of them nothing more than puddles of wax. Dracula had a slightly different reputation in Romania than in the West. Many still regarded him as a hero for standing up to the Turks. "It would not be here."

Arkady looked sharply at him. "Why do you say that?"

"There is too much negative energy here."

"This is a place of God." Brother Teodor's voice dripped with indignation.

"And there are some things that are definitely not of God." Adam pointed to the portrait. "This grave is one of them. Say what you will, this is not consecrated ground. The medallion wouldn't be protected here."

"Somewhere else in the chapel then?" Arkady suggested. "Behind a wall?"

Adam regarded the nearest mural, a line of saints' portraits. "Unlikely. The frescoes would be disturbed, and Mihai would never destroy works of art like that."

"You're wasting your time," Brother Teodor said.

Adam tried to focus. He paced the chapel, looking for any sign of the medallion's secret hiding place. Some said the grave in the church did not belong to Vlad the Impaler, but that he was buried elsewhere on the island, outside the monastery grounds, because the sacred soil would not accept him.

"It's not here." Adam ran past Brother Teodor out of the chapel.

He grabbed up his satchel from where he had left it and sprinted around the monastery to the wooded part of the island. Time was running short. The sun was already high in the sky. Once it set they wouldn't be safe anywhere except inside the monastery.

"What are you looking for?" Arkady asked, close on Adam's heels.

Adam didn't dare slow down as he crashed through the underbrush. "I'll know it when I see it."

At length he spotted a small tree whose bare branches grew in a thick bramble. A hawthorn tree. When he reached the base, he began to clear around the trunk. The tree was old, its bark rough and split. The thorns stuck Adam as he pushed back the branches, but he didn't dare stop. Finally he uncovered a small circle of stones with four larger stones at the cardinal points.

Adam grinned. "*Sub rosa*. Clever."

"What does that mean?" Arkady asked.

"Some associate hawthorn trees with witchcraft and death. Supposedly the wall between life and death is very thin at hawthorn trees. It's a popular tree for carving stakes to destroy vampires. Mihai made a compass rose at the base. Roses are symbols of secrecy. It's here." Adam knelt and tried to push his hands into the hard ground. "I need a shovel."

A minute later one of the monks returned with the requested implement. Adam pushed it into the earth while the others watched. It seemed the whole world held its breath while he dug. The wind died, and the sounds of the forest quieted even as the sky darkened with heavy clouds.

Eventually, the shovel hit smething. Adam threw the tool aside and dug the last few inches with his hands. He pulled a canvas bag out of the hole and opened it with trembling fingers. The dull metal fell into his palm, a dragon, its tail wrapped around its neck, a partially obliterated cross on its back and the Latin phrase inscribed around the outside: *O Quam Misericors est Deus, Pius et Justus.*

A gust of wind thrashed the branches of the hawthorn tree, and a lone wail echoed through the woods from the lake. Above the clouds had grown black.

Suddenly, Adam felt the cold barrel of a gun on his temple.

"Give it to me," Arkady said. "I'm taking the books as well. All of them."

Don't trust the Russians.

Adam remained still. "Arkady—"

"No, Adam. I'm not indulging you anymore. Thank you for your help in finding the medallion but it's safer with me."

"What about Clara?"

He wavered, but only slightly. "Do you honestly think she's still alive?"

"I have to hope she is."

"You're a fool, Adam." The edge returned to Arkady's voice.

Adam let the smooth, worn metal pass through his fingers. "Then what about Dracula ... and the others?"

"The medallion will be in a place he can never find it."

A shot rang out through the woods. Arkady jerked away, and Adam ducked. Four men emerged from behind trees, each holding a gun.

"Thank you, Arkady Danilovich, but the medallion and the books are ours," one of them, a tall bald man, said in Russian. "Please, Dr. Mire, you may hand me the medallion."

"Who are you?" Adam asked.

The man scoffed. "There's no need for you to know."

Arkady clutched his arm as blood ran between his fingers. "You might as well tell him, Igor. You're going to kill us all anyway."

Adam noted the positions of each of the four new men as well as the fact that the monks had disappeared. "Tell me what?"

"Shut up, Arkady," Igor barked, "unless you want a bullet in the other arm."

Arkady persisted. "They're all former KGB, sent here to tie up loose ends."

Adam didn't take his gaze off Igor. "What sort of loose ends?"

"Making sure no Russian secrets get out into the wild, now that none of our former 'allies' have to worry about Soviet tanks rolling through the streets of their cities," Arkady replied. "For decades there were rumors that Ceaușescu was conducting investigations into the paranormal, picking up right where the old fascist government of Romania left off. Those investigations included experiments on vampires. And so when everything looked like it was falling apart, the KGB came in to make sure he died. Did I get that all right, Igor?"

Igor glowered. "We did you all a favor. Imagine vampire spies, able to hear secret conversations through walls, to compel people to talk, or to kill them and absorb all their memories. Imagine vampire operatives assassinating heads of state and then disappearing without a trace. Imagine an army of vampires, moving through the night, slaughtering enemy forces before they even realized what was happening. Now imagine them all under the command of an immortal tyrant."

In the woods Adam caught a flicker of movement. "I'd rather not. Why don't you just let Arkady take the medallion and put it in his secret hidden sub-basement of St.

Basil's Cathedral? Doesn't that accomplish the same thing?"

"How do we know it will stay there? How many men of faith have taken it, promised to keep it safe, and then broken that promise? No, we are not going to leave this in the hands of the Church." Igor spat out the last sentence.

"What are you going to do with it?" Adam asked.

"Not something you really need to know, except I will say that Russia is approximately six and a half million square miles." Igor raised his pistol. "Now please, Dr. Mire, hand it over."

Brother Teodor and another monk emerged from the trees behind the Russians. Brother Teodor held the shovel. The other monk carried a candlestick like a cudgel.

Adam glanced at Arkady and then back at Igor. "Catch," he said, tossing the medallion into the air.

The monks struck, bringing their improvised weapons down on the heads of two of the four Russians. One of the Russians fired a wild shot, and the bulled chipped the bark of the hawthorn tree. Adam ducked around the trunk, but his eyes were fixed on the flash of metal in the dirt. He dove for it. His hands closed around the medallion, but Igor's boot came down on his wrist. Igor scooped up the artifact, a twisted grin on his face.

Adam slammed against Igor's leg, and the Russian tumbled to the ground. The two grappled back and forth until Igor managed to pin Adam down. His hands closed around Adam's throat. Adam struggled against him in vain. The edges of his vision darkened as he thrashed. Just before he blacked out, a dark shape rose up behind Igor.

The pressure around Adam's neck released. He gulped for air. Somewhere close by, a scream was cut off in a gurgle, and seconds later Igor's body landed with a thud next to him. Adam scrambled to his feet and backed away only to stumble over the body of another Russian. A hand grasped his arm to catch him. Adam spun around to find himself facing Arkady.

Adam didn't see any sign of the monks, but he and Arkady were not alone.

Three figures stood in the shadow of the hawthorn. First a man with a streak of white in his dark hair, the same one who had saved him from Serhan's men on the night in Thessaloniki so many months earlier. The grin on his face told Adam he would not be anyone's savior that day. Next, a woman with golden hair and icy blue eyes. Elizabeth. Finally, another woman, with the auburn hair and hazel eyes Adam had wanted to see for so long.

"Clara," he called, tears welling up and spilling over.

She tried to run to him, but the man jerked her back.

Elizabeth smiled and licked a drop of blood from the corner of her mouth. "Now that everyone's here, I suppose we can begin."

FIFTY-FOUR

Lake Snagov, Romania
19 December 1999

ADAM'S FACE WAS SMEARED WITH dirt, and he had a cut on one cheek. He hadn't shaved in a few days, and there were dark circles under his eyes. Arkady stood next to him. He didn't look much better. He clutched his arm where the sleeve of his coat was stained red. The others, the ones they were fighting, all lay dead, killed by Elizabeth.

Clara wanted to call out to Adam, to say she was sorry, to say she loved him, to warn him, but her voice caught in her throat.

Adam scooped up a round piece of metal at his feet and held it toward Elizabeth. "You want this? Let her go."

The medallion.

He found it.

"I can't do that, Dr. Mire," Elizabeth replied, "at least not yet."

"Why not?" Adam asked.

Elizabeth ran a finger down Clara's neck. "Because I need her."

Clara cringed. Elizabeth's touch was like a nail dragging across a chalkboard.

Adam's gaze flickered back and forth between her and Elizabeth. "For what? Bait? If Dracula wanted to be found, he would have returned by now. He's gone. Why is that not enough for you?"

"Because I can still feel him," she snarled. "He's in my head, whispering, telling lies. I want him gone."

Adam took a step forward. "He doesn't control you. He doesn't control any of you."

"He doesn't have to control me to keep me from what I want," Elizabeth spat. "Yasamin and Elena are happy with their petty kingdoms. Yasamin has a string of husbands she married for money. She surrounds herself with shiny, pretty things to fool herself that her days have meaning. Elena spends her time taking revenge on all the men who have ever wronged her. She has power now. She can get men to do whatever she wants, but she wastes her days in a tiny apartment in Sarajevo, the modern equivalent of her family's hovel in Kosovo."

"What do you want, Elizabeth?" Adam glanced down at the medallion in his hand.

She laughed. "What do I want? I want blood and war and death, the same as I've always wanted."

Thunder pealed in the distance. Adam stood immobile, as if waiting for something to happen. Clara couldn't read his expression. She only hoped he wasn't planning to do what she feared.

"Yasamin and Elena aren't coming to save you, and you're a fool if you think they would," Elizabeth continued. "They're no different from me. They'd kill you and everyone here without a second thought if it served their interests. The only reason you're alive is because so far none of us has wanted to kill you."

Adam locked eyes with Clara. With a slight shake of his head he seemed to apologize. "If it's blood you want, use mine."

His words hit Clara like a punch to the stomach. "Adam, no!"

Adam held up a vial of clear liquid, cold anger shining in his eyes. He must have palmed it while he and Elizabeth were talking. He crushed the vial in his hand and ground the glass into his skin.

Holy water.

Adam slapped the medallion into his palm where the blood and the water mingled. Lightning tore through the clouds as the wind blasted through the trees. Adam spoke in a language Clara didn't recognize.

Elizabeth and Jonathan both shrieked. Jonathan let go of Clara to cover his ears. As soon as she was free, Clara rushed toward Adam, only for Arkady to block her path.

"What are you doing? Get out of my way," she screamed.

"It's too dangerous." Arkady reached for her, but she avoided his grasp.

"You don't get to tell me what's too dangerous."

Adam's eyes were squeezed shut, and he grit his teeth. His knees were buckling.

He was in pain.

"Adam," she said through sobs, "Adam please stop."

He opened his eyes, but she couldn't tell if he actually saw her. Sweat poured down his face. His voice had diminished to a whisper. Clara reached for the hand holding the medallion. Arkady pulled her away before she could touch him.

"Let me go," she demanded.

Arkady shook his head. "I can't let you stop him. He's going to destroy them."

Clara watched as Adam fell to his knees. "He's going to die."

"He knows. That's why I have to stop you."

She jerked free. "No, there has to be another way."

Clara spun around and smacked the medallion from Adam's hand. Two things happened at once. Adam collapsed to the ground, and Elizabeth, consumed with rage, lunged toward her. Arkady shoved Clara out of the way, and Elizabeth, fangs and claws bared, barreled into him. Gore spattered across the ground as she tore open his throat. As the blood dripped from her face, she glanced up at Clara and smiled.

FIFTY-FIVE

Lake Snagov, Romania
19 December 1999

A DAM FELL THROUGH THE DARKNESS. He couldn't
see. He couldn't hear. He could only feel the re-
lentless rush of air as he plummeted. And then,
faintly at first, a voice came to his ears. The words were
unintelligible, but familiar somehow. As the voice grew
louder the words became clear. They belonged to the
chant he recited, but the voice wasn't his. It was deeper,
more guttural, more demonic.

The spell from the book of blood magic was mostly in
Old Hungarian with a smattering of Romany, Aramaic,
and Old Church Slavonic. It was intended to render vampires into the dust they should have become centuries earlier, if said a certain way. That was the clever thing about
the spell. Full of double meanings, it could also be used to
create a vampire.

He was using it to create one.

Adam slammed into the ground with enough force to

shatter every bone in his body. Instead the pain radiated from his torso into his limbs. He wanted to die, but he couldn't. The voice pulled at him, drew him in, threatened to consume him.

Another voice joined. A woman's, harsh and dripping in acid. She spoke in English.

"You fool. Did you honestly think the holy water would protect you? Did you think it wouldn't happen? Blood magic always demands a price. Sometimes that price is death. Sometimes it is more than death."

"No," Adam muttered through clenched teeth. "It will not happen to me. I won't let it."

A wicked laugh echoed through his head, threatening to make his skull explode. "You don't have a choice."

A blinding white light replaced the darkness. Adam opened his eyes to the gunmetal-grey sky above. He tried to sit up but could only manage to lift his head a few inches. Clara crouched nearby, her eyes fixed on Elizabeth. The vampire, face and hands bloody, stood over Arkady's lifeless body.

Clara would be next, and Adam couldn't do anything to save her. He tried to reach for her, tried to make his voice work, but his body betrayed him.

Then a black-robed monk, the third one, stepped in front of Elizabeth. He picked up the medallion from where it had fallen. Brave but foolhardy. Crosses and icons and chanted verses would slow Elizabeth down, but they would not stop a vampire as powerful as she was. The monk had merely doomed himself in addition to the rest of them.

Elizabeth's eyes grew wide, though, and for the first time Adam saw fear. The monk walked to where Adam had dropped his satchel. From it he pulled not the Roma book of blood magic, but the book Elizabeth had given to Adam while masquerading as Anya. *The Life and Death of Michael the Brave.*

The monk began to chant, low at first but growing in volume. He let the book fall open in his hand, its pages blowing in the wind. As the monk chanted writing on the pages glowed, but not the printed text. These letters were scrawled in a severe hand, spelling out words in a language long gone, recorded in blood.

Dracula's blood.

When the chanting ceased, and the wind died, the old monk was gone. In his place stood a much younger man, but not merely a man, a soldier, a warrior. Gone were the wrinkles, the yellowed eyes, the gnarled hands. He stood tall, shoulders back and chest forward. Thick, curly black hair fell on either side of his face. His gleaming green eyes brimmed with malevolent intelligence as he took in his surroundings.

He fixed Elizabeth with a glare. "You failed, my love."

A wary Elizabeth took a step back. "You shouldn't be here. The sacrifice—"

He gestured toward Arkady's body. "You provided it."

Elizabeth's expression was a perfect mixture of fear and hatred. "You should be in hell."

He raised an eyebrow. "What makes you think I'm not?"

"Don't start with your philosophical nonsense."

"It isn't nonsense," he protested. "There is a price to pay for what we are. I told you that on the first night we were together."

She lashed out, raking her hand across his face. "Don't ever talk about that night."

He smiled and caressed his reddened cheek, which was

already healing. "Do you regret it then? Would you rather be dead?"

"You made promises that night. You broke all of them."

He laughed, which only caused Elizabeth's scowl to deepen. "What promises have I broken? I offered you a life free of the rules that fettered you, free of the constraints of society."

Her eyes burned red with rage. "But you didn't tell me I'd be bound by your rules. I traded one cage for another."

"All you want is chaos."

"Don't you see? Chaos is the only thing that could ever bring us true freedom. We could have ruled, you and I together." Her tone was almost pleading.

He shook his head, regarding her as one would a petulant child. "You were wrong then, and you're wrong now. I don't want chaos. I've only ever wanted one thing, for my country to be safe, peaceful, prosperous. I made the ultimate sacrifice for that."

Elizabeth turned away. "You didn't have to try to kill me."

"You threatened everything I built," he bellowed. "There was almost nothing left as it was. You were going to plunge the whole continent into another war. I didn't make the decision lightly. I did love you once."

"You have no right to use that word." She pulled back her hand to slap him again, but he grabbed her by the wrist. She cried out as he squeezed. Jonathan rushed forward, fangs and claws bared. Dracula seized him by the throat.

"Why not?" he asked, holding the flailing Jonathan at bay. "You loved me at one point as well. You cannot deny you did." He indicated Jonathan with a nod of his head. "Do you love him? He apparently loves you."

Dracula threw Jonathan into the air. He crashed through the underbrush, coming to rest at the based of the hawthorn tree. The vampire staggered to his feet, prepared to launch himself at Dracula again in order to defend Elizabeth.

He didn't see Clara behind him clutching a broken hawthorn branch. With both hands she shoved the jagged end into his back. He collapsed forward, his body combusting and disintegrating into ashes.

As Clara stamped out the few tiny fires that managed to ignite in the undergrowth, Adam thought he saw a gleam of admiration in Dracula's eyes. Elizabeth's expression never changed.

Dracula released her. "Ten years ago, you tried to be rid of me, and you failed because you didn't have all the pieces. You tried again just now, but you still failed. Let go of this quest, Elizabeth. Leave now, and you may escape your lover's fate."

Elizabeth was silent for a moment, and Adam thought maybe she would listen, but the glint of metal in her hand told him otherwise. She sank the blade of the dagger into Dracula's side. The wound sizzled. The blade was made of silver.

"You will never tell me what to do again," she growled.

For Adam the entire world shifted. Everything suddenly moved in slow motion. The light changed and even the smallest details became crystal clear, down to the flecks of mud on Dracula's boots, the tiny pattern on the hilt of the knife Elizabeth still held in her hand. Sounds, too, amplified. He could count Clara's heartbeats from yards away, as well as hear the animals in the forest cowering in their burrows and the water lapping at the island's edge.

Someone held his hand.

He looked to discover Elena.

"Is this what it's like then?" he asked.

Elena nodded. "Always."

Dracula, knife protruding from his side, struck Elizabeth and knocked her to the ground. He extracted the dagger. Almost gone were his human features, replaced by fangs and claws and eyes that burned with hellfire. Elizabeth sprung back to her feet, her features changed as well. They charged one another, snarling and hissing like a pair of feral cats.

Elena helped Adam stand. "He is still weak from being restored."

"I know," Adam replied, not understanding how he knew.

"You've already made one decision," Elena said. "You wanted to become one of us."

"I didn't want to. It was the only way."

"To fight her."

His eyes narrowed. "To fight you all."

"What will your next decision be?"

Elizabeth and Dracula continued to battle. Blood smeared her face from a cut that had partially healed over, and Adam wouldn't have been surprised if one of her arms was broken, the way she held it. Dracula was weakening, though. Elizabeth forced him back, toward the hawthorn tree, toward Clara.

Adam watched them anxiously. "Did you happen to bring your crossbow this time?"

Elena smiled and shook her head.

"You're not joining this fight." Adam wasn't asking a question.

"It is not my fight," Elena said.

"But if Elizabeth wins—"

"If Elizabeth wins, then what? At this point her victory would be hollow."

She let go of his hand. The world stayed as it was, his senses enhanced far beyond a normal human's. Because he wasn't a normal human any longer. The changes had already started.

Elena knelt and picked up the medallion from where Dracula had dropped it. "This is what I was concerned about always. Now no one else can use it to cause chaos. No one is left, thanks to you."

Adam reached a hand toward her. "Wait, is that all?"

"Good luck, Dr. Mire." Elena smiled wistfully as the scent of lilacs tickled Adam's nose.

Then she walked into the forest and vanished.

A cry rang through the clearing. Elizabeth shoved Dracula into the hawthorn tree, impaling him on dozens of the thorns. The tree burned him anywhere he touched. Elizabeth watched him writhe with a satisfied grin.

Elena was wrong. It did matter if Elizabeth won.

If she won Clara would die.

The anger welled up in him, as did new sensations. His eyeteeth tore through his gums. The pain, unbearable at first, became strangely exciting, and Adam found himself giving over more to instinct than rational thought. He sprinted over the ground toward Elizabeth, his feet barely touching. He no longer felt the cold, just as his breath no longer came out in white clouds. He hit her at full speed, and together they tumbled into the snow and dirt.

She raked a clawed hand across his face. He dug his fingers into her throat. They grappled with one another until Adam slammed her into the ground and pinned her there with a knee to her stomach. She arched her back, struggling to break free, but Adam pressed down. She turned her head, exposing her neck for a moment.

Adam didn't hesitate. He sunk his teeth into her flesh, letting Elizabeth's black blood ooze into his mouth.

FIFTY-SIX

—◊—

Lake Snagov, Romania
19 December 1999

CLARA STIFLED A CRY OF horror as Adam bit into Elizabeth's neck. She wanted to scream, to cry, to retch. She stood from her hiding place behind the hawthorn tree, but a hand clamped around her wrist and pulled her back. When she turned around, she looked into Yasamin's dark eyes.

"Let me go." Clara demanded.

Yasamin's eyes flashed with annoyance. "You shouldn't have run away. This is your fault."

"My fault? You brought us here. How do I know you weren't going to use me as the blood sacrifice to bring Dracula back?"

"I do what I must, but I am not intentionally cruel. I do not inflict pain for the sake of it. I would never have brought you to the monastery. Your presence here has complicated matters."

For the first time, Clara noticed Yasamin carried

363

Adam's satchel. An old hidebound book with a tarnished silver clasp peeked out from the top.

"What do you mean I've complicated matters?"

Yasamin gestured to Adam. "He made himself into one of us so he could save you. If you hadn't been here, he wouldn't have done it."

Clara shook her head. "He would have just died."

Yasamin narrowed her eyes. "He is already dead."

Adam stood and wiped the blood from his chin with the sleeve of his coat. Elizabeth lay sprawled on the ground. Gone was her golden hair, now streaked with white, and her smooth porcelain skin was no more, now wrinkled and dotted with brown liver spots. Adam staggered away, as if drunk.

But Elizabeth rose up behind him.

Her ice-blue eyes at least retained their cold malevolence. She attacked, striking him again and again with her claws, slashing at his face and neck and chest. Adam held up his forearms to try to defend himself, but he couldn't stop her vicious assault. Covered in bloody gashes, he collapsed to the ground.

"Enough, Elizabeth."

She turned toward the sound of the voice, her eyes wide in terror as Dracula pulled himself free from the hawthorn tree.

"You bastard. You've ruined everything."

He stepped forward. "No, *you* ruined everything."

She rushed at him, but instead of blocking her or stepping aside, Dracula opened himself to embrace her. When she collided with him, he wrapped his arms around her and sunk the silver-bladed knife she had used on him into her back. The inhuman shriek forced Clara to cover her ears.

Dracula held Elizabeth and stroked her hair while he cradled her head against his chest. As Elizabeth whimpered, Dracula began muttering under his breath.

"No," Elizabeth said through gritted teeth, "no you wouldn't dare."

She tried to break away, but his embrace proved too strong. He continued to hold her as one would a wayward child returned home. His muttering grew into a droning chant. Elizabeth cried and pleaded, but Dracula did not relent. He covered her completely in the folds of his robe, his voice rising up to join the rushing wind. Lightning tore across the sky, and a thunderclap drowned out the last of his words. When he dropped his arms, Elizabeth was no longer there.

Dracula stumbled and almost fell, but Yasamin appeared at his side in an instant. He regarded her with a tired smile on his face. She offered her hand, and he took it.

"Wait," Clara called. She feared for a moment she had made a mistake as they both regarded her expectantly. "What happened to Elizabeth? Did you kill her?"

Dracula shook his head. "No. I did much worse. I did to her what she did to me ten years ago. She'll wake up somewhere, powerless, unable to remember what or even who she is, trapped in an old and useless body—forever."

Adam, still lying on the ground, groaned. Many of his cuts had healed, but he had lost so much blood.

"What about Adam?" Clara asked. "What's going to happen to him?"

A twisted grin spread across Dracula's face. "You'll find out in a moment."

Hand in hand, he and Yasamin stepped into the woods and dissolved into the shadows. The clouds overhead parted, revealing the blue sky once again. As soon as the sunlight touched Adam, he screamed.

FIFTY-SEVEN

—∭—

Lake Snagov, Romania
19 December 1999

ADAM WAS DEAD.
The story couldn't have ended any other way.
In the darkness.

In the silence.

Except the silence didn't last.

Voices chanted, not the harsh words of magic conjured by blood, but the deep, rich, resonant tones of monks singing the liturgy. He let the sound wash over him for a few moments, or hours, he couldn't tell. He wanted to stay there forever, to let the words of the monks quiet all the dark thoughts in his head, to cleanse him of the guilt and the shame, to banish the shadows forever.

But then he became aware of the hard, rough, cold surface beneath his back, as well as the fact that every part of his body ached. Each breath sent a spasm of pain across his chest.

Why was he breathing?

He opened his eyes. They refused to focus at first. Flickering orange light invaded the edges of his vision, though the center was still a black void. He tried to sit up, but a hand pressed on his chest and gently pushed him back down. He was thankful, because even that small effort proved excruciating and exhausting.

The image swimming in front of his eyes slowly resolved itself. The flickering orange light came from candles lined against stone walls. The walls, covered in murals, rose up beyond where the light could reach.

A face appeared, looking down at him. Clara's.

She smiled, though tears streamed down her cheeks. "You came back."

"Where ... where am I?" His throat felt like sandpaper.

"In the chapel of the monastery. The monks helped me drag you inside."

That was wrong. He shouldn't have been there. "How? How is that possible? I—"

"Made yourself into a vampire." Her smile faded. Her voice contained a note of regret.

He reached up and wiped away a tear on her cheek. "I'm sorry. It was the only way."

She took his hand and cradled it in hers. "I know. It was stupid. You shouldn't have done it, but I know."

Adam studied her in the flickering candlelight. He wanted to say so much to her, but he didn't even know where to begin. And he was tired. "My heart is beating. I can hear it throbbing in my ears."

A faint smile returned to her lips. "The monks don't know what happened. They say it could be the holy water you mixed with your blood, or the fact that I interrupted you before you had a chance to finish your chant. Or it could be that the sunlight burned it out of you."

He wished he could share in Clara's relief. He wished he could believe he had escaped the consequences of his decision, but that would mean believing a lie. The monster still lurked inside him. It would wait, biding its time until the moment he let his guard down.

And then …

He turned away from her. "Clara, you should go."

She sighed. "I'm not leaving you like this."

Exactly what Adam expected her to say.

"You can't stay. I'm serious."

"So am I."

"Clara, you don't—"

"Adam, look at me." When Adam met her gaze again, her hazel eyes held sadness, but also hope, hope galvanized by steel. She leaned in close, her face mere inches from his. Her breath warmed his skin. "Whatever the next battle, we're going to fight it together. "

Adam squeezed her hand. "I love you. I always have."

She kissed him softly on the lips before resting her head on his chest. "I love you, too."

Adam closed his eyes and soon found himself drifting to sleep. He had spent all his life searching, for what exactly he didn't know, but as he lay in Clara's embrace on the monastery's cold, stone floor, he knew his search was over.

ACKNOWLEDGMENTS

Thank you to everyone who has seen *Daughters of Shadow and Blood* through to the end. I wouldn't have made it without you.

I'm grateful for the friendship and advice of those in my writers' group, especially Darin Kennedy, Caryn Sutorus, Rochelle Bryce, Jay Requard, Traci Loudin, Eden Royce, and John Hartness. You gave me the courage to keep moving forward.

I'd like to acknowledge Misha Glenny's *The Balkans* and Robert Kaplan's *Balkan Ghosts* for their explanation of the legacy of the Congress of Berlin and their thorough analysis of Romanian history in the twentieth century. I also should acknowledge Lady Macdonell and Mary King Waddington, whose memoirs shed light on the life of a diplomat's wife at the end of the nineteenth century.

Of course, I can't go without mentioning Bram Stoker, without whom these books wouldn't exist.

Finally, as always, I want to thank my wife Lara for her support, her encouragement and her proofreading skills, and my children for keeping me focused on what's truly important.

ABOUT THE AUTHOR

J. Matthew Saunders, a native of Greenville, South Carolina, is the author of numerous published fantasy and horror short stories. He received a B.A. in history from Vanderbilt University and a master's degree from the School of Journalism at the University of South Carolina. He received his law degree in California and practiced there as an attorney for several years.

He is an unapologetic European history geek, enjoys the Celtic fiddle, and makes a mean sun-dried tomato-basil pesto. He currently lives near Charlotte, North Carolina with his wife and two children. To find out more, visit www.jmsaunders.com.